PRAISE FOR
Are You Somebody?

"You don't want the book to end; it glows with compassion
and you want more, more because you know this is a fine
wine of a life, richer as it ages."
—**Frank McCourt**

"This book has to be read. One of the most perfectly observed portraits
of female loneliness I've ever come across....O'Faolain brings a spiky,
independent intelligence that vanquishes cliche."
—**Zoe Heller,** *The New York Times Book Review*

"A beautiful exploration of human loneliness and happiness, of
contentment and longing."
—**Alice McDermott,** *Washington Post Book World*

"A lovely memoir that traces the growth of a woman
and her country over the last 50 years."
—*Publishers Weekly*

" 'I'm not anybody in terms of the world, but then, who decides
what a somebody is? How is a somebody made?' asks *Irish Times*
columnist O'Faolain. The answer can be found in her moving and
painfully honest memoir, a best seller in her native Ireland
that deserves as much attention here."
—*Library Journal*

"A funny, plainspoken, heartfelt memoir."
—*Elle Magazine*

"A lovely and complex mosaic out of the moments that
make up a life as it is being lived."
—*USA Today*

Best Love, Rosie

NUALA O'FAOLAIN (1940–2008) was one of
Ireland's best-loved journalists and writers.
She came to international attention for her two
volumes of memoir, *Are You Somebody?* (1996) and
Almost There (2003). She also wrote the novel,
My Dream of You (2001), and a history with
commentary, *The Story of Chicago May* (2005).
Her first three books were all featured on the
New York Times Bestseller list.

༃

nuala o'faolain

Best Love,
Rosie

GEMMA
Boston

First published by GemmaMedia in 2010.

GemmaMedia
230 Commercial Street
Boston MA 02109 USA
617 938 9833
www.gemmamedia.com

This edition of *Best Love, Rosie* is published by
arrangement with Sabine Wespieser, Éditeur.

Printed in the United States of America

12 11 10 09 08   1 2 3 4 5

ISBN: 978-1-934848-41-8

Cover design by Night and Day Design

Library of Congress Preassigned Control Number (PCN) applied for.

Acknowledgments

I would like to thank Dr. Lara Honos-Webb for
advice on depression quoted; Indiana University Press
for permission to quote from *On Aging, Revolt and
Resignation* by Jean Améry, translated by John D.
Barlow, 1994; and Alfred Publishing for permission
to quote from Cole Porter's 'Begin the Beguine'.

Introduction

I live in a cottage a few fields above the Atlantic ocean, in the west of Ireland. But for some years now, since my first book, *Are You Somebody?* had a big success in the United States, I've divided my time between Ireland and a room in Manhattan. I wanted to borrow the immigrant energy of the great city. I wanted to escape the despair and lethargy that still clings to the Irish countryside.

During these years, the most insistent narrative in my life has been the story of getting older. And getting older, I perceive, is an entirely different cultural experience on one side of the ocean than on the other. For example: the years roll off a woman from an old-style country like Ireland when her plane touches down on the tarmac in New York. I call it the JFK Effect – sixty years old becomes fifty years old in an instant. For another: the American sisterhood denies the self-abnegation of the European grandmother, defies ageing with every instrument at its command, and prefers not to dwell on death. I see, and it makes me both admiring and uneasy, that American women go on believing in their own importance to the end. Whereas in Ireland, the childless, ageing woman has no tribal function, and must invent her own self-importance.

Best Love, Rosie came out of these two preoccupations. What can the New World do to and for a woman formed in the Old World? And how does any modern woman – who has travelled, done interesting work, had lovers, been responsible for no one but herself – meet the challenge of that time late in middle age when these things begin to fail her? How does any person find new pleasures when the old ones have lost their savour?

What surprised me, as the story of what happens to Min and her niece Rosie unfolded itself, was how much fun I had with it. And I think that was because of the vigour with which Min – the older woman – seized her chance to get out of the Dublin milieu which was too familiar and had nothing new to give her. Her adventure in the book delighted me as much as it did her.

My head is with her. But my heart is with her niece, my dear Rosie.

She is a woman whose needs are too passionate and complex to be answered by America. Instead, she returns to Ireland and to the past. She retires, in many ways hurt by life, to the primitive house of her grandfather, beside the stone quarry where he worked on a remote and beautiful peninsula. She learns about the terrible lives that were lived there, especially by women. But even as she discovers the harsh truth of her own parentage, she is also encountering forms of love. Friendship; a small, loyal, dog; the splendour of the natural world; conscious efforts to redress wrongs done – things she never valued in her youth – are the resources she gathers as she pauses on the brink of the next part of her life.

Thousands of miles away, in the States, Min is also discovering new aspects of *joie de vivre* – the pleasure of being paid for work, for example, and the freedom of belonging to a transient, diverse and unjudging social underworld. Niece and aunt, who were silent when they were together, learn to speak to each other. Now that they have abandoned the roles thought appropriate to their ages and are separated only by an ocean, each have become pioneers.

There are dark undertones to all this, of course, and in the book, as in my own life, many good things have been lost for ever in the passing of the years. But *Best Love, Rosie* – my fifth book in ten years – is the book of my years of commuting between the melancholy of Ireland and the optimism of America. It insists on celebrating what those years showed me. That the world in all its shades of black and white is wonderfully interesting. That sorrow can be managed: it can be banished to a minor place within. And that even the most seemingly moribund life is open to the possibility of change – in youth, in middle age, and always.

Nuala O'Faolain
14 January 2008

Best Love, Rosie

nuala o'faolain

Part One
Dublin

1

I was in bed with Leo on Christmas morning in a chilly *pensione* near the docks in Ancona. It took courage to unpeel from his back and slide an arm out from under the duvet to ring my aunt in Dublin.

There was no reply, so I tried next door.

'Hello? Reeny? That you? Yes, of course it's Rosie. Merry Christmas, sweetheart, and every good wish for the New Year! I'm in Italy. Yes, with a friend – what do you think I am – mad? It just wasn't worth going home for the short break they give us at work. Listen – Min isn't answering her phone. Would you mind going out the back and calling up to her window? It's eleven in Dublin, isn't it? And I know she's going in to you for the turkey and sprouts. Shouldn't she be up and about?'

'Ah no, she's fine,' Reeny said. 'Don't you worry. She was in here last night watching *Eastenders*. But she's becoming a bit odd, Min is. There's days now she doesn't get out of bed even though there's feck all wrong with her. And – I don't want to ruin your holiday but I was going to tell you the next time I saw you – there was a bit of trouble there recently when she had a few drinks on her. The guards brought her back from the GPO of all places – nobody knows how she got from the pub into town – because she fell and she couldn't get up. Well, it was more that she wouldn't get up. She kept telling everyone she had to post a parcel to America. Anyway they were very nice and they brought her home, though the guard told me they'd a hard time stopping her hopping out the door of the patrol car, and only that she was a little old lady they'd have hand-cuffed her. She hasn't been out all that much since, and a few of the women talking about it in the Xpress Store were saying that maybe Rosie Barry should come home...'

'But Min doesn't want me!' I said, laughing.

'I know she doesn't,' Reeny said. I stopped laughing.

Reeny didn't notice. 'But that's the way they are with depression,' she went on. 'I saw a fella talking about it on the telly. They don't know what they want.'

'Tell her I'll ring her tonight, Reeny, and that she's to answer the phone no matter what. And how are you doing? Is Monty with you?'

Monty was Reeny's son, a big shy golf fanatic, somewhere in his forties, who my friend Peg had been going out with for decades. His father walked out on him when he was a little boy, and I always saw the golf thing as something he'd protected himself with while he struggled to make a man of himself. 'Tell him Santy's going to bring him a hole-in-one.'

Beyond Leo's shoulder I could see a corner of the Adriatic – brilliantly blue and white-capped from a stiff wind that was making the shutters rattle. There'd been an attempt at making love earlier, but neither of us had been committed enough to keep going. It was a good thing, I supposed, that we weren't afraid to show it when we were half-hearted. Still, low sexual energy was bad for the soul. Not to mention there were two more days to go in an under-heated room and there was nothing to do in Ancona when such attractions as it had were closed for the holiday.

Christmas Day. The very words used to shimmer.

'Leo!' I tried to wake him nicely by curling my arm around his belly and stroking him gently. 'Leo, sweetheart – go and see if the signora will make us a cup of coffee.' Lifting myself on my elbow, I was as shocked as if I'd touched a live wire to see that he was wide awake and staring at the window.

The next day we went to an organ recital in an exceptionally draughty unused church, where Leo disappeared into his completely attentive mode. You could stick pins into him when he's listening to music and he wouldn't notice.

Things would have to change, I saw with bleak clarity as I sat there growing colder and colder. We were once – but I didn't want to think about the marvellous lovers we'd once been. I could barely admit to myself that it was becoming harder and harder to lure him away, now that he had lost his villa, inland from Ancona, that he had hoped to turn into a small luxury hotel.

I thought about Min instead.

Somebody needed to be keeping an eye on her if

she'd reached the point where she disgraced herself in public, and with Reeny these days caretaking an apartment complex in Spain, for the first time since the two of them were young women she wasn't always at hand in the house next door. There was also the fact that in a few months I'd have finished my contract as a writer with the Information Unit of the EU in Brussels and I'd have a lump sum if I left – enough to keep me while I took my time looking around for the next job. Some of my colleagues actually retired at fifty-five, the ones who'd never liked their jobs and were good at saving. I couldn't retire, and I didn't want to. But I'd have enough with the lump sum to keep going for a year or two – maybe even three, if I went back to Dublin.

And – I sent my tongue on a delicate walk around behind my teeth – the dentists in Dublin spoke English. W. H. Auden said that thousands have lived without love, not one without water, but he might well have mentioned teeth. I had no future of any kind if I didn't look after the ones I had left.

It was completely dark now outside the single slender window, high up in a peeling, ochre wall. A navy-blue sky, with one winking star. There'd been a cheerful-looking *trattoria* on the way to the recital and we could go there as soon as we'd collected a heavier sweater and more socks from the *pensione*. Then, bed…

And what about all that? What about cafés and sex and sixteenth-century windows? One of the great things about Brussels was that I could very easily take a train to meet Leo. And I couldn't bear to be long away from him, even now. I kept my hair a tactful ashy-blonde colour, and bought my clothes in boutiques in the Flemish-speaking part of Belgium where even chic women loved bread and butter as much as I did and had the same build, and when I walked along beside him with my tummy held in and an interested smile on my face I felt like a woman alive in the world. In Italy, where we met more often than anywhere else, quite a few men had a good look at me before they turned away.

But in Kilbride in Dublin... My birthday wasn't till September but I'd be fifty-five then – barely tipping towards the second half of the decade, but heading that way. There'd never been unmarried women my age in Kilbride who considered themselves to be still in the game. Or maybe there had been, but they were too smart to let anybody know it.

The audience were applauding with tremendous vigour. They must be trying to warm up. Leo gave me one of the smiles he didn't know were lovely as he got to his feet. Music made him happy – well, music up to about the time women stopped wearing long skirts, no later.

Oh. An encore.

We all sat down again.

Home's most powerful lure, all the same, was an image, not an argument.

If I went home to look after her, there was a certain way Min might be. I was charmed by her face anyway – so small and white, the black eyes so round and childlike. But I'd seen long ago what it could look like when it opened like a leaf in the sun.

When I was a child, before my father died, the three of us used to go every summer to a wooden shack called Bailey's Hut, out on the shelly grass beyond the last wharf of Milbay Harbour. My father's mother, Granny Barry, could borrow us The Hut for our holiday because she worked for Bailey's Hardware and Builders' Providers.

There was no running water, so we brought a jerry-can of tap water for making tea and otherwise we used the rainwater in the barrel at the door. My father would also use the rainwater to wash Min's hair.

'Right you are, Ma'am!' he'd say, when she said this would be a good day to give her hair a good wash. He'd bring a basin of warm water out onto the grass, and then a bucket of rainwater. She'd kneel in her old skirt and her pink under-bodice that had a stitched cone on each side for her breasts. He'd sit on a box and with her head in his lap, he would shampoo her, using the tips of his fingers. 'Mind that stuff in my eyes!' she'd say. Then he'd leave her kneeling, her head bent, and he'd delicately pour the first trickle of rainwater onto her head and she'd jump and say 'Ouch! That water's freezing!' But as he went on, the water flowed more evenly. She used her hands to distribute the water around her hair and he followed her with his stream of water and poured it where her hands went, exactly. Then he put down the bucket, and wrapped the towel firmly around her head. She lifted her blinded face, and he dabbed it very gently with a smaller towel.

Her hair would dry then in the sun, combed forward to fall over her face, her thin shoulders peeking out at each side. Or she'd brush it in the hot air currents from the Aladdin heater they kept in the corner of the room behind chicken-wire, where I couldn't touch it, and it would take on volume and gloss and vibrate as if energy ran through it.

He'd say: 'See your auntie's hair? Your auntie Min has beautiful hair.' He'd sound wistful. He'd sound as if he were talking about something long in the past, though she was right there in front of him and was not going to leave.

I never forgot the way she lifted her unguarded face to his. He held it between his two hands for a few moments when she was waiting for him to dab the wet off, and she, who was always so wary and brisk, allowed herself to be held. Her eyes were closed but she rested in his care like a seabird coming down onto the water.

That was the face she might turn on me. She might be like that with me.

I'd take the lump sum.

I went back at the end of the summer, and for the first two or three months I didn't do much more than sit at the old kitchen table. It was as if I'd entered one of those forests in fairytales which surround the castle where the princess sleeps, where no leaves move and no birds sing. I was slowly thinking – you wanted this and you got it, but what do you do now? It was as if I'd been fractured from my own experience – as if most of what I'd learnt in thirty years of living and loving and working around the globe wasn't relevant to where I'd now arrived.

Nothing happened. It was an event when Bell the

cat walked across the table an inch from my nose on her way from the window to the stairs to go up to Min. She walked past again on her way back out. Sometimes she condescended to mew to show she wanted her dinner served up. There was nothing to stop me spending a long time wondering whether she really disdained me, or whether the situation was more complex than that. She could have chosen to walk around the edge of the room, after all.

'I always know where to find you, Rosie,' Andy Sutton said, and being Andy he said it every time he came to the house. Andy was in his early sixties, but he seemed even older because he looked after us all, including my friend Peg, and my friend Tessa, whose cousin in fact he was. Andy worked for a charity called No-Need and in summer he collected goats and hens and rabbits and pigs around Ireland and drove truck-loads of them across to Gatwick Airport in England, to be flown out to places that were so poor that the people could cope with only the smallest livestock. The rest of the year there were regular meetings at No-Need headquarters and he came up from the country for them and stayed with his mother Pearl, a few streets away in Kilbride.

He'd open the front door and stick his head into the kitchen.

'Is Min asleep?' he'd whisper.

And I'd whisper back, 'She either is or she's pretending to be.'

'Do you never move from that table?' he'd say, and go out the back to check the thermostat on the boiler or to fetch the ladder to change a high light-bulb. Or he'd stagger back into the room under a sack of logs from the trees on his farm.

My aunt, upstairs, would detect a presence and soon the madly animated voices on her transistor radio, or the sweet swoops of singers – she turned up the volume for singing – would filter down through the ceiling. Then whoever was in the kitchen could talk normally.

Other times, the quiet would be broken by dance music from next door and I'd know that Reeny was back from Spain and that she'd be in any minute to see us, tanned and jovial and carrying ham, or peaches, or chocolates – some gift that wasn't alcoholic. And once in a while the fellow who did old-age pensioners' hair in the home brought his gear in and I'd hand the kitchen table over to him. And every two weeks I'd tactfully go to the library when a psychologist and some sort of nurse assistant came to see Min as part of a service for elderly people with depression that Reeny – a virtuoso manipulator of the welfare system – had discovered. Reeny filled in the questionnaire too, but when the team came to assess her she had to admit that she'd only signed up because she liked getting something for nothing.

'Your aunt is very low in herself,' the psychologist would say reverently, when I was seeing her out.

'She goes to the pub too often,' I'd say.

But the lady didn't want to hear that. She stuck strictly to her own turf.

I'd turn back in to the kitchen and pick up my book, and the sound would come from upstairs of Min scrolling from station to station on the little transistor she kept on the pillow, so near to her face that it was half-covered by the frizz of wild, colourless hair.

And I could tell too from the rhythm of her heels on the stairs – I'd had the old carpet taken off and the wood stripped and varnished – whether she'd finally got out of bed for some plan that included me, or whether she was going to the pub.

'Rosie!' she'd exclaim in a friendly way as she came down the last two steps. 'What has you sitting so quietly?'

This was a rhetorical question, of course, and it made no difference whether I answered or not. During the autumn I had the back door open to the yard. I loved that, the lozenge of light on the kitchen floor, the little yellow curtains swishing softly in the warm breeze; and she'd smile too at the genial scene. But as it grew colder her eyes would go immediately to the hearth.

'That's a great fire you have there!' she'd say absent-mindedly, and she'd have already moved in to perch on the little blue armchair and pick up the tongs to add a few lumps of coal, or, if the fire was sullen, to carefully poke a few sticks into it at points where, when they lit, they would transform the whole thing. She was a genius at fires. 'Thank God for coal!' she'd say, shuttling fine slack onto her creation with the lightest of touches.

Sometimes, carried on by enthusiasm, she'd even refer to the fire in the range of the house she grew up in, in Stoneytown, out on Milbay Point.

I came to attention whenever she said that name. It was a quarry-workers' settlement on the edge of the sea that she dismissed, but that to me was as exotic as Shangri-la.

'Freezing we'd be in that oul' place,' she'd snort. 'If the boats couldn't make it over from Milbay to take the stone, we used to have no coal,' she'd say, and she'd draw her chair right up to our fire with a dramatic shudder. 'We could be weeks waiting on a bit of coal!'

I used to wonder why the fire mattered so much to her. Then one day I realised that in remote parts of Ireland in the dark, poverty-stricken 1930s, the fire was life itself. The range in a kitchen must have been the god of the house. People were completely dependent on it for cooking, for baking bread, for heating, for drying. There were woods near Stoneytown, Min conceded, but surely to God I knew that beechwood was no good for burning in a range?

She'd have her coat on ready to go out. But she got such satisfaction out of coaxing the fire to a blaze that she'd prop her big handbag on her lap and sit there peacefully looking into the flames, her face made young again by their pink reflections.

Not every day, but two or three times a week, she'd strain up then to the little mirror in the scullery to swipe on lipstick and drag a brush through her hair. A lot of people smiled quite unconsciously when they saw her because she was only four feet, eleven inches high and her eyes were as dark as a marmoset's. I knew that she was nothing like as cute as she looked, but I often smiled at her little ways, too. Helplessly.

Then she'd carefully detach the page with the crossword from the rest of yesterday's newspaper and go off to the Kilbride Inn. She did yesterday's crossword because the answers were in today's so she could look them up if she was stuck. It was accepted that I wasn't welcome to accompany her.

I'd say to myself, why does she bother going up there? She only sits by herself anyway. I don't understand her. And I don't know that much about her, either, beyond the fact that her mother died when she was ten, and her father disappeared a year or so after I was born. Then I'd think – what does it matter whether you understand her or not? You're stuck with her, anyway. She'd been a mother to me since the week I was born, but there's no law that says you have to understand even a mother, much less an aunt who took over when her sister died. And I'd think, without resentment, it doesn't bother her that she doesn't understand me. What's more, most of the people in the world don't try to understand each other. Analysis is a disease of the Western, educated classes.

And yet – I remember examining this thought slowly, sitting in the quiet kitchen with Bell for once content to be on my lap – people can accept that the partners they choose are separate, other people. They can make love – I had, often – without having a clue to what was going through their lover's head. They can look down on the dead body of a wife or husband and think, 'I never really knew that person.' But the woman who brought you up? I never in my whole life met anybody who didn't feel entitled to know that woman.

I doubted if I would recognise any of the places in Min's inner landscape. And what did she know of the miasma of images that kept me sitting dreamily at the kitchen table, as I wandered lazily among them. The seashore at dusk near Dakar, with the big crabs ambling down the sand into the even line of white foam. *Clack-clack* they went, and the waves went *shush-shush*. Or the oilcloth on the table on the grass outside a farmhouse on the Rigi and the taste of sharp cheese grated over fried eggs. Or schoolchildren, in Flanders, coming towards me in the dark on their way to school, on a causeway between fields of winter mud; the way the glow of their fluorescent armbands hung in the air as ghostly seagulls fed on the empty fields all around and dawn suffused the horizon. There was nothing to be done about the manner in which these images imprisoned me in solitary experience. It was life itself that had made me as distant from her as she, tip-tapping up to the pub with God knows what thoughts in her head, was distant from me.

My memories certainly didn't suggest any particular path I could follow into the future. I'd open my laptop and google the agencies I'd always got my jobs from – UNESCO, Overseas Aid, World Opportunity, the European Parliament. And I'd drift off into fantasy. Myanmar, now. How about trying to get into Myanmar? Rangoon must be a worn, humid version of somewhere like Valletta, say, in the 1950s. Tropical, but with stone clock-towers and municipal flowerbeds. British gentility overlaid on foreignness in a thick, humid atmosphere. But would it be right to work in Myanmar? There was a job going in Adelaide. I could manage a foreign language bookshop in Adelaide standing on my head. Someone told me that the wines in Adelaide were marvellous. Or Maracaibo. They wanted somebody to run a big school there where they taught the oil workers English. Men. But Latin men... It had always been hard to be the way they wanted, even when I was young and I was trying to please.

Guatemala was my best bet. I was just about the most qualified Teacher of English as a Foreign Language in the world, and the beautiful town of Santiago was full of TEFL schools. I downloaded an application form for Santiago Atitlán. But there was no urgency to what I was doing. My hands would fall idle.

It takes a while to come back to a place.

When I was moving countries every few years or so, I acquired the privileges of an expatriate with every move. I could invent myself everywhere I went. But my women friends in Kilbride never let me get away with anything. They were, apparently, experts on how I should behave, though Peg – who was always around because she was Monty's girlfriend – was six years younger than me; and Tessa, who'd been my friend since my first day working in Boody's Bookshop, was at least six years older.

She'd been the shop steward back then and had taken a brisk line with all of us, as she still did with me. Soon after I came back there was a party for her, because she was taking early retirement from the union, to which I wore a fabulous little Italian black suit I could still just about fit into, and three-inch heels.

'You really dressed up, didn't you?' Tessa said, when we were having a post-mortem. 'Everyone was talking about you, Rosie, though I suppose that's understand-able, you're still news. And that black suit is sensational. But what do you think? Could it do with a little some-thing at the neck?'

And, in a seemingly neutral tone of voice, Peg said, 'A lot of the girls there had come straight from work so they couldn't dress up.'

'Oh, give over!' I laughed at them. But they weren't even conscious of how they were always trying to teach me what a single woman in her mid-fifties was supposed to be like in Kilbride, Dublin, Ireland. One of them would say 'Are you going to the Eleven O'Clock?' as if they somehow failed to remember that I didn't go to Mass at all. And when I brought Andy along to the cinema, because he had given me a lift into town, they hardly spoke, even though they'd known him all their lives the same as I had. As good as telling me it wasn't the done thing to bring a man along on a girls' night out.

I knew that they were shaping me for the community, and that there was concern for me in that. But I kept the card my friends at the Information Unit in Brussels had added to the binoculars they presented me with, at a farewell feast in a Flanders tavern, where we danced all night to waltzes from a mechanical organ. 'Thank you for all the fun you brought into our lives,' the card said. There was a promise in the words. I might be a bit down now, but I had been up, and I would be up again.

I talked to the cat.

'Ulysses was away for twenty years and his dog waited for him. Did you know that? Argos, the dog? He was so old he'd turned white but he waited for his master and when at last he saw him come home he allowed himself to die. 'Thinking of dying, Bell, now that I'm back?'

She looked up from licking her fur to flick me an insolent look.

Apropos of dying, the insurance man wanted to know, did I want to top up Min's funeral insurance? For the first time, money began to worry me. Then the bill for the new central heating came. Then one day Min remarked, in a voice with genuine longing in it, how there were lovely legs of lamb in the butcher's, but at a terrible price. I had some substitute work in Kilbride Library every week that brought in a little cash. And I had enough savings for another year at the rate we were going, even though I'd bought a small second-hand car to take Min around in – not that she'd yet agreed to be taken around. I had a bond I could cash, even, to have the backyard glassed over and tiled if she ever said 'Yes' to the plan. If the yard was really nicely done, maybe she wouldn't go to the pub so much.

Not that she drank more than a very little at her lunchtime session, as far as I knew. But she'd have changed, all the same, by the time she came home. She'd be ever so slightly *wrong*. And sometimes something would bother her and she'd stay up at the Inn longer than a couple of hours. Then she'd come home and start doing something around the house, full of false elation, and my heart would be in my mouth, seeing how clumsy the drink made her. And a few times she came home and went to bed in the afternoon but got up again later and went out, and when she came back she had a smile like a grimace. I couldn't look at her. She had only done that three times to date, which was nothing compared to Mrs Beckett two doors up who was an alcoholic, not to mention a whole lot of the local men. But the thing was, I never knew when it might happen.

At the beginning, I sometimes went up to the Inn whether she asked me to or not. From the door I'd see her on the other side of the lounge, across a floor full of empty chairs and tables. I'd see the outline of her wild hair against the window there that she opened whenever she felt like it, as if she owned the place. She pulled an invisible space around herself in that big room, as if she was in a car and going somewhere. But she wasn't going anywhere. She had nowhere to go. It shocked me to see her, so that I was already hopelessly full of emotion as I crossed the greasy carpet. Even before she'd look up with her child's face.

But she didn't want me there.

The only time I caught a glimpse of her inner life had been in September, when there was a Mass of Commemoration on the first anniversary of 9/11. For the few days before it she talked a lot, telling me about that dreadful day and how she glanced at the television and thought the plane flying into the tower was a game, and she couldn't find Reeny's number in Spain, and the stew she had on was burnt so badly that she had to throw out the saucepan, and Andy Sutton brought down the bedroom chair and went over to get Mrs

Beckett because she only has RTÉ One, and Tessa came in after her work and made chicken sandwiches, and Andy went up to the Kilbride Inn for a dozen beers and a bottle of vodka because people were calling to the house all night. And all along the terrace front doors were open and you could hear the blare of television sets, and Enzo's son brought down fish and chips though the Sorrento didn't normally deliver, and then the boy stayed, watching the television with his mouth open.

'I had a terrible fright right at the beginning,' she said, 'when I remembered Markey Cuffe, that was your big friend when your nose was always stuck in a book, Florence Cuffe's boy that went to New York. I was asking everyone where did he work; he grew up out our back lane and he easily could have been dead; a lot of people around here had people over there they were mad with worry about and there was nothing they could do, the phones were all clogged up, you couldn't reach America. But then I found the cards I'd put away since last Christmas because he always sends a big one with gold on it and the address of his business, and it was in Seattle. Sure I know all about Seattle, Reeny and me used to watch *Frasier*.'

The whole of Kilbride, apparently, was going to the Commemoration Mass, and Min was ready early. She put on a moleskin coat so ancient that I could remember it on her coming into the Pillar Store when I started there at age sixteen.

'Min,' I began, but she cut me off.

'That coat cost hundreds of pounds,' she said grandly. 'That coat was in your father's mother's wardrobe when I was clearing it out, and it had hardly been worn.'

'But, Min—' intending to point out that it also smelled strongly of mothballs.

'And you,' she said, looking me up and down disapprovingly, 'you've a chance to wear your good skirt. Go on up and change. Throw us down the high heels and I'll give them a polish.'

In the church she was crushed against me by the crowd. Her eyes were closed and she took no notice of the liturgy. Instead – I was so close to her that I couldn't help but overhear – she prayed and prayed under her breath. 'Lord, Lord,' I could hear. 'Lord have mercy. Our Lady, help them.' I never knew anything like it from Min. Imploring was the very last thing she ever did.

The point she returned to earnestly, as if she said it often enough I'd understand, was that they were ordinary working people, the dead. 'They weren't doing any harm,' she'd say, looking at me, still baffled at the injustice. 'They were doing their best. They were going to work.'

But as the winter set in she went out less and less.

'What's wrong?' I'd say. 'Would you not get up?' I'd say to her. 'The car is outside the door, will I give you a lift up to the pub?' I asked her would she like to go to the Canaries, to take a bit of sun. To London. We could look at the clothes in the sales. I said, 'Will we buy a dog?'

She sprang into life. 'Certainly not!' she said. 'Bell hates dogs.'

'*Bell*.' I said, bitterly, as Bell's striped face with its level, golden eyes peeked out from the blankets under Min's chin. 'I think that cat is telling me to go back where I came from,' I said, but Min said nothing.

I dropped the idea of doing up the yard and took out private health insurance in case Min needed hospitalisation. But all that did was disqualify her for the services of the welfare psychologist who used to come to the house. When we found that out, Min was for once delighted with me.

'Good girl!' she said approvingly. 'I didn't know how to get rid of her. It's her that needs her head examined, not me.'

But that meant we were doing nothing at all about the situation. So I went in to town to Eason's bookshop and went through the self-help section – a place I'd never been before – looking for something that might help us. I brought home *Listening to Depression: How Understanding Your Pain Can Heal Your Life* and *Depression: the Mind-Body Approach*. For a while I read them to her every night, and she'd say they were great books, very interesting. But she'd go asleep after a few pages.

Our Christmas was very quiet and New Year's Eve dragged a bit, too, though there was wild good cheer on the television. Min was in bed and I sat at the kitchen fire and did my best to laugh at myself. Why couldn't I have been Angela Gheorghiu, the Romanian soprano? I muttered to an imaginary audience. To take just one example. Why was I born in goddamn working-class Dublin? Why couldn't heiress Doris Duke be born here and me in Newport or wherever it was? What difference would it have made to the universe? Why not me to be beautiful and rich and famous and wooed by tall, handsome men in wonderful long overcoats with fine silver hair that curls against their finely modelled necks? Placido Domingo, that kind of man. Why couldn't I have been the kind of woman Rilke fell for? All furs and a brilliant mind. With a castle. Those women didn't have to look after their aunts. Rilke didn't have to look after his aunt; as a matter of fact he refused to look after his mother. Rilke had it easy compared to people who have no choice but to look after their elderly relatives; a subject, by the way, on which in spite of it happening to nearly everyone, there is no literature. No writing, even, never mind literature.

I'd come across a thing on the Internet, a list of resolutions that if you stuck to them would help control your depression. Now I printed them out and took them up to Min with a cup of tea and a slice of Reeny's Spanish-style fruitcake. It was cosy in her bedroom with the new gas heating and the curtains closed against the winter night, and Bell surveying matters from her basket on the dressing-table and the transistor talking to itself on the pillow.

I began the lesson. 'OK. Number One. *Spend my time building on my strengths rather than patching up my weaknesses.*'

'Fair enough,' Min said after a pause. 'But what weaknesses does the person who wrote it mean?'

'Whatever ones you have,' I said. 'What ones do you have?'

There was a longer pause.

'She doesn't mean, does she,' Min said tentatively,

'like having a weakness, say, for butter on my potatoes?'

'No, I don't think so. We'll leave that one, will we, and try Number Two. *Ask myself every day, "What do I need?" and then take a step to meet that need.*'

'That's a great one!' Min said enthusiastically. 'Say I needed to bring Bell to the vet, I could ask you to ring him up and make an appointment!'

'Is there something wrong with Bell?'

'Not a thing – is there, Bella? Don't hide under the bedclothes, Bella. Come up here where I can see you.'

'The next one is *Make a list of activities that are delightful and do one every week.*'

'No problem there,' Min said. 'I was thinking of going to Mass somewhere else than Kilbride church. I don't like that oul' Father Simms. That's weekly.'

'OK,' I said cautiously. 'That's good. That's action. Now, Number Four. *Admit that I don't know* is what it says.'

'That I don't know what?' Min said belligerently. 'I do know.'

'What do you know?'

'I know lots of things. I left school the day I was fourteen.'

'I'm aware of that, Min. You've told me that five hundred times.'

'But that doesn't mean that I don't know things.' She was growing aggrieved now.

'Min!' I said. 'Who ever said you didn't? You're well able to do the hard crossword, for example, and you used to write me the greatest letters. Anyway, the last one is – *Say "NO" to myself on occasion and to others on many more occasions.*'

'No,' Min said.

'No what?'

'No to whatever eejit wrote those rules. No, they're no bloody good. No, I'm not going to do any of them.'

'That's right!' I danced around the bed. 'Right on, Sister!'

A bell to welcome the New Year began to ring. The first joyful binging and bonging came from Christchurch Cathedral, two or three miles away on its hill in the middle of the city, and then a wave of other bells gathered, rolling towards us from church to church down the Liffey and along the dark streets and across the canal and onto the roofs of our enclave of low brick terraces and little lanes. And suddenly all the ships in Dublin Bay on the other side of Kilbride blew their sirens to welcome midnight in competition with the bells. I threw the window open so that the room filled with a mad cacophony of hooting and pealing, and Min got 'Auld Lang Syne' on her radio and the two of us sang along and Bell began the New Year by stalking out the bedroom door in outrage.

From: RosieB@eirtel.com
To: MarkC@rmbooks.com
Sent: 11.25 a.m.

Dear Markey,

I got this address from your Christmas card from Seattle – I hope you don't mind me using it. I'm contacting you from – guess where? Right. Same old house. I came back because Min had become very reclusive and she was drinking (but only a little bit at the moment, fingers crossed).

Do you remember Colfer's shop? Mr Colfer who took about half an hour to serve a person anything? Well Peg, his youngest, who's a friend of mine and has been going out for ever with Reeny's son Monty (do you remember Reeny? She was very friendly with your mam though she isn't a bit religious) – anyhow, Peg gave me two books for Christmas – one by a priest I once went on a protest march with, and one by an American woman who used to be married to Seán Bán Breathnach who used to do the commentary on football matches in Irish. Books written to help you through life.

Peg told me that both those writers are now millionaires, and that it's because people think they're Irish – well not exactly Irish but Celtic. (It seems people think the Irish fall out of bars and thump each other, whereas the Celts have more class).

The question I want to ask you, Markey, is: Could I not write a book that would give advice to people about how to get through life?

I am as Celtic as the next person. And I am an experienced writer – I attach my CV and you will see that over the years, in a variety of jobs, I have written every kind of promotional and educational and infor-mational material. And I BADLY WANT work that I can do at home, where I can keep an eye on Min because sometimes I think she's very depressed.

I realise that Rare Medical Books is a book

business, not a publisher, but you must know people in the American publishing world? Would it be possible for you to put me in touch with an agent who specialises in this kind of thing? I know this is a long shot but frankly, Markey, from what I've seen, a baby could do better than most of the people who write these books. Their strong point seems to be their perky, optimistic tone, but I believe I could imitate that.

To give you an example:

Rosie Barry's Four-F Programme for the Middle Part of the Journey!

Are you as rich in experience as you are still young at heart?

And do you sometimes feel that neither the challenges nor the rewards of these vibrant years the world calls middle age have had the attention they deserve?

The Four-F programme builds on your wisdom, your joy and the love for others that a life well-lived has taught you. Don't let the years take you where you don't want to go. Instead:

Frolic like you always did!

Fear nothing!

Make every day a Fiesta.

And don't forget, but Forgive!

Thank you in advance, Markey, for any help you can give. Don't forget that if anyone in the self-help world would like to meet me to discuss this or any other idea, I can easily go to New York.

I haven't written to you since I sent you a card from Warsaw about Chopin a very long time ago, but I have thought about you and talked to you in my head many, many times.

Rosie Barry

2

'Markey, what time is it in Seattle? Your message said I could call any time. Are you busy? Can you listen for a minute?'

'Rosie, what's wrong with your voice?'

'Min is supposed to be asleep but she might come down. She thinks long distance is going to land us in the poorhouse, even when it's an incoming call. When Reeny rings from Spain, Min holds the receiver away from her ear as if electricity is leaking out of it and shouts, "All here are well thank God" and she tries to hang up. But anyway, Markey, have you any news yet?'

'One agent said she'd get back to me and I'll follow up again today.'

'OK. Thanks,' I whispered. 'Keep in touch.'

Singing was coming from the bathroom. Oh, yes, Saturday. I'd begun to insist at the end of February that Min get up on Saturdays. I said the bed had to be aired. She obeyed because I took her out to breakfast.

She was singing *'Là ci darem la mano'* in her own

home-made Esperanto. God alone knew what she thought that song was about, or any of the songs in Italian or French or, come to that, English that she made word-like noises to.

I sent her back upstairs to fetch her woolly hat and we went out into a wind that slapped us.

'O know you the land where the lemon trees bloom?' I said while we waited, shivering, to cross the main road. 'Italy,' I clarified.

'Well, away with you to Italy,' Min said. 'What's stopping you?'

I didn't bother answering that.

The man in the newsagent's in the shopping centre flirts with every woman who comes in. He tried with Min even though she didn't just look sixty-nine – she looked sixty-nine and quite odd. But she took no notice; said, 'Yes, yes!' impatiently and found the newspaper for me as quickly as possible, because she knew that if I had something to read I'd stay in the coffee-shop longer. I glanced at the news while she sat beside me surveying the scene, nodding, smiling and frowning at this or that like a kindly potentate. I knew what she was doing. When I was with her in public my nerves grew taut. I had to fend off the thought that someone looking at the two of us might think she was my mother and believe they could see in her what I would become.

Then I had to fend off the thought that no one ever did look at us.

Then I had to admit to myself shamefacedly that by 'no one' I meant no *man*. Kilbride just didn't have the kind of men who'd look with interest at a pair of women like myself and my aunt. Where, indeed, did? I was a proud feminist when I was young and I stirred up interest everywhere I went. But I never gave a thought then to what the passing of time might do to my self-sufficiency. It was only recently, after the affair with Leo cooled down, that I saw how I'd fallen out of a world that had men looking for women, and into a world that had mostly women in it, and gay men, and men very satisfied with their marriages. That world my boss in Luxembourg, a very bitter woman, told me about on my first day after I'd been posted there for a while by the Information Unit: of how demographically there were nine single women to every single man in that little country.

'And they're young women, mostly,' she'd said, looking at me.

The café was peaceful. An old lady on Min's left was making smiling faces at the infant sprawled in a buggy in front of a young woman who was chatting away to another young woman facing another buggy, who never took her eyes off her own calm baby. Both girls wore jeans and high heels and looked as comfortable in their roles as if they'd been practising them for a thousand years. Compared to them, what was the point of me and Min? Of the earth's resources being wasted to keep the two of us going? Today she'd insisted on a twist of chiffon scarf around her neck. 'A touch of colour at the neckline,' she said importantly, 'is always flattering.' I often wondered where she picked up the various little pronouncements about femininity which she issued as if they were holy writ. I only ever saw once – from far away and indistinctly – Stoneytown, the place where she grew up. All it had been even before it was abandoned was a terrace of grey houses and one more house out on its own on a rocky shore at the very tip of the headland where the Milbay River meets the sea, fifty miles south of Dublin. Not much chiffon around in those parts, I dare say.

We sat at our end of the banquette. Min's head was bent over her plate: she'd eat scrambled egg with appetite here whereas she wouldn't touch it at home. Her hair a vivid chestnut today, because of the recent visit of the hairdresser who did the elderly ladies for free. She got out of bed for that with alacrity. But once when I said, laying on the enthusiasm, 'There, Min! The hairdresser! There's an example of something you're receiving that you wouldn't receive if you weren't a pensioner!' the bleakness of her glance in reply made me truthful. 'What can be done, for God's sake, Min?' I burst out at her. 'I can't stop things being the way they are!'

Though for all I know, growing older isn't what's depressing her. A lot of people just accept life as it comes. I don't know how.

'I'll go and see what the desserts look like, will I?' I said. 'We might as well treat ourselves.'

Meanwhile the old lady, whose face had retreated around her mouth, leaving her teeth too big, had risen a bit unsteadily to her feet. 'I have to go to the toilet,' I heard her say to one of the young mothers.

'Well – go,' the young woman said. 'You're well able to go on your own.'

'By myself?' the woman said. She stood indecisively, holding on to the back of a chair. 'Where is it?'

I went up to the counter and brought back a fruit salad and an apple tart.

'Excuse me, is this lady with you?' A man in a manager's suit was now speaking loudly and accusingly. Behind him, the elderly woman was holding her handbag up to her face as if to hide it, her eyes shut but a tear rolling down beside her nose. 'She was found in the kitchen. Customers are not allowed in the kitchen.'

'I was lost!' she cried in a cracked voice. 'I didn't know where I was!'

'It's all right! Stop crying, for God's sake,' the young woman said; but the old lady couldn't stop.

'Oh, shut up!' the young woman snapped at her, so sharply that even the manager recoiled.

'I'm bursting myself, Missus,' Min was on her feet. 'I know where it is.'

She stepped around the buggy and was leading the old lady away before I had the tray down on the table.

We were nearly home when Min said, 'What time is it?'

'Twelve-thirty,' I said. 'Early,' I added in case she hadn't noticed my tone of voice.

'Are you finished the page with the crossword?' she asked.

In other words, she was going to go to the pub, no matter how early it was.

'We could go into town,' I said. 'Look around the shops, maybe buy Bell a new basket because that one is falling apart.' They say you shouldn't tell someone to stop doing something unless you can offer them something else to do. 'Or we could go somewhere in the car. It'd be great to get out of Dublin.'

'What's wrong with Dublin?' she said. 'I'll be home in an hour.'

And with that she turned in to the Kilbride Inn.

I got the bus into town and went around the self-help section of Eason's. And it's not that I'm teetotal. I love a couple of glasses of wine if the food deserves it. In the old days, of course, a few bottles wouldn't be too much, if it was a long lunch full of skirmishes and blushes and silences and hands that jumped apart from the shock whenever they touched. Never again? Is that what I had to accept? Yes it was.

Don't think about it.

Nothing. Nothing to help with ungovernable nostalgia for long, boozy lunches with people who fancied you. Nothing to help you cope with regret.

And that evening, my project touched rock bottom.

From: MarkC@rmbooks.com
To: RosieB@eirtel.com
Sent: 2.05 a.m.

I tried out the 4-F thing with various people who just sniggered. I'm afraid there's a problem with the letter F!

However one agent asked about you and I said you were as smart as paint. She then asked what you look like and I said I hadn't actually seen you for years but you looked very nice back then. When she asked how many years I was amazed to realise it's been more than 30! She said unfortunately the most important thing about selling in this market is how the author will tape, and if you're not young and good-looking, you have to be Shirley MacLaine.

But Rosie, don't give up. I'll keep looking for an agent/publisher. And did you mean it when you said you could come to New York? I'll be there for the Antiquarian Show in early June. Any chance you could make it then? The schedule's hectic already, but I could cancel the first morning and show you a few favourite scenes. Manhattan's not like Dublin – you have to get up very early to catch a good look at it.

It is a big thrill to be in touch with you again. Come if you can.

3

Tessa and Peg and I went for ice cream after the movie even though the skirt of the pink suit I was wearing was already showing some strain.

'You wear that to the pictures?' Tessa had said incredulously. All very well for her, she's a foot taller than me and stick-thin and has successfully modelled herself on Jackie Kennedy, little A-line frocks and all.

'I have to wear it sometime,' I said defensively, 'or I'll get no value out of it at all.'

I'd had no luck with that suit. Min, who was with me the day I bought it, informed the sales assistant that I must be off my head, that anyone with any sense picked a colour that didn't show the dirt. I remarked that I'd seen nomadic women in the desert near Isfahan who wear lots of pink and are covered in dirt and still look wonderful, and Min gave me her what-a-pain-in-the-arse-you-can-be look. I can't say I blamed her. Still, as I said to her, I did happen to have lived in all kinds of places and to have seen all kinds of things; and I could hardly stop them coming into my head just to be nice to a person who'd hardly been anywhere.

Min laughed heartily. 'Miss Hoity-Toity,' she said.

The ice cream at least stopped me sniffing: I'd cried so hard at *Babe* that Tessa moved to the row behind us on the grounds that she was getting wet. She looked attractively fit in grey leggings and a white singlet under a thick fleece with her legs strong on bouncy trainers. She never mentioned her exact age, but she must be nearly sixty-two, preparing for the old-age pension, though you'd never think it. A lock of pure silver, like a badge of honesty, swept back through her generally salt-and-pepper hair that I thought was natural but which Peg said might be a clever dye job.

'Four miles on the treadmill this morning,' Tessa said. 'How about that?'

'How do you not go crazy from boredom?' I asked. 'But it sure pays off. You look like a sexy games mistress.'

'The games mistress at my school was a fat nun,' Tessa said. 'Have you got the bridge book? Did you do your homework? Bridge is going to save us from Alzheimer's. And you're lucky, you have nothing to do all day.'

'No it won't,' Peg said sharply. 'If you're going to develop Alzheimer's you're going to develop it.'

Meaning, of course, the fact that her mother had had Alzheimer's before she died had nothing to do with the fact her mother had never read as much as a news-paper, much less played a complicated card game. Peg always got defensive about her parents.

'I do not have nothing to do!' I protested. 'I have an ambition. I'm thinking about writing a little book, a self-help book, you know like you find at the front of bookshops – ten ways to win your man or the four infallible tips for making a million? I bought a few self-help things for Min about depression and that's where I got the idea. I mean, I've written booklets and articles and publicity handouts. I can do it. So I'm going over to New York in June to see can I break in to the market. I mean, America is where they love those kind of books. By Irish people. Markey Cuffe is going to help me.'

The two of them stared at me. Words, apparently, failed them.

'Did you say you're writing a book about depression?' Peg eventually asked. 'With Flo Cuffe's son that sent her all the money?'

'Not depression.'

'Well, on what?' Tess asked.

'Well,' I said. 'I was wondering about growing old. I don't mean old like old people, I mean how about the changes people like us face, who aren't old at all but aren't young either? Don't people need help with that? Even a small thing, like the brown spots that come out on the backs of your hands – that comes as a shock. You wait for them to go away but they're never going to. And do you know what I saw in *The Irish Times* today?' I took the cutting out of my pocket.' "The average Irish-woman aged forty and over wants to weigh less than she did at twenty. Most women aged forty and over hate their naked body, according to a new survey, scoring it three-and-a-half out of ten compared with seven out of ten for the body of their youth." Isn't that terrible, girls? *Hate!*'

But Peg, who wore the same chain-store clothes since she was a girl, having moved maybe three sizes up over the decades, just smiled in an absent-minded way. Today she had blue jeans on her stocky, competent bottom-half and a blouse with a little frilly collar and puff sleeves on her top. Still, she was pushing it with a blouse as tweetie-pie as that.

'I wouldn't call it terrible, Rosie,' she said mildly. 'There's a lot of things I'd call terrible before I called that terrible.'

'What, like?'

'Well, cruelty, say. Cruelty to children, say. Or to animals, even.'

'Oh sure,' I said. 'But if hating ourselves is ruining our lives there's cruelty here, too. Women are being cruel to themselves on behalf of whoever hates women so badly that they can't accept their bodies whatever way their bodies happen to be.'

I was breaking an unwritten rule. The three of us never talked to each other about our physical selves. Weight, we talked about, nothing else. Though when we were young Tessa and I would sigh and giggle and lift our eyes to heaven and shake our heads at the goings-on of men; and Peg did the same, later, before she settled down with Monty; all this as if we understood each other so perfectly that we didn't need to use words. But the truth was that we would not use them. Our intimacy was based on reserve.

And so I'd brought along the cutting on purpose, to see whether we could move closer than that. How was it that the passage of time, all-destructive in so many other ways, didn't lessen the powerful ideal of being thin? The women in the study, after all, were older women; they weren't out there on display looking for a mate. Was it a modern woman's fate, to turn against her own body? Did my friends look with pain and astonishment at the signs of ageing, the same as I did?

'C'mon Peg,' Tessa said without taking her eyes off me – as if I were dangerous. 'Ask me a question.'

Peg opened the book. 'In calculating the value of a hand,' she read out, 'what points are given for the ten of spades in a hand where Ace, King, Queen, Jack of spades are the only honours?'

'Do you count it at all?' Tessa said anxiously after a pause.

'You do not. Good girl. Now, Rosie. What does an opening bid of one club signify?'

'That must be further on than page five,' I said, 'I'm only at page five.'

'We have to learn while we're still in our prime,' Tessa said. 'It'll be too late afterwards.'

'I hate those words, "too late",' I said vehemently. 'Too late for what? If I do manage to write something, it won't be in the shops till I'm nearly sixty, but what will that be too late for?'

'What shops?' Tessa said.

'What?'

'What shops?'

'All the shops. Everywhere.'

'Like – like *How to Win Friends and Influence People*?' Peg asked.

'Like *Sex and the Single Woman*?' Tessa asked.

'Well, that sort of thing,' I began.

'But what do you know about anything!' the two of them said in perfect unison, as if they'd rehearsed.

'Well, that's just it!' I said. 'I'm just like all the other poor schmucks who don't know what's happening to their bodies and their brains, nor what to do about it!'

They were silent again.

'And anyway,' I said, 'I have to do something about myself. You two seem to be content with the way things are for you, but I'm not. I mean, leaving Min out of it, what do I have in mind for my own life? Nothing, is the answer.'

There was an uneasy silence as we got into Tessa's car and queued to exit from the car park. Tessa was pretty contemptuous, usually, of women who 'let themselves go'. She might think that the least an overweight woman could do is hate herself. But I couldn't really predict what she'd think, even though we were old friends. When I knew her first, when I got a job in Boody's Bookshop after leaving The Pillar Department Store, Tessa was having some kind of relationship with Hugh Boody, even though she was the shop steward and he was the boss. For years the two of them went to the opera together all around Europe. We girls who worked in the store were inclined to believe that was all it was, a friendship based on love of singing. We were young. We thought they couldn't be sleeping together because Tessa looked like Audrey Hepburn and Hugh Boody, who looked like a gentle horse, was twice her age.

Their relationship had fascinated Min. 'Where are they now?' she'd say. 'Where are they now?' A temporary secretary once saw a receipt for a room in Parma for Signor and Signora Boody, but of course that *signora* could have been Mr Boody's real wife, a lady with grey hair and an English accent who never remembered our names.

'Where's Parma?' Min asked when I told her, making me point the name out on a map of Europe. Though I don't know that Min really understood how maps work – seeing she always made me show her which bit was Ireland.

Tessa and Hugh Boody were – whatever they were – for a long time, and his name would come into the conversation every time I came back to visit, until one day, about ten years ago, when Min in her roundup of gossip said she'd kept the newspaper with a write-up about Mr Boody, and a picture of him at the races only a week before he died.

'He's dead!'

'He died in a taxi,' Min said. 'The poor taxi man must have got an awful fright.'

She got the obituary for me and I read it later, up in my room.

I thought about writing a proper note of sympathy to Tessa, but before I did she heard I was back, and called to the house to see me. I intended to hold her hand or something like that and say I was sorry, but I didn't get round to it and eventually she said that she missed Hugh a lot, but that she'd been able to retrieve the money on their season ticket to Covent Garden. It was the perfect reminder I always got, sooner or later when I came back to Kilbride, of how people there kept certain emotions to themselves. You were allowed to be dramatic, but not really revelatory.

We were crawling now towards Kilbride, stuck behind a mobile home with a GB plate, when I said, to lighten the mood, 'Bloody English. Eight hundred years of brutal oppression and now this.'

'Nine hundred,' Peg said, 'because we're in the 2000s now. Did you know that it ended up that a Catholic wasn't allowed to own a horse? That's what my da told me. That's one of the reasons he always kept a few horses when he could find somewhere around Kilbride to graze them. He didn't even like horses. But he did it because the English came over and they took our land and they kept us down by force and they treated us worse and worse the longer they were here.'

'I didn't know you felt like that, Peg,' I said, surprised. 'I knew you were a Catholic – I mean, a real Catholic, sure we're all the other kind. But I didn't know you waved the green flag, too.'

'What's wrong with being a Catholic?' Peg said truculently. 'I go to Mass on a Sunday. Monty goes to Mass when he stays in our house. Eighty-something per cent of the population of the Republic of Ireland go.'

'There's nothing *wrong* with being a Catholic,' Tessa said in a soothing voice. 'Rosie didn't say there—'

'She implied.'

'She didn't imply.'

'If I didn't, I meant to!' I yelled. 'I don't know how you can kneel there, Peg – *kneel* – in front of a man who

41

calls himself a priest, who belongs to an all-male organisation that specialises – *specialises* – in bullying and frightening women. The Taliban of their day they were, and still are wherever they can get away with it. Telling poor African women with twenty AIDS-ridden children to be thankful to God they haven't committed the sin of contraception! Sitting on their fat arses in Rome as if it's the most normal thing in the world to sit around in frocks, making up things for God to say. No wonder I left Ireland. Everyone should leave Ireland. Women particularly should get the hell out from underneath the gunmen and the priests— '

'The priests aren't God!' Peg cut across me. 'It's all the people together who are the Church, and God is in the love they have for each other.'

'Tell that to the Pope!' I cried. 'Tell that to some poor woman crawling along with a prolapsed womb! Tell— '

'Jesus Christ!' Tessa shouted. 'Will you two shut up!'

I took deep breaths as silently as I could. Peg always got angry with me at least once a meeting. It always upset me, too. I'd tried suggesting to her a few times that though she had never left her childhood home, I didn't feel that I was any better than her. I'd said that though I'd travelled, travel is mundane enough when you have very little money. But it hadn't been mundane. There was a morning, a very early morning – and the memory of it is only one of thousands of memories – when I waited for a bus in a taverna in a village in the Mani, where the Greek men stood in the half-dark at the counter drinking their coffees and rakis, and the lamp flickered in front of a wall of icons, and a golden dawn moved across the cobbles of the old square towards the open door. Was I not indeed enviable, because there had been moments like that? If it had been the other way around, and it was me who had never travelled, I'd surely have envied Peg.

'I'm sorry, girls,' Peg whispered. 'I don't know why everything's getting to me these days. I'm taking Saint John's Wort but I don't think it's doing me any good. I think I'll go back to acupuncture.'

'Acupuncture is only a distraction,' I said. 'We have deep needs, all three of us, and— '

'You've hit the nail on the head!' Tessa interrupted me. 'Needs! Why don't we talk about *my* needs. Actually, I do have a bit of news you might be interested in.'

'Tess!' we said. 'What?'

'But since I've just spotted the only parking place within an ass's roar of Rosie's house...'

'Oh, Tess baby!'

'Wait!'

'Hurry up, can you, Tess?' Peg said. 'I promised I'd get back to my dad before eleven.'

'I'm tired telling you that you make a martyr of yourself to that man,' Tessa said, turning off the ignition.

I settled myself in happy anticipation. I enjoyed Tessa very much, and whatever it was she was going to do, it would be a practical, intelligent action. She acted where I brooded.

She waited a moment before addressing us.

'Girls, I am not satisfied with the way things are; the way Rosie said I was. I've decided to make a change.'

A bell somewhere far away rang the hour. Markey

used to know each Dublin bell so well that he could tell you which church it belonged to.

'I would have told you,' Tessa said. 'But, you know, I wasn't sure till today that I'd go through with it. But this morning I was in a bit of a confrontation with Paschal Kelly, director of the Counselling Training Centre – El Creepo as he is called by his staff – because I happened to say that I was thinking of going to a hotel for a spa break and he made a smart remark about you single people being free to follow your fancy but married men, alas, having commitments they could not escape. He actually said "Alas". Anyway, I said, "Paschal, your kids are somewhere around forty years old, so if they're still a burden to you there's something dreadfully wrong." But it got me thinking again, all the same, about being single, about the difference between it and being married.'

'But you've always been so contented, Tess!' I said, while Peg simultaneously exclaimed, 'But I thought you liked being single!'

'Remember the smell of the gorse around that place you used to rent up in Kilternan?' I said. 'Remember the party you threw the year the snow came right up to the windows? Remember Boody's was closed when the pipes froze and a gang of us got out to you somehow with a case of wine and enough smoked salmon to open a shop?'

'That was thirty years ago, Rosie,' Tessa said.

'*Thirty*?!' Peg said in a low voice.

None of us moved.

'I figured out that I wanted to make people's lives

better,' Tessa said. 'That's why I'm training for counselling. I mean, I was in the union for that too, but there was a whole load of Neanderthal men to get around first. But it isn't just other people I want to counsel –' she gave a little cough – 'well, actually, I want some insight for myself.'

She went on after a moment. 'So I'm thinking of linking up with Andy.'

I think my mouth must have fallen open. Andy! Andy was a kind of brother. Who, when he came up from the country to visit his mother Pearl, mended our broken appliances and brought us eggs and so on. But nobody had ever thought of him as a *man*. In fact, he had a slow, vacant manner that drove me, for one, nuts, even though I knew perfectly well that he wasn't vacant, that he was in fact a thoughtful person and a decent one.

'Does Andy know?' Peg said after a minute.

'He doesn't,' Tessa said. 'But who else is going to make an offer to a small farmer nearly sixty-four years of age, a real hard worker, but very quiet? The farm's not big enough for a young one who'd want a family and anyway he's always on the road collecting his animals for Africa. Auntie Pearl is well into her eighties and she worries about him night and day. And, like' – Tessa paused, because she never said anything sentimental if she could avoid it – 'I'd like her to die happy, the old lady,' she said, shyly. 'It would mean a lot to me.'

'But, Tess!' Peg and I said at the same time, before I continued by myself. 'Tess, you'd have to sleep with Andy. Clothes off, same bed, husband-and-wife kind of thing.'

'I know that, thank you,' Tessa said sarcastically. 'I know what it entails, even if we are related.'

'But Tess, what about Andy? Have you asked him?'

'Nobody asks Andy anything,' she said. 'Andy is *told*.'

Once again there was absolute silence in the car.

The evening star had already gone under the horizon but the pavement ahead and the branches of the apple tree in Reeny's yard that the kids didn't bother to rob any more were bleached by chilly April moonlight. I couldn't stop shivering in the house, waiting for the radiators to warm up. Min crept around turning them off no matter how often I told her we could afford the heating. Yes, she'd been down: the kettle was still hot and the kitchen radio was playing softly, someone singing Handel:

> *The trumpet shall sound,*
> *And we shall be changed,*
> *We shall,*
> *We shall,*
> *We shall be changed....'*

Marrying was different when you were too old for babies. Tessa could easily be a granny, couldn't she, say if she'd had a daughter at twenty and that daughter had a daughter at ... yes. A great-granny, even. Andy would have been a lovely father, too. Would he think about that – that if he married Tessa his chance at that was lost? He mightn't be what you'd call attractive, but he was as kind as you could imagine. That's why everyone pushed him around. His place in Carlow used to be a sort of depot for all kinds of pets. One of his cats, for instance, he'd found in a sack on a riverbank, with a leg broken. The leg had knitted in such a way that it dragged after the cat with the paw turned outwards, but it was a wonderful cat. He had beautiful, black hens that a Lady Something had left him in her will, as a fellow-enthusiast of rare breeds. And he looked after a floating population of horses and donkeys.

Almost every one of his pets had to be sent away when he put himself on call to drive his truck to England whenever there was a plane ready to take the No-Need animals to Africa. But not one of us had ever really thought about what the loss of his menagerie might have meant to him. That was what was so shocking about Tessa saying she was going to marry him: no one had ever taken his feelings seriously.

Andy could easily father a baby. It makes no difference to babies what their fathers look like. They gurgle away anyway, don't they? Saul Bellow looked like a sick basset-hound there towards the end, but his girlfriend was delighted to have his baby. Charlie Chaplin still looked great if you liked small old men, but God he was eighty-five, wasn't he, the last time? Wouldn't you think his willie would be just too tired to stand up? And then he'd hardly said hello to the child and he was dead. They said it was the Irish air caused the baby – he and the wife were on holiday in Kerry nine months earlier. Rostropovich. Did Rostropovich father a baby or was that some other Russian cellist with age spots? Not that growing older doesn't make some men even more attractive. Look at Bill Clinton: gorgeous to begin with and even more gorgeous since his heart thing. Women in their sixties had real beauty too, a few of them, but not the kind he had – not the kind that made your belly contract. People don't crowd around women his age, wanting to devour them.

I was climbing into bed when I remembered that once, outside Trinity College, a man was standing beside me waiting for a break in the traffic, and when we accidentally looked towards each other, I realised it was Paul Newman: grey cropped hair, eyes still marvellously blue in a handsome face, body limber under the perfect business suit as he set off across the street. Wait'll I tell Min that Butch Cassidy's out there somewhere! I thought. But after a moment I decided that he was a bit too tailored for me. A bit too perfect, whereas I liked my men rumpled.

I started to laugh at the thought of it – a nobody Irishwoman who lived with her aunt in Dublin turning up her nose at Paul Newman because he was too well-groomed.

But I drifted into sleep thinking about Tessa's last words.

Of how she'd swung around in the driver's seat just as I was stepping out of the car, and looked at Peg and me, and said, 'I see it in our counselling sessions all the time. People are dying of loneliness every day.'

4

I took a deep breath before I went upstairs. 'Min – where would you like to go while I'm in New York next month?' I was standing at the window, tidying the curtain into even folds. My tone of voice was a carefully chosen shade of *ennui*. 'I have to go over there but it's only for a week.'

Nothing.

'I have to go to New York. It's work, not pleasure.'

Nothing. I turned around and caught sight of myself in the mirror. Talk about dull-looking. All I needed was a flowered pinny and rubber boots and I could pose as a simple Irish housewife, circa 1950. A good haircut was the least I needed before Manhattan.

'We're not getting any younger, Min. I need to find work I can do at home. My lump sum is disappearing at the rate of knots…'

'*I'm* young enough, madam!' She shot upright in the bed, and Bell gave a startled wail. 'You go off wherever you want to and I'll stay here in the comfort of my own house.'

'As a matter of fact you didn't even have central

heating till I put it in,' I said. And, I added silently, I bought out the leasehold for you as soon as I was earning good money – how come that never gets mentioned? 'But anyway, you can't stay here on your own.'

'Yes I can. I was here for years and years while you were wandering the world and—'

'You were younger then and—'

'And I have no problems when you go to see the boyfriend or whatever that foreign man is who sounds as if he's reading the news.'

'Leo. You know his name is Leo. But I only go away when Reeny's at home. If you fell, Reeny would come in in a flash. Those stairs are a death trap. Or if you left something boiling on the stove. But—'

'I'm not going anywhere.'

I flounced out past the bathroom to the little bedroom that was my dad's so as to get myself under control, as I used to do when I was a teenager and Min was giving me various kinds of grief. I tiptoed across to the window and opened it to let in a bit of fresh air. All my life, even though my memories of him were so old they seemed in black and white, I'd tried not to stand on the strip of thin carpet between the bed and the wardrobe with its deep, secretive corners, because I thought of that as Daddy's territory. His dinner-jackets used to hang in a neat rank above his socks balled-up in a cardboard box and his brown-paper packets of shirts and the brush-and-polish kit for doing his shoes. The mirror on the wardrobe door was the hinge between the two sides of him: the man in rumpled pyjamas who came downstairs with the cat in his arms and put it down to give me my kisses; and the cinema manager who gave himself a last looking-over – myself seated on the bed watching him adoringly – straightening his dickey-bow, plucking the crease in his pants to hang right, smoothing his hair back with rapid, alternate strokes of his lightly brilliantined palms, and going off in his black gabardine coat like a film star himself.

I sat on the edge of the bed, which sagged, just beyond the iron frame.

'You used to climb out of your cot in Min's room and climb in here, and go back to sleep beside me,' my dad told me when I was small. 'Maybe you remembered that your Mam slept in this bed when you were in her tummy. But she had to go to Heaven, then. So I sent a message to the priest in the place she came from to tell her father that she'd gone to Heaven, but that she'd left her little girl to mind me. That was you,' he said, smiling at me, and he absent-mindedly touched my cheek. I knew that if I held up my face in a certain way his hand would not be able to resist the caress.

'So then Min turned up. I didn't even know your Mam had a sister.'

He made a face of comic astonishment, and I laughed with him.

Four or five years later, when he was in bed a lot and I used to do my homework up in the room beside him, he remembered that again.

'Min wanted to stop you coming in here,' he said. 'But your Granny Barry told her to let the poor motherless child go to her father if she wanted to.'

He gave me a smile that was frail but mischievous. 'Of course, Min didn't like that. As far as she was concerned you weren't motherless at all. And neither were you. Minnie was only fifteen when she came to us, you know, but she was as good a mother or better than a woman twice her age. But she should have been having fun. I think of that when I see the fifteen-year-olds that come into the Odeon. They never stop laughing – they're having a great time.'

'Why did she want to stop me coming in here?' I asked. All my fights, when I was growing up, were with her, not with him. It was her I had to understand.

'She wanted to toughen you up,' he said. 'She thinks she's tough herself.'

And he smiled his tender smile again.

But Granny Barry didn't like her at all and my Dad pretended he didn't notice. I saw all that, even when I was small. We used to fetch the key to The Hut from Granny Barry at the beginning of our holidays. I'd run up the crooked stairs to the flat over the archway above Bailey's Yard where my grandmother lived, praying that we wouldn't be delayed there. There it'd be – the gold rimmed tea-set, the leaf tea in a perforated, chrome ball, paid out on its chain into the boiling water like a diver, the sandwiches – squishy egg or dry ham – in two columns on a leaf-shaped platter.

'Sit over at the table, you must be dying with the thirst,' she'd say, kissing me and my dad.

He sat in the armchair that was called 'Billy's chair', smiling, his head resting on the embroidered white cloth that was there to protect the velvet. An *antimacassar*, Granny once said, and I was delighted, years later, when Markey told me that macassar was an oil men used to wear on their hair. All Granny's things were perfect, Edwardian things. The chenille tablecloth with bobbles and the Turkish carpet and the bamboo stand for a china pot in the window and the stiff plant in the pot. Granny Barry used to rub Pond's Cold Cream into its leaves. You could do a production of 'The Dead' with them if you made a play out of the story – though how would you do the end? You'd have to have a film coming out of Gabriel's head. Granny knew who James Joyce was because every day when she lived in Bray she went to the same Mass as one of his sisters.

Min wandered around restlessly, longing to escape out of there. But she didn't dare say anything. I took the opportunity to show off. I'd read out bits of the Papal Blessing certificate that was sent from Rome to bless Granny and Granda's marriage – not that Granda was all that blessed, since he died, Granny always said, when their wedding cake was still in the tin. The Blessing was a framed scroll that had always impressed me. It was draped with an olive-wood rosary with beads the size of eggs and hung to the left of an equally imposing Sacred Heart. Jesus could see the Blessing, I once assured my father, if He just squinted a bit.

At last we got away and drove to the bottom of Main Street where we passed the rusted winches and rotting wooden sheds and crossed a creek of the Milbay River and came to a stretch of thin turf with bald patches of gravel and shell behind high fencing, where our hut, standing on concrete blocks, looked out to sea. In my memory it was always a perfect late-summer afternoon when my father unlocked the wire gate and drove us in and then went back to snap the padlock shut. He'd be wearing a short-sleeved shirt. Always. His straight, silky hair would fall across his face. That's how I remember it. He'd lift his head to breathe in the salty air, and twirling the key with a flourish, he'd walk jauntily back to the car. Then he'd move the driver's seat of the Ford Prefect forward with a thunk and Min would get in and drive – oh, the excitement! – across the sandy grass.

'Brake! *Brake*, woman!' It was wonderful how they laughed. She'd do no more than move the car at a snail's pace about fifty yards but it would change her to do it. Her eyes would glint with pride. They'd seek out my father's eyes, and he'd nod, as if to say, 'Oh, yes!'

Then Dad would push open the door into air thick with the smells of splintery plank walls and tarpaper and dusty coconut matting. He'd bring in a Calor gas cylinder for the two-ring cooker and a few jerrycans of water from home. Min would have left the floor covered in newspapers the year before, and I'd squat and try to read bits which she'd keep pulling from under my eyes. Then she was knocking down spiders' webs with a brush and prising open the window and dividing the bag of bedclothes between the iron bed in the inside room where she and I slept and the rubber mattress in the corner of the front room which my Dad would blow up last thing for himself with a bicycle pump.

We lived in our bodies in The Hut. I saw everything.

That was maybe the main reason why I so loved being there. We were close. I was near enough to the other two to understand them. Min would put our supplies out, for example, and I could see by the way she arranged them her pride in them because we never otherwise bought much at a time. We began each holiday with untouched packets of salt and tea and sugar, a stack of tins of baked beans, two cartons of eggs, a pound of sausages, a pound of sliced ham, a big fresh loaf with a black crust and a whole box of Afternoon Tea biscuits. She left everything out for a few hours but then she had to put the things a mouse might be tempted by into old biscuit tins, which she put regretfully away.

Last thing, when all the chores were done, she'd hang her old polka-dot bathing suit on a nail in the partition wall. She didn't swim in it; she didn't swim at all. But she loved it and she hung it up as though it were a banner.

I stood up from Dad's bed, dreamy with memory, and a watery version of myself stood up in the mirror of Dad's wardrobe. The room – the whole little house – was as silent as the tomb.

Dad didn't die till I was fourteen years old. Towards the end, he lay downstairs in the kitchen on the special bed Reeny got from Homecare, where he coughed and coughed, and was too weak to make much difference to the household. There was really nothing left of him by the end. Min did everything for him – fed him, emptied his bedpans, washed him, gently cleaned his teeth and his eyes and his ears. She wouldn't let him be taken to hospital.

'I promised him,' she said, no matter what the doctor or the neighbours tried to say.

I know my father heard her because I saw his hands rise from the coverlet as if he wanted to applaud.

On the last day she held a cigarette to his lips for a few minutes and he tried to suck on it, and she poured a little shot-glass of whisky and smeared some of it onto his tongue. Then she put those things away and combed his hair and lightly sponged his face and held one hand, while I held the other, until Dad came to his last breath.

We sat frozen for a minute or two minutes, not able to believe the silence where his breathing used to be.

'Open the door!' she cried. 'Quick! Quick!'

I opened the front door a fraction.

'More!' she commanded. She was standing up, her eyes coal-black in her white face. 'Wider!'

Then Reeny came in. She gave me a kiss and said to Min, 'Will I give you a hand washing him?'

Min hadn't moved from where she was standing, and still looking at the door, didn't answer.

At that age I was mad about boys, who were on my mind even in the hours after my father died. Though it wasn't boys themselves so much as the intensely exciting world me and my girlfriends had discovered, where we watched and were watched by boys and talked about them all the time. I went up to this room, Dad's old room, and I stood just inside the door and I tried to clear my head of everything but him and pray for him to rest in peace.

I could all but see grief sitting in the corner, beckoning to me, but my own life surged in and out of my mind. I was in the top gang of girls for the first time now that I was boy-crazy and they didn't have to ostracise me for liking lessons. We hung around outside Colfer's shop and the Sorrento chip shop and the back lanes, and the boys shoaled up and down and sat on walls and jeered at us as we passed with pink cheeks. And now that my dad was dead downstairs it filled me with anxiety that I'd have to walk around wearing black with everyone looking at me. And I'd be trapped in the house.

I heard Min come up the stairs. All my life she'd hop-skipped up and down them like a mountain goat, but today she was slow. I thought she was going to her bedroom, but she came into the room behind me and I think she rested her cheek against my back for a second.

'We'll have the removal tomorrow,' she said, 'and the funeral the next day. And then – you go out with your friends, Rosie. You were his pride and joy, don't forget, and he wouldn't want you to be stuck in the house.'

Then her voice got stronger. 'He had a great life so he had,' she said. 'I know that's not what it looked like, but it's what he said to me a thousand times and he never told me a lie. And he's happier now than he ever was. Did you not feel his spirit going out the door? Did you not feel how happy he was?'

I closed the window in Dad's room again. To think – that day, the day we lost him, Min was only twenty-nine!

I went back past the bathroom to her room, where she was a lump under the bedclothes.

'Is it OK if I turn on the light?' I said. 'OK? Listen, Min, I was having a think there about New York and it might just be a waste of money. I was really only going for one meeting. To tell you the truth, the meeting was with Markey Cuffe from out the back lane, and nothing might have come of it. So I've decided not to go.'

'No,' she was swinging her child's legs out of the bed. 'No,' she said without looking at me. 'You go. I should have said to you, go.'

'I really can't,' I said, 'unless you'll stay somewhere for me.'

'Choose me somewhere nice, then,' she said.

If it had been our custom to hug I'd have crushed her. As it was, I gave her a lift to the pub because it was raining.

Part Two
New York

5

I splayed like a starfish in the Harmony Suites Hotel so as to feel as much as possible of the sheet, my heels and elbows slithering across the fine surface, before turning over to feel its silkiness on my breasts and on the fronts of my feet. I even relished the sound that rose up to the room, a distant roaring and grinding beneath the traffic noise, which the doorman told me was rehabilitation going on around the clock at the World Trade Center. He also told me that it was unseasonably cool for New York in early June. But even though I'd turned off the heating I was as snug as a baby under the soft blankets and extra comforter that I'd taken from the second bed. Not to mention delighted with the luxury of everything after the plainness of Kilbride.

And for nothing, almost! The room cost less, on a special offer, than the midtown places I'd stayed in when I'd come to Manhattan to attend a conference on Violence Against Women at the UN or to shop with Tessa. Those rooms had smelt of stale air-freshener overlaid on city dust with windows that looked out on walls a few feet away. But this room had a wrap-around window, full of the lurid, night sky over New Jersey and of the dour river below, jostling down towards the harbour.

I delayed the bliss of falling into jet-lagged sleep, turning the pillow to recover the crispness of an untouched side, and thinking how a person could give a party in a bed like this, like the couple in Evelyn Waugh who lived a busy social life in theirs...

How come I never thought of our beds in Kilbride when I was bringing Min presents? The sheepskin rug the man in the airport in Perth said would be $100 excess but then let me check in in exchange for a kiss – a great kiss, too. Fully meant. Or the lampshade I had to hold on my lap the whole way from Helsinki. Or the Provençal oilcloth and matching napkins – which I bought in lieu of a day's meals in Arles when I hadn't a bean. Does she still have those? And if so, where would they be...?

Oh God, I should have rung. But the Sunshine Rest Home doesn't allow phone calls after 9 p.m. and in Ireland it's ... oh God, I'll be a wreck when Markey comes if I don't sleep.

I slipped across to the bathroom, then stood for a moment enchanted by the huge swags of lights in the office blocks over on the New Jersey shore. The enormous sky was pricked all over by stars but ragged, inky clouds were moving in to blot them out. Down below a fire flickered where someone homeless must be living, on the rough ground behind the hoarding across from the hotel.

My soul doth magnify the Lord, I began. But I never got

much further than that before I forgot I was saying a prayer of thanks – I was always just too happy.

I waited in the silent foyer at half-past-five the next morning. Even the traffic noise had died away outside, the receptionist asleep in her chair behind the desk.

'Shoes?' Markey said, as he charged through the swinging doors.

I lifted one foot to show him a sneaker with such instant obedience that I could feel him laughing as he held my head for a moment.

'Rose!' he said into my hair. 'Rosie Barry! It's been much too long!'

At least he couldn't see my face, which was blushing with shock. How, how on earth, had Markey Cuffe become so handsome? Cuffo – that's what the other boys called him when they needed him to come out for a game – but it was Spiderbrain the rest of the time, because his arms and legs were so long and thin and because he was always reading; always 'had his head stuck in a book', as reading was described in Kilbride. He had greasy curls all the time I knew him, nor had it ever crossed my mind that underneath them there lay the shapely skull you could see now that his silver hair was close-shaved. He'd had really bad spots, too, which were the first thing I'd noticed when I first got talking to him, at fourteen, on the steps of the little branch library whose librarian threw everyone out anytime she felt like it, so she could go and play the slot-machines at the back of the pub. But then, Markey hardly ate anything; he was so poor that the Brothers left out a loaf every day for him to take back after school to the cottage in the lane behind our house where he lived with his mother. The only good clothes he'd had was a man's suit that was too big, which I happened to see on him once when I was going out our back gate, and he was opening the door of the cottage to the priest.

In those days the priest went around bringing Communion to the sick, with his gown flapping around his ankles and Holy Communion held high up in front of him in a kind of silver box.

'The Eucharist. Not Communion,' Markey corrected me when I mentioned it. 'A pyx, that's what that box is called.'

He had always loved unusual words and he had always loved putting me right. And typically, he didn't say anything about whatever was wrong with his mother. He never did say anything about his home life.

Even when he grew up and the spots disappeared – even then, his eyes weren't the intense grey they were now – though whenever I'd visualised him, I would begin with those grey eyes. But it was the skin around them that had actually changed, maybe from living over in Seattle where everyone is outdoors a lot. Somehow it had become a grainy, olive-brown.

The fact was, he was beautiful now.

'Are you ready?' He was practically pawing the ground. 'If we don't get going now, by the time we reach Canal we won't be able to see across the street for traffic.'

He was turning away when he remembered his manners.

'How's Min?'

I didn't answer for a moment. I couldn't say that I'd ever known her to look at me with such comprehensive bitterness as she had when we'd passed, the morning before, a ragged queue of old ladies outside the dining room of the Sunshine Rest Home. Some of them propped in wheelchairs, and one of them calling 'Mammy! Mammy!' in a heartbroken voice as she stroked the wallpaper.

I couldn't say that the last thing I'd said was 'I'm sorry, Min', and that she had looked at me as if she'd never seen me before and said nothing. What could she say? This was the same woman who a few nights before, after I burst into tears in front of the television at the sight of a row of little North Korean children with bloated stomachs and twig limbs, had strode across and changed channels, and had hissed at me, 'People die, Madam! They die! Or they're got rid of because there's no use for them. Life is *hard*.'

I didn't say how when I got into the car to leave the Home, I couldn't drive because I was shaking so much. I wasn't sure in the end that I'd done the right thing. The last few days before I left she not only didn't go to the pub – she got up in the mornings and was out in the yard before I came down, putting new bedding plants in tins and old pots and in the hip bath that she was laboriously filling with soil that she stole in increments from the public park at the bus stop. She asked me did I want an egg for my breakfast? She was going to whitewash the coal shed, she said.

But even so...

People who drink fall, and they set themselves on fire, and they walk into traffic.

I'd left her sitting on her bed in the Sunshine, glowering at me. I'd been trying to help, when she went to the bathroom, by unpacking the bag she'd insisted on packing for herself. But digging into the chaos of it I came across something hard, and when I peeked into the foil I saw that she'd wrapped up some old pieces of toast from breakfast and a couple of greyish chicken legs from the fridge and a carton of yoghurt that was already leaking. I nearly wept. She must have been afraid there'd be no food.

I heard the toilet flush, and threw her things back into the bag. I didn't want her to know that I knew. I emptied my wallet of all the money I had in it and left the pile of notes on the locker so that she'd have enough for anything she wanted. Then I told her I was sorry and somehow got out of there to the car.

'Min's fine, Markey,' I told him instead. 'Physically speaking, but she doesn't look after herself. I solved the problem of coming over for this week by booking her into a kind of rest home. I think she'll grow to like it.'

Should I return his polite enquiry? I didn't actually know what his living arrangements were, but if I said something like, when he had to leave his home to go to booksellers' conferences and so on, did he miss it? Wouldn't that tell me? But maybe he'd only enquired after Min because he used to know her; that is to say, to know to come round to our house as seldom as possible, because she thoroughly disapproved of all the lending of books and going on walks he and I went in for. He wasn't her idea of a boyfriend worth having, as she made crystal clear. She thought four years older than me was too old. She thought that we were poor but he was shamefully poor. And she thought – she said it so often, I was sick of hearing it – that he looked like something the cat dragged in.

But by heavens he didn't any more. He looked unique: someone good-looking and confident and well dressed and at the same time someone who knew Kilbride. Everybody in Kilbride should come to America. Look at his *nails*. Look at his marvellous teeth. Look at the energetic way he was moving ahead of me holding himself straight. The men at home seemed to be perfectly content as they were, to put it mildly. Take, for example, Monty, who had spent his life playing golf and yet his tummy never got any smaller. It spilled over his waistband, while his bottom had migrated halfway down the back of his thighs. And Andy, though he ate like a horse, was so thin that we all said if he turned sideways you wouldn't know where he was. And neither of them – no man, probably, in the whole of Ireland – would be caught dead wearing a long black coat with a kick pleat at the shoulders and a blue scarf made of something softer than cashmere and a fine black sweater and blue jeans and black loafers. And a hat! Oh my God, a wide, black hat! I hadn't known a man who dressed like that since I lived in Italy. In my early thirties, I'd been – a good age for living in Italy.

There was a faint swathe of pale light in the charcoal-grey sky away to the left where the ocean must be. But it still felt like the dead of night in the street, apart from the faint dance music I'd thought I heard from behind the hoarding opposite the hotel.

'It's a hidden city,' Markey was saying. 'The old Manhattan. The meat market's still hanging on – the streets and the buildings, anyway – but the fish market's going soon. But just look at this' – we'd reached Canal – 'isn't this just like the main street of a Russian merchant town if you raise your eyes? See the wooden storefronts, those windows and the shuttered cellars? Here's a glimpse of the old commercial, immigrant city – not as good as the Lower East Side but as good as we're going to manage in the time we have and still fit in Soho. See? Over there? Those buildings were warehouses. See the hoists? Those wonderful materials, granite, and cast-iron.'

'You haven't changed, Markey!' I cried.

Then hearing myself, I added in silence – not changed? Are you kidding?

It was me who was the good-looking one, when we were young. Did he remember that? He used to walk with me as far as one of the other girl's houses on a weekend night when I was going to a dance, in a cloud of whatever perfume the Pillar Department Store was giving free squirts of that week and a pencil skirt and a bra that yanked my breasts up to point at the sky, and all the while he'd be talking about Claudel or Robert Lowell or the urban models the planners had in mind when they rebuilt central Dublin after the 1916 Rising. I'd be tottering along in my stilettos. I should have been against high heels, since they're a form of bondage, but even after feminism came and changed everything I continued to love it up there – where it felt sexy. Markey was just about the only part of my life that wasn't twanging with the sexual. He'd turn away and go home to read, and me and my friends would go out on the town.

Which was where Min wanted me to be. She wanted me to work in the Pillar and go to dances and meet a husband. She knew, when I didn't realise it at all, that I was being made unfit for my destiny by being Markey's apprentice.

He'd checked my shoes first thing, too, the day we started off on our first-ever exploration of Dublin.

'There was a big distillery here once,' he said as he led me through a district where alleys between massive walls opened onto tracts of waste ground. 'See? Workers' housing,' he pointed at a terrace of redbrick houses isolated at the edge of a derelict square. 'They had bathrooms,' he said. 'There was full employment in Dublin at the time and they had to make the houses good to attract workers.' High gates hung open and grass grew between the uneven paving stones of the wide yards. 'The horses were brought over from Lincolnshire. I often wondered whether they were buried at the end of their working lives. People grow very fond of horses. Have you been to the Royal Hospital, where the old soldiers used to live? We'll go soon. Wonderful topiary, and there's a horse buried there. Upright. The officer who owned him wrote a poem that's on his gravestone. At the end it says that there are men who believe that:

Dumb creatures we have cherished here below
Will come to greet us when we pass the pearly gates.
Is it folly that I wish it may be so

Markey stood in the weeds in front of what must have been a warehouse while he recited the lines. I'd never before heard a poem recited outside school.

Then he took me to an ornate pub and bought one mulled port between us. 'These old drinks are dying out so it's our duty to drink them,' he said, before showing me how to tell original Victorian tiles from replicas. He then told me that a crowd came over from Hollywood and made a spy film in this district, pretending it was Soviet Berlin. 'This is the only total backwater in Ireland that ever got a premiere in Beverly Hills,' he said.

It was dizzying, being with him. I already loved The Hut, but apart from when I was there I was hardly conscious of place. But from the day I started walking with Markey, place has mattered more to me than I am able to explain even to myself.

By Spring Street I'd fallen to the rear like an Arab wife and the gap between us was exactly the same length as when we were young. But he then waited for me on the corner to show me where the seventeenth-century spring had been.

'Did you know that Kafka knew what Manhattan looked like from watching newsreels?' I told him between shivers from the cold.

'Really?' He looked at me with respect, then absent-mindedly unwound the scarf from his neck and tucked it around my neck. 'That's interesting.'

We hurried on, side-by-side now, but he still didn't match his step to mine. He never had. I used to think that was one of the ways he was always trying to prevent me from saying anything personal, just as I was always trying to trap him into saying something – anything – about me or about us.

'Min can't make up her mind whether Sister Cecilia is a bad influence or not,' I'd once said, for example, about the nun who'd come to teach music in my school. 'Well, she knows for sure she's a bad influence, but then again she can't be, because she's a nun.'

'Do you know what that's called?' Markey said over his shoulder.

'What what's called?'

'Having to believe things that contradict each other.'

'What?'

'Cognitive dissonance,' he said, turning around again.

'I suffer that at you and me going around together,' I said, would-be playfully. The kind of heavy hint I used to give.

He said nothing, of course.

'Seriously,' I said. 'What's a girl like me doing with a boy like you? I mean, you're brilliant and you'll be at college in the autumn and I'm going into the Pillar Department Store.'

Silence.

I tried to back-pedal. 'What did the Martian say to the jukebox?' I said to his hunched shoulders.

Still nothing.

'Do you give up? "What's a slick chick like you doing in a joint like this?" '

I saw in the bathroom of Soho's Moondance Diner that apart from a purple nose I looked normal enough, though I neatened my eyebrows with a wet finger. There'd been a lot of water under the bridge since I'd wiped off my precious PanStik because Markey said he didn't like makeup on women, though I was by no means sure at the time that in *women* he included me.

I used to push open the heavy door of the church near the Pillar, and feeling my way past the leatherette curtain and into the warm air the congregation had left behind, I would pray to Our Lady, 'Make Markey love me the way I love him!'

But She never did pull it off. When we went to the pictures in daytime cinemas that smelt of smoke and disinfectant, I'd hear breathing and swallowing and lips un-sticking from each other when the soundtrack went unexpectedly quiet. But Markey would be sprawled at ease, his knees on the back of the seat in front, and his face bright and mobile at the thought of something inside his head. As soon as the lights went up, he was talking again.

And the truth was that though I pined for him romantically for years, it was all in my head. A boy came to work in Despatch in the Pillar who I fancied so much my legs could hardly carry me when he was near. I loved being with Markey, even if there wasn't a word for what our relationship was. But my body didn't want him.

I wiped my breath from the mirror in the diner bathroom. Don't forget that, Rosie Barry. Don't start that oul' pining all over again.

Back in the present, Markey was talking business.

'I did some calling around, Rosie. A fascinating field you've got us into! I found there's one company that supplies news-stands and supermarkets and gift shops all over the Midwest with booklets – nothing literary, of course – just humour, home decoration, health issues, and cookery. Louisbooks & Collectibles it's called. Google it. It's huge.'

Somebody must have told him once that people should smile even when they were in earnest. Either way I smiled at his smile. Even the waitress, an agile, hefty blonde, was smiling. She even took back the eggs on my corned beef hash when I grimaced at how runny they were and got them fried on both sides. She plied us with coffee every time she passed us in her patrol of her lively patch, calling out to the men behind the counter and dealing out great plates of food to the talking, laughing customers. In fact the diner was such a scene of sparkle and abundance that anything seemed possible.

'Then I realised that I know the CEO,' Markey continued, 'though I've never met him. His name is Louis Austen and he buys books from us. He's a real connoisseur, too. I have great respect for him: he turned down a Galen notebook that even the specialists believed in, and he was right. But I called him about your idea and he said that sure, his company is in the market for inspirational topics and he'd be glad to have his inspirational guy take a look at anything we send him. I told him you wanted to do something on the mid-life crisis and he said—'

'The mid-life crisis isn't really what I had in mind. That's a glib way of looking at it.'

'*Get* glib, Rosie. He told me Chico – Chico's his guy on the inspirational side – says the Celtic thing is over, but Wise Women are still very in.'

The waitress was back with the coffee. 'Where you from?' she asked.

I'm sure she meant Markey, but he said, 'She's from Dublin. Do you not hear the lovely accent?'

Ha! Same old Markey: he doesn't even notice she's trying to flirt.

Elvis was singing 'Hound Dog' on the jukebox and by now I had a whole pile of French toast swimming in maple syrup and everyone in the diner seemed to be laughing. Was it only an hour since we'd shivered on the empty streets of a different Manhattan? A grave, lonely place it had been, in the cool dawn.

We ran with the fantasy. I'd be the writer and Markey'd be the agent. He'd edit what I wrote and pass it on to Chico. Why not try it? Someone wrote all the inspirational bestsellers. Why not us?

Markey half-stood and, leaning forward, gave me a kiss on the forehead, after which the people at the next table clapped and he blushed and sat down. Then the waitress, arriving to write the check, mimed smacking a kiss onto his head, at which he blushed again.

'Know why you're the right person?' he assuredly said as we were shrugging into our coats. 'It's because I think us Kilbride people aren't Californian New Agey and we aren't East Coast Smart, either. We're natural Midwesterners. I'm a hopeless writer – photography is my thing – but you're great with words. And you're not a cynic; anyone can see that from just looking at you. And neither are the people in Ohio and Idaho and all those places where Louisbooks are on sale. So it's a fit!'

He practically danced out to wave for a cab, delighted with himself.

'I'll call you,' he said. 'And there's an Inspirational Books Fair in the Sheraton on Friday that I can't stay for, but you're to promise me you'll go. And keep dinner free tomorrow. And Rosie' – sticking his head out of the window of the cab – 'go and buy yourself a hat on Seattle Rare Medical Books.'

I waved his scarf at him but he shouted 'Keep it! And Rosie – *be positive*. This is America! OK? And we're gonna have *fun!*'

I imagined Markey's sparkling eyes on me when I went into Century 21 and bought a velvet cloche with a scarlet flower over one eye. A very old lady shuffling past the mirror where I was trying it on quipped, 'That's right, Honey, keep 'em guessing', which struck me as another reason to buy it.

On the way back to the hotel I also bought a pink notebook.

In the room I got back into my gorgeous bed and inscribed the first page.

NOTES FOR (title to follow).
by Rosaleen Barry (New York, 2003)

Then I racked my brain for a wise thought, but I couldn't think of a single thing.

So I ran a bath, with the intention of saying a prayer for our little venture while I was soaking, but I was too delighted and too jet-lagged and I couldn't concentrate. Also, when I sat up in the water it just so happened that I could see myself in a particularly flattering mirror. So I got out and put on the new hat and got back in and sang the 'Flower Song' from *Carmen* at top volume instead.

I then took out my laptop to check my email.

From: MarkC@rmbooks.com
To: RosieB@eirtel.com
Sent: 12.00 p.m.

It was great to see you this morning – just great. And you haven't changed a bit. I'd forgotten how your face lights up when you're interested. Of course God help everyone when you're not interested.

I called Louis as soon as I had a break and he wants to know the working title. Any ideas?

From: RosieB@eirtel.com
To: MarkC@rmbooks.com
Sent: 12.30 p.m.

How about *A Wise Woman's Thoughts for the Middle of the Journey*? Or – seeing as how I have to put my specs on to type this – how about *The Bittersweet Years*? Or if you think that's too downbeat, how about *The Cheerful Book of Growing Older*? Or – to lay my cards right on the table – *Making the Best of the Middle Years*? Alternatively, I noticed in the plane on the way over here the little icon of the airplane inching across the map. Wouldn't *Time to Destination* be a great title? After all, the main thing about middle age is the consciousness that time is running out.

From: MarkC@rmbooks.com
To: RosieB@eirtel.com
Sent: 12.40 p.m.

Lay off the European gloom! Next thing you'll be quoting Sam Beckett. I was talking to the women who serve coffee at the convention centre – they're no chickens and they say they're having the time of their lives. So we could call it – *50 Plus – The Time of Your Life*!

From: MarkC@rmbooks.com
To: RosieB@eirtel.com
Sent: 1.30 p.m.
STOP PRESS!!

Chico just called. He said the maximum wordage for a Louisbook is 1,500.

From: RosieB@eirtel.com
To: MarkC@rmbooks.com
Sent: 1.45 p.m.

That's not too bad. That leaves room for epigraphs, statistics, etc.

From: MarkC@rmbooks.com
To: RosieB@eirtel.com
Sent: 1.50 p.m.

1,500 words for the whole thing.

From: RosieB@eirtel.com
To: MarkC@rmbooks.com
Sent: 1.55 p.m.

WHAT IS THIS? A JOKE??? The greatest writers and philosophers and religious teachers have spent centuries trying just to approach, never mind give advice on, how to live. I SINCERELY HOPE YOU ARE KIDDING?

From: MarkC@rmbooks.com
To: RosieB@eirtel.com
Sent: 2:10 p.m.

I checked with Chico.
1,500 is what's on the table, ol' pal.
So, are you in or out?

From: RosieB@eirtel.com
To: MarkC@rmbooks.com
Sent: 4.45 p.m.

OK, OK!
In.
I'm a pro, after all. I write brochures.

So here's an example of a kind of 'Thought' @ 150 words:

Attachment # 1: The Age of Miracles

Many of the experiences of our youth seem to pass without leaving a trace. But they do not. It's just that, like plants put down for spring in the depths of winter, we don't know which of them will flower or bear fruit.

We have to wait to find out.

In the middle years, the wait ends. What we planted earlier in life we harvest now.

This is a great truth: that you have to keep living to find out which bits of living come right. You can never be sure of what you're laying down for the future. You have to wait for the future to happen, to find out.

The miracle is that even when the past seems to be lost ground, as long as you continue to live, it is not.

And so, middle age becomes the age of miracles. When, at last, you too can know how rare miracles are!

From: MarkC@rmbooks.com
To: RosieB@eirtel.com
Sent: 5.30 p.m.

I sent the 'Thought' on to Chico right away and he's just called to say that Louis thinks the Irish are well-known to be very sensitive, and he goes right along with that.

Of course, people over here are polite to a fault, and we don't have a contract or anything resembling one.

But can you do ten of these things? I mean, I couldn't do even one. Are there even ten different ways of being inspirational in 150 words?

From: RosieB@eirtel.com
To: MarkC@rmbooks.com
Sent: 7.00 p.m.

No problem! They're for people our age, aren't they? Well, if I look around my own life I see that the rewards come from my body (not often enough!), from having a little money, from friendship, the arts, travel, food, and animals – even Min's cat Bell, who doesn't much like me, gives me endless pleasure. And not giving up: keeping going is itself a source of value. That makes nine topics, doesn't it, if you keep the one about how miraculous middle age turns out to be? Which it is. Who'd have thought that you and I would be doing this, for example?

I'll think of the last one when I arrive there.

OK?

From: MarkC@rmbooks.com
To: RosieB@eirtel.com
Sent: 7.10 p.m.

Brilliant.

Working title: *Ten Thoughts for the Middle of the Journey*.

Dinner tomorrow – I'll come to your hotel
around 7.00.
Sleep well, Rosie.
Wot larks!

6

Sometime during the evening the phone rang. I thought it was Markey of course. 'Rosie? That you, Rosie? Hello? Peg, there's something wrong with this. Are you meant to press the green button, hello? This is Monty O'Brien speaking. May I speak…?'

'What's wrong? What's wrong?'

'Nothing, really,' Monty said. 'Nobody's dead or anything like that. It's just Min. Little bit of a kerfuffle here. Your auntie was found out at the airport, in the ladies to be precise, and the security people there got Reeny's number off her and Reeny's in Spain and I answered the phone so they asked me if I could come and fetch her. I went out for her with Peg, but she wouldn't come home. She said she has a ticket to New York and she's going and that's that. The New York flight tomorrow – no, wait now, that's today, isn't it? She said she's had her passport in her handbag since she went to Nevers with the parish. We rang the Sunshine place but the woman there wouldn't take her back, so we booked her into a guesthouse down the road that has a shuttle van because Peg has to go home to her da and I've a tournament first thing in the morning. So that's the story.'

'Had she been...?' No, I wouldn't ask. Instead I said a long thank-you to the two of them. 'So let her come, and welcome! I'll only be here for what – five days? Monty, could you go in and open a tin for Bell till we get back? They're in the cupboard – oh, you know. Yes, leave the bathroom window open. See you Tuesday and thank you and I'm really sorry for the trouble. She sure is a hoot!' I ended, attempting a pleasant little laugh.

But I banged down the phone, then jumped out of the bed and pounded the floor over and back to the window, trying to contain myself.

You're always ruining everything! I was shouting inside. *Always*! Even when I thought it was going to be my first day at school you ruined it. I was on the floor and I'd grabbed the new schoolbag that had nothing in it and you said, 'No, no, you can't go till you're four,' and you walked away. You walked away! You were always trying to be wherever I wouldn't be. When I was a child you made me go out and play all the time. You didn't want me near you...

But this wasn't that, was it? This time, wasn't she trying to be near me?

And certainly she'd never wanted that before. Even three or four years ago, when I went from Brussels to deepest Burgundy on Sunday trains to meet her when she was on a trip to the tomb of Saint Bernadette of Lourdes, she still didn't welcome me.

She was standing in the hall of the railway station in

Nevers, small and furious, in the buttoned grey raincoat and matching sou'wester hat that she put on, even when it wasn't raining, if she was going to be with respectable people.

'I was waiting ages,' she said.

'You could have sat on that,' I said, pointing to the wide step of the weighing machine. She gave me a theatrically sarcastic look. 'You could have spread a piece of paper down over it!'

'Where would I find a piece of paper,' she said, 'when I don't speak the language? I can't stay out too long,' she added. 'We have to be back at the bus at 4 o'clock on the dot – there's a very nice man in charge of our bus. He has the same name as what's-his-name that used to be the real gentleman type – the real ballroom-dancing type— '

'Maurice Chevalier?'

She nodded impatiently, as if it had been perfectly obvious who she'd meant. 'Him.'

Then she told me that one of the ladies from Dublin had paid two euro yesterday for a cup of hot water to put her teabag in, but the lady might have got it wrong because she didn't know how much money she'd had to begin with because her daughter sewed it into her hem.

'I wish I knew how to talk a foreign language,' Min said miserably, as we walked out into the grey town. 'Sure you might as well otherwise be in Kilbride.'

And… yes! What was it she'd said next? It came back to me now. She'd said, 'The only language I can talk is English. So the only faraway place I could ever go to is America.'

I settled with my Proust on the white sofa, while a pigeon on an overhang just below the window fluffed its feathers and looked at me shrewdly. In the light of a streetlamp I could see into the vacant lot across from the Harmony, where behind the hoarding a homeless person was hauling something across the broken ground to where a pile of bedding as untidy as a magpie's nest lay beside a fire. The clouds massed over the buildings across the river were pale, but as I watched they turned grey-black and the lights on the far shore dimmed. Oh! The rain-shower moved towards me across the choppy river and I waited, transfixed, until it dashed onto the window in front of me. Such a beautiful thing, the lights coming back through the watery glass as it cleared, sparkling more diamond-bright than ever.

Soothed, I took my emergency apple from the secret compartment of my suitcase and ate it while I read about the first time the narrator saw Saint-Loup. Then I brushed my teeth again and – by now raising an imaginary hat to Min – got back into bed.

It happened some kind of carnival troupe was flying into Terminal 4, and so Min arrived in America amid a welter of little kids dressed up as mice and adult-sized costumed bears carrying purple fairies on their backs. I watched as she stepped, neat as an elf herself, through the sliding doors of the arrivals lounge, and stopped to look wonderingly up at the escaped balloons that jostled lightly under the glass of the roof. So much her ordinary self that she looked extraordinary, wearing the ancient black sweater which she always referred to, with a self-important pursing of her mouth, as her 'best'. She had a little repertory of women's conventional expressions; the frowning way they all scrutinise a piece of clothing; or the way they all coo over another's woman's baby; or the stern look at a man on a market stall when he's picking out the tomatoes they're buying. I knew that my own expressions copied Min's. But where did Min acquire hers?

She'd stopped again to watch a very big black man who had a marmalade kitten in the breast pocket of his jacket. He was talking to another man as if there wasn't a kitten there, peering from side to side in keen inspection of its surroundings. Min looked on like a child: immobile, impassive. Her hair, that often got matted when she'd been in bed for a long time, had been brushed and pinned back, and it still had a richness even streaked with white and silver that caught the eye. Altogether she cut a sturdy little figure, with a bulging shopping bag in one hand and her ancient black moleskin coat that smelt of mothballs over her arm.

'Minnie!' I called to her, as a trio of tip-tapping young women daintily pulled aircrew bags across her path. 'Min,' I called again, at which her head turned unhurriedly. She might have been fascinated by her surroundings but she was perfectly self-possessed.

'I was going to keep my money in my knickers, Rosie,' she began without a preamble, 'but I got talking to an Irish lady who lives over here and she told me there isn't the same level of theft at all. They want for nothing here, she said, the most of them, so they don't have any call to feck things. I had two pairs on, to slip the wallet between, but when she told me that I took one off in the toilet. Sure I can't be going around afraid of my own shadow.'

It was an afternoon of high wind blowing in strong gusts that bowled people along, clutching hats and skirts, across the roadway to the parking lot. Min had dropped back, and I turned to see her watching the small plume of smoke that was coming from a trashcan attached to a pole, and the two heavy men in uniforms who were circling it, speaking self-importantly into walkie-talkies. They were waiting for the fire tender, I heard one of them say, when a boy walked up and emptied his can of Coke into the smouldering trash. The wind then took the can which the boy had dropped and blew it, bouncing and rattling, across the road.

The black taxi driver pulling in beside us was laughing uproariously as a huge fire-truck thundered up. But Min had been struck by something else. 'Did you see that?' she said. 'A whole can of Coke when he could easy have got water.'

Typical. Never asked me how I was, or whether by any chance there was anything I'd rather be doing than hanging around Kennedy Airport to attend to her. Never apologised for all the trouble she'd caused. Didn't enquire where she'd be sleeping. But ... it was such a change to hear her talk after the silence of Kilbride! She was babbling even, perched on the very front of the seat, her head swivelling this way and that.

'Rosie, aren't the houses awful small? You wouldn't think houses would be that small in America. When the people are so big – the ones that come to Ireland, anyway. And— '

As we were coming over a rise, the driver interrupted her to say that there was Manhattan now.

'It's nearly the same as the Sorrento!' Min cried.

And she was right. A version of a Manhattan skyline was picked out in red tiles on the wall of the Sorrento Fish & Chip, and all our lives we'd had nothing else to look at while Enzo riddled the chips out of the fryer and whooshed them into paper bags. A magic shape doesn't have to be exact.

She was delighted by the tollbooths. 'They should do that in Dublin,' she said – 'make everyone pay to come in and give the money to everyone who lived there already!'

There was nothing she didn't have a comment on: a white stretch-limo, music pounding from it; the people who streamed in front of us at stoplights and the different kinds of hats they wore; the number of dry-cleaning shops; a panhandler singing and joggling his paper cup who she said would make a fortune at home, he looked so happy.

I pointed out the UN.

'Where's the Irish flag?' Min said. 'Wrap the green flag round me, boys!'

'That Ireland,' the driver said. 'That is one sufferin' country.'

'Ah it's not so bad now,' Min said. 'It's gone very quiet since President Clinton came over and made the Northerners talk to each other.'

'Is that so?' he said. 'Well, thank the Lord Jesus for that.'

'Where are you from?' she asked.

'I'm coming from Sierra Leone, Ma'am,' he said. 'In Africa. A sufferin' country, too. Which you understand, coming from Ireland.' He was silent for a moment and then he said, 'But you tell me the good Lord is sending you better times. May it please the Lord Jesus to send His peace to Sierra Leone, too.'

'Oh,' Min said, 'you're right there.'

'Let us pray,' he said.

We were on the West Side Highway now and near the hotel.

'Our Father,' the driver began, 'which art in heaven…'

We picked up the prayer and finished it with him.

She did agree that our room was like something out of Hollywood. 'A white carpet! Thank God I don't have to clean it.' And she also remarked that the girl at the desk was the image of your one who was married to Bobby in *Dallas*. But otherwise, she had gone back into her old silence, and her eyes kept straying now to the window where the sky showed a wild mixture of magenta and black above the chasm of the highway and the river. I began to feel the usual soreness. 'Dreams That are Brightest' had been the one I liked best of the opera aria 78s she used to play on her wind-up gramophone, and this was as near as we were ever likely to get to make a dream come true. Surely she might say something like that? We were on holiday in a room that had a white sofa as long as the window for looking at the astonishing sky, and two big beds covered in silk and velvet throws and cushions, and a telephone beside each bed and one in the bathroom. It was beyond a dream – that one day we would be in such a room, in such a city. And a man who looked like Clint Eastwood – like he looked when he was in his prime, not now – was taking the two of us out to dinner. She had me to thank for that, too.

But 'What happened back home?' was all that, within our etiquette, I could say.

'Ah, that Sunshine was a terrible place,' she said. 'You wouldn't put your worst enemy in that place. You should have heard them crying! And we had to sit in front of the television all day and watch the racing.'

'You had a room of your own,' I began. 'You didn't even have to come out except for meals. And if you were going to run away you needn't have caused all that trouble in the airport; you could have gone home. If you're well enough to turn up in America, you were well enough to go home.'

But it so happened that I brushed against her as I was saying this. She was in the kitchen alcove, fumbling in her shopping bag for the teabags she'd nicked from last night's guesthouse, and there wasn't room for the two of us when I leaned across her to fill the kettle. So my side touched her side. And when it did, I almost exclaimed aloud. Because I felt from her slight body a deep, anxious quivering that she could not control, even to keep it hidden from me. She was as nervous as a dog. That must be why she'd stopped talking: it must be taking all her energy to keep her face and voice normal. I ran the tap so that she wouldn't know I knew. I'd glimpsed how much there was, from her point of view, to fear. My anger, now that she didn't have the presence of the taxi driver to protect her. My questioning; my control over this place. The loss of the expertise she had in her own house.

And there were other challenges. Here was a woman of nearly seventy who'd always lived as simply as anyone well can. Who every week, when she cashed her pension, divided most of the money between the tins marked ESB, Bell's Food, Gas, Insurance Man and TV Licence and put the rest in a zipped purse in the innermost pocket of her handbag, and that was her administration, done. And here she was flying the Atlantic for the first time, going through US immigration for the first time, making tea with an American kettle for the first time.

'How about a little nap, Min?' I suggested.

To which she obediently wrapped herself in a Harmony Suites bathrobe many sizes too big and went asleep instantly on the coverlet.

I stayed on the other side of the room.

I was going to be sleeping a few feet away from her.

That hadn't happened since Bailey's Hut. The partition between the two rooms there didn't reach to the ceiling and when I woke in the early morning I'd hear my father snoring or breathing loud and shallow or mumbling. Once, I heard him singing. I liked his night noises the same as I liked everything about him. When he was showing me how to swim, with me on his back, we snorted and spat and coughed and threw water at each other and fell in and out under the waves and his body was a safe thing that made me fearless. But Min didn't swim. Min didn't really go in for touching people at all. The reason I remembered every detail of a night she stayed up with me, on the rug in front of the fire carefully dropping warm olive oil into my ears, was that it was exceptional. She touched me in a matter of fact way every day, of course, dressing me and undressing me. But that night was the only time she wasn't hurrying. And she wasn't giving me instructions. She just turned me gently first onto one side, then onto the other.

Then one year a sports field opened a little farther out the wharf road from The Hut, and Min had the idea of her and me using the shower in its changing room — because we had an Elsan chemical toilet but no running water in The Hut. She said that if anyone caught us sneaking through the fence with shampoo and soap and a towel in a supermarket bag we'd be laughing stocks but we'd be clean laughing stocks. So for a few years the two of us took a shower every evening.

We were never caught. We'd wait in the late summer light for the last shouts from the sports-field and for the caretaker to cycle back to Milbay town past our wire fence. Then we'd make a run for the pavilion across the dark grass. Min would hoosh me up and I'd slide my hand inside the window and open it outward. Then I'd let her in and we'd undress in the dark and squeeze under the showerhead, bumping against each other all the time, soapy limbs vying for the one trickle of warm water.

I was never as close to her body again until, in the years after Daddy died, when we hadn't a penny, and the rates man used to call every quarter, and we had to pretend we weren't in. We'd squash into the cupboard under the stairs as soon as we got the word he was coming along our street. We were used to it, and he was used to it and Reeny next door, leaning against her doorjamb while he knocked and knocked on our door a few feet away, was used to it. I usually brought the hairbrush into the closet and gave my hair a good brushing. I was quite happy in there. He'd peer in the letterbox and we'd have left the door to the kitchen open and he could see there was nobody there. Then he'd go away.

But it was around that time that Min started going to the pub. She ironed all day, to keep us going, because she wasn't entitled to a widow's pension – she hadn't been married to my da – so until I started in the Pillar we had only supplementary welfare to live on. After five or six hours of ironing she went up to the pub. Then she got into the habit of it.

That was the end of wanting to be near her. Nowadays, when I went up to the Inn myself in the hope that she'd come home with me, she sometimes linked my arm or even tried to hold my hand on the way down the street. And I hated that. Her fingers felt like claws. You don't mean it, I'd think. You've been drinking. It's not love. I'd make her arm drop from mine as soon as I could, not caring if she realised what I was doing.

I looked down on her now where she was deeply asleep on her side with one arm over her face and the other by her side. Before she slept she'd gathered her important things close beside her on the bed. Her battered tin spectacles case. Her wallet of leather worn as thin as paper. No fewer than six miniature salt and pepper pots acquired on the plane. A small snapshot in a perspex cover of Reeny and Monty leaning on the wall between our backyards, with Bell when she was a kitten perched between them. A blue plastic bottle in the shape of the Madonna that was presumably full of water blessed at Lourdes. Her hand lay near these objects, as if to quickly defend them. The flesh at the knuckles was loose and the back of the hand was sprinkled with brown spots.

If you came at her through the modesty of her belongings, it seemed absurd to be as angry with her as I often was. The hand, with its grimy fingernails, was as small as a child's. Was she not childlike? I knew Min had no idea how to behave like most women – how to dress herself to be attractive, how to chat, how to use the little, insincere words everyone used to be polite. I knew she'd had no instruction in those things. There was no one to instruct her. Her mother died when she was ten and – because of that – her elder sister, my own mother, ran away.

'She said she was heading out,' Min once, very reluctantly, told me, 'and when I asked why she said "I'm not staying in this place without Mammy." '

The dead speak through us, Freud said. And then Min's father had disappeared a few years later, when she was already taking care of me up in Dublin.

Was it possible to see things a little differently from

usual, in this wonderfully new place? Take touch, for example. When Min had fumbled for my hand on our way home from the pub, mightn't that be something she was trying to say, that she could not say unless she unlocked herself with alcohol?

I lifted her limp hand and held it for a moment.

Nothing. No gush of feeling. I didn't feel a thing. All the same, it was the first time I had voluntarily touched Min in many years.

'And beer?' the waiter said. 'Cobra beer from India?'

Min might have been Markey's own mother, so tenderly had he seated her in the Shalimar Balti House, making sure she was comfortable enough before calling over the waiter to explain the menu to the visitor from Ireland.

I waited to see what she'd say about the beer. The barmen in this city were hardly going to be like Decco in the Kilbride Inn, letting her sit there all afternoon, and then nominating one of the men who'd come in for a pint on their way home from work to give her a lift to the corner of our street. Look at her now – oh, I hoped she wasn't going to drink too much! She looked as young now as if she'd been only hiding during the bad years, rather than growing old. Seated bolt upright with shining eyes, and giving Markey a hard time about ordering the Indian dishes that would be most like Irish ones.

Sometimes at home her eyes shone, too, when she came back from the Inn. But that elation had nothing to do with where she was. The exact opposite was the case. The drink at home got her to a place that wasn't home, to a place where she could be not herself.

'Fine,' Markey nodded absently at the waiter. 'Min – beer? Water? Tea?'

'Tea will do. With a drop of milk, don't forget.' Of course, Min had known Flo Cuffe. There was a Mr Cuffe in London, the father – people said he was a Protestant and the family had run him off – but Markey hardly ever went over there and when he did, all he was interested in was making it to the second-hand book-shops on the Charing Cross Road. But he loved his mother. He handed her up all his wages – he got a civil service librarian job straight after school and went to college at night – even though she would send off nearly the whole amount to some priest she knew who ran an orphanage in Calcutta.

She'd had an influence on my own life, too, Flo had.

Three years after Markey left Ireland I was in my first year at college – thanks to support from Hugh Boody, my boss in the bookshop where I now worked. I was coming home very late one night from some crisis at the student magazine I helped out on, when a form approached through the mist full of refracted light that had settled on the black street. And when we met on the median I saw that the figure was Mrs Cuffe.

'Who's that? Is that Min's Rosie?' she said, looking up at me from under her hat. 'I'm late for Mass, Rosie. I think the clock must have stopped.'

She was so distressed that I had to be careful, so I looked elaborately at my watch. 'I think the clock was maybe fast,' I offered casually. 'Because it's not late you are – you're actually a bit early for the Eight O'Clock.'

'I'll wait in the church,' she said in a panic-stricken voice. 'I'd rather wait than maybe be late.'

'The only thing is, but,' I said, 'they won't be opening the doors for a while yet. And you could catch your death in this oul' drizzle waiting outside.'

'You're right!' she said, looking up at me helplessly. 'But if I go home the clock's broken.'

So I persuaded her to come with me. Min came down from bed when she heard me talking, and I saw her taking in the fact that Flo had a shoe on one foot and a boot on the other. She knocked on the wall and Reeny came in in her dressing-gown and the two of them started to build up the fire and make tea and talk in an everyday, unhurried way to the old lady.

And that was when Flo had influenced me. I suddenly saw myself standing there, useless. The women didn't need me. I didn't fit in.

Markey's mother eventually said, shamefacedly, that she must have forgotten to eat her dinner she was that hungry, and they made her scrambled eggs and toast with the crusts cut off. And when she began to grow sleepy, they put coats on over their nightclothes and took her across the back lane to her own house. They tried to extract Markey's telephone number in America from her, but she didn't know where she'd written it down, so they said they'd come back in the morning. Then they took her into her bedroom, and settled her down with her prayer book and a bottle of Coke before they left.

'She was never the same after that night, so she wasn't,' Min had taken up the story for Markey. 'I remember Reeny telling you on the phone that you didn't have to come home, that any of us who had houses with back doors onto the lane would bring Flo her dinner and so we did and it worked out great. She loved her grub, your ma did, and she lived in comfort in her own house until a month before she passed on, and by that stage she didn't know who she was – you know that yourself.'

Min was earnest as I'd seldom seen her.

'Honest to God, Marcus, she hadn't a care in the world. For years when you'd go into the house – you'd just knock and go in – you'd hear her talking away and she'd say Oh Mrs Connors or whatever your name was – she knew who everyone was – I was just talking to The Little Flower. That's Saint Teresa. Or Saint Bernadette. Or I was just talking to Blessed John Sullivan – that's a priest there was in Dublin that was very holy – and he was telling me about Heaven. It was never God or Our Lady, I don't know why. Maybe she wouldn't have been as comfortable with them. And she had friends from the days when she used to clean the church and from the Sodality and the Third Order of Saint Francis and they were always calling in. And give the priests their due, they brought her back water blessed in Rome and rosary beads from Medjugorje and things like that. And she had money galore, with all you sent her. It wasn't anyone's fault what happened to her in the end. Her poor old brain just wore out.'

'That cottage was more than a hundred years old,' Markey said after lifting his bowed head.

'None of us could get over it,' Min said. 'It was the

grandest little place. It was always warm in there, no matter what it was like outside. Is there any more tea?'

'Two-foot walls,' Markey said.

'I can see why a Protestant would have wanted to escape out of there, all the same,' I remarked.

They both looked at me coolly.

Markey was so strikingly handsome that nearly everyone who passed the booth looked back at him and then at her, a small woman with silver and grey hair piled up in a haphazard cottage-loaf above a face alight with response. The pair of them were having a great time bantering about Kilbride, the way it used to be when there were hardly any cars and the milk was delivered in rattling bottles and the bread van did the rounds.

He's so much more relaxed with her than with me, I thought. Seated close to her. Laughing with pleasure at her. Maybe he savoured a woman of his mother's generation? Or maybe he remembered how he and I had nearly been a couple and that made him wary of me still.

He must have known, the day we went walking down to the Pigeon House, that it would devastate me to be told that he was leaving Ireland – and not sometime in the future, but that very night. Maybe that was why he was being so nice to me about this inspirational booklet idea. Maybe he wanted to make up for that great hurt. Like I'd said in my first 'Thought', miracles of restitution offer themselves in middle age.

'Rosie's going to write a little book about how to make the most of the middle part of life,' Markey was telling her, full of enthusiasm.

'She's *what?*' Min said. '*Rosie* is?' She surveyed me sternly. 'Sure what does she know about it? She's only a young one.'

'Can't I find out from you?' I smiled at her.

'Yes, now's your chance, Min,' Markey said to her. 'What do you think about middle age? Compared, say, to being decidedly young or definitely old?'

But Min couldn't rise to the change of subject. Jet-lag had caught up with her, and I could see she wanted to bow out of the evening. 'I was nearly a writer myself, once,' she said vaguely. 'I lived in a house that James Joyce the writer lived in. The first time I was ever in Dublin, the bus from the country stopped in Rathmines which I thought was the middle of Dublin so I asked the driver to let me off and there was a sign in the window saying "Room to Let". So I had a room there for a few days when the baby' – she gestured abstractly towards me – 'was still in the hospital. Anyway, there was writing on a stone outside my window which said that James Joyce had lived there between when he was two and five. So I often thought, he must have learned to write while he lived there. He couldn't have been a writer if he didn't learn to write. And if I'd have written anything when I was staying there, I'd have been a writer too.'

'I'm older now than he was when he died,' Markey said. 'But,' he said, half-laughing and half-concentrating on the tangled sleeve of the coat he was trying to help Min into, 'I won't be leaving as much behind.'

'Have you no children?' she said.

'I meant books,' Markey smiled down at her.

She couldn't leave it alone. I turned away. Of course I used to think about having his children. That was how all girls thought, when I was a girl, about the boys they thought they were in love with.

'I have no children of my own,' Markey said. 'But my partner had children who are grown up now and their children call me Grandad. Billy and I are both in the Grandad's Club in our community; we're taking the kids to Disneyworld soon.'

There was no life in the sky behind the New Jersey office blocks.

When Min was in the bathroom, I slumped on the sofa. Of course, I hadn't had a specific expectation but nevertheless it felt once more as if there were a dark lake inside of me, from which at a particular cue – five minutes, even, of being looked at with interest and approval – a monster had reared up, dripping with need. I'd already vaguely seen myself as Markey's special old friend, if he were on his own and needed someone. And I was angry, again, about how I'd been misled by my ignorance when I was a teenager. There weren't gay people then. There were a few homosexuals in books all right and live ones – actors, mostly – in the centre of Dublin, but there weren't any in places like Kilbride. I was always gargling in case I had bad breath and that was why Markey didn't try to kiss me. I thought he was too fine, and that the boys who grabbed at me were a bit coarse. If only I'd known there could be a gay person I might actually, personally know, I could have saved myself a lot of bother.

When Min came out, I managed a smile, but she wasn't even looking at me.

She treats me like the confidante in an opera, I thought – there to listen to the heroine's thoughts, not to have any thoughts of her own.

She was arranging her things carefully on the night table. Markey's card, I noticed, with his private number heavily circled, was now one of them. I noticed because he'd circled it on the one he gave me, too, and for one moment I'd thought he'd made a heart shape.

'That's an awful pity about Marcus being a grandfather,' she said chattily.

I prepared myself for defence. I couldn't bear it if she pitied me and I couldn't bear it even more if she laughed at me.

'Why?' I said, feigning surprise. 'What's wrong with being a grandfather?'

'He'd have suited me down to the ground,' my aunt said.

'*What* did you say?' I asked, not believing my ears.

She was climbing into her bed, wearing the fancy nightdress I'd bought her for the Sunshine House, the same one that she'd declared she wouldn't be caught dead in. Her hair was sticking out all over her head.

'What's wrong with you?' she said crossly. 'Nine years difference is nothing over here. They're always on the television. Demi Moore and what's his name, or that fella, the lorry-driver, that Elizabeth Taylor met in the place they all went to for taking drugs.'

'Ten years.' I said. 'Ten, not nine – his birthday's after yours. Min – Min, you never liked him! And the way he is now—' but she'd obviously been too jet-lagged to properly hear who Markey had said his partner was. 'You don't know anything about Markey, all you've done with him is have an Indian meal.'

'I know that,' Min said. 'But anyone can see he's a grand man. His mother was a lovely woman, too. And I made up my mind, you know, when you put me in that place with the gaga old ladies. I want to have a life. That's why I came over here. I'm not ready to be...'

And she fell asleep on the word.

From: RosieB@eirtel.com
To: MarkC@rmbooks.com
Sent: 11:10 p.m.

Min and myself are going to do Manhattan from top to bottom in the time we have left. So I'm not planning on doing any work the rest of the time we're here except go to the Inspirational Book Fair. But I wonder whether we should ask for more words? Or just take them. An Introduction occurred to me – this is just a first draft, of course.

'This is a short book, but although short, I hope it will not be little. It is a book about a place – that plateau between the end of our prime years and the beginning of old age. And it is also a book about time. A profound German thinker once said: "To meditate about time is not natural and is not intended to be so. It is the work of human beings who are horrified, who are no longer at peace with themselves because their disquiet does not leave them in peace..."'

I would then go on to discuss the temptation we all face to avoid the whole subject of ageing altogether. What do you think?

7

Markey rang when I was still asleep and I thought at first that I was dreaming, because he seemed to be giggling. Early morning sunshine stretched from the pinnacles of the New Jersey office blocks to our lovely beds. Min's bedclothes were thrown back: she must be in the bathroom.

He *was* giggling. 'Where, oh where, Rosie darling, did you find the German thinker? You made him up! Go on, tell me you made him up!'

'I certainly did not! Jean Améry is famous – at least I think he is – for his reflections on ageing. He even killed himself. I'd never heard of him but then I saw him quoted somewhere as saying that after a certain point in life one thinks of nothing but time.'

'Rosie…'

'And I think that's true. Suddenly you become conscious of—'

'Rosie!'

'What?'

'No German thinkers. Particularly, no suicidal German thinkers. That is Rule Number One.'

'He wasn't German, but I didn't dare say "Austrian", which is what he was. But the thing about pessimism is that it's realistic.'

'How is it more realistic than optimism?'

'Markey, the man was an *Auschwitz survivor!*'

'No Auschwitz survivors! That's Rule Number Two. Listen, Rosie. Do you remember Debbie Reynolds? Do you remember Gidget? Do you remember the young Judy Garland in *Easter Parade*? That's who we're trying to sell to, those girls, getting on in years, nice, open-faced women who look about fifty but are sixty-four, who still wear hats and are dear people and *ignorant* of bad things, Rosie.'

'But Markey,' I shouted, *'that is not how it is.'*

'You think Joan Rivers thinks about nothing but time?' he cut across me. 'Warren Beatty? Henry Kissinger? George W?'

'No,' I said impatiently, 'not that kind of person. But Philip Roth does.'

'Philip Roth thinks about America,' Markey said firmly. 'First and foremost. Now why can't you do another one like the first "Thought"? Why can't you fall in with the American habit of looking on the bright side?'

'And you really must make it along to the Inspirational Books Fair. Tell Min I said you were to go to it. And wait'll you see, Rosie, there won't be a single German thinker in the place.'

The bathroom was empty and I rang reception in a panic. But Min turned out to be right there, talking to the elegant blonde receptionist. Rila by name and from

Tashkent, she told me. When I got downstairs I found them practising their English.

Rila came around the desk and pointed a leg at Min. 'Tights,' Min said.

'Pantyhose,' Rila said. Which came out 'panteeowss'. 'Where please is Daffy?'

'Where is Daddy, please?' Min tutored her.

'Daffy is a clothing discount store. Very good money.'

'Very good *value* for money, Rila. But where is Daddy? There's a few things I have to buy.'

'I'll take you, Min,' I said. 'It's on Broadway.'

'Oh, I know where that is,' Min said. 'I was there this morning.' She began to sing. "My feet are here on Broadway this blessed harvest morn." '

'Morning,' Rila said.

It turned out that Min had woken early, confused by the time difference, and, taking dollars from my purse, had gone looking for breakfast.

'I was hungry,' she told Rila. 'All I got last night was Indian food, no wonder Indians are all so thin.'

'And did you have your breakfast?' I asked.

It seemed that she hadn't, but whether she'd come back to the hotel for my sake, or simply because she didn't know how to order food in this city, wasn't clear.

That confusion was a feature of the next four days. Half the time Min astonished me by what she could do and knew; and half the time by what she couldn't and didn't. She wouldn't let us go to the launderette, for example; insisted that the only washing machine she could trust was the one in Kilbride. So the elegant hotel room was turned into a Neapolitan slum in no time, with her T-shirts and her horrible black, cotton tights hanging from the lamps to dry. She wouldn't take taxis and she didn't like the subway, but there seemed to be nothing she didn't know about the bus system and, what was more, Frieda, the woman who cleaned our room, gave her a Metro card some guest had left behind which had nearly twenty dollars on it. Of course she always knew about anything she'd ever seen on television; she knew a lot about the Depression, for instance, and, for some reason, a lot about the history of Central Park. But though I'd heard her sing traditional songs about Napoleon back home, it had somehow emerged that she didn't know who he was. Nor what nationality Shakespeare was, either. And now every morning I gave her a sheaf of dollar bills which she carefully put into her pocketbook, but without even looking to see what denomination they were. She had no real sense of money as spending power.

It's because she really and truly never had any to spare, I thought with a kind of shame. She has led a subsistence life.

We began that morning with a bus – her treat – uptown to the Empire State Building, to find our bearings.

And after that, in a mere three days, we did Saint Patrick's Cathedral and Bloomingdale's and the Fraunces Tavern and the Negro Burying Ground and Radio City and the Dakota. We went to Barney's to look at the women doing their shopping. Women as slender as pencils on long, bony legs and beautifully made up, every single one of them with glossy long hair, and all in black and stepping so lightly that their feet barely touched the ground.

'They're like what do you call them with the horns?' Min said respectfully.

'Antelopes,' I said.

'Do you see how many carrier bags they have, Rosie? Do you see the way they all smile? In Kilbride, thin women have something wrong with them, but here thin women are the happiest.'

I got bored. 'Will we go and look at some real antelopes?'

So we took a bus all the way out to the Bronx Zoo and went on an elevated train through a park full of exotic animals, of which Min particularly liked the elephants.

'Someone told me they're the only animals that dance,' I said when we were eating a hot-dog at a picnic table.

'Bell dances,' Min said, looking at me levelly, as if daring me to contradict her.

'All right. But they're the only animals that mourn their dead.'

'Oh do they?' she said, impressed. 'Do they?' And she jumped up to go back to the elephant house again, and when I said one old chap there, with sad, raisin eyes in grey, wrinkled cheeks, looked like a politician, she gave me a reproachful look.

'He could be thinking about his dead friend,' she said.

That afternoon we stopped off at the Chrysler

Building because Markey had made me promise to go to see it. The security man let us examine the beautiful tiles and frescoes and the inlays on the walls and floor and doors even though, because of 9/11, he wasn't supposed to allow rubberneckers in.

Min was most impressed by the craft work. 'You'd never see anything like that at home,' she said. 'The Irish are only good at the heavy stuff.'

That reminded us to walk across the Brooklyn Bridge. Another bus. But it was so breezy up there that we only got halfway across before we had to go back to Chinatown to buy her a jacket, which she was delighted with because it was allegedly a $100 jacket on sale at $15.

On the third morning we went to the South Street Seaport and watched a fabulous fragment of movie that some sailor had shot long ago when he was rounding Cape Horn in a small boat in a storm. Min made no comment until, when we were having coffee afterwards, she looked at me with a yearning face and said, 'I've never been anywhere on a boat since I was fifteen.'

So to cheer her up I took her on a ferry ride I'd read about in the guide book. We caught a big commuter catamaran from a dock near the Seaport which sped out into the harbour past Governors Island and skirted Staten Island and arrived at a little town on the New Jersey shore which was a resort in summer. Min had stayed on deck, revelling in every minute of spray and speed. We battled the wind up Main Street, past boarding houses and apartments-to-let, and seaside attractions – gift emporiums, T-shirt shops, ice-cream stands – all still shuttered on a weekday in spring.

Min's cheeks were a wonderful pink from the fresh air and the ferry ride. She looked like a good child, in her neat little padded jacket.

'There's a sign that says "Seafood, Open",' she said. 'Up there, at the top of that hill. Why don't we have that? Sure didn't I grow up on periwinkles?'

This was new information. Usually, she claimed that she couldn't remember anything about what she ate as a child except that she didn't eat enough of it. It reminded me of all the things she never told me. 'But you'd have to climb the hill to reach there, Min,' I snapped at her. 'I thought you weren't up to much exertion? I thought you had to stay in bed most of the time because your legs are so weak?'

'What made you think that?' she said blandly.

I stopped dead in the middle of the sandy road and barked at her, 'Because you never got out of bloody bed, for one thing! And when you did you went up to—'

'I didn't climb out of bed when I'd nothing to climb out of bed for,' she mildly replied. 'If I climbed out of bed in Kilbride I knew what I'd see.'

The smell released from the plank walls of the clam shack reminded me of The Hut, as did Min's happiness. We were the only customers in the place, and Min was now perched on a high chair at the counter, chatting to the girl behind, who asked her whether she wanted a glass of wine or a beer with her sandwich. I nearly snorted when I heard Min cheerfully reply, no thanks, drinking at lunchtime made her sleepy. But I was content, and so opened my *New York Times* to steal a look at the news.

Though I wasn't really reading.

Being on holiday with a female relative de-sexes a person, I was thinking. Did Miss Mysterious, my aunt, by any chance feel that? Had she any thoughts on being a woman, as opposed to, say, a man, or a jellyfish, or a cloud? What had she meant, after all, when she said that Markey would have suited her fine? Could she possibly have meant, in bed? She couldn't! All my life when I went in to Reeny's, and Min and Reeny and maybe Andy's mother Pearl were watching television, I'd see the same expression on their faces as they looked at someone like Zsa Zsa Gabor, say, who'd had multiple husbands. They wouldn't even bother to sneer. They just stolidly looked at the woman with the facelifts and the divorces and the snow-white teeth, as if she were so self-evidently crazy that it wasn't worth a comment. If someone talked about love, their faces became even more neutral. Yet they must have heard and used love words once. Everyone knew that a month after Reeny's husband walked out, he sent her back a card to say he loved her – the postman ran down the street with it, shouting. And Andy famously sent his mother a Valentine's card every year for the last twenty years or more. He said his father would have wanted him to.

But Min... Very likely she'd never heard and never said love words. She came to us when she was fifteen. My father died fourteen years later. That was all that happened to Min. Subsistence level there, too.

By the time we left the seafood place – 'But Rosie, they never even heard of periwinkles!' – my aunt knew the name, background and immediate plans of the girl behind the counter. And when we got back to the Harmony Suites I knew she'd disappear, through the door behind the desk, because she'd been going to evening Mass the past two nights with some of the Latin Americans and Eastern Europeans who worked in the hotel. And she had already met other people from the get-together they had in the presbytery of the vast, redbrick Catholic church they all went to, down near Fulton Street.

She'd also been out to an evening of ethnic dancing, even, the previous night, with an older Mexican woman called Luz, who was twice her size, even discounting her pink turban. Luz had a beaming face and an astonishing, upper-class accent which she had learnt, Min told me, when she worked for Directory Enquiries. Now she was a cook, because the money was better. Min said she sent nearly every penny back to Mexico where her daughter had seven children.

'Your aunt gives us the best advice!' Luz had said to me as they headed off to the dancing, and I'd teased Min about that when she came home.

'How in the name of God are you giving advice, Min Connors? You don't know the first thing about New York!'

'I give *general* advice,' she said loftily. 'People are not that different from each other.' She was silent for a minute. 'You know how you were asking me why do I take so long to get back from Mass? Well, we stop and say a few prayers at the World Trade place, there at the wire where they let you stand. The lights would blind you, so they would. The people that were killed there were working people. Working people are the same the world over.'

Coming back from New Jersey that afternoon was too windy on the deck, and so we huddled together in the cabin. Lights were coming on in the great cliffs of offices around Wall Street as we zoomed across the harbour towards Manhattan. Min gazed out in silence at the sky already streaked with night.

Eventually she summed up. 'I thought back over everything since I came here, Rosie, and I have only one complaint.'

I waited in real suspense.

She didn't approve, it seemed, of the doors on the stalls in American public toilets. They didn't go all the way to the floor and you could see people's feet and it wasn't nice.

'Oh, Min!' I said. 'You know a lot more than that! American people have lovely manners but a lot of them believe terrible things. And their government goes around interfering with other countries.'

'What do you mean, *their* government?' Min said aggressively. 'What about other governments? They didn't fly the planes into themselves.'

'No, but there were reasons.'

'Oh, and there's another thing, I don't like switches on lamps. Why can't you press the little switches in and out the way we do at home? Why do they have those little wheels? They have either little wheels or a little knob-thing that sticks out that you have to twist with your fingers. They're useless.'

'You know full well what I'm trying to say,' I said.

But she wouldn't have it. OK, they didn't know how to make a decent cup of tea. OK, you never saw a white woman pushing a pram. But otherwise, the USA was perfect.

8

Min went off to meet her friends that last full day we had, and I went up to the mid-town Sheraton to the Inspirational Books & Collectibles Fair.

'You should be here,' I said when I rang Markey from a payphone in the foyer. 'There's a crowd here who publish something called *Father Murphy's Irish Chicken Soup*.'

'Oh my,' he groaned. 'Oh, why didn't we think of that first?'

'Anyway, they've decorated their corner with giant shamrocks and bunting in green, white and orange, and there's a kind of Celtic maiden with long blonde plaits leaning out of a round thatched hut that's supposed to be ancient Ireland. And there are portraits of Joyce and Yeats and Beckett embedded in the thatch – oh, and Edna O'Brien!'

'So what's wrong with that?' he said. 'Anything for business.'

'Well, I dunno,' I said. 'I would've thought that if ever there were a writer who wasn't in the self-help-inspirational category it was Samuel Beckett. But you're right, it works: there's a crowd around that stand there isn't anywhere else, half of them in green baseball caps with *Celtic Chicken Soup* that the publishers are giving out.'

'Great idea!'

'But the whole place is like a big playgroup. No, it's like the chorus in an opera. You know the way the chorus is always looping in and out with tambourines or baskets of fruit or wedding garlands? Grown people wandering around doing silly things? It's like that here. As for the blonde with the plaits – you remember what some critic said about Ava Gardner, I think it was, when she played Queen Guinevere? "She may not be a convincing medieval lady, but she sure knows how to lean over a balcony." '

Markey was laughing and I was laughing too. But all the same, I wanted to double-check that what we were doing was definitely not in the same category as the Father-Murphy-soup thing.

'It's all very jolly here, Markey, but it's infantile,' I said. 'The books themselves, particularly. I don't know how our project will fit in.'

'Why not?'

'Well, because it's about something that isn't jolly. There's nothing jolly about the part of life where you still think you're young but no one else does. Plus in middle age you have to prepare for the next part of life which will be really and truly testing. People you love will die, for instance. And there's your own dying. One of the things I want to learn is how to walk towards the darkness…'

'Rosie!' Markey yelled down the phone. 'Rosie! Come off it! You're not walking anywhere. You're a mere toddler!'

'All right,' I said grudgingly. 'But I don't want to hear you're giving out free T-shirts with my "Ten Thoughts".'

'Why not...?' he began, but I cut him off.

'I have to go back to the hotel to start packing. And I've picked up a book for Min to read on the plane, if "read" is the word I'm looking for. *Your Inner Golden Girl* it's called. At least me and Min are getting on better than we ever have, so there's one good thing that's already come out of the self-help idea.'

'I don't know why you sound so surprised,' Markey said. 'Surely most women of your ages figured out long ago how to get along?'

'No,' I said.

'No?'

'No.'

I bought apples for tomorrow's journey at the cluster of stores around the subway exit, and Maybelline mascaras for Tessa and Peg, maple syrup for Reeny and a packet of organic catnip for Bell. Then I walked home to the Harmony Suites in bright sunlight and a snappy wind, wondering when I'd last felt so well.

This was the way it had been the first time ever I'd lived abroad – a time that had given me a lifelong taste for being somewhere foreign. I was still supposed to be working in the Pillar, but Sister Cecilia at school had somehow fixed me up with a summer au pair job in Roubaix, in France. Min couldn't do anything to stop it, and so for three months I'd shared a loft over a bakery with a wonderful music student called Lalla. I still remember one morning that I came out to go to my job, picking my way through the jumble of scooters in the courtyard with North African music playing somewhere, when a boy whistled from where he stood above me on a loading bay and ran to the edge of the platform to keep smiling at me for as long as he could. I felt a perfect fit with the world, that morning. And today, though I knew I was graceless as I scurried along, I was just as joyful. I was *more* joyful. I had Min, and she was fine; a couple of glasses of wine every day, but nothing at all to excess. And I had Markey, if only on loan.

Hey, there! That woman there was Min! She was walking ahead of me towards the Harmony Suites with another woman, both carrying plastic bags and bouncing along at speed. I was so amazed at Min walking like that that I fell farther behind, as if hiding.

Up in our room I found her rinsing out an electric-green bathing suit, which, she explained, was a loan from Rila, the receptionist from Tashkent.

'But you can't swim!'

'I know I can't. But I never tried in a swimming pool before. I was never in a pool. I was only ever in the sea, and I don't like the sea.'

She went into the bathroom to towel her hair.

'The water was lovely and warm,' she called to me, 'and I had a great time splashing around in the kiddie pool. The girls said it would shake off all me aches and pains and they never said a truer word.' I could hear in her voice how delighted with herself she was

Then she came out and told me how Rila's little girl ran up on the altar at Mass that morning because she thought it was a stage and began to sing 'Our Love Will Go On.'

'She turned around and belted it out!' Min said. 'I nearly wet meself laughing.'

She wandered about putting stuff in her big shopping bag, as I had a last look at the pink and purple melodrama of the evening sky.

'I'll tell you something, Rosie,' she began. 'I'm worried about the house. I'm not sure I emptied the pedal bin under the sink before you put me into that Sunshine place. That attracts mice, you know. The place could be overrun with mice.'

'Sure isn't Bell climbing in and out the window?' I said. 'Why would we have mice now when we never had them before? And anyway, you'll be home soon.'

'No,' Min said. 'I'm not going home for a while.'

I just gaped.

'But you have to go home!' I said. And all I could think of to persuade her was the cat. 'What about Bell? Bell doesn't like anyone except you.'

'You go home,' Min said. 'I'm not going. I've hardly seen anything and the ticket cost a fortune and I asked the air hostess and she said I could change it. And I asked the man in the airport to tell me what the stamp they put in my passport means and he said I don't have to go home for, I think, it's ninety days. And that suits me fine. This place alone would give me enough jobs to keep me going for nine hundred days – I know the whole score here, they're crying out for babysitters that can speak English and it isn't even against the law; if you do babysitting for someone who's staying here it's nothing to do with the Harmony, it's the guests who pay you. That's what the girls downstairs explained to me. And I was asking the priest about somewhere to stay and he said it straight: as long as you're white and you can speak English and you're willing to work, you'll never starve in New York. They all go to him, you know, because he speaks Spanish the way the most of them do, but even some of the Chinese go to him. I told him I was an experienced laundrywoman,' she ended. 'I said that for a laugh, but it's true. I'm working all my life, but that's the only job I ever got paid for.'

'You're not well,' I said, at a complete loss now. 'Even if he is a priest those are illegal jobs you're talking about. It's disgusting, so it is, exploiting a poor old woman to do under-the-counter laundry.'

'Who's disgusted?' she said vigorously. 'I'm not disgusted. No one I know is disgusted. You just have a bee in your bonnet.'

'Min!' I said, and I didn't even try to stop myself. 'You were a disgrace! You fell down in the General Post Office and you had to be brought home and all the neighbours saw you not able to walk. Carried in to your own house. Dirty. *Drooling.* You weren't able to mind yourself. That's why I came home. God knows what would have happened to you if I hadn't come home. And for the last year, anyway, you've often spent days in bed and you hardly ate if the food wasn't smuggled into your mouth. When you did go out you came back smelling of drink. It seemed you hardly knew my name sometimes. It was horrible. That's what put you into the Sunshine Home, OK? And where did all this come from, anyway? You've hardly moved outside Kilbride since I was born, and all of a sudden you're the independent type?'

'I like it here,' she said simply. 'I have something to get up for here.' Then she changed to a more combative tone. 'And I didn't worry about you when you went off round the world, even though you hadn't a pick of commonsense and you were in places where you didn't have a word of the language. You found your own places to stay and your own jobs and so will I. So don't you worry about me.'

'But if you fall sick, Min! If poor people fall sick in America they're sunk.'

'Is that what was worrying you when you were going into jungles and deserts, that you'd fall sick?'

There was silence.

'Were you serious about liking Markey?' I began again. 'Because if you're looking for a man—'

'I was just messing,' she interrupted me. 'Sure I know Markey's type.'

'How on earth would you know his type?' I said furiously. 'What "type", anyway?' Though of course she hadn't meant anything like that.

'You know one man you know them all.'

'I never heard such nonsense,' I said. 'And you didn't know even one man, by the way. Not as far as I'm aware.'

'Is that so, Miss Smartyboots? I knew my father,

didn't I? And I knew your father.'

'Oh Min…' I nearly started to cry. 'Min…'

I knew there was nothing I could say to stop her. I shouldn't stop her, anyway. The more I emphasised how self-destructive she had been, the more I had to agree that this was maybe, just maybe, a great idea. I should be taking my hat off to her. And she was right that people could be young in America no matter what age they were. She was an Irish sixty-nine, which was about fifty-nine in the States. A fifty-nine-year-old could do everything, even at home. Well, she couldn't do anything that could look as if she was looking for a man, but Min wasn't looking for a man, it seemed. That is, if she was telling me the truth. But she always did tell the truth; there was just a whole lot she didn't tell at all.

After she went into the bathroom, I cried as silently as I could. It was shock. She'd planned this! She hadn't come after me at all! She must have meant to do this all along, or why would she have checked the duration of her tourist visa with US Immigration? And all that research into jobs – she did all that without even giving me a hint. Wasn't I the fool to think maybe she'd followed me to New York because she was lost without me!

Hadn't it counted for anything, then, that I'd come home to look after her? Did she put no value on that?

She'd needed me too at the time, no matter what she might think. I know she did. I'd get home from whatever days I worked in Kilbride Library around seven o'clock, and when I came around the corner I would see our house down at the end of the terrace and I'd make it a point not to lift my head. Because if she wasn't up in the Inn, I'd glimpse, out of the corner of my eye, the twitch of the curtain at the upstairs window. She was standing behind it, watching out for me. When I went in I'd hang around for a while in the kitchen to give her time to recover from her rush back into bed. Then I'd go up and chat to her about the day and whether there was anything special she felt like eating, and often I had some little treat – I'd have gone to the Italian deli for good sliced ham or I'd have made a detour to the fish shop for a fresh bit of cod or I'd have nipped up to Tesco for the early new potatoes from France. I sometimes even stopped at the off-licence and got her one of those little quarter-bottles of wine to lend a festive touch and to stop her wanting to go out – a couple of glasses of wine was no harm.

And it wasn't just that I tried to encourage her to eat and kept the house clean and cosy and I talked to Bell when she wouldn't. She signed for the old-age pension every week and collected it herself, but she'd never done anything about her other entitlements – to free chiropody and to a pair of glasses if the optician said they were needed. I fixed all that up for her. And I tried to keep her mind alive. I'd save up things that happened during the day to talk to her about. Any news that Tessa or Peg or Andy had, I'd pass it on. And events in the world – if she came down in the evening I'd make sure to switch over to the 9 o'clock news and talk to her about that.

But so, apparently, what?

'But what will I go home for, if you're staying on here?' I said to her, when she eventually came out of the bathroom. 'I'm not doing anything much at home these days.' I somehow couldn't bring myself to say out straight, 'Will I stay on, too?'

Min didn't reply in words. She smiled very sweetly. She gave a little shrug of her shoulders and she held the palms of her hands out to me. Saying, I think, 'Don't ask me what you should do. I don't know.'

I did notice that her eyes were red-rimmed, as mine too must have been. But that could have been from washing her face. All she did when passing the sofa was to give me a quick little pat on the top of my head. And all she said was, 'Don't forget to check the pedal bin the minute you get in.'

From: RosieB@eirtel.com
To: MarkC@rmbooks.com
Sent: 3.15 p.m.

Just to say, I'm going home tonight, but Min's had her own 'miracle in middle age' and she's staying on. She has offers of more jobs than she can handle – illegal, of course, she's on a tourist visa – but it's all provisional. She moved into a hostel called the Estrelita today; she's next door to her new friend Luz and very happy.

This unexpected development means I should be able to knock the 'Thoughts' off in the near future, no problem.

I know you're afraid I'll be too European, but the problems of middle age are mostly to do with ageing (yes, in Europe it is spelt ageing). Ageing leads to death. If anybody has found a cheerful, positive side to having to die it would have to have been an American. Do please let me know if anyone springs to mind.

But maybe right now I'm a bit more sensitive than usual to the passing of time. It will be strange to go back without Min to the house that always, without fail, had Min in it.

It's been a great week, all the same. Thanks, dear Markey, for everything.

From: MarkC@rmbooks.com
To: RosieB@eirtel.com
Sent: 3.30 p.m.

That Min always was a law unto herself! I wish my Mam had lit out for the Territory too. Those were great women and they deserved better than they got.

Min is right to take off. Nobody over here would believe that she owes you anything at this stage. And she is in the right place. It is different here from Ireland, at least how Ireland was in my day. Remember the way the older guys hung around Kilbride? That bench they used to sit on all day? Well, here no one makes you retire when you're this age or that. There are jobs here for anyone who will work. Age is not an issue. It would be illegal for me to ask someone who came here for an interview their age. Do you ever see Joan Rivers on Irish television? Joan Rivers could give Min a few years but she has what people here admire: sass and energy.

Markey

PS. I was gone from Dublin before the Joyce Symposium arrived, but I remember the first American academics. I remember you saying, 'O brave new world that hath such people in it'. They used to come into the library. The men – do you remember? We'd never seen loafers before or corduroy trousers or chinos or cashmere scarves or those soft cotton shirts. Or white raincoats – oh God, the raincoats! I'm sure those raincoats were why I emigrated to the States, though by the time I got here I wouldn't be seen dead in a white raincoat (a 'duster', they turned out to be called).

9

On the plane, I passed up *Legally Blonde,* and gazed instead through a sliver beneath the blind at a moon that spread its radiance along a floor of fluffy cloud as far as the curve of the earth. How is it we humans manage to forget that we're spinning in space? I thought, then shivered. Bell, if she was in a good mood, would tuck into the curve of my body when I got into bed at home, and I'd be grateful. Animals are at the other end of the spectrum from such cold emptiness; they're compact and warm and specific and they don't seek for answers because they don't know there are questions

I twisted this way and that, trying to be comfortable, but I couldn't sleep. Then I dozed off for a few minutes and woke with the seatbelt buckle pressing into my thigh. The unnatural feel of myself sent me back to the first time I ever realised that I had a body, when I was – what? Less than four years old, anyway. Children were allowed go to school when they were four.

Self-consciousness had begun then, with me sitting on a wooden floor while far above Min's voice snapped 'No! No you can't! They won't let you in. You can't go till you're four.'

I'd climbed on a chair to take down the new school-bag and then I'd taken my coat off its hook and now I was on the ground with the coat draped around my shoulders because I couldn't manage the sleeves by myself, and I was sitting on the bag so no one would take it from me. I knew even in my fury that I was learning what a floor is – the dense feel of it on the back of my legs as I drummed my heels on it, the flat of it against the round of my bottom, the way my shrieks bounced along it.

She walked away and left me with a bad taste in my mouth. I noticed that.

And most anything I knew from then I knew through my body.

Like that time some neighbour woman must have told Min that warm olive oil would soothe my earache; might even have come to our door with the loan of a little bottle of Goodall's Medicinal Oil of Olives. Min knelt on the rug in front of the fire and held me across her strong thighs and poured a little of the oil into one ear – careful in what she was doing as she seldom was – then placing a towel against that ear she turned me over to do the other. Then waiting with me while – this was what people believed then – the wax in the ears would soften. While my face pressed into her belly brought me to where I wanted to be. And whether it was because of that, or because it was the middle of the night and she wasn't in a hurry, or whether it was the soothing heat of the fire – which I can still remember – the pain did go away.

I likewise learnt whether Min loved me or liked me

or was indifferent to me from one minute to the next by what she did. It was physical. It wasn't just in how she touched me but in her breathing, the speed at which she moved, the lightness or heaviness of her voice. It was all sign.

How does anyone come to knowledge of another person except through the body? That was so obvious I didn't even think about it. Of course, I went to the Gresham Hotel with Dan. I'd been aware of him watching me with a serious face every day during the Joyce Symposium, where I minded Boody's bookstall in the hallway outside the Old Physics Theatre in Newman House – a special room, because Stephen Dedalus had had an edgy talk about aesthetics there with the English Dean of Studies.

The smiling, polite Symposium people came out and milled around my books four times day and Dan was always at the back of the crowd, tall and blonde. And young, compared to the others. He smiled every time I looked back at him from under my lashes. Which I was well able to do at twenty-one years old. I'd been indicating to fellas on the other side of dancehalls for years that I liked them, too.

He walked me to my bus stop.

'There's a free day tomorrow,' he said. 'Any chance you could show me around a bit? I haven't seen anything outside.'

The bus-driver snapped open the door of the bus and yelled at the queue as if it had been keeping the bus waiting, 'Are youse getting on or are youse not getting on?'

'Oh, here!' I cried. 'Wait, Mister! Goodbye, Professor!'

and I jumped on the bus.

'Goodnight, you mean,' Dan called after me. 'Not goodbye. Midday at the hotel!'

'You have your marching orders now, Sweetheart,' the bus driver said. 'The Yanks are back in town.'

At home I shaved my legs, even though I'd decided to wear my jeans.

The interminable night in the plane ended at last, and with sore eyes and a stuffed nose I came out of Dublin airport. Shouldering my bag, I walked to the car park for the pleasure of seeing a cool, clean spring day break in my native place. I walked down concrete paths past passive workshops and offices whose shut doors reflected the first glints of dawn. Spiders' webs on the railings glittered as light spread and the sky changed without moving. Sparrows were already bustling about, and crows squawked amiably amongst themselves as they went about their business.

A group of cleaning women, far younger and more blonde than Irish cleaning women, leaned against a wire fence while they waited for something. I called to them, 'Good morning, beautiful ladies,' and one of them, anyway, waved and smiled at me.

I found the car and began to drive home.

Min never missed a trick. She wanted to know that day why I was wearing jeans to work. I'd sworn when I was under Lalla's influence, in the bakery loft that summer in Roubaix, that I would never lie to Min – feminist women did not lie to other women. But it would start a really major row if I said I was going to meet an American professor. That was exponentially incompatible with Min's goal of turning me into a version of Kilbride Woman. I could not say either that he was staying in the Gresham. Min knew nothing about hotels except that they cost money and they were not homes. She'd been in a hotel exactly once in her life, as far as I knew, when she had to take me into the ladies in Wynn's on Abbey Street once, during the Saint Patrick's Day parade, when I was crying from the cold and wanting to pee. She didn't trust them.

So I told her that we wore jeans when we were stock-taking in Boody's. Sisterhood would have to wait. And even if Markey had been around, I'd have sped towards Dan as I did that morning, my heart beating, running the length of O'Connell Street.

Markey had never even taken my hand, even to say goodbye, that grey, October day we went walking down past Ringsend and along by the dumps and container depots out to the South Bull Wall where the Liffey flows into Dublin Bay. A bad smell came from the sewage works and there was litter caught in the marram grass and lumps of oil coagulated in the clumps of sea-weed that marked high tide on the beach side of the road. And the wind blew sand across the tarmac. Of course, all this suited us because what we were doing was finding the exact location of the place where Joyce had set the encounter between the boys and the pervert in *Dubliners*. We'd already done the locations of the other stories.

I wondered afterwards: did I sense some new

distance opening between us? Why else did I start talking about Monty next door, and how he'd never been what you'd call normally lively since his father walked out? 'His father left his tie hanging on the rail of the bed – you know, there where the knob is. And it's still hanging exactly there. The exact same place. Monty won't let anyone touch it and it's been something like eight years.'

'How long it's been makes no difference,' Markey said. 'Time is meaningless on certain levels. Freud says in *Thoughts on War and Death* that the primitive mind is, in the fullest meaning of the term, imperishable.'

'Look at the size of the granite blocks!' I said, to stop him starting on Freud.

'Do you know who built this sea wall?' he said. 'Go on – guess!'

'I give up.'

'Captain Bligh. Captain Bligh was the harbourmaster in Dublin, before he took the post of Master of *The Bounty*.'

'Wow!' I stopped dead. 'Marlon Brando!'

Markey took that as his cue. Walking as always a little ahead of me, he said over his shoulder how he might be seeing Marlon Brando with his own eyes soon; that he was going to London that night and, as soon as he put the fare together there, he was heading for the States.

I stumbled, but he didn't look around, so I followed him miserably through waist-high weeds to where he was pointing out the carved stone lintels on a ruined building. 'A former fever isolation hospital,' he said.

'Everything that ever happened out here was sad,' I

muttered. In those days America was so far away that people who went out didn't come back for years, if they came back at all.

'Oh no,' Markey said, and quoted with relish the opening line of a poem. ' "I will live in Ringsend with a redheaded whore…" '

'The word you really notice in that line is "I",' I said angrily. 'I, I, I! And "redheaded" doesn't tell you anything about the woman. What would calling me "wavy-haired" tell of what I'm like as a person?'

'That's irrelevant,' Markey said, 'the poem is about him, not her.'

'Well, then, why bring her into it at all? And what does he mean, "*I* will…" What about asking her? How does he know she wants to live with him?'

'Oh for God's sake!' Markey snapped. 'Why have I been wasting my time on someone as thick as you!'

'You weren't wasting your time,' I said, almost crying.

Markey turned around and looked at me for a moment with his full attention. Then, beginning to smile, he twirled back towards me. With the sea to his left and his right and the lighthouse behind, he revolved towards me, arms outstretched. 'Goodbye Dublin!' he shouted – a beanpole in a herringbone tweed overcoat that had lost its buttons and swung out behind him. The last revolution brought him skidding up against me and his face touched mine. We had never been cheek to cheek before. I went absolutely immobile.

But he didn't say anything. He didn't do anything. And after a few moments I had to open my eyes.

Dan the American was waiting for me outside the Gresham, leaning back on his heels, peering up at the façade. His blonde hair was blowing in the sunny breeze and when he saw me coming he ran to me and hugged me. He was thrilled, he said, kissing both my cheeks, to be in the hotel Gabriel and Gretta went back to after the party in 'The Dead'.

'And that's not the only Gresham thing,' I said proudly. 'Shelley – you know Shelley? – Shelley came to Dublin in 1812 and threw pamphlets down from this hotel urging us to rise up against British oppression.'

'Which window?' he asked. 'My room is at the front.' Then he looked down at me with a kind of goofy, nervous, half-smile. 'Would you like to come up and see it?'

'Well,' I said, and stopped dead.

I'd never been in a hotel bedroom, much less in a hotel bedroom with a man. 'Well. Maybe we should see a few things first.'

So we crossed the road and I sneaked him into the Rotunda Hospital to see the baroque chapel. 'Isn't it marvellous?' I whispered. 'The exuberance of it! The way it's both very plain and very decorated.' I was quoting Markey, of course, showing off because Dan asking me to his room had given me confidence.

'It's kinda not Dublin…' he said.

'It's the Dublin of then,' I said. 'Dublin changes. I was born in this hospital – my dad told me the whole story in bits and pieces when I was growing up – but my mother had TB. You know? Tuberculosis? You've heard of it? She caught TB in the same sanatorium she was a maid and my dad was a patient in. So they sent her back there as soon as I was born because she was infectious and she was dying. So when she died,' I heard myself telling Dan, 'she'd never seen me. They wouldn't even hold me up for her to look at me through a window. They didn't even tell her she was going back to Peamount Hospital. But one thing I think about is how everyone always says that about a mother who dies – that she never saw her child. But what about the child? I never saw her.'

He took my hand. 'Poor little Rosie,' he said.

We then walked out to the abandoned Jewish cemetery in Fairview whose wall I used to climb on my way home from school. It had a funny date carved on it – 5904 or something like that. I was guessing Dan was a Jew because his name was Cohen, but I'd never met a Jewish person to talk to.

'Don't let me fall! Link your hands and give me something to stand on!' I had one foot in a crevice I knew of old, the other dangling in mid-air. Dan was laughing, just below me, and now he had one hand on each buttock and was trying to push me straight up, but I was laughing too, and fell back onto him, and we had to start all over again. This time he grabbed me between my knees with one hand and shoved, so that laughing helplessly I more or less fell over the wall onto the high bank on the inside, and in a moment he was beside me. And so we found ourselves sprawled together on soft grass in a secret place, a quiet, walled rectangle where old tombstones rose above a tangle of bushes, weeds and ivies, our bodies poised to fall into warm puppy play.

But then he saw the names on the nearest graves, and became solemn. A thing that's just a fairly sad fact on its own is a different thing entirely when it applies to a whole people. I understood perfectly that he might mourn for these Lithuanian Jews who'd set out for the New World and got no further than Dublin. To me, too, my mother's death was about all the people she stood for as well as about her. That nobody respected her even when she was dying because she had no education and no money.

We headed back into town on the top of the No. 23 bus, me sheltered inside one wing of Dan's windcheater and willing to stay in there for ever.

I hauled my stiff body out of the car in Kilbride, lugged my suitcase to the door, and fished the key on a string up through the letterbox. I'd often pointed out to Min that the burglars were locals too and so knew perfectly well where the key was kept, but she said they wouldn't burglarise her or Reeny because Monty would kill them.

In the quiet kitchen I stepped gratefully out of my stale clothes.

That day of the Gresham Hotel, we'd wandered from the bus up across the waste ground of what had been the brothel district where Leopold Bloom and Stephen Dedalus had ended up. And then, without saying anything, we reached O'Connell Street and walked past the porter and up the grand stairs of the hotel. It was a late summer afternoon. Shafts of light came in through the tall windows in oblique slants. How could I do anything but lie down with Dan and let him do what he liked. Didn't I think that that was how you did things? Wasn't I right?

It was blissful, the first half. My consciousness shrivelled to a pinprick, like the last dot of light on a television screen. But then he ruined all the swooniness by saying, 'Don't move!' and hopping in to the bathroom to fix himself up.

I stayed on the bed, I had to. I couldn't possibly just get up and leave. And anyway Dan was by far the most glamorous man I'd ever snogged with, with his silky-soft sweater and his sneakers, his straight blonde hair and his honey-coloured skin. And he knew about not having babies which was more than most Dublin fellas knew at the time.

And in the end there was amazement and pride at the effect on him of what we did. To be able to do that! To a man! To a man like him! *Me!*

When he was dressing he slipped a white T-shirt over his head. I'd never seen one of them before in real life, though James Dean, of course, wore them in the movies. But then again, Dan was the first man I'd seen go from nothing on to everything on.

Reaching through the white curtains, he touched the frame of the window.

'Could it have been from this window?' he asked.

Well, not exactly, I was going to say, because it was obvious the present windows weren't one-hundred-and-fifty-years old. But he looked so hopeful that I said 'It could easily have been' instead. After all, not many people, even back then, cared all that much about Shelley.

I said I had to go home, in order to get away and be by myself. But I couldn't head for Kilbride till the usual time so I waited in a chip shop in Marlborough Street, drinking tea and reading *The Great Gatsby*. Thank God I happened to have one of the most wonderful books ever written in my bag on that occasion. Not that I was traumatised, the way girls in books often were after they'd lost their virginity. But I felt different – both heavier and shakier. I was sore, too, and a mess down below. I'd have to throw away those panties. But Dan hadn't forced me at all, even though when the thing was over I didn't see the point of it. No way had I been going to refuse to learn what my body was ready to teach me.

I still allowed for the body in my plans. Today, I'd arranged to go to the dentist because I knew I'd be so exhausted after the long flight that I wouldn't be as afraid as usual. When I got back from the dentist I drowsed in Min's blue armchair with Bell on my lap. Then I trudged up to the Xpress and got rashers, eggs and the paper and came to life a bit. The old tin clock ticked away the afternoon. The fire made small noises. Monty came in next door and I could hear him watching something that kept breaking into cheers and claps. A golf match, what else.

I rang New York. 'Señora Connors!' I shouted. 'Min. Meen! Una señora muy pequeña.'

But the woman who answered the phone in the Estrelita spoke Spanish with an accent I couldn't understand, and after she abandoned the conversation in the middle of a sentence, there were only clangs and echoes from concrete floors and steel doors. By the time I gave up, the call had cost me 10 euro for nothing.

After that, I wandered around the house restlessly. I'd never been so much at a loss. There was a cold atmosphere around my heart, like the twilight space around the moon. For the first time, there was nobody to turn to. No body.

Unless I tried with Leo again. But how could I try? It had been harder and harder for several years to arrange weekends with him. In Macerata we hadn't even lasted a weekend; I'd left at the end of the first day.

No. Don't think about Macerata when you're tired and teary.

Think instead about the marvellous years when he, too, could hardly speak when you met. When he, too, couldn't pick up a drink because when he was near you after a separation his hands shook too badly to hold a glass.

At last I could allow myself to go to bed. But first I showered and made a tuna sandwich and ate it on the hearthrug in the light from the fire. I could barely think or feel, but I could remember the way lovemaking had once made perfect sense of being alive. Usually, whatever I was doing was inadequate, compared to that. Lovemaking, somehow, made time dense. It was the only completely worthwhile use of time I knew, apart from reading something like Proust.

Leo had come towards me, a tall, courtly figure, carrying two glasses of chilled *sekt*, in the interval of a concert at the Bregenz Festival, when I'd come over for the night from Strasbourg and was wondering whether I had the energy to queue at the bar in the heat.

'You look thirsty, Madame,' he said. 'May I? One for you, one for me.'

Like a hero in a romance.

But I was quite natural with him at first. I knew the way of the world – an elegant, beautifully groomed man in a wonderful suit with an expensive wristwatch on a fine, olive-skinned wrist wouldn't be personally interested in a woman in her forties with a bit of a tummy and soft, matronly breasts in a commonplace dress. The people who came up to him in the most deferential manner to make comments about the music – which he replied to briefly in a variety of languages – ignored me as I expected to be ignored. It turned out, when he walked me back to my guesthouse along the path under linden trees that goes along beside Lake Constance, that he was the occasional music critic of a Zurich newspaper and he had written a biography of Brahms. By then I was too dry-mouthed with excitement to say what I might have blurted out in the first few innocent minutes, that when I used to baby-sit I often tried to put a child to sleep by humming Brahms' *Lullaby*, and how it never worked.

In the nine years since that night, I'd met Leo in various places in Europe, generally near airports. Also, when I had a little time and a little money, I'd gone back to some of the same places, by myself. I had gone back, for example, to that hotel on the linden path and insisted on the room over the front door with a window so low that from my pillow I seemed to be on an exact level with the silver surface of the lake. Such moonlight there had been, the night I met him! And such silence, apart from the little gobbles and cries of water-hens or coots who'd wake for a moment before rocking themselves to sleep again on the water. I'd lain awake until dawn, unmoving, transfixed, because when he was shaking my hand goodnight – our hands were the only part of us that touched that night – he'd bent to me and whispered, 'We will find each other again.'

At one point, maybe a year in, when I was working in Brussels, I rented a tiny wooden house with a lipstick-red door surrounded by a picket fence in the sand dunes near Ostend, while Leo was in Amsterdam working on an article about the Concertgebouw. He came to me for four weekends. I still hadn't learned. I thought – four weekends, he must love me! He'll leave his family! I'll bring him home to Kilbride! Wait till Tessa and Peg get an eyeful of this!

He made *gratin dauphinois*, slicing the little waxy potatoes so fine that – as I'd laughed and showed him – you could read print through the slices. He brought interior-design and garden-design books with him, and told me in the smallest detail how he was going to turn the villa he had recently bought into a boutique hotel. He'd make scrupulous sketches to show me, while I'd be faint with longing to go upstairs to the four-poster with the linen sheets where, when he opened the window in the dormer, the hum of traffic from the Amsterdam–Brussels motorway overrode the shush-shush of the sea behind the dunes. I never heard the sea, except in that hour or so around dawn when he often woke me, wordlessly stroking me.

But though he'd stand beside me to dry the dishes, we never jostled each other. And he never joined me either in the early mornings when I'd get up and sit on the back stoop in my nightie and drink a cup of coffee, though I patted the threshold beside me. He sat instead behind me at the kitchen table and studied his interior-design books.

Even when we were still mad to meet each other, I was already retracing our steps. I went back to the Albergo Cosima in radiant, autumn weather though he and I had been there in a cold spring. I went back to the Holiday Inn near the East Midlands Airport where I'd met him for one night when he flew in to England to visit his sons at boarding school. I went back to the Hotel Tritone in Ravenna, where the mistral was so bad I stayed in bed and read my Proust and the housekeeper brought me a Happy Meal from McDonalds. I went back to the Excelsior Intercontinental in Zürich, where I'd taken a room, three months after we'd met, and sent him a note to tell him I was there.

The door of the same room was propped open while it was being cleaned, and I told the chambermaid I might have lost an earring down the back of the sofa – the one where Leo and I had first been naked together – and she helped me as I pretended to look for it. On that night, he and I had roamed this same room with its coffee-tables, armchairs and lush rugs as naturally as baboons in a rainforest. I'd had lovers, of course, before. But Leo was the one. Leo who brought to life something that had been dormant ever since the Gresham Hotel.

And he'd known he would. I couldn't get over that.

That first night when we were our public selves again, our hair, wet from our separate showers, tidily combed, he turned around from the window and said he had known that we would suit each other perfectly.

'Your face is full of adventure,' he said. 'Do you know that?'

I was beginning to simper when he added, 'Also, of course, you are the right age.'

I stood in the hotel room, that time I went back, and the poor cleaning-woman went on searching down the backs of the sofas. She could see I was in distress.

'You take this please!' she said, offering me her own earrings, and I blushed with shame.

I went back to those places because I could not endure to leave the affair as stark as it really was, with hardly a kiss, or a commiseration, or a joke. The Christmas before last I had told him what I was doing, at a time when I still hoped we might break through to some new understanding, when his marriage had ended and he was living in a room in Ancona. I never saw the room. We were staying as usual in our *pensione* near the docks.

He listened carefully to me telling him that I had gone back to various of our rendezvous.

'Do you want to know why?' I'd said.

'I know why,' he said, and he smiled his lovely, slow smile.

And that was it.

And the next time we met was that May in Macerata.

Bell condescended to come with me when I collapsed into my bed at nine o' clock, but she wouldn't move off the pillow. It still felt like heaven. The room was dark and warm and full of ghosts. Four o'clock in the afternoon in windy Manhattan. I hoped Min was OK. And maybe she'd acquired something better for her head than that beret which blew off in anything resembling a breeze.

Had I so wanted to be enfolded by a lover because Min kept herself to herself, even when she was near?

There was often bad weather on our holidays in The Hut, when she and my father and I were the happiest we ever were, and my father and I would become for a little while as self-possessed as Min. We'd put on socks and coats and calmly hunker down until whatever it was blew over. There was no bustling around the place. No scullery or yard or street or cinema for anyone to disappear to. Min had no option but to sit in one of the old cane chairs beside my father in the other – a queen side by side with her king. I would sit at their feet, the three of us quiet, looking out through the door that was always open to the lip of sandy turf and the strip of shingle shore and the sea. Sometimes the silver rain would come down in diagonal stripes everywhere except right at the door where it fell in heavy, unlovely drips; sometimes a misty drizzle gusted by; sometimes thunder cracked and rolled in from the horizon, or lightning played across a low, glowering sky above waves that were suddenly agitated and foamy. We watched the weather as if we were an audience too polite to leave. And, when it passed, and we began to move and turn to speak, it was slowly, as if we were coming back with effort from somewhere magical.

Passages of fullness that never came again. Never such intimacy, not even in the hands of the most skilful lover, not even skin to skin.

From: RosieB@eirtel.com
To: MarkC@rmbooks.com
Sent: 4.15 p.m.

'Thought' No. 2: the body.

These are the four necessary things.

1. Eat clean, pleasant food.
2. Do not squander your wellness in drink and drugs, but take a sleeping pill or a tranquilliser if you need to indulge yourself.
3. Walk and stretch. If we don't like our bodies enough to celebrate what they can do, why should they like us?
4. Make love as often as possible, but appropriately. The guidelines above apply to sex, too; make it careful, clean, throw in the occasional treat, and use it to celebrate.

If you are not in a position to make love with another person, deconstruct what you receive from lovemaking – sensual pleasure, connection, physical relief, delight in your own powers – and tap those resources in other ways. Think about:

swimming,
domestic pets,
gardening,

masturbation,

massage,

yoga,

how to cook gourmet meals.

Or just lie naked in the sun, like a heroine out of D.H. Lawrence.

(150 words)

From: MarkC@rmbooks.com
To: RosieB@eirtel.com
Sent: 5:45 p.m.

Listen to me, Rosie!

You have been to New York about four or five times in your lifetime, apparently to visit department stores. I have lived on both the East and West coasts of the United States for more than 30 years and for the last 20 of those I have run a book business which, admittedly, does not make money, but which has given me happiness and made me many friends. My partner and I brought a seafood risotto to a neighbourhood potluck supper last night. On 4th July we'll be toasting marshmallows. We belong. We like that.

We are contented citizens of Middle America. And I have to inform you that it is a very, very prudish, decorous place.

So bodily functions are OUT, except for sex.

And within sex, anything explicit is totally OUT, especially masturbation.

As for D.H. Lawrence, a quarter of a century ago

the phrase 'the author of *Lady Chatterley's Lover*' would have had a measurable effect, even in Idaho or Alabama, among people who read books. But nowadays:

a) Nobody reads books in about forty-seven of the fifty states, and

b) Nobody at all reads D.H. Lawrence.

From: RosieB@eirtel.com
To: MarkC@rmbooks.com
Sent: 5.57 p.m.

Doctor Bowdler, I presume?

Markey – you can like it or lump it, I am fed up being demure! The first one I sent was much more helpful, but herewith a 'Thought' about the body, second draft:

We cannot keep our physical fabric young. But we can take youth's components – energy, adventure, openness, optimism – and make our present circumstances creative of those qualities.

We can identify the experiences that bring us a new kind of physical youthfulness. And we can be glad that now, in the middle of the journey, we at last own our own bodies. At last, our best comrades are fully ours. We're not sending them out to compete for a mate. We're not bearing or rearing children with them.

We should look with affection and gratitude on those loyal friends, our bodies. But let us gradually, also, privilege those things that are not body. The spirit and the body must part some day, and the body moves through time towards that eventuality. But spirit does not age. On that day, your spirit will be just as young as on the day you came into the world.

(150 words)

From: MarkC@rmbooks.com
To: RosieB@eirtel.com
Sent: 6.13 p.m.

Forgot to say: NO DEATH!
DON'T EVEN HINT!
People buy inspirational books to be cheered up.

From: RosieB@eirtel.com
To: MarkC@rmbooks.com
Sent: 6.19 p.m.
Subject: TRUTH

I am a normal, well-favoured, woman of the first world in excellent health. I am in what I consider earliest middle age, my mid-fifties.

Yet every day I spend much time in painfully bewildered anxiety because:

I lose my spectacles and money and keys.

My hot flushes are so bad that they leave me dazed. They make me hate the Creator.

The forgetfulness I cover up now is different from the ordinary forgetting when I was younger. Now, single words fall out of the sentence I am assembling as if they'd been picked off by a sniper.

The white hairs in my eyebrows are few but they mock the dark ones with their strength.

I have blotches on my legs and a deep wrinkle around each ankle.

The dry skin on my legs flakes.

I am frightened. I took hormone pills for the hot flushes and now I'm afraid I will die of a woman's cancer…

But aw shucks! I mustn't use the D-word, must I?

From: MarkC@rmbooks.com
To: RosieB@eirtel.com
Sent: 6.19 p.m.

Don't think I don't understand what you're saying. I could make a list of my own, too. It's a choice, Rosie, whether to keep these things to yourself and allow the world to enjoy you – and believe me, looking at you and being in your company is thoroughly enjoyable – or whether to share them for the sake of 'truth', I can't tell you what to do in your life. But you have to remember with 'Thoughts', if we're to have a chance with Chico, that this is not an in-your-face culture. The USA strives might & main to be cheerful and genteel. Your 'Thoughts' if they ever exist in book form, will be on deckle-edged paper with a flowery border and a little ribbon.

Death just doesn't fit in.

Part Three

Stoneytown

10

The letter came about a week later. I'd been up since early and Tessa and I had been to the café for a weekend breakfast. Then we'd gone to the garden centre and now we were out in the backyard in spring sunshine, planting frail Petunia in the old hipbath.

'You know, we're doing this for Min,' I said, 'but when I tell her about it on the phone I bet she'll just say "Very nice, Rosie". The only time she seems a bit homesick is if I say anything about Bell or about bacon. Or a fresh batch loaf. I mentioned the other day that I had a fresh loaf on the table and she said she was going straight to her boss in the restaurant to talk to him about bread. The thing is, Tess, you'd think a woman who spent her entire life in the home – you'd think she'd be homesick? Otherwise, what's it all about?'

Bell had heard her name and sprang onto the wall from wherever she had been sunning herself.

'Sorry, Puss,' I said. 'I can't help it that I'm not Madam herself.'

'People change,' Tessa said. 'I thought I'd never move out of the old place, but now I couldn't be happier with the townhouse. I'm thinking of putting down a real oak floor instead of the laminate. Oak is for nothing in Belfast.'

'Min's place now is no townhouse,' I said, remembering the Hostal Estrelita. 'The window only opened at the top and the bed was about three feet wide and there was a lamp in a kind of recess beside it but its base was bolted down. I turned around to say for God's sake we can do better than this, but she had an expression on her face like she was opening her Christmas presents. So I said, 'well come on, we'll go and buy a few things, but she said Luz had a friend who worked in Kmart who'd get her a discount. She wanted me gone; wanted to start her new life by herself. You wouldn't have recognised her, Tess. I know people change when they're young, or even middle-aged. But you don't expect them to change when they're old.'

'It depends,' Tessa said cautiously. 'Nelson Mandela was in his eighties when he got married to what's-his-name's widow from Mozambique.'

'That's right. But getting married isn't really changing. Not compared to a senior citizen with a drink problem smuggling herself to New York and finding work and a room. Anyway,' I said – though Tessa is so fanatically commonsensical that she rejects even the suggestion that human personality is mysterious – 'I don't think that Min has changed. I can't get over the feeling that it's natural for Min to be doing this.'

'Oh Rosie!' She predictably cut across me. 'You're just sorry for yourself.'

'I'm not so much sorry for myself as bewildered,' I

said. 'Should I mind as much as I do? Or is there something wrong with me? Nobody ever told us what this part of life would be like, did they? That's why I don't know what to say in the little booklet I'm trying to do with Markey.'

'Oh my God!' she groaned. 'That oul' drink of cold water!'

When I first met Tessa, in Boody's bookshop where we both worked, she was bandbox perfect and Markey was a lanky, decrepit, absent-minded junior clerk in the National Library who cycled everywhere on a lady's bike.

'People change,' I said. 'You just said so.'

'Yeah,' she said, 'but people don't forget what people were like before. I don't care if he's God Almighty now. I'd still see that stinky old raincoat every time I looked at him.'

It might be as well to change the subject.

'She wasn't any good at cooking, Min wasn't. She was like someone who'd never seen it,' I said.

'When she was in Reeny's,' Tessa laughed, 'the two of them always stopped some kid passing the door and sent them up for chips and smoked cod, even though Reeny is a brilliant cook.'

'And now there's a whole shelf of gourmet cooking magazines up in the newsagent,' I said. 'Women like Min, Reeny and Pearl are dinosaurs in the twenty-first century.'

'They had each other,' Tessa said.

That was true. Reeny would bring Anadin upstairs with a glass of water after Min had had a hard night or feed Bell if no one else was around. And Min had taken over when Reeny collapsed after her husband walked out. They lent each other everything. And not long ago I heard from up in my bedroom Reeny saying, 'I went to Mass with Monty this morning in Fairview church, Min, and there are only two steps there, not like the God knows how many there are in Kilbride.'

'Yeah,' Min said. 'And it's no distance on the bus.'

That was that, then. An arrangement made to cope with their ageing bodies. Without saying 'age' and without saying 'body'.

I'd felt like an alien, listening to them.

Why was I so driven by my body? Why were other women not?

A shower was coming in over the rooftops. 'That always happens,' I said, 'when a person has just finished watering.'

We stood inside the open door, listening to the sound of water sliding down slate above, and from behind, the kettle's growing assertiveness.

'I used to love this room first thing in the morning,' I said. 'I used to get up early because I loved school so much.' The kitchen would be like a warm cave, with whatever cat we had at the time abandoned in sleep on the hearthrug, and the morning light just about to strike the scarlet Busy Lizzies that thrived on frequent drenchings from the dregs of pots of tea. I'd heat up my porridge and eat it in the gathering day. My father in his bed in the corner would still be asleep, but I sat beside the bed anyway, and if he opened his eyes I was the first thing he saw.

'My mother used to get up to make me a flask of soup,' Tessa said fondly.

'Well, Min didn't. Min didn't really want me to go to school at all. "I left school the day I turned fourteen," she'd say, every time the subject came up, "and it didn't do me a pick of harm. Did it?" And I'd have to say, "No Min, it did not." "What use was school in a dreary oul' place like Stoneytown," she'd say, "a few houses and an awful oul' wind that'd nearly knock you over?" And I'd say, "This isn't Stoneytown, you silly old bat" – well, I'd say that to myself. Out loud I'd say, "This isn't Stoneytown" and she'd ignore me.'

It was all so vivid to me that I looked, now, at the fire. Nothing. Just the pinecones painted silver that Mrs Beckett, who used to be waiting at the door of the pub in the morning when Decco opened it, made in rehab.

Tessa called from the scullery where she was washing her hands. 'Come down to the gym with me. Balance training – that's what you need. Whatever about the meaning of life, we have to learn not to fall down and break our hips.'

'But Tess, don't go! I have so much to ask you! You always know everything. I wanted to ask why do you think the older generation never mention hot flushes? Min, or Pearl, or Reeny? And how come I've never come across anything that might be hot flushes in a novel? And another thing, Tessie – tweezing. If I tweeze out each white hair that appears in my eyebrows, will more than one grow back, or does it make no difference?'

But I turned away then so that she couldn't see my face, because I was blushing scarlet. That hadn't been a tactful thing to ask Tessa, whose own eyebrows were a suspiciously even auburn.

'Why do we go through all this anyway?' I mumbled. 'You'd think there'd be a reward for how brave and clever we are about ageing, but instead we just get to die.'

With that, she stopped putting on her jacket and, coming over behind me, gave me an awkward hug.

'Take it easy, Love,' she said, and of course tears came to my eyes at bossy old Tessa being so kind. 'And stop worrying about everything! You think like people in books think, but most people don't. I don't know why we're on earth and neither do most people and it doesn't bother us.'

'You're a born Head Girl,' I said affectionately, seeing her to the front door.

Though I was wondering — what happened to the getting-married-to-Andy-Sutton plan, then? If life is as easy as she's making out, how come there hasn't been another word about that?

I sat on at the table after she went. The grey was settling in, and the rain was becoming more insistent on the windows. So I opened the laptop and banged off a message to Markey, just to see if he was there.

From: RosieB@eirtel.com
To: MarkC@rmbooks.com
Sent: 12.55 p.m.

How about calling the 'Thoughts' book *Last Exit before Tunnel*?

Back it came with a ping.

From: MarkC@rmbooks.com
To: RosieB@eirtel.com
Sent: 12.57 p.m.

Aw, lighten up!

Yep. He was there.

I'd managed to assemble a mental survival kit over the years – if I hadn't I'd have despaired time and again at ferries kept in the harbour by high winds; parties I wasn't asked to; dates who only wanted me to caress them, not vice versa; flatmates who decamped leaving bills unpaid; jobs I didn't get; places that when I got to them weren't there. I saved for a long time to travel to Athens and then I had to climb up to the Acropolis on a path of rocks worn to glass behind a plump woman in hot pants and high-heeled mules, in a sun so hot that the Parthenon swam in front of my eyes; and when I scrambled down again I discovered my money had been stolen from my back pocket.

But what I did then, before even looking for a policeman, was count my blessings. I remember that I did it on my fingers, under a pine tree. Blessing number one was the shade of the tree.

Where was the pink notebook? There. I crossed out the few words on its first page, and wrote:

Tips for The Bad Times

1. Count your blessings.
2. Wash your face and fix your hair.
3. Tidy your handbag.
4. Establish as best you can your exact financial position, even if it is fairly dire.
5. Do a good deed for someone else.
6. Smile at everyone you meet – they won't know you don't mean it.
7. Make your bed with clean sheets.

I couldn't think of any more. Besides, what if you were in a hotel? You'd be crazy to make the bed. And No. 7 was a bit housewifey. I needed to think up some unisex ones.

I typed the list into an email and sent it to Markey, to show him I wasn't sleeping on the job.

Then, out of pure idleness, and because finding something else to read would involve standing up, I opened the top envelope of Min's mail. A brown envelope with a harp on it, a State envelope, not sealed, so it couldn't be anything personal – which it couldn't be anyway because Min never got a personal letter in her life, unless you counted what she got from me.

The Department of Defence/ An Roinn Cosanta
  Re. South Milbay Air Corps (Junior) Training Camp.

To whom it may concern,

The Minister for Defence, Mr Hal McFadden TD, is pleased to announce the relinquishing by the Department, on foot of a review of the Department's aviation needs, of the lands at Milbay Point taken in charge under the Act for the Defence of the Realm (1892) and formerly seized under emergency powers. A substantial project of reclamation of the site is envisaged in the near future, to comprise the provision of an access road, steps to a public beach, wood coppicing etc.

It has come to the Department's attention that a single dwelling house at Milbay Point, in the townland of Baile na gCloch (Stoneytown), was not acquired outright, but instead made available on a long lease, dated September 1948, per agreement with its owner Mr Joseph Connors. It is further specified in said agreement that when said lease is vacated, the property (to include rights of way, former haggard, orchard and sundry outbuildings, foreshore rights et alia cf. Land Registry Map no. Wex/39/577) should revert to his daughter, Marinda Connors. The lease has now fallen in and the aforementioned property has accordingly reverted to the said Marinda Connors. According to the Register of Electors, a Miss Marinda Connors is resident at the address in Kilbride, Dublin at the top of this letter. A copy of the lease can be made available on request.

Access to the property can only be arranged at present through the Air Corps Buildings Maintenance Division, Casement Aerodrome, Baldonnel, where a key to the gate of the former training camp may be provisionally issued to Miss Connors or her assigns, together with the original house key. Reference Milbay Point/Private House in any enquiry. It should be noted that this property, though requisitioned, was surplus to the requirements of the Air Corps. The house, therefore, has never been refurbished and has not been entered for many years.

Yours faithfully,
Followed by someone's signature.

I looked at the clock. Borderline. But possible, to reach there and back.

A light knock sounded, together with the front door opening, and Andy Sutton put his head round the kitchen door.

'Hiya Rose! I'm heading from Pearl's place to the airport so I thought I'd say hello and—'

'Andy! The very man! How do you go from here to Milbay?'

He was delighted. 'I've the new AA atlas in the truck,' he said, boastful about that when he was never boastful about big things. 'Nothing else is any good with all the new motorways and all.'

He wasted a lot of time going out to the truck to fetch his atlas and then going back out to fetch coloured pencils to draw alternative routes. I had to keep yelling at him that if he didn't hurry up it would be dark before I got going.

'What's your hurry?' he was asking. 'Can't whatever it is wait for another few days? I could take you down in the truck if you gave me a bit of notice. I know that part of the country like the back of my hand from taking the animals to Rosslare.'

But I couldn't wait. 'I'll tell you a secret, Andy! I'm going to the place on the other side of Milbay where Min and my mother grew up! If I can get in, I'm going to see their house! I'll be able to touch it, maybe.'

'You never saw it before?'

'I saw it from the sea, miles away. That was all. For a few minutes. When I was nine or ten. Oh, keep your fingers crossed for me!'

It happened once that when we arrived for our holiday my dad saw that a small rowboat had been pushed into the space between the concrete blocks The Hut stood on. He sent me crawling in there to see were there oars in the boat and there were – two fine oars!

'C'mon Rosie,' Daddy said. 'We'll have an adventure.' So we dragged the boat out and across the grass and down onto the pebbly sand of our little beach.

'See can you catch us a fish!' Min laughed. A joke, as my father wouldn't know one end of a fish from another, but it showed what a good mood she was in.

It was a high summer evening, with the sun just beginning to decline towards the west, and the Milbay River so wide and calm at the point where the estuary met the sea, that the pink of the sky lay reflected in it. My dad rowed us slowly – the boat small and ourselves low in the water – across the pink which broke, slow and sleek, and became black where it was turned over by the oars. The evening air was still and everything was quiet, even the seagulls, floating high up, fragmentary against bars of delicate cloud.

It was then that I first heard the name of 'Stoneytown'. My father, resting on the oars as the boat gently rocked, said it as he pointed it out to me. Earlier, from out in the middle of the estuary, he had pointed back to where we had come from. To Milbay, on the northern side of the river, with its quayside and its roofs and its two church spires. And there, where the old warehouses and wharves ended, at the last bit of flat ground, you could just about see The Hut.

But then he had made me look ahead again, to the

south side of the river, the side ahead of us, across from the town. Inland were thick woods, and then a tall mast with lights that were always winking, and a windsock, flying next to a building that looked like a small office block. Then, nearer the sea, a smooth green hill with dark gashes in it. And then Daddy started to row again, and the boat fairly glided along, and soon we'd gone so far that we were now off the point where that southern shore met the sea. Tucked in between the hill and the water, facing Milbay across the river, was a terrace of grey houses. I'd seen them before, when the weather was clear. From the far distance they had looked normal, but I'd already noticed, playing around The Hut before bed, that lights never came on in them.

'That's Stoneytown,' my father said, 'and if we go on a bit you'll see the house Min and your mother grew up in.'

I was amazed. I knew they were from somewhere along the coast, but I thought it must have been a place hundreds of miles away from Dublin. I didn't know it had been on my horizon every summer.

'Did Min ever tell you that?' he said. And when I shook my head, he said, with one of his smiles, 'Don't say anything, then. It's her business.'

We were within sight of it now, a house that stood alone, beyond a jetty that had partially fallen into the water and was covered in barbed wire. It was a sturdy house, of blocks of stone, with a roof of stone flags. That's all I could see, and I wanted my Dad to row in farther so I could see more. But out here was where the river mouth became unsheltered sea, and the water was choppier than before. It was time to turn around, Dad said.

'Why are there no people?' I asked.

'The government took it over when there was a war between England and Germany,' he explained, 'and nobody knew what would happen to Ireland. The people had to leave. They were a law unto themselves, before that. They worked in the quarry. Do you know what a quarry is? See the hill? The stone from that hill was famous. You know where we go to Mass? That church was built with blocks from this hill. And after the war, when the people were still all gone, the government kept it for the air force that was just starting.'

I was as breathless with excitement now, having finally set out from Dublin, as I'd been then. My heart fluttering with excitement, as I drove past Milbay on a new bypass that crossed the Milbay River upstream of the town. After the bridge the road went directly into woods that had to be the same I'd seen on the inland side of the winking mast from Dad's boat. Yes. Here was the tall perimeter fence of the camp, and in a mile or so, its wide gateway. I pulled in and sat in the car for a moment, taking deep breaths. A gusty, greying evening, it was. An hour and twenty minutes from the house in Kilbride. Not bad at all. Though in summer there'd be far more traffic on the road.

We were soon into water as smooth as silk after my dad turned the boat around with one oar and started making with steady strokes for home. Then, suddenly, amazingly, as we moved across the river mouth, a thing that looked like a small typhoon sped across the calm water towards us, coming in off the Irish Sea.

'Mackerel!' Daddy shouted. 'A shoal of mackerel, by God!'

The surface of the water broke as the gleaming green, blue and grey-black mackerel surrounded the boat in a rush to pass it by. Squeezed up out of the oily water by their own number, they made silver arcs as they jumped, transforming the whole scene in a frenzy that was strangely silent, except for the splash after splash of water, and the hard slap of mackerel bodies against the wooden bottom of our boat where nearly a dozen fish that had slipped over the side now writhed.

My father was thrilled. 'Wait'll we tell Min! Bringing her home fish when we didn't even have a fishing rod!'

He pulled the boat up when we got to the shelly beach under The Hut, and then taking off his shirt and tying the sleeves, he filled the bag he'd made with plump fish. He then set off ahead of me, dying to astonish Min.

But just as we got to the edge of the lamplight that spilled from the door, he stopped and bent down to me and said, quietly, 'Don't tell her we had a look at Stoneytown. She doesn't like talking about it.'

We then burst in like people out of a film, my dad half-naked and laughing and proud as punch of himself; and me, nearly as important, and delighted to be home again.

The gate to the camp was too high to climb. And I couldn't see. The greys of twilight were turning very quickly to night, just as they had that evening after the fish danced past our boat. I'd need a torch to take a good look at the chain and the padlock, and needless to say I had no torch.

'But I'll be back,' I whispered. 'Just you wait. I'll be back in the morning to claim our house.'

And – as if I had been heard – the scene suddenly, dramatically lit up.

A hundred yards beyond the camp gate, two powerful security lights mounted on high poles had switched on and now illuminated the broken windows of the nearest building, beside an asphalt roadway with grass-filled cracks and holes, and a barrier of weeds intertwined with the mesh on the camp gate, and on either side of it, drifts of dry leaves half-filling what once were sentry boxes. The woods however stood motionless beyond the light, darker than the night sky.

Wait till Min hears this! That she owned – owned! – her childhood home! I'd better get cracking and tidy up in Kilbride. She'd be on the first plane back. I'd also better give Bell a thorough combing or there'd be hell to pay. Flowers, by the way. Welcome-home flowers. Do a supermarket shop. Hide the luxury sheets I'd bought in New York.

I jumped into the car and turned for Dublin, my head dizzy with anticipation.

From: MarkC@rmbooks.com
To: RosieB@eirtel.com
Sent: 11.15 p.m.

Just to continue the point I was making, Rosie:
    The people of the USA, who are mostly fine

people, use growing older to dye their hair, get married for the fifth time, cycle up Mount Rainier, re-train as carpenters, have plastic surgery, travel abroad, contribute to their communities and so on. They keep busy. Many of them – and I speak for myself – especially enjoy making money and the company of their grandchildren.

Do you have broadband, Rose? I want to send you the latest *MORE* magazine. *MORE*'s target audience is women of 40+ which is exactly the demographic we would want to hit with 'Thoughts'. The words on *MORE*'s cover are: Successful/ Stylish/ Healthy/ Adventurous.

The kind of words Irish grumps and sourpusses use do not appear in *MORE*, for the very good reason that they would depress the hell out of anyone who is not as young as they used to be.

From: RosieB@eirtel.com
To: MarkC@rmbooks.com
Sent: 11.32 p.m.

Forgive me if I'm being slow or something. But don't American people grow old the same as other people do? They die, don't they?

But just in case you by any chance meant me when you refer to grumps and sourpusses, the truth is that today, life really is WONDERFUL! I have a WONDERFUL surprise for Min that I'm dying to tell her, but I'm having a hard time getting an answer to her pal Luz's cell phone.

Incidentally, I came across a possible epigraph for our 'Thoughts' in The Notebook of Malte Laurids Brigge (which you, as a matter of fact, gave me when we were going through our Rilke phase):

'I pleaded for my childhood, and it has come back, and I feel it's still as hard as it was then, and growing older has been of no use at all.'

What do you think?

From: MarkC@rmbooks.com
To: RosieB@eirtel.com
Sent: 11.37 p.m.

Tell me you're kidding!

From: RosieB@eirtel.com
To: MarkC@rmbooks.com
Sent: 11.39 p.m.

OK. I was kidding.

11

Nobody on earth knew where I was when, two mornings later, I opened the camp gates with the keys I had got from the Air Corps and stood in the soft, lively air, listening to the rooks announce my arrival from the branches of a beech wood whose grey was flushed with green.

I could feel the beat of my heart actually shaking my ribcage as I locked the gate behind me.

I was on territory of my own, now.

There was no road to the shore, but a track went around the back of the camp, where Nissan huts so old that their tarpaulin roofs had perished lined one side of a cracked and uneven airfield. The track then skirted a lush meadow and gradually ran out at a green ridge, gashed with quarrying, that must be the last thing between the land and the sea. I left the car there, backed in across the floor of a bushy semi-cave. As I came out, rabbits bolted into a nearby dump of rusted machinery smothered in the white flowers of a strangling weed.

Convolvulus. Another good sign on this day. Reminding me how Markey had once stopped to show me the vine the flowers grew on. Had asked me did I know the word *convoluted*? 'Same root,' he said. 'A twisted thing.'

'How do you mean?' I asked – after all, I was only sixteen and I worked in a department store.

'To say someone gives a convoluted explanation means the explanation's all twisted and turned like this stem.'

For the first time I understood that words have histories and how they can differ but have the same ancestors. I looked at him, so pleased I couldn't speak – at which he gave me a little kiss.

I was now climbing the low ridge, as limber with joy as if I were sixteen again. Is there a guide to grass? What would you call grass as dense and short and smooth as this? A small rabbit scuttled past, brilliantly white against the emerald turf. Still distracted by it, I was assaulted by a marvellous breeze from the sea and, lifting my head, took in the shining roofs and spires of Milbay across the glossy river and the sea ahead and what had once been Stoneytown below, all of it serene and smiling in the morning sun. Below me to my left stood the terrace of houses in ruin, behind the broken jetty onto which great chunks of masonry had fallen. The backs of the houses were half-smothered by a riot of briars, nettles, ivies, hazel and hawthorn scrub; at their front, countless storms had piled boulders alongside the top of the shore, outside what had once been their doors.

But what mattered most to my dazzled gaze was the settlement below me on my right, facing straight out to sea. There was a house roofed in big stone flags, beautifully encompassed by a high-walled enclosure full of trees at one gable end and a stone barn at the other, and at the back by a line of sheds that, together with the barn, enclosed a big yard. The waves, now at full tide, seemed to dance almost up to the front of the house. There was no path along the ridge that ran down to the yard, but I saw a deep, grassy cart track that came down on my right between the ragged hedges of a couple of overgrown fields and ended at the yard gate. So I ran down the ridge to it, and, immersed in its shelter, I walked towards the house, the sound of the sea filling the air with every step. Eventually I passed beside the sheds and the barn and stopped to stand some fifty feet from where green waves and white foam curled and slapped onto glistening black rocks.

Turning then, I looked at the house my mother and Min grew up in. The house my dad had shown me on the mackerel night.

And then, as if I knew exactly how to do these things, I clambered over the storm-tossed rounded boulders and pushed, ungainly, holding my bag in front of me to protect my hands, through the nettles on the strip of ground between me and the front door. Pulling down a bramble that had grown across it, I jumped on it till it flattened on the ground. The wood of the door was soft and bleached with age, but the old dirt that had filled the keyhole was almost as hard as stone. I picked at it with the point of my nail scissors, all the time babbling under my breath, 'Oh please, oh please.' Finally I worked the dirt out and, as gently and slowly as I could bear, breath held, eyes half-closed, I spat onto the key, then inserted it.

It did turn, too; and I heard, as if it were a miraculous sound, the heavy click of the lock. Thank you, thank you, I breathed, as I slid to the ground, my knees trembling too badly to hold me up.

Eventually I stood and shoved with all my might against the door, thumping my hip against it repeatedly. I got it open just enough to squeeze through and see that a hazel bush, which had grown up through the cracked flagstone of the floor and now reached towards the dim light of a mottled window, was what was blocking entry. So I grasped the bush and pulled and pulled. I was determined to fill the house with light and air and I couldn't do that until I could open wide the door. Unable to budge the bush, I squeezed out onto the shore again and searched the debris there until I found a sharply pointed stone. I then went back and, squatting at the hazel bush, loosened its roots with my stone. Like a hominid ancestor with a flint tool. Like a child, patiently playing. And after a while I was able to pull the bush out and throw it to the side. Then kicking fallen plaster and dirt away with my foot, and slowly scraping dirt from the floor to smooth every half-inch of progress, I wrenched open the door and sunshine entered a room that had been dark for more than half a century.

I laughed out loud! And told myself proudly I was a changed woman already. It was evident that no one had penetrated to this remote house since it had been abandoned. The nearest person, too, was miles away. But still, when before – if ever – in my whole life, had

I not cared how much noise I made? When had I ever shouted out loud with joy? When had I thrown my head back and laughed all by myself? What's more, I had an appetite for the work that opening up this house took. I panted and grunted. Bashed and banged my way through the rusted buckets and basins which littered the floor of the back kitchen, where they must have fallen, over the years, from hooks where once they'd hung. I dragged at the thick back door and I squealed with its squeals. Nothing checked my barbarian's progress, not even the iron rims of cartwheels that had been laid to hold down the planks that covered the well.

But the planks themselves were too heavy for me.

I slumped to the ground and sat on the grassy flags with my back against a wall and waited for my body to stop shaking. The stones of the wall, where they faced away from the south-east, were thick with lichens – bluey-green, silver-white, palest yellow. Yet the stones where they faced south-east were as bare as if they'd been scrubbed that morning. So now I knew where the prevailing wind came from! I laughed, ridiculously pleased with myself for having figured out this little thing.

I sat in the peace of the yard, the waves whispering throatily on the other side of the wall, and ate half the chocolate I'd brought. I always had some chocolate around since the man friend before Leo, who'd been a keep-fit fanatic, told me how a person's blood sugar level could plummet dangerously low at any time and everyone should carry chocolate to boost it back up again.

I had passed this on to Min who said, 'Well, why isn't everyone dead, then?'

I said, 'What?'

'People in olden times, who didn't know about chocolate, why didn't they all drop dead?'

I tried to remember that man's face, but what came back instead was the day in Austria, cycling along the Danube, that we had begun to part. He had refused to come with me to visit the Mauthausen Concentration Camp. What was the point? he said, adding that there was a whole Holocaust industry these days. I said – I remembered both saying it, and the bedroom with pine walls and frilly curtains where it got said – that I understood his being too emotionally lazy to visit a scene of real suffering, and too spiritually lazy to confront real evil, but did he also have to be so intellectually lazy that he repeated other people's clichés, like the one that attempted to denigrate the Holocaust experience by using the word 'industry'?

No wonder that you ended up with Leo, I told myself now, as I hauled myself up to go back into the house. Leo who says so little that even you can't jump on him.

All but one of the four plank steps to the loft were still in place, and so was most of the loft floor. The part where the floorboards had rotted and you could see into the room below was in a corner, so the rest was safe enough. There was a mirror, milky with age, hanging still from a big nail between beams, and linked by huge festoons of grey spiders' web with the iron bedstead beneath. The cobwebs wavered in the disturbance I was making, so I stood immobile till they stopped moving. Life would have centred itself around the range in the room below, but this loft would have shared in that life, there being only a layer of floorboards between upstairs and downstairs. It would have been warm here from the range, and because the stone roof-flags were insulated by plaster that had been roughly spread between the supporting beams. Down behind the bed, between the low, last beam and the floor that was thick with dust, there was a small expanse of plaster, and because the spring base of the bed had rusted away, I could see that there were marks on the plaster. That corner was crowded with them, though there were none anywhere else. I hunkered down to study them. They were lines or ticks, bundles of down-ward lines, scored into the plaster with what must have been a sharp piece of burnt stick. Each bundle was of six downward strokes and each had been finished off with one diagonal stroke across the six. Every four bundles there was a bundle of just four vertical lines, also crossed off by a diagonal line. Twenty-eight days to each cluster.

Then, I didn't guess, I just knew. I knew because I'd just been remembering the quarry at Mauthausen and the horror in the air there, where the captives worked till they dropped or the sadistic guards killed them for sport. I knew that a distant and tiny echo of horror came from these marks, too. They'd been made in desperation – you could see where the plaster had been gouged, not lightly marked – and they'd been made by a desperate woman. My mother's mother was the first woman to live here, the wife for whom my grandfather built the house. I'd hardly ever thought about her. That she died of appendicitis when my mother was fifteen and Min was about ten; that was all I knew. Min had no photo of her. Nothing, as far as I knew, was known about her. Not her maiden name. Not her age when she died. She was like most women born on this planet: no trace of all that she had been was left behind, except her children.

Her daughter Min.

And her granddaughter Rosaleen Barry. I put my palms up and felt my warm cheeks. Me. She'd left me behind.

This calendar – surely it was hers? Out in even as remote a spot as this, and even in the utter bleakness of what it must have been like in the 1920s, a woman would have known that there were days when she might conceive and days when she might not. Maybe she was desperate not to go through pregnancy again. Or maybe it was the opposite – maybe after two girls she was trying to find out when she'd be fertile, because in a place like Stoneytown a woman wouldn't have counted for much without strong, male children. I'd been in hardscrabble places all over the world where women who had not produced a son were pariahs.

'What's Min short for?' I'd asked my aunt once when I was small and she'd said it was short for 'a minute, which is all you've got to finish your homework'.

I asked her again a few years later.

'Marinda,' she said. 'That's my real name, Marinda Connors.'

'There's no such name as Marinda,' I said. 'There's Miranda.'

'That's right,' she nodded. 'They got it wrong. I was told that before.'

'Who got it wrong?'

'The women,' she said. 'My mother was in a terrible state in the hospital in Milbay, and the women came over from the Point – that's what they called it, they never called it Stoneytown – to fetch me. But I had to be baptised before I'd be let out of the hospital, and they picked Miranda only they got it wrong. They saw her in a film, Carmen Miranda.'

'I thought you had to have the name of a saint or an Irish name, or the priest wouldn't baptise you?'

'Well, maybe Marinda is one of Our Lady's names?' she said hopefully. 'Isn't it nearly the same as Maria?'

I thought that was that, but then she burst out, 'It didn't matter! Nobody cared what a girl was called! You never heard your full name!'

Whoever had made these scratch marks was trying to have control over the tides of her own body. What a statement, in a society where the men undoubtedly had control of everything, from bringing food in to bringing the dead out! I went to touch one of the bundles of marks, as a gesture of respect.

But my hand jumped back before I made contact.

They couldn't have been made by my own mother, could they? Fifteen years old when she ran away from

Stoneytown. Why would she have been trying to keep track of her monthly cycle? Or Min?

No.

I stood and listened to the sighing of the sea. The marks burned in their corner.

We might as well have been disembodied spirits, Min and I, for all the femaleness we'd ever acknowledged in each other. And while she lived half her life within a few feet of a man – her own father, or my father – the fact she was a woman was very probably never spoken of. I knew by instinct not to go to her when I was shocked speechless by my first bleeding; instead I went in to Reeny and waited till Monty had gone out before starting to cry, and pointing to where my belly ached. Reeny must have gone to Min because every four weeks after that, until I got my first wages from the Pillar, there'd be a half-crown coin for me in the front pocket of my schoolbag. But we never spoke about it.

Even when I was going out to demos, marching and protesting about this and that women's lib issue, I never talked to my aunt, woman-to-woman. She and I never talked about wanting babies or not wanting them, much less about wanting lovemaking or not wanting it. The nearest she had ever come to showing me her inner self was in the last few years, when the drink and the silence must have been her way of tamping down something like rage.

I turned away from the cobweb-shrouded bed and made my way down from the loft, placing each foot exactly where – I imagined – her girl's foot would have gone. And, like a nimbus around her footprint, I imagined the slightly bigger footprint of my own mother.

I must have been in hundreds of houses in my lifetime, I thought. I've lived in tens of them. But this is the house that was waiting for me.

I'd have to go back to Dublin. My mobile phone didn't work out here and I urgently needed to find out about health insurance in the States for a soon-to-be-seventy-year-old. But before I left I went out to the backyard again. It was lovely there. The stone walls were so high that the sea breeze passed over – you could feel its lively presence, yet it couldn't come down to disturb the sleek warmth of the flagstones and grasses and weeds, and the old wood of the barn doors and the faded, whitewashed stone of the row of sheds. The shed beside the back door, where the board seat with a hole in the middle would have had a bucket beneath, must have been the privy. There was a tiny window in the back wall there – the wall above the shore – its glass crazed by age and weather and a rusted latch. Yet when I shoved it open the sea sounds rushed in.

But then when I squatted to pee on a corner of grass, the sea receded again, back behind the overgrown hedges and the thick wall. I could feel the June sun suave on the skin of my thighs and my bottom, my eyes half-closed to the dazzle of blue sky, green grass and lichened stone.

Last thing, I tried to move the planks that covered the wellhead again. Calm now, I worked them patiently to the edge of the low, circular wall where eventually they thumped to the ground. When I went down two stone steps to peer in, a surge of such pleasure went through me that it nearly made me giddy. The water that rippled almost imperceptibly from whatever spring was feeding it was so clear that I could see each individual cobblestone of the beautifully made lining. It was living water. Rich water. It gave a heart to the house with its walls of granite blocks, its stone roof-slabs, its lintels and window frames and doors of weathered wood. The words '*He is not dead but sleepeth*,' jumped out of nowhere into my head.

Finally I climbed back over the ridge to the car. At the top, I stood in the mild afternoon under a filigree of lark song and looked down on the roof of the house, on the little beach to its left leading to the broken jetty and the tumbled terrace of houses, on the rocks and gleaming mud of the estuary where the tide was coming in all foamy waves, and on the deep channel of water between this side of the river and the homely huddle of Milbay town. Wading birds on the mud below made helpless calls and a snowy-winged guillemot flew down from the blue with a raucous cry like an overseer rebuking his workers. It sang with life, the whole, wide vista. The house, though battered and worn, was alive, and so was the seashore where the cormorants stood on black rocks, and so was the hill with its velvety ridge above its gashed and hollowed sides, and so was the fecund meadow and the sparkling beech woods and even the old offices and dormitories of the Air Corps camp. And I – the world having granted me a new connection with it – I sang with life, too.

The message light was blinking in the corner of the kitchen in Kilbride.

'How's it going there, Rosie? This is Min here. I wonder if Bell knows that it's me talking – hello Bell!'

Min was shouting as if that would help us hear her across the Atlantic.

'There is a homeless lady opposite the Harmony Hotel and they gave her an apartment but she doesn't want it because she'd have to pay part of her Social Security so Luz and me took it and we're giving her twenty-five dollars a week each – sure I receive that for a few hours in the restaurant kitchen. It's money for jam except I have to put me hair up in a white cap like an ambulance man and I have to take a bus and then the subway. Anyway you can ring Luz's phone any time except not at work; we go to work at 5 p.m. and we do nine hours including our break. I saw a coat in Macy's sale, lovely brown wool that would suit you down to the ground, Rosaleen. I'm going to buy it on Saturday if it isn't gone, I'll be going up that way to choir practice at our Lady of Guadeloupe, I often heard of her, the Black Madonna. So bye for now. I'm having a great time, but the problem with the hostel was the thieving; we hadn't been there three hours when Luz's little bag with all her cosmetics was fecked while she was in the shower. I'll give you another ring tomorrow as soon as I buy a card with numbers like Luz has that she's always ringing Mexico with. Bye now. Bye Bell – be a good cat for Rosie!'

I went out the back and called for Bell who came and sat on an old newspaper while I combed her and we listened again to the message. She didn't react at her name, but then she could have been hiding what she felt.

I did react. I went up to bed full of happiness.

I'd found a magic house, and it belonged to my family. It *gave* me my family.

And Min must be missing me, because she only called me Rosaleen at her most affectionate.

12

I was terribly anxious the next morning, however, waiting for Min to ring. All my life she'd mentioned Stoneytown only reluctantly, and always with more or less loathing. How could I describe the place to her in such a way that she would at least keep an open mind? How could I convey to her that as far as I was concerned every single thing about it was utterly magical? That this could be the biggest thing ever to come between us?

I went up to make my bed. How austere it was! I must buy a few silk and velvet cushions, at the very least; you'd think it was still the bedroom of a bookish girl earning very little. On the shelf of honour, right above the bed, were the Penguin Joyces, limp with use, that I'd read under the counter when I was on Irish Souvenirs & Gifts in the Pillar. Yet I'd only read half of *Ulysses*, though I finished the book, because I couldn't stand Stephen Dedalus. I'd skipped the hard bits, too, though I could remember trying and trying again to understand them. I let myself be oppressed, in those days, by what seemed like huge things: not understanding Joyce, not having money, not having clothes, not having a father, wanting to stay on at school and being stopped by Min. Or by not having straight hair.

'I wouldn't mind if it was *curly*,' I said to the girls in the Pillar. 'But wavy is the pits.'

I went back down to the kitchen table, and gloomily transcribed a note into the pink notebook. Ashley Judd, apparently, had spent forty-seven days in a Treatment Center in Buffalo Gap, Texas, suffering from 'co-dependence in my relationships, depression, blaming, raging, numbing, denying, and minimising my feelings'. After forty-seven days she came out happy. 'It's so simple, really,' Ashley said. 'I was unhappy and now I'm happy.'

I mean, if it was as simple as that, why bother to write even a booklet for gift shops?

2 p.m. Min was surely up by now? I tested the phone. It was fine. She just hadn't rung.

The number I had for Luz's phone had never yet been answered.

Another thing: I didn't know Luz's second name.

Well, I wasn't going to waste a whole precious afternoon. The house at the Point could do with a good cleaning no matter what was going to happen. The thought filled me with such pleasure that I sang like Figaro when he's measuring for the bed, as I gathered a brush and pan, a mop, Flash and Windolene, plus teacloths, towels and a few old blankets that were bound to come in handy.

I looked in the *Golden Pages* to see whether by any chance Bailey's Hardware and Builders' Providers was still in existence. It wasn't, but there was another hardware store on the main street of Milbay, so I went in off the bypass and parked right in front of it.

'Nails, Mister, please,' I said to the man in the low, cluttered shop. 'And a hammer.'

'What size nails?' he said.

'Small nails, medium nails and big long nails,' I said. 'And a plastic bucket and a basin and a portable charcoal barbeque and a little camping gas stove. And a torch and a bucket I could put ashes into. And one of those.'

'My God!' the man said, springing up to take down the folding step-ladder I'd pointed to. 'Here I was thinking I should quit the business and in the door you come.'

'And tell me what else I'd need to give an overgrown old house a good going-over.'

'You need a screwdriver,' he said. 'Is there electricity? Well, I could give you a nice battery-operated one. I'll throw in the batteries. And a wrench and pliers. And is there brambles? I've a shears here'd cut down an oak tree. How about a Stanley knife? And is there ever a window in the place at all?'

'Oh good,' I replied, 'the knife'll be just the job for scraping off bird droppings. That reminds me, have you a bucket with a lid for the toilet? With some of that smelly, chemical stuff? I hope there's no mice, but have you anything for them in case there are? Something that wouldn't hurt them? And firelighters. And matches – wow, I almost forgot matches! And a few knives and forks and spoons. A roll of garbage bags. Some of those rubber car mats – say six of them, they can go down on the floor. Oh, and a teapot! And black lead for making the range nice and shiny.'

'It must be a quare long time since you cleaned a range,' the man said. 'I stopped stocking black lead years ago.'

'That's right,' I beamed at him. 'My name's Marie Antoinette.'

While he was packing the car, I went down the street and got soda-bread and smoked salmon and butter and milk and tea, plus a lemon and apples. And the newspaper. If I felt like sitting on my butt and reading, that's what I'd do.

At which I ran back to the store to tell him to throw in a couple of wooden stools.

The head of a traffic warden appeared around the door and the man said, 'Take it easy, Comrade, I'm just finishing loading up for Her Majesty, Queen of France here' – and the head disappeared.

And off I went, whistling.

A swathe of Russian ivy had grown overnight across the gates of the Milbay Camp so I got to use my clippers straight away. But that was almost all I did with my new things. Showers kept coming up from the south through the soft, grey sky, and I had to time my journeys up and over the hill from car to house for the intervals between them. I'd buy two little carts, next time, and leave one in the cleft of the quarry where I parked.

I put all my stuff away on the wide shelves of the back kitchen, with the sound of the sea coming through the open back door. But apart from that, all I did was shove to the side, with the back of the sweeping brush, the thick layer of flaked plaster and dust and twigs that covered the floor where the hazel bush had been. A wagtail bobbed in the open door at a run and then, seeing the avalanche of dirt coming towards it, backed out as quickly. I then swept the clearing I'd made, revealing flagstones so strong that only two or three had cracked in all the years they'd lain there. But they'd been laid on dirt, so that weeds and stunted things had grown up between them, even in dimness.

I worked with a knife on prising open the two small leaves of the windows, after lavishing oil on the rusty hinges, and noticed my hands because they were in my line of vision. A constellation of brown freckles. The story of my skin's ageing had hardly begun though there'd been some thinning and corrugating and discolouring – nothing much, but nothing, either, that was ever going to be reversed. Min's hands were blotched as well as spotted and the skin on her face was covered with a network of hair-thin lines, like the craquelure on the varnish of an old painting. On her last birthday I'd insisted she get up and we all go up to the Kilbride Inn to blow out the candles on a little cake and sing 'Happy Birthday'. And she'd slapped on makeup and put on the black jumper she still considered a treasure, along with a pair of my jeans from twenty years ago, and so had ended up looking wiry and wild-haired and neither old nor young.

What did she think about that? She'd seemed very pleased, and shy, a thing she never usually was. What did she think of the sixty-nine years since she'd been an infant laid, very likely, on the settle bed on the other side of this room?

My own body set off into the world when I was about fifteen. It moved out to learn about other bodies. When had hers ever had a chance to do that?

She was fifteen when I was handed to her. And that was it. No hot desires for her. No giggling. No self-consciousness, her little pointy breasts and her flat tummy never to fill and swell. No conception, no contraception.

She ironed nearly everything, even my father's drip-dry shirts that didn't need ironing, and when Reeny caught her at it one day, she laughed at her. 'Do you not realise, Min, that drip-dry fabric is the most important invention since the pill?'

I waited to see whether Min would say 'What pill?'

But she didn't say anything.

Little did Reeny know that Min ironed his underpants, too, and his sheets and his hankies and the little napkins she put on his tray when he wasn't able to sit at the table for his meal. A flower, too, she always put there, as I knew to my cost because she nearly killed me when I once pinched the last bloom from her pot of chrysanthemums. Reeny didn't know about the trays so delicately arranged, though she thought she knew everything. If anyone came into the house, in the second between the bang of the front door and their entry into the kitchen – hey presto, my father's tray disappeared.

The newly freed windows creaked in a gust of wind. I hurried out the back for a quick look around my kingdom before the serious rain came. One last strut of a wooden gate hung between beautifully made piers of flat stones at the furthest corner of the yard, and beyond, the deep cart track which ran up to the woods. The tangled, wet grass was speckled with a tiny blue flower. Cornflower, maybe. At least I knew that the flocks of chattering brown birds that swooped from the briars of the bank to grasses that swayed with their weight were field sparrows. They had some other name, but that was what my dad called them. He didn't know much, but he took an interest. Min didn't. Min didn't have names for anything. And yet, this was Min's home place.

I turned to go back to the house.

She who'd never owned anything owned all this.

A first drop of rain splattered onto my nose. I ran down the track and across the yard and gathered my picnic from the back kitchen and spread it at the front, on a car mat, just inside the threshold – my bag of food and my new knife and fork and a mug full of crystalline well water. A soft screen of rain was wafting in from the sea, but I could still make out the distant point of land on which Bailey's Hut had once stood. I could identify it because there was a container park there now, with its containers stacked up high. Milbay had always been a town with a workaday harbour full of dirty coal boats and high-smelling trawlers, not attractive at all. But I had loved it. I loved the Milbay River. Who would have thought that I'd be so blessed by it? That I'd be completely happy on both of the points of land where the river water surrendered to the sea?

I had to go home for the call Min had promised. After eating, I locked up as slowly as possible, smoothing the soft old wood of the doors with my palm to feel their silkiness.

I climbed the ridge in the pause before twilight where everything in nature stops moving and holds itself still. The container park where The Hut had stood was clearly visible across the estuary in the low evening light. It was as if Min's sweetness when we were there on our holidays now infused the whole wide scene. It was the sweetness of a pure person, I thought. Of a young woman who was alienated from her own past, who had no parent or lover to celebrate her, who worked full time for no pay, who was looking out at the summer rain with someone else's child at her feet and someone else's widower at her side. But those negative things didn't define her. She could be as perfectly happy as a child, and when she was, sweetness came from her like perfume.

She was unspoiled. She'd had the protection of the position of mistress of a household; and yet she'd never been on display – never had to offer herself around. Her body had never been currency.

I hurried to the car. I shouldn't have thought of that – her unspoilt body and my used, compromised one. For over a year now I'd buried, as deep as I could, any thought of what had become of Leo and me. But now Macerata broke into my memory and there was nothing I could do but remember it.

The cab from the airport was air-conditioned that day, but I was almost faint with uneasiness. I knew that Leo hadn't wanted me to come to Italy, even though he was too polite, too reticent to spell it out. But he'd mentioned, when we were leaving Ancona after that not very successful Christmas, that the Macerata Opera Festival people had invited him to a meeting in the spring, to which I said it was an easy place to reach – would he let me know where he'd be staying? When I dared to peek at him, he was looking at me and smiling helplessly, like a father giving in against his judgement to a child. He murmured something, but I didn't really hear.

The sky was white-blue with the heat, though it was only early May. I gasped, stepping out of the car, and hurried towards the shade of the vine-covered patio where Leo was slowly rising from a wicker chair. He came towards me, courteous as ever. But stooped. He was not at all what he had been before his boutique hotel project went wrong. At lunch, when he took off his sunglasses to read the menu, I saw, along with a reflection from the water jug on the table that danced merrily under his chin, a blueish-white tint to the half-moons of soft skin under his eyes. He did manage, at one point in his meal, to smile at me with the old charm, but he hardly ate.

'You look very well, Rosie,' he said. 'Always your eyes are shining.'

I suppressed a humorous remark about shining with lust: the affair with Leo having never been noted for its jokes. Only this meeting quickly became not just serious, but grim. Worse than grim.

'I'll remember this heat till I die,' I said, when I was in his room. The doors to the balcony were open and streaks of sunlight too hot to walk on fell across the parquet floor.

'There is nothing but these between us and the sun,' he said, pulling the curtains closed. 'We melt away, like the planet.'

It was my own fault. All during our time on the bed the heat was like a second assault. The breeze from the sea would lift the curtains or furl them, and the sun's rays seared wherever they fell: on my arm or my stomach or on the back of my thighs. Nor had Leo any energy to spare, to help me out of my misery. Instead he burrowed and rooted, in-turned, as if he were being whipped on, his breath coming in sobs.

He wouldn't say anything either, even though I implored him.

'Stop it, Leo! Talk to me! Leo, please talk to me.'

What he'd done for pure self-satisfaction when he was well, he did now in desperation, trying to bully the vitality that once flowed between us into flowing again. It was the saddest, loneliest parody of what we had been. And I'd made him do it. He knew desire had deserted us. He'd tried not to let us end so badly.

In the airport that evening I crouched in a corner. I could see a phone from which I could have rung him to say I was sorry – meaning I was sorry for him and for myself, as well as ashamed of myself; but he was a man for not saying things. In the plane I pulled the airline blanket across my head and wept silently behind it. And the fabric against my cheek called to memory my face pressing into the cotton apron Min was wearing that night when she had turned me towards her, her hands moving gently on my head as she dropped in the oil that would cure my earache. Half a century later I could still smell the clean cloth. But it didn't help.

When I was in my twenties and thirties I didn't know fear. It wasn't that I could have any man I wanted – far from it. But everyone always knew I was there. I was never not sniffed at and scrutinised; I interested people, even when the other person didn't know he was interested. And a very decent man had wanted me to be his mistress when I was twenty-five, and three or four times after that someone fine saw something special in me, and moved towards me, bypassing seemingly superior women. Nothing lasted, but being chosen at that level made up for the many times ordinary men didn't value me.

And I never stopped picking and choosing, myself. It was like an obbligato accompaniment to the rest of life. I never had a love affair with a woman, but I knew there were women I found attractive and ones I didn't, so everyone who came my way got a quick, unconscious glance. The only category I excluded – and I did it without even noticing – were people who seemed old to me.

And then I began to move through my forties. The game, the hopeful interplay, was so much the motive and interest of my life that I could hardly believe it was closing down. It was as if a crowd had emptied from an arena and I found myself alone, out there in the middle of an empty place.

Then Leo and I met, and after we came together in the Excelsior in Zürich the passion was mixed with gratitude and relief. Of course it was. I'd found my old place again. I was warm and supple and womanly again.

And now? Now, without him? I saw how time had diminished my place in the world every time I went up to the Kilbride Inn. I'd come in the door and the men who lined the bar would glance up at the mirror behind the bottles to see who it was. And once they saw me they looked down again and went on with whatever. They didn't even change expression. They didn't even smile. Waste of time, noting the entry of a woman who as far as they were concerned was invisible.

Luz answered her phone, for once.

'Min's girl!' she said. 'Why, hi Honey!'

She was delighted to talk to Min's Rosie. I was one lucky girl to have an auntie who was the life and soul of the party. When the boss moved her from the kitchen to front of house, everyone's tips went up.

'And here she is now looking good enough to eat!'

'Min! At last!' I could hear some kind of banging in the background and a voice shouting orders. It brought it home to me that I wasn't talking to the woman who used to sit in the door of The Hut in the morning sun. This was a busy worker.

'Let me send you money for a holiday, Min,' I begged, 'then you can come home.'

'Ah, I had enough holiday,' she said. 'The work is a great change.'

'If you want to stay for the summer, till your visa

expires, I've an insurance policy I'd be glad to cash in. You could move into a proper apartment.'

But she was all gaiety. 'Why would I mind working when I'm well paid for it? And the Chinese lads are the best of company even when they don't know a word you're saying. We went out to this racetrack on a bus to bet, and I thought I'd be seeing horses, even though it was the middle of the night after work. And guess what, Rosie! The horses were on television! They were in China!'

But her chatter stopped dead when I told her about the letter giving her back Stoneytown.

'And I got the keys and went down there,' I said. 'There's no one at all there. It's a ghost place. But I got into the house.'

I waited, but she didn't say anything. 'That's a house that was built to last!' I said nervously. 'And it's in a beautiful spot. If there was electricity, it could be fixed up.' My voice died away.

'My father left it to me?' she said.

'Yes.'

'In a will?'

'Not exactly a will.'

'Does that mean he's definitely dead?'

'Of course he's dead! No one's heard from him for over fifty years. Have they?'

'I don't know,' she said. 'I never met any of the others after I came up to Dublin to fetch you. And I only heard from him for a year after I came up.'

I couldn't stop myself. 'There were marks, Min, on the wall beside the bed upstairs. Someone was counting the days of the month and marking the wall. Was that…?'

'That bed was for married people,' Min said, 'and my dad. They didn't put children there. I don't know why there'd be marks. Me and your mother slept in the settle at the back of the range. I often thought about that settle. It was the best bed I was ever in. I went back once – there's a place to squeeze through the fence behind the phone-box on the main road – with your father. I wanted to show him the settle bed to see could we ever carry it out, but the house was all locked up. We only got as far as the barn. It was an awful cold night. Anyway it was a terrible oul' kip, that house.'

'Well, you're not exactly living on Park Lane now,' I said. 'Are you?'

'Me?' she said. 'I don't have a worry in the world! There's three of us now because the woman that's supposed to live in our place, who camps opposite the hotel, she comes over to us a lot. She doesn't like some of the men that have moved onto her patch.'

'But is she not a wino?'

'Our place, you could eat your dinner off it. Luz has it beautiful. She keeps it perfect because she has a weak chest and she has to not have any dust. She has a machine to make the air wet.'

'I'm sure. But the fact is you're an old-age pensioner, you're living in social-welfare accommodation with a derelict person, and you're working eight or nine hours a day for half-nothing.'

'I have money!' she cried, and even on a bad line with a lot of noise behind her I could hear the passion in her voice.

'You had money here! You can have my money!'

'I have *my own* money! I can come and go as I please! That Stoneytown – the flags on the floors were wet from September to June so they were, even with the best of fires you couldn't draw out the damp. We don't even have to light a fire here, the heat comes on by itself, we don't even have to pay. Give them back the place. Tell them to give us the money instead.'

There was a burst of confused talk on the other end.

'Take the money, Rosie! I have to go now, the boss is roaring.'

Luz took the phone. 'Be good, Honey!' she said cheerfully. 'And if you can't be good, be careful!'

Bell was asleep on top of the laptop, so I lit the fire and put her basket in front of it, with a bit of cooked ham on the blanket, to help her over the trauma of being woken up. The I began to type.

Kilbride, Dublin

My dear Leo,

A wonderful thing has happened to me and I've just realised that you are the person I want to tell about it. It must be because you loved the villa you had so much. I don't know anyone else at the moment who would understand what it is to fall in love with a house.

It turns out that my aunt is the owner of a small stone house, unused for decades but not derelict, in a beautiful spot on the coast south of Dublin. My aunt is in America, but I went to see it and I can't tell you how happy I felt there. I think that's why you are on my mind...

For Leo too had had a response to a house which, although both he and it were infinitely grander than me or the Point, had been of the same kind as mine. And he too had had a vision of the ideal. Peacocks were going to wander through the grove of magnolia trees, and just beyond the marble flooring at the end of the pool would be a secret door in the old wall, under the tumbling, antique roses, so that guests could come and go from the upper piazza of the village. He was going to make up for the music he hadn't composed, and for the family he hadn't kept together, by creating the world's most elegant inn. And so he had plunged towards the future as if it would transform the past.

...*What I'm afraid of now is that my aunt will ruin everything. Suppose she sells the place? I don't know how I'd forgive her.*

I used not to understand why, when you lost the villa, you lost interest in everything. I was too young, even though it is not all that long ago. But then, five or six years ago, I still believed myself to be in the prime of life. I didn't understand until recently the difference age makes to one's emotions, how much more serious they become with each passing year. How urgent it becomes to realise a dream.

I hope this will find you. I want you to know that I send you my very, very best wishes for your health and contentment,

Rosie

PS. If a dream is unrealisable, it is also necessary to accept that such is the case. I am trying to write some little thoughts on middle age, and acceptance is, I think, a key to contentment there.

I printed the letter out to take to the post-box as soon as I found a stamp. Then it occurred to me: if I was Leo, I wouldn't think much of that as a letter. A bit dry. So I added a final sentence.

I think of you very often with warmest gratitude, mainly for your-self, but also for teaching me about the Schubert Quintet in C Major. You're a superb teacher, you know!

I then printed that version out to post.

After which I opened the 'Thoughts' folder.

Wasn't it interesting, in a mild kind of way, that I hadn't wanted to waste one of my 'Thoughts' on the subject of passion? When it had ruled great swathes of my life? My experience of being so crazy about Leo that I would have walked through fire to be with him had retreated to the corner of my head, where I parked those questions I couldn't answer no matter how hard I tried. What had all that been about? I often asked myself. But without any hope of answering.

I then tried to write a 'Thought' about the corroding power of disappointment. The way Leo's life had gone wrong suggested the words. He had invested his whole self in his dream, but after the local hoteliers thwarted him, and his wife's lawyers forced a sale of the villa, it turned out that his whole self wasn't enough. It needed a stronger self.

From: RosieB@eirtel.com
To: MarkC@rmbooks.com
Sent: 1:05 p.m.

Markey,

I attach a 'Thought' on disappointment, and another on money which is on my mind because I'm about to have a huge fight with Min who wants to sell my grandfather's old house and I passionately don't want her to.

Let me know what you think! You're supposed to encourage me. What's-his-name who edited Scott Fitzgerald and Thomas Wolfe... Perkins... couldn't you be like that?

Attachment #1: A 'Thought' ... about balance

A man set out to open a fine small hotel. It failed, and the failure half-destroyed him. A woman politician fell in love with the surgeon who did her hysterectomy and bought him a fishing river, because he liked to fish, but when he wouldn't see her any more her life collapsed. A boss was passed over for the top job; he became a sullen presence among bewildered colleagues, and left one day without saying goodbye.

These people broke their own hearts.

They lost their balance.

There is a cull, somewhere around the middle of the journey. Some people march on. Some, who did not manage to keep dream and reality in balance, limp alongside the marchers, bitter, reproachful and disappointed.

Risk yourself still. But remember, recovery time is shorter now than it ever was. Respect the way things are. Ground yourself not on what might have been, but on what is.

(150 words)

Attachment #2: A 'Thought' … about money (First Draft)

'Gold is the old man's sword' (P. B. Shelley. English poet, 1792–1822)

A challenging aspect of the middle years is the realisation that your identity is less and less underpinned by the interested regard of other people.

An excellent protection against feeling of no consequence is money.

So, consciously deploy your money to invigorate your own presence in the world, thereby lending it, in the eyes of others, light, usefulness, originality and charm.

Organise events. You can't buy friendship, but you can underwrite opportunities for meeting and entertaining people, which is the first requisite for making friends.

Create employment or improve the environment where there's a need. It doesn't invalidate philanthropy when it has the side effect of validating you.

Patronise the arts. It can't do any harm to art itself or to artists. And if the meaning and purpose of art gradually reveals itself, it will both absorb and succour you.

(150 words)

13

I was going to Peg's for Sunday dinner, which was always a treat. But I kept waking up, hours before I needed to, as tides of regret about Stoneytown rose and fell within me.

Just before dawn, when the birds in Mrs Beckett's tree two doors up were beginning to urge each other into song, I threw some clothes on and, leaving a tin of sardines for Bell, who was out clubbing, set off for Milbay. The sun came up just as, somewhere south of Wicklow Town, I saw a sign for a beach and suddenly turned down there, as if wanting to face due east and bathe my troubles in the sweet light of the new day. I followed the lane to where it widened above a small bay and opened the door of the ticking car beside a ditch that emptied clear water onto the beach in runnels of mud and pebbles. Flocks of seabirds lifted ahead of me as I moved steadily across the firm sand towards the distant line of the sea. But they settled again, and I walked among them where they scuttled and pecked.

Be here now, I said to myself. The calls of the birds, the hum of the sea, the breeze lifting my hair with its fingers and touching my head like the ghost of a loving mother. Out near the shining water the incoming tide was silently filling the fine rib-like patterns on the brown sand.

I turned back before it could cut me off.

Be here *now*.

Afterwards, I wondered whether it was because I'd in some way prepared myself, that the dog had let me see her.

I'd left the car at the camp buildings and was making my way across the meadow, feeling my sneakers become soft with dew, when something made me look over at the beech woods, where I saw a small black dog come out of the trees, stand in the shadow-play of sapling leaves, and watch me for a long moment. She then plunged into the meadow grass, her black back making its green more vivid, and lolloped towards me till she was at my feet, looking up at me with confident brown eyes. I wondered had she been left behind when the Air Corps moved off this headland, but if so, someone had been feeding her.

I didn't make much of greeting her, though she was charming. She was someone else's. She was just passing by, I thought.

But she stayed with me. And her presence made the quality of time different; indeed it made the experience of all that morning different. Because she was so interested in everywhere I went, and so frankly curious about everything I did, bounding forward and coming back, circling and shepherding me, my own movements and actions took on significance for me. And later, when she crouched on the floor beside me to watch with keen attention, the flames reflecting in her gleaming eyes, while I tried out the range to see whether a fire could still be lit in it, I talked to her – not out loud, but in my head. And it was such a pleasure to do so that I realised I must be lonely.

'Min isn't one bit lonely,' I said to the dog.

It's a strange thing, I told the dog, as the flames flared between twigs, that all along the terrace of houses the roofs have caved in; trees are growing in hearths, and nettles are crowding the window spaces where all the wood has rotted away. Yet very likely every range would light up at the touch of a match, no problem. Imagine if you went from house to house and had twenty of these old iron ranges roaring with fire. They'd see it over in Milbay – the chimneys that have been dead for more than half a century puffing out smoke. But they won't see this one. My grandfather's house is in a private place.

The fire was well alight now and I closed the little iron door and began to rise, stiff. Glancing down, I saw the dog had fallen into sleep on her side, her front paws crossed at their white tips, her silky flank peacefully rising and falling.

'You weren't listening, Darling,' I said to her.

She hadn't understood I'd come by car, and the instant she saw it she held back. I saw her sleek back once or twice more as she skulked along the edge of the meadow before disappearing. By the time I opened the door, she was gone. So that was that.

205

But on the radio on the way back to Dublin they played a piece of choral music, and I happened to be paying attention when the announcer said it was called 'O Magnum Mysterium', and that the words the music was set to were these:

'O great mystery, that animals should have witnessed the birth of Christ.'

I'd never thought of that before, and I was delighted.

'When's the bus coming?' Mr Colfer kept saying. 'Is it time to go yet?'

Each time Peg yelled at him that there was no day centre today, and he would sit there disgruntled by that, until he forgot and asked again.

The phone rang.

'It's Tom, from Canada,' Peg said. 'Daddy – Tom's on the phone! He's ringing to ask how you're feeling.'

'Tell him I'm not feeling too well. Tell him God bless and ring me again when I'm feeling a bit better. Don't be bothering me with them, Peg. You talk to them.'

'Daddy, Dympna and the kids called as well, and they sang "Perfect Day" for you.'

'Why doesn't Dympna come home and help out here?' Mr Colfer petulantly replied.

'Dympna's married in Manchester this years,' I said, trying to help.

'And why doesn't Reeny's boy get a move on that way?' Mr Colfer snapped at me with sudden sharpness. 'What's he waiting for, may a person enquire?'

'Now, Da,' Peg said, serene as ever.

'All the same, I don't blame your father for asking,'

I said, when she had at last settled her father down for his nap, dentures in a glass of water, commode at the ready, cordless phone beside him. She'd mashed up sprouts and potatoes in a bit of gravy for him and chopped up a big spoonful of stuffing. No chicken. The old man was always choking.

'And what about?'

I knew she knew what I meant. 'I mean, when even Tess is thinking of finding someone to help her through the night.'

'She's gone to Fatima with Pearl,' Peg said. 'They're divils for punishment, that pilgrimage crowd. Andy's down the country collecting rabbits. It's only for a long weekend, Fatima, but Tessa said Andy's really grateful to her for going with his ma because otherwise he'd have had to go and he's been umpteen times already. Give me Las Vegas! This year Monty and me are thinking of going back there, because the food and drink is for nothing, and you can keep all your money to lose on the slots. I mean, Fatima was nice. Only the place we stayed in was too religious: the men were on one side of the building and the women were on the other.'

'But that's just it, Peg. On your holidays, you and Monty, don't you ever…?'

She shot me a look to make sure that I'd really said what she thought I'd said. We never talked about this kind of thing.

'Don't forget,' she said, deciding to go some way with me. 'I brought up the younger ones for my mother. By the time I was twenty I never wanted to see a baby's bottom again as long as I lived. Not that I minded,' she added quickly, having strayed a bit too close to self-assertion for her comfort. 'I wasn't like you, I was never any good at school. The nuns didn't know I was alive.'

Wow! Was there a hint of bitterness there? This long afterwards?

But it was true. She'd done most of the work of raising the younger pair, who were huge babies. The whole of Kilbride wondered how her tiny mother managed to have children so strapping by Mr Colfer, who was fragile-looking himself, and famous for the snail's pace of his work around his shop. He was usually to be found at the piece of waste ground out the back where he'd given himself permission to graze a horse, leaning on the wall and looking at it. Every time Mrs Colfer began to look pregnant again there were jokes cracked about how it wasn't the wall Danny Colfer was leaning on at home, anyway. They weren't made to his face, even in the pub, because he was big in Fianna Fáil: he knew people who could put in a good word for a job or a house.

'But just as a woman, Peg, do you not feel the need...?' I stopped, remembering how Tessa accused me any time I so much as mentioned a man and woman in the same sentence of being obsessed with sex. That side of things did fascinate me; I couldn't help it. Even at Mass, on the rare occasions I went, I'd sit at the back and watch the respectable neighbours shuffling back from Holy Communion, picking out the ones who looked fulfilled.

'Well, you're a woman, too, Rosie,' Peg said. 'I don't know why you're picking on me. What about your own needs? You don't even have someone like Monty to go on holidays with. Not since that dried-up oul' stick of a Frenchman that stayed in Tessa's house once. Nobody that me or Tess know about anyway.'

'He wasn't French,' I corrected automatically. 'And he wasn't a bit dried up back then either. Never judge a book by the cover.'

'That's what I'm saying to you,' Peg said. 'Never judge a book by the cover, me and Monty included.'

She broke off to ring the woman next door to ask her to keep an eye on the place while we went out for a couple of hours. I liked watching her stand with the phone to her ear, idly looking at her own outstretched hand, her lips tightening into a frown as she listened, then curling into an unconscious smile. I liked looking at her. She had fine lines, now, around her blue eyes, and a tiny dusting of grey in her blonde hair just at the temples, but I thought she was prettier than ever. Heretofore she'd been too like everyone her age, but now the delicate marks of time had made her herself at last.

'Where'll we go?' she said, bright-eyed with anticipation. 'I love going out as long as Da's down for the afternoon. I even love bringing the rubbish down to the recycling bins.'

'Will we go out to your house?' I said. 'Monty never mentions it, so I don't know how it's advancing.'

'Well, OK, if you want,' Peg said, 'but that's not much of a treat. And I'll need to be back soon, because Da grows kind of restless.'

'But Peg,' I said, starting the engine, 'how is it you've spent the whole of your adult life looking after your parents? Is it natural? That's not how the generations are meant to be, is it? Why don't you at least ask one of the others to come home from time to time, to give you a break?'

'It's meant a lot to the others that I'm here,' Peg said. 'Those marriages haven't been plain sailing, you know. They don't spell it out, but I know that it was a help to them when things weren't going so well, to know that everything was under control at home. And you don't understand – I watch Daddy when he's sleeping to make sure he's breathing right. It doesn't matter to me even when he doesn't know me. I know him. I'll be lost when he goes.'

The car was slowing as we turned off the narrow back road behind the airport into an even more narrow road. There were raw, new houses all along the way, though when Monty bought this site it had been empty countryside.

'Next turn right,' Peg said. 'It's only a boreen. Monty picked the place for the privacy.'

'How do you mean, "Monty"? Sure, isn't it your house too?'

'To tell you the truth, Rosie,' Peg said, 'I like living in Kilbride. I like being where there's a bit of stir. Here…'

Across the distant fields the Belfast motorway flashed with traffic in the afternoon sun, but the place itself was perfectly quiet except for birdsong. In front of us the foundations of the bungalow had been lined with hardcore, and a cement mixer stood on a patch of the bare earth. But the foundation trenches were full of mud and weeds, and a load of breezeblocks, dumped long ago, was covered with scotch-grass and nettles.

'This'd be a great place for a dog!' was all I could think of to say.

'I can't drive,' Peg said. 'I'd have to learn if I lived here.'

'Why did you never learn? Sure Monty's a genius at teaching.'

'I never needed it,' Peg said.

I stole a look at her, her face half-hidden by strands of curly hair blown across her face.

'But is that the way to live?' I said.

'I just stuck to whatever came my way,' she said. 'But the thing is, Rosie, I look around me and everyone on the television is getting divorced and the other half are miserable. And Tessa is really tense. I mean, it's a bit much, picking on Andy to marry her. The poor fella won't know what hit him. And even you, Rosie – I wouldn't say you're happy, Pet, even though you're always running around this country or that, trying out different things. Yet me – I'm happy. I'm very happy, even though I'm going nowhere. Whatever happens is OK by me. If I live here I'll live here, and if not, something else will happen. The only thing I pray for is that Daddy will feel no pain, and that God will leave me the rest of you, and let us all grow old together, Monty and you and Min and me, and let all our loved ones be well...' Her voice trailed away.

'But what about love?' I could not stop myself from bursting out, tears in my eyes. 'What about fancying someone rotten? I'm not able – no matter how hard I try, Peg, I'm just not able to accept that though I'm full of life, the world says I'm finished with, and that's the way things have to be.'

'Don't be upset, Pet,' Peg said.

We began to walk back to the car.

'Why didn't you stay on in America with Min? That'd suit you better than here,' she offered gently.

'Ah, she wanted to do it her way,' I sniffled. 'I'd have cramped her style. And I'm not raring to go the way she is. I *went*. I've *been*.'

'She's dead right to do what she's doing,' Peg said. 'I see people around here and they don't realise that time is passing them by. They're full of oul' talk that they're going to do this and they're going to do that, and the next thing I hear the bell from the chapel and the hearse is crawling past the door with them inside. And they never lived! Most Irish men don't know they're born. You'd think one of them would have a bit of sense and see what a great person you are, Rosie.'

'Yes,' I said, blowing my nose. 'And pigs might fly.'

But in the car I made an effort. '*Que sera, sera!* – that's going to be my motto from now on,' I said. 'Same as Doris Day. Though I think Doris had it hard towards the end.'

And with that I raced the engine and wheeled out of the field.

That night I moved around Min's kitchen restlessly. I was a tiny bit miffed that Peg thought all that was wrong with me was that I needed a man. Whatever it was I longed for, it was bigger than any man I'd ever known, not to mention any man I was likely to know in the future. What's more, there'd been a distinct implication, in what she'd said, that I'd been trying and failing to find a man. But that wasn't so. I'd been protected from all that by having Leo. Also, if I thought a man would solve my problems I knew how to set about finding one. I could manipulate the statistical odds. For example, I could look for jobs in places like Canadian airbases. I could sign up for classes in how to master the internal combustion engine. I could teach in prisons.

But what man, now, would ever know the me who'd lived for a time in a hut among the tamarisks and trumpet vines on the edge of a bay south of Kalamata so that I could read my Proust from start to finish with no interruptions? The me who could tell you where to buy the best buffalo mozzarella in Rome, or where to stay in Bayeux if you went to see the tapestry, or how to reach the ruins of Persepolis if ever you were in Shiraz? The me whose feet had sunk into the cold, silky sand inside the mosque in Timbuktu, onto which the sun had not shone since the mosque was built centuries earlier with the desert as its floor? The me who'd walked back to my room through the smoke and mist of the alleyways of an Indian village above Lake Atitlán all one icy winter, after days spent teaching English to Guatemalan boys who could not sit still?

And what man would realise that when I made a list like that, I was not showing off, but that I named the places as tags, as shorthand for the myriad memories that had shaped me?

I could have avoided solitude by staying home in the first place, the way most of the women in Kilbride had done who now had partners who knew all the same events and people as themselves. Min had wanted me to have the security of that. But I wanted romance. And now – suddenly the opera programme on the radio was playing Leontyne Price singing 'Un Bel Dì' and as her impassioned voice surged up into the great assertion that her lover would return to her – my heart twisted with regret.

Quick! Where was the pink notebook?

I turned to the *Tips for the Bad Times* page. How many did I have already? Six.

So I added:

7. *Do not listen to the great romantic arias when you are melancholy.*
8. *If you accidentally do, do not sit down. Keep moving. Keep busy.*

The phone rang then, and I almost cheered out loud.

'Min!' I began.

But it was Peg.

'Just to say goodnight, Pet, and to make sure you're feeling all right. You're not, are you? I can hear it in your voice. Listen, Rosie, just have a good night's sleep and who knows how things will look tomorrow. And Rosie – don't bite the nose off me – I just want to tell you that I think you're a great person and I'm a lucky woman to have you for my friend.'

I muttered something grateful.

She's like Browning's Last Duchess, I said to myself as I hung up. 'She liked whate'er she looked on, and her looks went everywhere.'

But for once I heard my own destructive tone.

The fact was that Peg had meant what she said.

And note well, Rosie Barry, I said to myself, the reason people love Peg is because Peg goes to trouble for other people. Peg took the trouble to call you.

The phone again. This time it was Min on the other end.

'Hi Honey!' Pause. 'Did you hear what I said, Rosie? Hi Honey!'

'Congratulations,' I said. 'That's a great thing to be able to say. But don't be going native over there. Remember home? I keep thinking about Stoneytown. Could you not come down there with me and see could it be done up? The fire works in the range and all. It doesn't make sense, Min, for you to be in boiling-hot New York, breaking the immigration laws so as to work in some greasy spoon.'

'Ah, give over, Rosie,' she said, not very affectionately. 'I'm not even in New York. It was becoming too hot there and Luz's chest couldn't take it. So we hopped on a plane to Portland – very nice, Portland is. Nice and rainy. I don't know how long we're staying, but where she goes, I go.'

'Portland, Maine?'

'No, Portland, Oregon.'

'How do you mean, you *hopped on a plane*?' I said, astonished. 'Whatever about clear across America! Do you not remember when the ticket came for me to go to Roubaix? Do you not remember slamming in and out of the scullery saying God forbid that you'd ever go up in the sky in a plane? Do you remember asking me who's the patron saint of flying because you wanted to pray to him, and I said why couldn't it be a woman saint; why did you always think that if it's anything important it has to be a man?'

'Sure a plane is nothing to me now,' she laughed, 'after I did it by myself from Dublin. And we have a mobile home here for half-nothing in a place beside a river you can go fishing in for your breakfast, and I'm starting a new job tomorrow; it's in the kitchen of a pub, run by a fella from Galway, so that's all right.'

I had never asked Min straight out whether she was happy because she had a certain flat way of ironically repeating the word whenever I used it about other people.

So I asked instead, 'Are you OK, then?'

'I'm grand!' she said. 'Never better!'

They'd been to some place near Portland for an Old Time Irish Night. They'd slept in a lovely warm chalet that was really for people who climbed mountains. There was a husband and wife teaching Irish dancing and you didn't need a partner, eight people all danced together, or four if you couldn't find eight; the teacher told you which eight to go into and if you were lucky you got a partner who knew the steps. Her partner had a pension from fighting in Vietnam.

No, she never did it before.

No, there was no dancing in Stoneytown.

'Are you joking?' she said in disbelief. 'Dancing? Where would you dance, out there? Who would you dance with? There was no music! And boys and girls weren't let go anywhere near each other and the married people never did anything like that. The men had their places outside where they drank, and the women brought them the drink. End of story. The old people sang, specially the old women, but only if they were good singers. It used to make the dogs howl; there were always dogs everywhere even though the boys used to drown the pups. But there was no dancing. It was the same all the time, except the men drank in the houses in the winter.'

'Well,' I said, quite coolly. 'That's more than you ever got round to saying before.'

'They're interested in the old times here,' she said. 'There's one fella, every time I open my mouth he's pushing his little recording machine at me. He wants to know about the songs, but I only know a few.'

Bell was mewling outside the window. 'Hang on,' I said. 'The cat's getting wet.'

'I was thinking of applying for a Home Improvement Loan,' I said a moment later, 'and doing a real job on the yard. I was reading about it. An outdoor room, they call it. Bell'd love it.'

There was a pause.

'Rosie,' she said. 'Spend your money on yourself. You're not growing any younger and you need the money for your teeth. I'm saving up to have myself American teeth. I'm cleaning a few of the trailers during the daytime for the extra dollars, so I have to say good-bye now and God bless, as I've my cleaning to do. And you won't be able to have the money for the old house anytime soon, will you? I was talking about it to Luz. She was saying there might be rules and regulations.'

'But Min…'

'Rosie, I'm as happy as Larry. I really am. So don't you worry, child.'

Gone.

Quick as I could I dialled the number of Luz's mobile phone.

'This number is not responding. Please consult your directory.'

The radio opera programme was ending as I went around turning things off for the night. That was a piece of advice Hugh Boody had given me once when the two of us were behind the counter in the bookshop and things were quiet: 'Go to the opera in wealthy countries only,' he said.

But Lalla and I went one December in Budapest when Hungary was still under the Soviets, and the country had no money and we had no money, and though the tickets were cheap the opera was marvellous. If someone in the plot died, and the audience wanted to hear that part again, they just clapped until the character came back to life. In *Tosca*, Scarpia came back twice, and Tosca herself reappeared from behind the battlements she'd just thrown herself over, and killed herself all over again.

And when we came out, full of laughter and delight, the bells were ringing for Christmas Eve and snow was falling.

I went up and brushed my teeth. God! Were they going yellow? The dentist in Kilbride didn't approve of whitening your teeth with peroxide, but he wasn't a single woman of a certain age.

I never even brushed my teeth at night till I knew Lalla. See: those three months in Roubaix weren't just blissfully happy; they were full of learning.

The loft Lalla and I shared smelled beautifully of bread because it was over a bakery, and boys made comic by the dusting of flour on their hair and eyebrows used to whistle at me when I tripped down the outside staircase in the mornings in the miniskirt that barely covered my thighs. I'd walk to the house I worked in, where I'd give the children their breakfast and escort them to school, savouring every detail that was different from Dublin; the lettering of old French advertisements on the sides of houses; the way lace was hung on the windows in two borders instead of a single curtain; the fruity smell of beer on the air from the open doors of taverns; the way people waiting for buses belted their coats exactly at the waist even when they had no waists. Being abroad pulled my attention into the immediate present. I walked as light as a deer.

I tried to learn from Lalla about boys, because the girls in Kilbride never told you anything important. I told Lalla that I was crazy about someone at home, but that we never touched, even when we were lolling side by side in an empty cinema.

'That is very unhealthy,' she said disapprovingly. 'For the boy especially that can give bad migraines.'

This response confused me completely because she had only recently rebuked me for bringing boys back to our apartment.

'I'm only kissing them,' I said tentatively. 'I don't go all the way.'

But Lalla just blushed. She had skin so fine that you could see the action of the blush, like Mary Queen of Scots, whose throat it seemed was so white that when she drank a glass of red wine you could see it go down.

Every day I looked forward to the night, when our room became a warm cave and the two of us bunked into one bed under the puffy duvet, head beside head, and talked, low and earnest. I'd always believed other people felt me to be restless and unreliable. But Lalla made me feel valuable.

'To work in a department store is not your destiny, Rosie,' she said. 'It is how you think of yourself that makes your life big or small. My grandmother and my mother were doctors. That is one of the good things about being Jewish. Women have always been allowed to have education.'

'I thought Jewish women were always having to be purified by the rabbis and all that?' I said. 'The same as Catholic women have to after they have a baby? You know that? That we have to fetch a witch doctor called a priest to sprinkle water on us to make us clean again after we dirty ourselves having a baby.'

'What's dirty about having a baby?' Lalla said.

'I suppose all the blood,' I said.

'There isn't necessarily any blood,' Lalla said.

'How do you know?'

'I saw a baby being born. Our cook had a baby prematurely and I helped my mother.'

'Oh, Lalla! Tell me the whole thing— '

'Go back to your own bed. I have to go asleep…'

We read every book by American women we could

get our hands on, and read and re-read, until they were threadbare, the copies of *Ms Magazine* that had found their way into foreign-language periodicals in the main library of Lille University.

'My mother is a captive wife,' Lalla said, 'who plainly does not know why she has ended up in a villa on the coast of Algeria with a stranger who says he is her husband.'

'Min doesn't fit any of the descriptions in the books,' I said. 'They don't have women like her in *Ms*. But for most of the women in Kilbride the family is their whole life. Someone like Min who's a bit different even if she's different by accident – they don't take her seriously.'

'De Beauvoir is right,' Lalla said, 'about what men do to women, but what women do to women can be the worst. My mother will decide my future, and she is not interested in my freedom because she is not free.'

'Your mother is always on your mind, Lalla,' I said. 'And I think a lot about Min, who's more or less my mother. So what do you make of it that Kate Millett and Gloria Steinem and all those don't seem to give so much importance to mothers? Do you think it's because there's so much room in America? Everyone moves to somewhere. The mothers don't know what the daughters are up to.'

'I don't think mothers would be so hard on daughters if fathers didn't exist,' she said. 'I think women do men's dirty work for them.'

'Still,' I said. 'They mark you out if you don't fit in. Even the day of my First Communion, the women wouldn't let me think I was wonderful. My father was sick that morning and we were late making it to the church and all the girls were gone up already, hand in hand. I had to go up at the end after all the boys, by myself. The only child on their own. Everyone was laughing at me.'

'You'll remember that till you die,' Lalla said.

I was warmed to the soles of my feet by how tenderly she smiled at me.

'But women are good to each other as well,' I said. 'Min would have no life if it wasn't for Reeny next door. And' – I pushed on, blushing – 'and look at the way you've shared everything with me here.'

'Yes,' Lalla said. Then, half-ironically, half-proudly, she offered, 'Yes, sister.'

You'd swear that sometimes she loved me just as much as I loved her.

Of course, there can never again be a first time. The first pride in yourself. The first ideas that belonged to you and your kind and to no one else. The first adored friend.

At one point when I was working in Sydney I didn't make it home for three years. Min got Monty to bring her to Dublin airport to meet me – the only time she ever did that. On the way home she filled me in on the local news, which was always gripping, especially the way she told it. It was around then, for instance, that Peg's dad, the newly widowed Mr Colfer, developed a passion for the plump young wife Enzo in the Sorrento Fish & Chip had brought back from a trip home to Italy. The woman who cleaned the garda barracks over-heard the garda sergeant telling Mr Colfer he was barred from the Sorrento, and Mr Colfer calling the Sergeant a 'Blueshirt' and a 'West Brit' who should be ashamed to lift up his head in an independent Ireland.

I was in the armchair, stroking Christabel, who was the cat at the time, looking forward to hearing more. Min sat down on the chair that she kept to stand on to pull the blind down, and studied the back of her hands.

'They sent a message up from the school,' she said. 'They were after receiving a phone call from that place you were in Belgium years ago. Some nun over there wanted to ring Sister Cecilia.'

'Roubaix is in—'

'Anyway, Sister Cecilia isn't living in the convent any more; she's in a council flat in the city with the lowest of the low and has no phone, so they had to run for her from the shop nearby and shout up that there was someone foreign on the phone. It must have cost a fortune, hanging on like that, long distance.'

I waited. Min smoothed her apron.

'Apparently she speaks great English,' Min said. 'The other nun.'

'What?' I began. 'What's wrong?'

'Apparently the other one said, does the Irish girl – that's yourself – know about Lalla?'

'What about Lalla?' I asked, with whom I'd fallen out of touch.

'So Sister Cecilia said, what about her? The nun said Lalla and her husband were in a hotel somewhere in the mountains and Lalla – well, maybe she slipped but anyway she fell off the balcony.'

'Well,' she said after a pause, 'it was in the paper of

whatever place it was and the paper said she'd jumped.'

'Why?' I couldn't stop staring at Min's mouth.

'The paper said she was cremated and the ashes sent back to her family.'

I must have been staring at her with pure hostility.

'My mother went off in the boat to Milbay wrapped in a blanket and we never even got the blanket back,' Min said, bitterly. 'A few years later I thought I'd see my sister, just to say goodbye even, but when I went to collect you, they'd sent her body back to the sanatorium and no one said anything about taking me there to see her. My father disappeared a year later. And your father! I was still a young woman, to my mind anyway, when your father got so sick. There's no way to rely on anyone in this world. You saw yourself how sick he got. It was a merciful release when he went. Your precious Markey that was your big friend headed off to America, didn't he? Your Lalla is dead. It's all the same. Put your trust in nobody, Rosie Barry, for I can tell you now that there's not a being on earth worth the bother. She must have been so far down in the dumps she couldn't get herself up. It's a terrible thing sure enough, but you don't see much of it around here. If the women round here got a chance to stay in a hotel, they wouldn't waste it by jumping off a balcony.'

I couldn't look away from her.

'People die, Madam,' she said desperately; and I went up to my room.

From: RosieB@eirtel.com
To: MarkC@rmbooks.com
Sent: 10:45 p.m.

A 'Thought'... about friendship

Your heart doesn't stay strong by itself. You must take action, to keep it in working order. Friendship is what keeps it limber. Friendship is the ordinary, everyday operation of the heart.

Bad friendship kills. The people of Okinawa live longer, in better physical and mental condition, than any other people on earth. They believe you should identify, even in the people closest to you, the toxic ones. Then let them go.

Love your friends. Be as careful of a true friend as you want a friend to be careful of you, even when the friendship is not the warm, easeful thing your laziest self wants it to be. Keep a friendship going, like an accompanist vamping until the singer comes back, even when it seems to have disappeared.

You can make yourself a private Okinawa. The more you generously respond to friendship's demands, the stronger the beat of your heart.

(150 words)

From: MarkC@rmbooks.com
To: RosieB@eirtel.com
Sent: 10:54 p.m.

I have problems with this one, Rosie. Maybe you should begin with something like: 'Although you already have more friends than you can cope with, you can expand your circle by ....' People need to be reassured that they have friends.

The problem with the Okinawa thing is that it's telling people to get rid of other people, which might suggest someone is likely getting ready to get rid of them too.

On the other hand, what you said about 'toxic people' reminded me of how I left my car mechanic who's been putting me down for years, and you wouldn't believe how much happier going to a new guy has made me.

How's Min doing? And how are you doing? There can't be many more 'Thoughts' left to do. I hate to think our little project is nearly over.

14

It lashed rain on Monday from a sky that was low and leaden, and the gutters in the yard gurgled and spurted and I had to turn on all the lights in the kitchen to see to make tea. Bell sat on the window sill and looked at the water sheeting down the glass with eyes that kept closing from sheer boredom. I felt the same myself. America, apparently, had reached out and touched us. Some hurricane had spared the Florida coast only to spin our way instead, and this deluge was its tail end.

That'll teach you, I said to myself – that'll teach you to have a fantasy of casual Mediterranean living in an island that sits low in the north Atlantic.

But my imagination wouldn't abandon Stoneytown. Instead it set to work altering the details of the fantasy. Now I wasn't lying on the hot stone flags of a sun-drenched yard; rather I was lying, somehow in cosy warmth, somehow in comfort, under a roof satiny with rain, in an ark that sailed between a sea white with foam and a meadow of rain-polished grasses.

I found an umbrella upstairs in my father's wardrobe. He was the last neat person to live in this house.

Once, on the stairs outside Granny Barry's flat in Milbay when we were going to tea there, he took out his comb and with his body blocking Min from moving, he combed the front of her hair. She was still flushed with anger during the evening. But she was quietly mutinous, anyway, whenever we went to Granny Barry's place. I could remember many of the remarks Granny made with a little laugh, to show that they were jokes. 'Min looks as if she just escaped from the ruins of Berlin' was one. Or 'All Min needs is a big stick and she could be herding cattle'.

My granny would take me into her bedroom and teach me deportment: to cross my legs at the ankle and not to speak until spoken to and always to leave something on the plate. I was miserable until I could crawl in to sit beside Min's feet in the house that I made under the table, behind the chenille tablecloth with bobble edges that came to the floor. I pretended I had a gaslight down there – I made the flapping noise Granny's mantle made when its flame burned blue – and adjusted an imaginary see-saw lever. I took her miniature dustpan and matching brush in there and swept imaginary crumbs off an imaginary table. Once I got into big trouble with Granny. The mirror on her dressing-table was loose; left to itself it hung forward, and all you could see in it was the floor. So it was wedged at the side with a copy of *The Messenger of the Sacred Heart,* which was the only printed matter in the house. And on that visit I took it out of its place and squirreled it in under the table, and licked its scarlet cover till its red dye ran, and I gave myself red lips, like a woman.

Min said nothing if I was in trouble or if I was praised in Granny's place. You'd think she didn't know me.

The grown-ups had their supper of beige chicken legs on lettuce with mounds of white potato chopped up with yellow salad cream, and then they pushed their chairs back and peeled off the tablecloth. My granny always had different bottles, and she plonked them, half-full, on the table.

'The usual?' she'd say, and she'd pour Min a small sherry – the only drink I ever saw Min touch until after my father died.

Then they'd have a bit of a singsong. The window behind my granny's head would be wide open to the summer evening and swallow-like birds wheeled and swooped in the dusk over the yard. My granny sang old-fashioned songs like 'I Dreamt that I Dwelt' or 'Roses are Blooming in Picardy', which Min could hum as soon as she heard them once. But she had no interest in old songs. She told me once, when we were watching Enya on the television, how a lot of the songs the older women sang when she was a girl were in Irish – the Stoneytown people had come up from a place in Waterford where there were copper mines where everyone spoke Irish. But she didn't know what the words meant.

She liked the songs that were popular around the time she came to Dublin. 'I'm All Yours in my Buttons and Bows!' she'd sing. Or, as the evening wore on at my granny's, 'Jealous Heart'.

'Jealous heart, oh jealous heart stop beating!' she'd sing, and my father would nod and point at his chest as if to say those were his exact sentiments.

I listened from my hidey-hole under the table, or watched from the depths of the red sofa across the room.

I'd do a bit of indoor research, I thought, so I drove south in the rain to see whether there was anything about Stoneytown in whatever local history they might have in Milbay Library. I hadn't planned to go out to the Point itself, but as I got clear of the city, the rain stopped. And seeing as I longed to know even small things, like what colour the stone flags of the roof were after rain, and what the stream that flowed out of the hill and under the wall of the yard to the shore was like when it was full, I decided to go as far as the ridge and look down; it wouldn't take much more than half-an-hour.

I parked at the telephone box at the lay-by in the woods and walked back up the drying road to the main camp gate and then up the path, dodging the puddles that shone in light that was beautifully clear in the aftermath of rain. I followed the perimeter track past the cave where I usually left the car to the hill at the back of the house, bending towards the short grass as I climbed, and hearing it, whenever I held my breath, respond to sun after rain in a thousand, secretive rustlings.

I straightened up as I reached the ridge, and all was well below. The tide was right up to the boulders in front of the house, but the place was in no danger. The waxy, dark-green leaves of the thick hedges around the yard were shinier than ever. There were pools of water under the eaves of the sheds because the gutters had perished – rain must have cascaded onto the yard. Yes, the cover was safely on the well. My eye travelled on. A small, black bundle had been left outside the back door...

No. That wasn't a bundle.

I described what happened next to Andy, when he came in to see me from Reeny's that evening.

'The sea beyond the shelter of the stone sheds was so calm in the rain,' I said, setting the scene for him, 'and silent birds were drifting like pale fragments into the dark of the woods, like twists of paper—'

'I know what you mean!' Andy cut in. 'You have the right words for it! I'd never have thought to say that that's what the birds look like.'

'Yeah,' I muttered. Not that I received so many compliments that I could afford to be picky. 'But the thing is, the bundle moved!'

'What?' Andy cried, a strand of spaghetti trailing from his mouth that had fallen open in surprise. I leaned across the kitchen table and pulled it out, then dangled it in front of his face.

'It was the dog,' I whispered to him. Then I jumped up and whooped around the kitchen, bursting with the joy I'd felt. 'It was the little black dog I'd seen a couple of days ago! She was waiting for me!'

I'd whistled – not the real, clear thing, but a breathy woman's whistle, broken up by emotion. And I saw the dog rise and turn and without even looking up at me on the ridge, begin to climb rapidly towards where I stood. It came up the turf towards me, much thinner, it seemed, than when I'd last seen it, perhaps because its coat was wet.

I didn't ask her to come with me however; in fact, I hardly even looked at her. Who knew where she really lived and how soon she would go back there? But she followed me of her own accord across the meadow and into the woods where it seemed still to be raining because of all the drips and flurries of drops. I realised I was carrying my Dad's umbrella and I put it up, but the trees were closer on each side to the narrow path than I'd realised, so I stowed it in a hollow trunk as conveniently placed as the umbrella stand at a restaurant door.

'There!' I said to the dog. 'I'm furnishing the place.' At which she leapt to attention, brightly looking now at the stashed umbrella, now at me.

She followed me then through the gap in the hedge behind the telephone box. And watched me intently while I unwrapped a sandwich I had for myself in the car, and when I offered it, took it delicately in her mouth. Then she ran behind the telephone box to eat in private. She came back and slurped up rainwater from the gutter, and I sat sideways on the back seat, my legs out on the grass, my face up to the afternoon sun, while she snoozed, half across my feet, front paws neatly crossed.

The night before, I'd been comparing myself to Peg, and – though I was half-laughing at myself for being so morose – I'd decided that if I wasn't loved as well as she, it was because I hadn't loved well myself. So I'd opened the pink notebook and written down:

TIPS FOR THE BAD TIMES:

9. Don't be aggrieved because life is unjust to you. There is no justice.

But was this not love, this warmth that I felt towards the dog at my feet? Surely this was love, even though the dog was only a dog? The desire to protect her, that flooded out of me, that almost pained me – what was that, if not love? One small, thin animal ran towards me, and inside huge, heavy doors slid back and my dam began to gush. Even my feet, that I never gave a thought to – were today precious to me because the dog, trusting me, slept across them.

She wanted to be near me.

And where was the justice in her choosing me? Nowhere! I happened to be there, and she happened to need me.

It was a marvellous thing, that there was no justice!

When I got back to town I'd inscribe the next Tip:

You can't win 'em all; but you can't lose 'em all, either.

But she would not come into the car. When I lifted her, she scrambled urgently out of my arms and ran behind the phone-box and into the woods. Pure misery went through me. Then I heard a small, tentative bark. She was on the other side of the fence, twenty feet away, but she was looking out at me; she wanted me to see her. I opened the car doors and beckoned her to come back and come inside. I bent down to the fence and implored her: 'Come, Sweetheart! Come!' Then I stood and repeated it imperiously. And then I whistled. I got into the driver's seat and out again, all the time keeping my eyes on her. And all the time she sat in the dense greenery, her smart little head held high, watching me.

Then she disappeared, and there was nothing I could do about it.

Once, I saw a photograph of a man dying in a hospice. He was in gaunt profile, lying on a high hospital bed under a square of sheet, pale body under pale cloth against a pale and featureless wall. But his right arm was hanging down so that his hand could rest on the head of the fine dog sitting beside the bed – body calm, intelligent head alert and mild. The man was dying in an aura of purest love.

I'd talk to Markey about it, only it was 7 a.m. on the west coast of America and I could hardly ring him at his home to talk about dogs. But I risked calling Portland from the phone box.

'It's rainy here, too,' Min said when she woke up enough to talk. 'But the funny thing is, Luz wouldn't mind going somewhere rainier. It's something about her chest, she needs to keep the tubes in it damp. But she's doing great for now.'

She didn't exactly have a conversation with me then, so much as deliver one of her breakneck summaries.

'There's people here that have been in mobile homes all their life and they all stick together the way they used to in Kilbride years ago. The man next door gives me a lift in to work in the afternoon because that's when he goes in himself; he has to be dragged away from the river he's such a mad fisherman; and I'm sent home in a car after my shift. I know all the drivers, they don't go away till I'm in my door with the light on, they're the best. And there's a cat that's waiting for me on the doorstep every night. A beauty, a pure beauty. Somebody left him behind, they should be shot. Edward is his name and it suits him. Is Reeny back? Tell her I'm having the time of my life, she can shove her oul' Spain where the monkey shoved the cabbage.'

'But what if there's an emergency?' I said. 'You'd better give me your work phone number now, and the name of this Galwayman's place.'

'I never knew where you were,' she said mildly. 'For years. Many a time I didn't have a number for you that I could have got Reeny to phone if I fell down the stairs or anything.'

The phone gave a warning. I put in another two-euro piece.

'Poor Bell wouldn't be in the same ballpark as Edward at all; he's a cat that's worth money, you should see the fur on him. And I take my dinner at work, so what more would I want? Even the weekend – next weekend we're going to some sort of Irish party.'

'There was nothing stopping you from going to Irish things here,' I said sulkily. 'Stoneytown is about as Irish as it gets.'

'Is that where you are?'

'Ah, I just came down to have a look. It was raining. Now I don't know what to do because a lovely dog is after following me and she won't get into the car.'

Beep beep beep. Another two euro.

'Min, if I give you the number of this phone – you know where it is, on the main road halfway through the woods – would *you* ring *me*? It's about ten times cheaper from a private phone in America than from a public phone in Ireland and we wouldn't be interrupted all the time. We could have a date. Say Saturdays, around the time you get up? There's only another few Saturdays till you're home, but it would be nice…'

'I'll write it here,' she said. 'Give us it. But sure you won't be out at the Point that much, will you? What would you be doing out there?'

'I have to sort out the dog.'

'Listen, Rosie. Find your own dog. Don't be getting mixed up with stray dogs.'

'Thanks, Min,' I said. 'Does the same go for cats?'

'Do you know what I can't get over?' She wasn't even listening to me. 'I can't get over the way the women here keep themselves lovely. The lady across from me, who rang me up to come over and have my nails done when she was having hers, and that lady won't ever see eighty again. A very nice woman she is too, she paid for my nails as well as her own, you should see them, they're gorgeous.'

'How come you…?'

'But the thing is, when I look back on it, the women that lived on the Point, they were old before their time. They looked twice the age of the ones here. They hadn't a tooth in their head, most of them. But there's a girl at work is going to take me to her neighbour who's a dentist…'

'But you never said a thing about teeth,' I shouted. 'Why didn't you…?'

Another warning beep.

'When will we…?'

236

But we were cut off. I had no more coins, and Min didn't ring back.

Finally I gave up on calling for the dog and went into Milbay, to the garda barracks on the quay. The car park was above the jetty where the Stoneytown boats would have tied up when the quarry was going. A light, drifting rain had come back to dapple the river, but I could see quite clearly the terrace of roofless houses where the workers once lived. I was delighted that I couldn't see my house at all – could only imagine it around the headland, facing out to sea.

A young garda looked at me blankly and went into a back office and came back with an older one, a sergeant. I explained again that I wanted the guards to know that I was coming and going over there beyond the camp, that my family had a property there. I began to look in my bag for the letter from the Department of Defence, but the sergeant made a gesture that took in my face and clothes and indicated there was clearly no need for proof of identity from a respectable woman of my age.

He wasn't from the area himself, he said, but he'd heard of the Stoneytown people alright. He broke off and called out to an old man at a desk in the far corner, who looked to be watching ice-dancing on a small television set.

'Paddy was a garda here for years and still gives us a hand answering the phones. Paddy! Do you know anything about Stoneytown?'

'Certainly I do,' the old man said, after coming forward with alacrity. 'Certainly I remember Stoneytown! Is it you that wants to know, Missus? I was just starting off here when the people from there were moved into the town. It was near the end of the war and everyone was afraid the Germans would come in off their submarines or the English would or the Japs or some shower would. So the whole gang from over there was evicted and brought over and put into chalets here behind the church, useless yokes, the wind whistling through them. But sure there was food rationing then, and no coal to be had, and the lot of them would have died if they didn't come in off of where they were.'

'And are they still there?' I said, hardly able to speak for excitement. 'Min and I could …'

'Ah no. They disappeared before you could say Jack Robinson. They went off to Wales and Yorkshire and them kind of places. And do you know how long it took Martin Blake to pull those chalets down? The whole row of them? Go on, give a guess! Half-a-day it took him. That's as bad as they were.'

'But there could be descendants?'

'There's no descendants,' he said. 'Their kids went with them – sure they wouldn't leave one of their own behind. Thieving scum, they were. There was no jobs going and there wasn't a pub would let them over the door. They were sent on their way from the town here as soon as the trains and the boats came back. My sergeant at the time was preparing to go over to arrest the last of them, the fella that was their leader when they were working. The bossman, like. They couldn't order him off the Point like they had the others because he'd built his house himself; there wasn't anyone who could tell him what to do.'

'That was my grandfather,' I said.

'You're not serious!' He gaped at me. 'He was a fine man by all accounts,' he added. 'There was never anything known against him. He just wouldn't go when the government told him to. He said there was no law that said he had to leave the Point. But they'd made a law after the war was over, to do with the Air Corps, and he went off in the end, and then the whole place was put out of bounds.'

'When did he go?' I asked.

'Jimmy!' He shouted in to someone behind a partition. 'What year did Cavan beat Mayo by a point?'

'1948, ya oul' bollocks, do you know nothing?'

'That's right. 1948. I remember the people outside the pubs trying to listen to the match through the windows. And the sergeant was getting ready to go out and arrest him. But then the government sent men out there and they fixed it all up legally and he went away.'

I had to sit down. I went to The Harbour Coffee Nook, a place that hadn't changed at all since my dad used to take me there when we were on our holidays in The Hut. I had thought it the height of glamour then, but now it reminded me of the little dairy bars in forgotten outback towns in Australia, or the tea-rooms in places like Gdansk, or Yerevan – places with oilcloth-covered tables and jars of dusty plastic flowers and painted shelves sparsely decorated with pyramids of empty tins. I ate a cupcake with lemony icing in memory of my dear dad. And of Min. We never went to the Harbour, my dad and I, without bringing Min back a cupcake.

The Electricity Supply Board office was next door, so I went in to make an enquiry about extending power to the house.

'No,' the supervisor said, even before he said, 'I know where you mean.' A handsome man with clear brown eyes and a powerful mouth, his wavy grey hair carefully combed.

'I saw Stoneytown many times when I was a child,' he said. 'The islanders, as the old people called them, though the place isn't strictly an island, built a bonfire on the shore every Midsummer's Eve, and the Milbay people went across in boats. I went across myself, when I was a little fellow. The islanders threw stones at us but they couldn't reach us. No. There won't be power. There's no plans for cabling out there.'

He simply stopped speaking then, as if to signal that he wasn't going to waste more time talking to an ordinary-looking woman too old to be worth the effort to charm. Or was I being paranoid, on account of him being so attractive? He and I were likely much the same age, but since when did that make us equals?

My lowered eyes kept falling on his sinewy arms and hands – where I had to look, or else brave the frown he didn't even know had taken possession of his face.

'The house was built by my grandfather,' I said.

To which he refused to make even a polite exclamation.

It isn't my fault, I snapped at him inside my head, that I bore you because I'm not young enough to flirt with. But each time his eyes flicked discontentedly across me, my head hung a little lower.

Still, he was somewhat interested in the subject. 'We didn't tie up,' he said. 'We just shipped oars and watched the Stoneytown people sitting there around the fires.'

And he was a man of powerful presence too. He would have been a formidable flirt.

So I tried to coax him with smiles and humble body language. To think, instead of becoming more truthful as I got older, I had to deceive! I had to hide it deeper than the worse shame, the fact that I thought he was very sexy. I didn't think I was so bad myself – OK, very slightly thickened and wrinkled compared to my younger self, but juicy still, and soft. But I knew he'd have been outraged at any suggestion that I was worthy to fancy him. And the playing field would never become even either. For some reason my dentist had a Harvard Alumni magazine in his waiting-room, and I'd seen in its personal ads how even the retired professors – eighty-eight years old, some of them – specified women in their sixties.

'Everyone was afraid of the quarry people,' the man was saying. 'Very rough people, and hard on the poteen, too. Women as well as men. And that stretch of the coast where the river meets the sea – that was supposed to be guarded by the little folk too, though that's a story put out anywhere there's smuggling.'

I adopted an air of genteel interest. Began to fantasise about what that man's mouth might do ... To who, *me?*

'No,' he said. 'It'll never happen. Sure they're only heaps of stones, those old houses,' he said. 'I've had a look through the binoculars when I'm out fishing. You couldn't wire those. The quarry people would have lived in caves for all they cared about houses. They worked hard and they played hard.'

'The men may have played hard,' I said. 'I'm sure the women just worked.'

'You'd want to be careful,' he said, looking at me almost with distaste. 'Out there on your own. You'd never know who'd be going out there to drink their cider.'

'My grandfather's house is not a heap of stones,' I said coldly. 'It's weatherproof, and there is a strong wooden bar that fits into notches behind the front door and another behind the back door. And I have a book contract, and to do my work I need electricity.'

'Well, you won't be having electricity. I'm sorry. Unless by any chance you're a millionaire, and even then the ESB wouldn't countenance connecting up to a ruin that'll be gone any day now when the developers get their hands on the old camp. That'll put a stop to the cider parties, when the money moves in.'

'Why would anyone travel ten miles by car,' I asked him, 'to the gate of the Air Corps camp, and then find a way of climbing the fence, and then walk half-a-mile or so to reach an abandoned house that it would be very hard to break into – just to drink their cider?'

'You'd be surprised what people will do,' he said.

But he did give a hint of a shamefaced smile.

The library would be open for another half hour, so I ran in there to recover from the ESB man. Though what written record could there be? The Milbay people were afraid of the quarry people in addition to despising them, and which of those drunken, pugnacious people themselves could possibly have lifted their heads from breaking stones to write?

But I was in luck.

What I found, tied by cloth tape between paper boards, was a thick, brown book called *Notes on Milbay and its Surrounds* by C. Ó Conchubhair, 1956, 'printed at the *Milbay Herald*, patrons M.J. Bailey and Family'.

I turned to the index where the words 'Milbay Point' somehow jumped out at me from acres of small print, under the entry 'Language, The Irish.'

Linguists from the Institute of Higher Education were at one time interested in the patois of the semi-nomadic people who settled along the southern Milbay shore at Milbay Point to work a granite quarry there c.1920–1943. The patois was, according to surviving teachers from Saint Jude's National School (which was sporadically attended by island children) replete with words taken from Irish and Welsh. During the Emergency, the Department of the Gaeltacht aided in the resettlement of such families as remained, the foundations of whose homes, though temporary in intention, are still to be seen behind the former Methodist Chapel and Temperance Hall.

When transatlantic travel was resumed at the end of the Emergency, a number of the quarry people were said to have moved to the USA, thanks to the fortuitous survival of the pilot of a light airplane which crashed near the quarry in 1942, and who, the Milbay Herald *reported, invited his rescuers to visit his home city. The*

present writer, however, is of the opinion that this invita-
tion was never taken up, given that there is no record of any
passport applications by the destitute quarry workers, who
had by then been absent for several years from their sole
place of employment.

I called Bell first thing when I got in the door, same as always. When she didn't spring immediately onto the window sill, I went out and looked over the wall into Reeny's yard. Music, yes! At last, our Reeny was back from Spain!

I ran in and hugged and hugged her, reluctant to let her go. She knew, of course, what I was also saying: 'Isn't it terrible that we don't have Min?'

There was the ritual admiration of her bare, brown legs and her blonded hair and her figure toned by swimming. Then she opened a litre of the Rioja she always brought back in huge quantities.

'No one ever knew what was in that woman's head,' she said, settling down to talk. '"That's just like Min," I said to Pearl when I heard what she'd done. Off like a rocket once she got the chance. Remember when she was going to be an opera singer?'

I would have been about twelve, with my father already sleeping in the invalid bed in the corner of the kitchen because he couldn't manage the stairs. But he was still well enough to sit up. And trying even to help me with the bane of my life, which was maths, the night that Min came in from the pictures. She could go any night she liked because my Dad had known all the other cinema managers in Dublin, and they all knew Min was rearing me for him.

But that night she came in and looked over at us as if she could hardly see us. Then, taking off her coat, she proclaimed, 'I'm going to be a singer!'

'But Min...'

She'd sung a bit in recent times, after Sister Cecilia had sent for her to sing with the choir in the convent. And she'd managed all right because Sister Cecilia had written out the words of the 'Panis Angelicus' and 'O Salutaris Hostia' on a card – not the real words but a makey-up version that sounded like the Latin. But it was the film she'd just seen that had captured her, a film called *The Tales of Hoffmann*, which Reeny saw later that week and said was about an opera singer who, if she sang, was going to die, and she did sing and she did die. Reeny also said things could be worse, that Min could have gone to *Jailhouse Rock* and come home wanting to be Elvis.

Of course, Min had no idea how or where a singer was trained. So all that happened was every time I annoyed her – every time not just for days, but for weeks – she would threaten to leave me and my dad and go to England and find a job in the theatre while she broke into the opera business.

'Even if it's washing the floors!' she used to say, to which I'd say, 'Oh, it *would* be washing the floors.'

At which my father would come to life and say, 'Watch how you talk to your aunt, Miss.' But his voice would be shaking. She was making him dreadfully anxious.

'Do you remember, Reeny, she had the same two books out of the library for ages, *Stories from the Opera*, Volumes I & IV? I used to say to her that she needn't worry about missing the volumes in between since she never read the ones she had.'

'Your father used to wind that old gramophone for her,' Reeny said.

'Oh, yes…'

A wind-up gramophone that she had got from a junkshop, with a front of fretwork and faded plush, and a big tarnished horn. Andy Sutton, who'd have been twenty-one or so at the time, helped lug it home to our kitchen. We still had some of Granny Barry's things, one of which was a shopping bag full of heavy 78 rpm records, each in a brown paper cover emblazoned *The Great Voices Collection*.

For a time Min played the frail, exquisite voices while she did her ironing. If she sometimes hadn't an arm free to wind the handle, maybe sprinkling hissing water on the sheets, Dame Nellie Melba or Gigli or Rosa Ponselle would begin to wobble and waver to a slow, bass groan. But my father, seated in his pyjamas beside her on a kitchen chair, would get up then and wind the gramophone, bringing the voice up to pitch, like a creator breathing life into the creation.

'I'm going to learn to be a singer in an opera,' she'd declare, as she thumped the iron up and down. 'As soon as I have a chance.'

I didn't look at my father anymore when she said it. He couldn't do anything about it, whatever was wrong with her. But it wasn't funny. She could read and write very well for someone who'd only gone to school occasionally, and left it for good at fourteen; but you couldn't imagine her handling a score. She didn't know a word of any foreign language. Plus we had no money. We didn't even own the house; we paid rent every week, and the man wrote it in a little book.

Above all, she didn't know what an opera was. I knew, though I'd never been to an opera. 'Do you realise, Min,' I said more than once, 'that there aren't just songs in operas? There's bits in between where they only talk. You'd die of boredom.'

She looked at me as if I knew nothing.

In the end, I went to Sister Cecilia and told her Min was making home a horrible place, and all for nothing.

'I had to,' I said to Reeny. 'It was driving us nuts.'

'I remember,' Reeny said. 'I saw Sister going into your place.'

I had gone out and hung around in the street while the nun was inside. I was so afraid. Supposing Min told Sister Cecilia she was going and that was all there was to say about it? What would my dad and I do then?

Sister Cecilia beckoned me to fall in beside her as she sped back to the convent. All she said was, 'Your aunt is not sick. Just wait, and it'll pass over.'

I only saw now that she could not say, 'Your aunt is twenty-seven years old and she has no life of her own. Your aunt is looking at you turning into a fine girl while her girlhood has gone for nothing.' She couldn't say, 'For these and other reasons your aunt is unhappy.' Unhappiness wasn't a recognised condition in the Kilbride of those days.

'What do you think, Reeny?' I asked. 'I mean, I can understand that she didn't have much of a life back then, with me at school and Daddy so sick. But now? Flitting from coast to coast over beyond? She's sixty-nine years old! Why would she do something like that now? When she didn't even go on package holidays all these years? I'd have brought her anywhere she wanted to go, but she never even got a passport till the Bernadette of Lourdes trip.'

'I said it to Pearl,' Reeny said judiciously. 'It was because it was America. She must have thought it was her last chance at America.'

'But I would have taken her to America if she'd only said…'

'I mean America the way it would have been if she'd got there when she was supposed to get there. Doing it her way. Did she ever tell you that was where she was supposed to be going? She thought there'd be no stopping her. The war was over and even her father had said she could go. She had the money, then. But then the priest got the message that your mother hadn't long to live, and there was no one to mind you. And all the years you were coming and going, she never really had any money. Not enough to go to America. No one around here had.'

'I don't think it was money,' I said, as I got up to go back to my own house.

I was thinking instead of the way she listened to the *Great Voices* collection. Our life in Kilbride was innocent, but still she must have longed for their more perfect innocence. Min was a person who knew longing.

I didn't turn on the light, back in my own house. I just sat at the table in the shadowy room. For a minute I thought of working on the next 'Thought', but the profusion of things in my head – the dreams Min had once had, and the undertones to my interview with the electricity engineer in Milbay, and my worry about where the dog might be, and whether I would ever see her again – conspired to put me off the whole inspirational thing.

That must be the main reason self-help books are so dead, I thought. They never mention the ordinary things that crowd every second of your life. They don't capture the density of being alive. And they don't pay attention to the contexts of your experience, like whether you're a man or a woman, young or old, Irish or American, poor or rich, educated or not educated. Or whether you've been brought up in a proper house by people who thought you were precious, or in some other scenario altogether. The self-help books I'd studied were full of little parables about puppet people who floated around in some dimension where there were no localities, no particular time in history.

And the people they talked about – all those Brads and Carols and Ethans and Rachels, all of them furnished with a few details like a job in advertising or PR or web design – you'd think these people were just pure will. That they only had to be told how to improve matters and next thing – Hey presto! – matters had improved. It was as if the people who had the problems weren't real to the people who wrote the self-help books. The advice they dispensed might be real, but not the people they dispensed it to.

Smoochy dance music was creeping through the shadowy room. Oh, Reeny was at it again! There were nights when she played Chris de Burgh singing 'Lady in Red' over and over. Maybe ten times. She was dancing with herself, I knew. Up and down the kitchen. '*Lady in red*,' she'd intone along with the song. I'd seen her do it. Her arms curved in front as if she were holding a partner; her head inclined to one side as if another head lay next to hers; her eyes half-closed. '*Lady in red...*'

And if Monty came in while she was dancing, he'd roar, 'God almighty, Mammy!' and slam the CD out of the player.

I whistled softly for Bell and sat for a last moment with her on my lap in front of the embers of the fire.

I was thinking of something else Reeny had said.

After I'd asked, 'But, Reeny, if she wanted to go to America, why did she wait so long?'

And Reeny had said, 'Well, Rosie, we all go along in the same old groove, not even noticing what we're doing, don't we? And then one day it's time to make a change. Like, she wasn't here for longer than you were away. Why did it take you so long to come home? Why did it take her so long to leave home? It's the same thing, isn't it?'

I set out for town with the pink notebook in my bag, so as to make notes for a 'Thought' on the arts if inspiration struck. The subject made me nervous, but remembering the thrill of learning from Markey when I was young, and how that had helped shape my life, I'd decided I couldn't leave art out.

The critic George Steiner once remarked, I jotted down while the bus warmed up at the Kilbride terminal, *that 'we are an animal whose life-breath is that of spoken, painted, sculptured, sung dreams.' And what is the dream, but to stand with the eternal art object against the individual body's dissolution?*

Yet most of us...

Most of us *what?* Most of us don't really know where we are in relation to art. I wonder did George Steiner take buses? He probably did, living in Geneva. But did he listen to the old ladies on them talking about the bargains in the sales? Did he manage to think out his ideas even though the man beside him was anxiously enquiring of him what he fancied in the Derby? *The gap between popular taste and high art...*

The bus was now stuck in a traffic jam in Talbot Street. The man beside me said it was always the fuckin' same. *One of the great opportunities of the mature life is that most of us have leisure at last to express the artist that lives within us all...*

The bus lurched forward and stopped again.

All? Monty? Enzo up in the chip shop? No. *Many of us.* No. *Some of us.*

We were now passing Marlborough Street where there was a record store run by a nice man, back in the days when records were 33s and 45s. I was like Nora Joyce, I used to think, after reading somewhere that when Joyce was writing *Finnegans Wake,* Nora used to go out to record shops in Paris and listen to opera. I often thought of that: the loneliness of the wife, going out to listen to romantic music. Markey was as big a genius to me as her husband was to Nora, but knowing him hadn't stopped me longing for rapture. If anything, Markey had made the longing worse.

Music was the only art where he had been uncertain. Except for madrigals: the day he discovered madrigals he climbed our yard wall and sat up there, trying to sing a four-part harmony all by himself.

I had the advantage of Sister Cecilia who would stride into the convent assembly hall in her neat boots, survey us in a silence that lasted until we could hardly breathe, then whip open the piano and make everyone jump sky high with a great crashing chord. One rainy afternoon she played a Chopin ballade just for me, the one in A. At the end, as I sat still dumbstruck, she flung herself out of the place as if she'd done something wrong. I made Markey come into town to the record store, where he listened to Rubinstein playing it. He didn't move, though he was not as still as Leo is when he listens.

The bus finally stopped at O'Connell Bridge, where I saluted the shore of mud and pebbles, just upstream, that just might be the exact spot where medieval Dublin men in hooded cloaks hauled up the ships of the Vikings. I could all but see tall men with great, golden beards climb the bank and make their way through the smoky, cluttered alleyways.

'Is that a notebook you have there?' the man beside me asked.

'Yes,' I said firmly, and jumped off.

In the bookshop opposite Trinity I found the first treasure of the day – a book of lithograph portraits by a German artist; portraits, not of whole faces but of eyes. Each pair of eyes was set beside a haiku-like poem by W.G. Sebald. I didn't understand the relationship of the words to the pictures, unless it was tonal. But one pair of eyes were those of Sebald's dog, and as sorrowful as his own. I bought the book, and walked on up to the National Library, composing a defence in my head.

One of the advantages of growing older is that you grow in confidence about your own reactions. For example, pundits will tell you that a pure aesthetic response must be free of sentimentality. That responding to depictions of dogs, for example, can have nothing to do with the questions of colour or form which have always occupied visual artists…

I was late for Tessa, but still I paused to surreptitiously touch the granite entrance pillars when I got to the library, because James Joyce himself had leaned against those very pillars, as had my young self and Markey too. We used to talk on the steps among them on my day off from Boody's, the same as the young people in *A Portrait of The Artist* had, and about much the same things, too. Then I'd go back up to the Reading Room and sit at my desk and tilt my head back and dreamily watch the tiny feet of the seagulls that walked around on the glass of the domed roof overhead. Or I might put my book under my sweater and go down to sit in a stall in the old-fashioned ladies room and read and smoke.

'What's this?' Min had said, when I'd asked her to sign the form for a reader's ticket. As if she'd never seen a form before.

'It's for the National Library.'

'Do you not have to ask a man to sign it?'

'No,' I said, 'it says "guardian".'

'That oul' bitch in the library in Milbay wouldn't give me a ticket,' she bitterly replied. 'She said I had to ask a man to sign it.'

You could have picked me off the floor with astonishment.

'I thought anyone could go into a library and take out a book,' she said. 'I thought they were like post offices, that you were entitled. There was no television then, and you'd be so bored in the winter you'd blow your brains out. The only thing there was at home was a radio with an acid battery that my father took to the garage in Milbay to be topped up, only he'd forget and anyway it was hard to hold it in the boat. But you had to have the library thing signed by someone who voted in elections and the island men never put their names to anything and they never voted for anybody. Anyone wanting to know anything about them, the only person to go to was the priest.'

'But could they read?'

'Of course they could read!' she said crossly. 'Sure we had to go to school whether the school liked it or not. A good few of the women could read. Prayers, they read. They had them on little cards, real old-style words. Hard words. And anything about cures. Or film-star magazines, they often brought great ones back from Wales.'

'Why didn't you tell me that before?' I said.

'I forgot,' she said.

'You did not,' I said.

I also remembered one day saying to her, 'There's death everywhere in *Dubliners*,' which I'd picked out from the paperbacks we had for sale in the Irish Souvenirs & Gifts section of the Pillar Department Store where I was working. 'There's all kinds of death in the best story and it's even called "The Dead". It's about a husband who's depressed because he can't really understand his wife…'

'Pity about him!' Min cut across me with sudden savagery. Standing in the scullery door, she let me have it with both barrels. ''Reeny had a small child when her husband went to the shop for cigarettes and never came back, and she had to keep going, depression or no depression. Your father wasn't well enough to work for how long before he died? Two years. Two years, do you hear me? Nothing coming in except the Disability. You have a great job, and you're only sixteen years old, and you're fed and clothed to beat the band, so let me hear no more about this depression!'

In other words, she didn't want me to be different from her and the other women around. And in a way I wasn't different, especially then, when I was only beginning to read. I was learning the world both from real people and from people in books – and they were both much the same to me. Dilly Dedalus was the same as the girl whose mother was in the sanatorium my dad had once been in, who was always hanging around outside the Kilbride Inn waiting for her father so that she could get a few bob for food for her siblings. Or Min saying, 'What's that word? What kind of a word is that?' – the word being 'haberdashery' – which was no different from Molly Bloom asking Poldy about metempsychosis, except that I had to go to the library to look it up because that was before Google, and Min looked at me defensively when she asked, as if I might mock her for wanting to know.

Maybe, even, she was hostile to my reading because nothing had stopped me doing it, whereas everything had stopped her.

'Rosie!'

After I finally released Tessa from our greeting hug, I tried nudging her in front of me in the self-service queue so she couldn't see what I was choosing.

No luck.

'Not quiche *and* tart, that's two kinds of pastry.' Hissing so that the civil servants munching away at the tables around wouldn't hear.

'What's it to you, Bossyboots?' I hissed back. But I didn't take the tart. Otherwise I'd receive the lecture about self-discipline I always got, along with the addendum about health and fitness that she'd added in the 1980s, together with the further addendum about the earth's scarce resources that she'd added recently.

She'd used the phrase 'comfort eating' once and, stung by the implication, I had snapped back, 'You could do with a bit of comfort yourself,' and she'd reddened with shock. But she *still* couldn't stop talking about carbohydrate counts, sometimes with a little tinkling laugh, as if the subject had somehow just popped into her head.

'Tessie,' I said. 'Give over, OK? I'll have a salad this evening, I give you my word of honour. Meanwhile, which of the arts is your favourite? Which art means most to you in your golden years?'

She let me distract her.

'Golden my foot,' she said. 'Anyway, what's different now except that we can afford the tickets?'

'Well, go on.'

'It used to be opera,' she relented, and a beautiful smile spread slowly across her face. I knew without doubt that she was remembering something from the time with Hugh Boody.

'Now, I never listen to long things,' she said, realising she'd been halfway through a sentence. 'Isn't that awful? To tell you the truth, I have the television on most of the time. Did you see the documentary on what's-his-name the artist whose wife was always in the bath?'

'Bonnard. No. I hardly ever think of turning on the telly. Only if there's a war. Are you having a coffee?'

'Well there is a war. Several. No, thanks, even decaf wrecks me nowadays.'

'Do you like Yeats?'

'I did at school,' she said seriously. 'Come away o human child.'

'That's baby Yeats,' I said. 'Before his genius kicked in. Fairies, I ask you! Fairies! A grown man. But finish up and we'll go over to the exhibition on him next door.'

'Speaking of men,' Tessa said, 'whatever happened to Doctor Death?'

'Are you by any chance, Tessie, referring to my distinguished lover?'

Tess was the only person I knew who'd ever met Leo. I had booked a holiday at a Club Med near Ajaccio sometime in the early madness when I knew he'd be at a conference there, and I'd asked her to join me because I was paying for a double room anyway. I didn't actually tell her about Leo – he mightn't have turned up, after all. But he did turn up, and I spent the three days he was there either in bed with him, or sitting in silence with an explosively disgruntled Tessa. I didn't see her again for six months, but I knew what she thought of him when she pointedly didn't refer to him in any way. Still, a few years later, when he was in Dublin and so was I for a spell, she lent me the solid, bourgeois, redbrick house her late parents had left her. I wanted Leo and me to be like a married couple – for once not in a hotel. Min thought I was on some training course, when I came in at midnight and went out at 8 a.m. Or at least I think that's what she thought.

'You know,' Tessa said. 'I'll tell you something. When I was trying to decide about becoming a counsellor, one of the things on my mind was wishing I knew how to help you escape that weirdo.'

'Weirdo?' I murmured, as if I wasn't quite familiar with the word. I was moved, all the same, to think she'd worried about me.

'Ah well,' she said generously, 'sure we'll all settle for anyone if we're desperate.'

'There was nothing desperate about being with Leo,' I icily replied. 'He was what I wanted. I pity any woman who doesn't know what a man like Leo is like.'

'But where is he now?' she said, with the touch of a sneer. QED is what she meant.

'He's in Italy, as a matter of fact,' I said lightly. 'He's fond of Italy. But he'll be coming over for my birthday, I hope.' A complete invention, this. 'You'll come to the party too, won't you, Tess? September 5th, death of Flaubert?'

I don't know how that came into my head, but it worked.

'Oh, I didn't realise you were still with him,' Tessa said – humbly, for her.

'Look at us!' I said, rising to my feet. 'We're a disgrace to womanhood! We come here for W. B. Yeats and within minutes we're talking about lovers!' Though I still hadn't asked about her and Andy.

I was speaking too loudly, startling a little bald man at the next table whose hands jumped, knocking his newspaper off the water carafe where he'd carefully propped it.

I sent Markey an email that evening when I was having my supper – I'd drawn the kitchen table over to the fire and had everything I needed within a few feet of my chair, as if I lived in a yurt and there was trackless tundra all around. Even Bell was agreeable to sit in her basket at my feet and vigilantly watch the flames, as if, were she to relax her gaze, they might do anything.

I told him that I'd tried to do a piece on the arts and ageing, in his honour, but that I couldn't – that there was too much to say:

If you're so blessed as to be an artist, growing older is a further blessing. I saw it today in Yeats – how great his old age was – and the same would be true of Titian and Wallace Stevens and Verdi and Beethoven. Art deepens. And even people like me and you, who are not artists but who do care, we grow in understanding, too. We may be only stumbling after the practitioner, but we're all going in the same direction. It means more to us all the time, the reading and listening and looking. For one thing, where else does an ordinary person have access to something that's intended to be larger than the individual, and intended to last longer than a single lifetime? What's more, art takes us away from money and wealth and all that. Because you can't really buy art. You can't instruct the arts to be of consequence. They choose their own time to strike you with their significance.

I can't do it, Markey, not in 150 words or any number of words.

In bed, before I went to sleep, I apologised to W. B. Yeats.

'Who is to say,' I said to him, 'that there aren't fairies all over the place?'

I then imagined the birdsong there would be in the Milbay beech woods when the good weather finally came. Light that would dapple down through the leaves, wood-pigeons making their imploring cries, and in those glades where the trees thinned near the edge of the camp, there would be butterflies at work above the silky grass. Or dragonflies even, with their double wings of black and silver.

I used to ask my dad to catch a dragonfly so that I could see its tiny face, like the faces they had in the illustrations of a children's book I'd seen at school. Min had told me how he awoke one morning towards the end of his life, when his mind sometimes wandered, and informed her that he'd just come back from the Phoenix Park, where he'd been catching dragonflies, and that she was to give them food.

'They're over there,' he pointed. 'They're in the pocket of my good coat.'

From: MarkC@rmbooks.com
To: RosieB@eirtel.com
Sent: 9.05 p.m.

My dear Rosie, that is as fine a 150 words on the arts as I've ever seen. Big thinking in a little space.

It is as well, however, for the simpler citizens of the Midwest, the ones who buy cute little mini-books with brocade covers, that the last three 'Thoughts' be on easier subjects. Travel, food and – I forget what the last one is! But we're nearly there.

You are a great girl and you always were.

16

'Come to the pictures this afternoon?' Andy called down the hallway. 'I can't go later; I have to be back down the country tonight to go over to England at the weekend. *Ocean's Eleven.* You can look at George Clooney and I can enjoy the movie. I rang the bell for you last night, but you didn't answer the door.'

'C'mere, Andy? For once I'd locked the front door, but I didn't hear the bell.'

'I'll have a quick look at the wiring so,' he said, and he started crawling along the skirting-board. 'Make us a cup of tea, will you? Sure when Min's here the kettle is on before I'm in the door. Well, if she's in a good humour it is.'

'She's always in a good humour these days,' I said. 'Travel suits her. Same as your Pearl – Pearl's always on the go.'

'This wire is all corroded,' Andy said. 'And my ma doesn't really travel. You should see her suitcase. Packets of oxtail soup, a load of them, in case the food is foreign. What else would it be in Spain but foreign? I told her. She brings Lyons' teabags and Tayto crisps too, but she's not as bad as some of them. There was a lady on the Fatima trip, Tess was telling me, whose suitcase was so heavy they could hardly shift it – and what was in it only two litre bottles of water from her own tap at home.'

'How's Tess?' I asked. Now was his chance to tell me if there was any news.

'She's great,' he said cheerfully. 'She's gone to Belfast to pick out her new floor. She's going to do up her whole house, the floor is only the first thing.'

Oh, poor Tess! I thought. Peg and I would have to pretend that she'd never said anything about their hooking up together.

'She was saying to me,' Andy was still chatting away, 'that you should have one put in, too.'

'Typical Tess,' I remarked. 'Always knows what someone else should do. But this is Min's house, not mine. And anyway, I know where I'd like to live if I could have my choice …'

And once again I put my heart and soul into describing Stoneytown to him. Beginning with a description of the track that led behind the Air Corps barracks to the big meadow, I then climbed to the top of the ridge and painted the picture for him of the terrace of ruined houses on my left that faced, across the wide river, the quays of Milbay town, and on my right, facing out to sea, the solitary house of my grandfather, with its yard, ancient walled orchard, barn and haggard, plus two little fields that stretched back to the woods. I told him what the old man in the Milbay garda barracks and the supervisor in the ESB had told me about the past of the place.

'I'll say this for you, Andy,' I finished at last, 'you really, really know how to listen.'

Because I had noticed, as I talked, that something happened when Andy was interested and thought no one was looking at him: his eyes, usually blurry and secretive, would open wide. And that in turn settled his face, so that his features sharpened up around them. I'd known him since I was a child and wasn't a bit shy with him, but just as I was about to tell him what I was thinking, he amazed me by saying something similar about me.

'D'you know what, Rosie? You look completely different when you're talking about that place! Well, not different, but more the way you used to look when you were working in Boody's bookshop, dashing around mad with enthusiasm. You looked like a child then, but, of course, you were a child.'

'I was not!' I cried. 'I'd been away, so I had! I'd been in Roubaix with my friend Lalla! Min was urging me to go back to work in the Pillar so I'd meet a nice fella, and I wanted to show her that that kind of thing was all in the past now, and that what I was going to do instead was read every book in the world, because my whole life had changed.'

'I know.' He was smiling at me. 'That happened to me, too. I went on that charity hike to Tanzania with the lads from the GAA club, and I wasn't there a day before I was trying to figure out what I could do to come back.'

'Ah, it's not the same,' I said. 'You people in No-Need are helping other people. I wasn't helping anyone. I just wanted the best for myself.'

'What do you think I'm doing?' he asked, laughing now and looking around for his jacket. 'I'm in it for myself, too. Come on, Rosie, run up to the bedroom and I'll ring the bell and tell me can you hear it now.'

I got out the laptop while I was waiting for Andy to return for the pictures. As if sitting there gazing at it was marginally more productive than sitting there not gazing at it. The kitchen was too hot, but if I went upstairs I knew I'd flop onto the bed and after a while fall asleep and then there'd be the grey waking-up. I'd be overcome again by the feel of the house as I had been in the days after my father's death. Never mind amazed once more at how this knowledge of desolation that lives inside me never went away, but shows itself only if I sleep in the afternoon and wake up at dusk.

And look what else has been buried in there! A man's regard, resting on me.

I'd forgotten what it was like. How *other* a man is, even a thoroughly domesticated one like Andy. The distance across which his gaze had travelled somehow woke an antique response. No wonder even women who were satisfied with the lives they'd made, who knew perfectly well that what kept them going was their women friends, would like to have a man. For the *flavour*, if nothing else.

Travel, I typed. *A draft.*

Had Andy always noticed me? Or was it just when I was young in Boody's? At Tessa's retirement-from-the-union party my high heels were the only high heels in the room. Mind you, last week he saw me out in the yard in my dressing-gown that looks as if I've been sick all over it, from the time I spilled the bleach. I called his mobile because Bell was up Mrs Beckett's tree and wouldn't come down, but of course wouldn't you know it, by the time he came around she had.

Anyway. This was getting me nowhere.

Ever since Saint Brendan set out in his leather boat to find America, the Irish have been wanderers.

It had been the tiniest of frissons, but a frisson it had been. And did that mean that I was hopelessly deprived? Without knowing it? Margaret Mead once said a woman needed three men in her life: one to give her passionate sex and children; one to protect and nurture her and the children; and one to be the friend and companion of her declining years. Well, I wasn't declining, physically. As a matter of fact, I'd never felt better. And I obviously didn't need children, or a protector for them. So that left passionate sex.

I looked around the kitchen. Passionate sex? Here? At home? Ah no, the last person who'd gasped and cried out in this room was Daddy. And anyway, sex doesn't happen in the house of your childhood where the wood at the bottom of the doors is marked by the claws of cats you loved more than anything in the world. Not if you're romantic. Sex is more like a lush fruit that grows in exotic places. A girl walks quietly beside a handsome American up the wide stairs of the Gresham Hotel – she's trembling for many reasons, one of which is that the porter might call out after them – and along a quiet corridor where he bends to open the door to his room, where sunlight suddenly blinds her from tall windows whose white curtains billow in the current of air, and friendly noises of traffic and people rise from the street below, and the young man turns to her and folds her into his arms. Or a man on a plane to a new place who says, 'I'd be happy to meet you tomorrow to help you find your bearings'. Or the shape beside you in the dim aquarium which turns into a man who smiles and says, 'Which one's your favourite?'

It is *somewhere else*, the possibility of passion. It beckons you to come and find out.

As places do.

Was that what people had at the back of their minds when you asked what wish of theirs was still unfulfilled, and they replied, 'I'd like to travel.' Funny how they never outright said, 'I'd like to have lots of sex.'

Ever since Saint Brendan set out... the Irish have been wanderers. Lugging the suitcase to the airport, standing in line, the hazards of the flight, its after-effects, and then, of course, the adjustment of body and mind to the new experience: all this draws on the resources of practicality and flexibility you have accumulated over the years.

But travel doesn't have to be...

Once, on the Albanian side of Lake Ochrid, I had been in a battered village, a former resort for Hoxha's elite, but now a dirty, broken place. The blocks of workers' flats had decayed back into something premodern, their balconies stacked with wood because any heating system in the buildings had long been broken and vandalised. In the hotel that smelled of rot, most of the water pipes had been wrenched from the walls, while the one in our bathroom gushed boiling water. I was with a woman who worked with me in Luxembourg; who'd been everywhere in her day, but even she lost her nerve when we tried to walk along what had once been a promenade above a stony lakeshore covered with litter and lined with pillbox bomb shelters that stank of human excrement, and where little boys attacked us. Feral children, sneaking up behind us to hit us, because we carried nothing they could steal.

On one side there are the logistics. On the other side the richness of experience that only travel can bring. And middle age opens the person to that rich store. At last there's time and some money and knowledge and a seasoned opportunism...

And yet an old woman had whispered a welcome to us, in French, from behind the gate of her cottage. And while we clung to each other for warmth in the damp bed, the lilt of a band rose from the dancehall below us in the hotel, along with the laughter of dancing people. And in the morning we walked in brilliant sunshine to the border, a mile away, and after we crossed over into Macedonia, and began the long walk to the nearest Macedonian town, an empty double-decker bus had appeared from nowhere on the country road. We flagged it down for a joke, but it stopped, and the driver drove us, helter-skelter, right into the middle of the next town. We got a room in a house for the night – a son's bedroom, bedecked with soccer posters – and at last we ate, on a deck over the crystal-clear lake. We had sausages with crisp skins and potatoes and glasses of golden beer, and my colleague smiled for the first time since we'd left Greece a few days before. I smiled back and ordered another beer and relaxed into my chair, as sparrows came and bustled around our feet.

And I saw, in those exaggerated circumstances, why I always, always moved on. What I wanted from travel was the achieving of it. It was about moving through the solution of problems to ease. It was about fending off threats to the ideal state that beckoned me on. It was about fighting my way to temporary homes – homes that had nothing but happiness in them.

I knew from before I began that I had made a sacrifice in order to travel.

In my old document case where I kept treasures and important things was the newspaper obituary of Hugh Boody – worn now along its folded creases – that Min had saved for me. Nobody knew it was in there.

I cherished it.

When I was twenty-five, and in my final year of college, I had a scholarship and so didn't need to work in Boody's bookshop except on Thursday nights. One Thursday, Mr Boody came in on his way to collect Mrs Boody from a golfing dinner. He asked me, as if it was the most normal thing in the world, to meet him at 4 o'clock on Sunday afternoon in the back bar of a hotel near Heuston railway station. It wasn't a completely ob-scure hotel: Markey, in the course of giving me a condensed introduction to the philosophy of Wittgenstein, not one word of which I'd understood, had told me Wittgenstein stayed there. But I'd never been inside it before.

Sunday came round, and the barman, once he'd

served us, went forward into the lounge where a football commentator was bellowing from a television. There was no one else at all in the bar.

Hugh Boody had hands with long, thin fingers. He poured out my lemonade and pushed it towards me and sat there across the table behind his little glass of whiskey, perfectly calm. I was bemused but in no way worried – I'd known him as a very pleasant boss for years.

'Rosie,' he said, his fine face candid, 'I want you to be my woman friend. I know in my bones that we'd hit it off better than anybody else – both of us, not just me. I mean regularly, Rosie – I mean as an arrangement, like in the old days, but a secret, of course. I've had the idea for a long time that we'd suit each other down to the ground, so I hope you'll just think about it. You're a truthful person. Anyone can see that in your face. So that's why I'm risking it, telling you the plain truth. I'd find you a nice place. And open a bank account for you, of course.'

I don't think I used words. I just shook my head, over and over.

'If you're sure about saying no,' he said, his face flushed now, 'that's the end of it. No problem there at all. Forget I spoke.'

I said, standing up to go, 'I want to see the world. I want to travel.'

He looked up at me and our gazes locked just for a moment and, yes, he was right about the fit between us. Now that I was alert to him, excitement swept over me.

'I'll be going away soon,' I managed to say, and I walked out.

From that moment on I thought about his proposition as little as possible. I didn't ask myself: What kind of man is this? I didn't ask myself: Why me? I didn't imagine how it would be making love with him. I didn't let practical questions into my head, like what he had intended to do about his wife and Tessa.

Because he'd wounded me. It hurt me very much to think that there, with my life before me, there already was a road not taken. What you're trying to do when you travel, why you keep on planning and moving and avidly learning, is to cheat your way into fullness of experience. But thanks to Hugh's offer, I had been conscious from the beginning that there is no way to have it all.

Very occasionally I'd allow myself a glance back. It would have been so peaceful, I'd begin to think. It would have been like living with my daddy in peace and order. I'd have been able to accomplish anything –

No! And I'd put the memory of that afternoon away again.

I had put it away now, too, by going back to work, and an hour later I was able to dial up and send to Seattle.

From: RosieB@eirtel.com
To: MarkC@rmbooks.com
Sent: 12.47 p.m.

Markey,
    Herewith a draft of 'Travel'. It wasn't as easy as it looks: I have 150 words to say about every inch I've ever travelled.

This one is Number 7, isn't it? We have:

– The miracle of middle age
– the body
– disappointment and its traps
– money
– friendship
– the arts
– Yep. Number 7. And I'm drafting 'Animals' and 'Food' now.

OK? I remember you saying you had a tortoise in Seattle that waited by the door for you to come home and made noises when you scratched his poor old head. So I'll try to find a place for tortoises.

Did I tell you about the macaw I once met in London in a B&B? A huge scarlet and blue bird? The owner told me how in spring it follows young female guests around and pads upstairs and waits in a lovelorn way outside their doors. But it doesn't bother about older women.

Isn't that terrifying?

Attachment #1: draft, travel

Ever since Saint Brendan set out in his leather boat to find America the Irish have been wanderers. It is not a comfortable calling, wandering. The suitcase, the airport, the line, the hazards, the adjustments of body and mind: all these draw deep on reserves of patience and flexibility, and sometimes exhaust them.

Sitting under a café umbrella in a piazza, we proclaim the glory of the world. We endure dislocation to arrive at the condensed richness of experience that only travel provides. And this is a richness, both sensual and intellectual, which grows in savour as we grow older. At last there is time and money and skill and self-knowledge with which to shape the travel experience.

However luxuriously done, or however crudely touristic, travel is always about creativity. It celebrates our ability to feel and see and think in new ways – to open ourselves to the surprising world.

Beep beep from a truck in the street. Andy's truck. *Bang!* The front door. His smiling face peeked around the kitchen door.

'Fetch your coat, Rosie, George Clooney's waiting for you.'

'Andy, I know you're always doing me favours, but this time I want you to do me a *huge* favour...'

'Break it to me,' he said. 'When did I ever say no to any of you?'

So I asked him to skip the cinema and to come to Stoneytown with me on his way to his farm. Well, his farm was in Carlow, so strictly speaking Milbay wasn't on the way, but cross-country, near enough.

'And – brace yourself, Andy – I want you to bring my bed from upstairs. *Please.* I want to sleep in the house if I pluck up the courage, but I couldn't sleep on the floor in case there'd be mice. I have the bed clothes packed into my own car already. Because I know you'll say yes. Because if you don't, Andy, I'm stuck. No firm will deliver a bed to where there's no road and a hill to climb. But I'll help you and then I'll buy a new bed for here. So will you do it for me? You will, won't you, Sweetiepie?'

'What about my grub?' he said. Andy Sutton was famous for always being hungry.

'I have two burgers here, lovely, juicy burgers, Andy, ketchup and all on them already. Grilled rolls. I can have them on the table in a minute. And I can buy the stuff for a picnic in Milbay. You won't be hungry. Please, Andy, this is my only chance, and you're going away. *Please.*'

'Have you a wrench?' he said. 'And is there mustard on the burgers? And where's Bell anyway? What about Bell? Will we bring Bell?'

'She's on Min's bed, where else.'

'Here, Bella, Bella, Bella!' he called at the foot of the stairs. 'Here, Chuckie. Come and have some burger.'

After the cat padded down the stairs, he scooped her onto his lap, kissed her, and began to stroke her under her chin.

'We can't bring her,' I said. 'There was a dog, and she might still be around. They mightn't hit it off. You'll go in next door to Monty and be good, won't you, Isabella?'

She gave me a level stare, and yawned.

I kept looking at the sky as I dodged up and down the main street of Milbay, adding the newspaper and a rhubarb tart and tomatoes and apples to the bread and ham. The Hut food, and even the same shops as before. It was an ordinary, grey day, and I was afraid there might be rain. Andy had gone off to the hardware shop to buy a little handcart, to carry stuff from his truck to the house. I told him to tell the owner of the hardware shop that it was for the Queen of France.

My fingers were crossed that the weather would improve, and the place would look lovely by the time we got there, and my wish was granted, the woods and the meadow even more delicately green than I remembered. The two of us carried the base of the bed up the springy turf to the ridge where we stopped in the air to survey the vista of sea and river, all soft and pearly and simple. I was dying to look at Andy, though I knew his face never showed emotion if he could help it. But I knew that he was impressed, because he was extra quiet. We then went back to the car and got the mattress and carried it on our heads, up and over the hill, like a bier. Andy brought the last pieces down in the cart and set up the bed in the loft, while I started the fire and got water from the well. After that, he went out and walked the fields and the barn and the sheds, then came back in and prowled around the house, knocking on walls and pulling at beams and poking at floors and ceilings; not speaking, but making the little grunts men make when they're in inspecting mode.

I was setting out our picnic on the window sill, which I'd been using as a table, when he said to wait a minute and went off around the corner to the terrace and came back with an ancient-looking door. Laying one end on the window sill, he balanced the other on a neat plinth he made with big stones he'd taken from the shore. Then he spread out the car mats to cover the floor, on which we sat side by side, like people do on carpets in Arab houses, and ate contentedly, the door open beside us to a sea and sky now of the palest, most delicate blue.

Then, without a sound, the black dog slipped in. I didn't even notice till I felt a cold nose sniff along my arm towards the hand holding a ham sandwich.

'Hey!' I yelled, and fell over backwards in surprise and laughter, and the little dog, thinking it was a game, jumped on my stomach, while Andy was saying something like 'Well, well, well, look who's here!' – and tickling the dog who was licking my face as I was still trying to eat my sandwich and the three of us were one joyful mass on the floor, the dog mock-growling and jumping all over us and the makeshift table in great danger of collapsing.

'Come here, Missy,' said Andy, finally calming her down. 'We'll give you a dinner of your own.'

The three of us then finished the meal. Perfectly at ease. Though my heart still shook every time I took in again how ill she looked, and how listless, after the first exuberant welcome, she showed herself to be. All she seemed to want to do was slurp up bowl after bowl of water. So we didn't go for a walk. Andy cleaned and coaxed into use the old shutters on the two little windows, and worked in the back kitchen on the door that squealed. Myself and the dog just rested.

Last thing, Andy made a dash back to Milbay to buy me a couple of folding chairs, an oil-lamp and a bag of dog feed, and to have the key to the gate copied. He said he couldn't be looking for my key every time he came here to bang in a nail. I turned away so he wouldn't see how delighted I was to hear the words.

He also brought me back a rotisserie chicken from the deli, a bottle of wine and a corkscrew.

'You know what, Andy?' I said. 'The women in your life have had a wonderful influence.'

But as it became time for him to leave, he grew more and more anxious. 'If only there was mobile phone coverage out here!' he kept saying. 'Or if you'd come down to the farm with me.'

But I knew the dog wouldn't climb into his truck any more than into my car. So I told him there was a short-cut through the woods to the public phone-box and that if anything went wrong I'd ring him. Not that I would. What use would he be, forty or fifty miles away?

'And have you euros for the phone?' he said. 'Show me. Count them. And have you my Carlow number written down?'

Before he went, he saw the dog begin to revive. Not that she ate the chicken, but she went over to the plate it was on and lay with her paws on either side, sternly guarding it. She didn't want to leave it when Andy took her for a little walk down the shore, last thing, but he insisted. I watched them from the door, as he picked his way slowly through the rocks, and all I could see of her as she followed him was her black tail.

I ran around the orchard side of the house then for a quick pee among the stunted trees. The lights of Milbay were beginning to twinkle in the gathering dusk, and the evening was cold.

'We'll stay in after you've gone,' I said. 'It's strange here, still. But – thanks!'

We hugged as we'd always done.

I went in and put the wooden bars across the doors. He then pushed against them to show me no one could force an entry, and called goodbye, telling me to go to the phone-box first thing in the morning – he'd be waiting.

I was already learning from the dog who was staying very quiet. She slept against my thigh and didn't move even when I had to stand to feed a bit more driftwood into the range that burnt low but vividly. I usually hadn't the patience to sit doing nothing, but for her I delayed the chores until the sky in the little windows was darkest blue. Then I washed the dishes in a basin in the back scullery by the light of a couple of candles Andy had stuck into a tin can full of earth. I made the bed, up the four steps of the loft, by more candlelight, as the light from the open range danced on the low ceiling. I then squirted Windolene at the mirror above the bed, buffed it with kitchen paper, and looked solemnly at myself in its new limpidity.

The last face that mirror had seen could easily have been my mother's.

I lit the paraffin lamp, figuring I had about forty minutes of power in the laptop battery, and tapped out a 'Thought' for Markey at the new table. The dog had moved into the shadow under the stairs, sitting up with her eyes open and gleaming, but she didn't move and I left her alone.

'Thought' No. 8: Animals

Maybe there is no one to love your loving heart. Maybe your own heart can no longer shrug off the dryness that has settled on it over the years.

But we can forget how difficult loving is when we smile at animals, admire them, praise inventive nature for such colourings, such silken coats, such gentle muzzles, such lustrous eyes, such fluffy tails, such grace in moving and sitting and sleeping, such nakedness of feeling, such fine instinct, such wealth of personality and character. Not wanting to change them but honouring what they are, we love them.

Feel the heart unclench when a living thing puts its powerlessness in your charge – a dog, a cat, a parrot, an iguana, a tortoise, a donkey, an old horse. A love grows that is so purged of the need for reward, so attentive to the otherness of the other, that it can make human love seem almost coarse.

Animals are Creation's gift to the human animal.

(162 words)

I'd send that from Milbay Library in the morning.

I took up all the car mats, and after making a pile of them on the floor of the loft, I put a towel on top: if the dog wanted a place of her own, but also to be near me, she could sleep there. Or she could stay where she was. On my way upstairs I crouched beside her for a long minute with my hand lightly on her head, but then I left her in the shadows and went to bed myself. It was amazingly cosy in the loft. Where the far corner of the floor was missing, I could see the glow from the fire and I could hear the sea. Making the same noise as Bell makes when she's very happy: a deep purr, slow and steady.

Even the marks on the wall on the plaster below the bed didn't seem tragic to me, now. There was will to them, wasn't there, and energy? My grandmother had done her best to take control of her destiny, hadn't she? Like her daughter Min was doing. Like I was doing…

And just as I was beginning to swirl towards sleep, the dog came up to the loft. I heard the light click of her paws on the wide wooden steps. She jumped onto the bed and after a few moments surveying the possibilities she curled into the small of my back. She wasn't at ease at first. Shudders riffed through her. I could hear her quiet panting. I could feel her mouth work. Oh what babies must go through, I thought, if a little dog who is perfectly safe can be as anxious as this!

Then she finished gumming her jaws, and with a last long sigh that made me smile, because it was just like a sigh of Min's when she considered herself hopelessly overworked, the dog fell deeply and silently asleep.

Part Four

The Party At The Point

✦

17

The following weeks of July into early August were a life within a life. I became serene, and so did the dog. Within a few days she began to sleep without the yips and shudders of nightmare, though there was something about the night, still, that weighed on her consciousness, and I often came awake to find that she was awake too, sitting immobile, looking into the dark. In the morning, then, she'd be as grumpy as a human being, and try to cling to sleep when I got up. But I made her come with me. I needed her. It was fine summer weather and I'd found a little cove of dark sand not three minutes away from the house where if I left my shoes on a certain rock I could enter the water without encountering a single pebble. I took a towel and went down there most mornings, and the dog had to come, too.

If I'd had email in the house I'd have told someone what I'd discovered: that you can do almost anything on earth on your own and not notice you're alone, except go for a swim. You can't run splishing and splashing into cold water, howl as you reach down, and then swim a bit, gulping at the air, and then warm and expand and discover that it feels marvellous, without feeling the absence of someone to witness all that.

It was such a pity about Leo. He didn't swim at all, now. Once, years ago, I'd stayed in a village on Lake Lucerne for a week near where he lived, and he used to meet me on the pier so early in the morning that the sky would still be pale and the mist still thick; we'd swim until it was broad, blue daylight. Then he'd jump into his car in his robe to go home, and I'd go up the path to the guesthouse that smelled, freshly, of coffee.

Oh, well… He was a wonderful man in many ways, but he had no sense of humour. When I told him once that Joyce said a pier was a bridge that got disappointed, he didn't even laugh. Humour would help him now. Growing old must be as bad for a vain man as for an ordinary woman – for anyone who has always been first and foremost looked at. Bad enough being me, watching the crevices deepen in the loose skin of my upper lip; but what if in my day I'd been Marilyn Monroe?

I swam nude, as I always did when I could. After all, I'd lived in a shack on the beach south of Kalamata, the first time I read Proust. Here there was nothing but sea between me and Cardiganshire; and I didn't have a bathing suit.

There was one at home, not that it was likely to fit me: the polka-dot bathing suit that Min had kept all her life though she had never even attempted learning to swim. But I'd noticed that its corsetry and thick nylon fabric were still in surprisingly good nick, when I'd opened her bag in the Sunshine Home. I'd smiled when I saw it, having forgotten that she brought the suit everywhere, even to Nevers, when the Ladies' Pilgrimage went to the tomb of Bernadette of Lourdes in the very heart of landlocked France. It meant 'out of the ordinary' to her, that suit. And to me. Before my father got sick, its appearance signalled that The Hut was near. The neighbours would have begun to trek out on the bus to Dollymount Strand with their primus stoves and sandwiches wrapped in the greaseproof paper from sliced pans, and Min would take down from the shelf in the wardrobe the brown paper bag, worn to softness, where she kept the suit, protected by a grainy mothball whose pungency declined each year.

I never got a straight answer as to where it had come from.

'It's a bandeau type,' she answered me once, so I thought she must have ordered it from a magazine or a catalogue, since 'bandeau' was a word to marvel at in our house. The suit had puckered sides and an inch of flat curtain along the top of the thighs.

'I saw the same on Esther Williams in the pictures,' she said another time.

'But Esther Williams always swims,' I said.

Min took no notice.

Over the years, its big white dots turned yellow and its boned bosom began to lead a life of its own, while Min got thinner within it. But my father's objection to it never changed.

'You're not going out in that, are you?' he'd always say. 'Are you, Dear?'

He called her 'dear' when as near to angry as he ever got with Min.

And she'd come as near as I ever saw her to taunting him.

'Why wouldn't I?' she'd say, and she'd haul the cane chair out of the hut and ostentatiously sit on it in the suit.

I was striding back from my swim one magical early August morning, the towel knotted around my waist, my breasts drying off in the morning sun, when the dog suddenly ran back towards me and away again, barking madly. Glancing up, I saw Andy, fifteen or so feet away, on the grassy bank just beyond the rim of boulders at the top of the shore, turning away from me.

'I'll put a kettle on!' he called over his shoulder and hurried on towards the house, while I untied the towel and tied it again under my arms. A blush had spread all over me, but at the same time I said to myself, forcefully, 'It doesn't matter! It's nothing! It's not going to spoil anything!'

Because I'd been feeling lately – if timorously, holding my breath – that I might finally be perfectly happy, now. For maybe the first time in my life. I counted my blessings in bed every night, beginning with the clean, comfortable bed, larding my ecstatic thanks to whoever or whatever was up there with phrases from every prayer I could think of. I had this exquisite place. I had the dog who came from nowhere. I had my friends nearby. I had Andy to help me. Soon I'd hear from Markey, and whether or not the 'Ten Thoughts' ever saw the light of day, they'd started our relationship off again. My Min was on an adventure, but soon she'd be home. And – hell, I was in Ireland, which, bad as it was and, especially bad as it had been, was not so bad that a person couldn't live in it.

Which I literally had not been able to do in many countries. In Mali because the malaria medication made me so sick; in Osaka because the district the school was in was unbelievably noisy; in Managua because of the dominance of machismo. I hadn't been able to bear the violence against women that I knew was all around me in Cape Town, even though the men I worked with were lovely. I could have lived in a palatial villa in Lahore, and earned very good money writing a report on a distance-learning project for UNICEF, but once I glimpsed the brothel district where girls of ten and eleven years old had painted faces and sores on their poor arms and legs, I turned the job down cold.

Those countries where contempt for women was institutionalised were also absolutely out; I was damned if I was going to be forbidden to drive or drink or if I was going to walk three paces behind someone just because he had a penis. And I couldn't bear the sadness in countries that went in for mad drunkenness – I couldn't take that stuff any more. And I wanted to be where I could speak my native language. Even in Italy, where I fitted in very well when I was thin and dramatic and smoked all the time and hennaed my hair, I'd become lonely for English. And for peace and quiet. Like this peace. This marvellous quiet.

Ireland was great. Even if the older Irish man was a perfect study in shyness and repression.

'Gorgeous morning, isn't it, Andy?' I called out chattily as I went in to the house.

He had his back to me in the scullery, fetching the mugs and plates for breakfast.

'I went over to the phone-box last night,' I continued, on my way up to the loft, 'to ring Min, because she has a landline now and she can ring me back for half-nothing. I was reminding her about when we used to be on our holidays in a hut down past the wharf in Milbay, and we used to nip in and steal a shower in a sports ground.'

I was dry now and slipping into my raggedy track suit.

'Because swimming doesn't make you clean, Andy, did you ever notice that? I'm filthy. There's sand and grit between my toes all the time. And I'm having a hard time washing even my face, never mind the rest of me. A full bucket of water is a bit too heavy for me. She'll be home for my birthday party,' I said, coming to the propped-up door we were still using as a table. 'Will you be in Ireland? Oh say you will! It'll be no good without you!'

I noted, when my gaze flicked over him, a small, red flush still on each cheek. I was overdoing it, I could hear. Since when had Andy Sutton been essential to a party? Mind you, since when had he been so extra good and helpful? Which led to:

'Why are you here, Andy? I mean, I'm delighted to see you but...?'

Oh God, I shouldn't have started off like that.

'Min's different, Andy,' I babbled on. 'We talk to each

other differently, now. She's not as prickly, and I'm not as superior with her. I just hope it lasts. But it won't, will it? When she comes home, it'll be her house again. Her Petunias, her cat, her blue armchair, her niece.'

He was trying to make toast, holding the big slices up to the bars of the range; but there wasn't enough substance to the fire this early in the morning.

'And we don't agree about this place, her and me. I had to hang up without arguing with her, because I'm frightened in that phone-box, you know, when the trees are creaking and you think someone is in there breaking off branches. But she made it crystal clear before I did that there isn't going to be much more of Stoneytown. I made her bring her actual ticket and her passport to the phone and read them out to me. She's booked to leave the States on September 4th so as to be home on the 5th – my birthday. And on the 6th, she said, and I quote, 'even if I haven't had a wink of sleep I'm going into town to whoever has the biggest offices for buying houses and I'm going to throw the letter from the government down on the desk and I'm going to say, "Right, Mister! How much will you give me for that?" That's what she said.'

I'd been talking for a ridiculous amount of time. I'd have to stop.

'So I said that I have to stay here because the dog can't be got into anything with an engine, and that I love it here. But she said that with the money she'll make for the place she can have a great life. She said if she had some money she could travel. I said what was wrong with people these days that they couldn't stay in the one place? But she reminded me that whenever I came home she used to look at all the stamps in my passport and ask me about them.'

'Rosie,' Andy began, 'I've a surprise for you.' He sounded perfectly normal, having had enough time to recover. I couldn't have been all that exciting, anyway, with my hair stuck to my head and my skin purple from the cold water. I had hardly looked like Ursula Andress coming out of the water in *Doctor No.*

His big surprise was that he'd brought Bell from Dublin, who he was combing now to help her get over the experience of the drive. She had eventually settled down, he told me, on his lap and put her paws on the steering wheel as if trying to steer. Another surprise was the cat's utter indifference to the dog, and vice versa.

'I brought her in case there are any mice about. Because I'm worried about you, Rosie,' he went on. 'The candles alone are a fire hazard. And you could put your back out with the buckets – Pearl put her back out just climbing off a train. I was thinking that there's no problem rigging up a little water pump – I do it in Africa all the time – but of course I need electricity. And there's something that came up at the last No-Need meeting. About Rosslare Harbour. There's a problem there with stock that are rejected by the vets or that make a load overweight. We've nowhere to keep them till I'm back from Gatwick with the truck and I can collect them and bring them up to Carlow. We had a lairage there, but the Council has taken that for parking because the harbour's so busy. They'll have to give us somewhere else but it won't be sorted out for a while.'

'I could help!' I jumped in. 'I have the two fields! I mean, Min has.'

'That's not enough,' Andy said.

'Oh, I'd have liked it,' I subsided.

'No,' he said. 'I'll tell you the point. You're right that you've the makings of a lairage. But the point is that there's rules and regulations about lairages. They have to have power.'

'Oh well...'

'So if this place is made into a lairage, the ESB has to lay on electricity. It's the law. And in fact there should be no problem. I checked and there's a live feed as near as the airfield.'

I must have looked at him like an adoring starlet might look at a famous producer who'd just given her a starring role. I was genuinely speechless.

'I was speaking to the agriculture boys in the ESB, and, according to them, there'll be a team here first thing tomorrow.'

I was about to say a heartfelt thank-you when he finished: 'So you'd want to have your clothes on.'

I leaned across the table and kissed him smack on the cheek, laughing away the last of the embarrassment. Well, who'd have thought that our Andy could crack a joke! Especially when he had – I'd felt it too – been genuinely upset by the little incident. Wait'll I tell – well, no. It mightn't be the best anecdote to tell Tessa.

At that the table began to tilt and the dishes to slide towards the floor. 'Furniture,' I said. 'I can see why it was invented.'

There were three Saturdays left in August, on which Min and I had a firm date to talk to each other at 9 in the evening. I could hardly wait till our date to tell her how amazing the change had been, after I flicked a switch, and the worn walls of the room leaped forward out of their dimness, and I saw the dirt at the edges of the floor, and the rot along the base of the settle bed.

We ran through the meadow towards the phone that evening, the dog and I. She was fully herself, now. It was a wonder to see how glossy her coat, more like a skin of thick, black silk now, had become. Her ribs had disappeared under a fine, round sausage of a body, and her black eyes shone like onyx. One ear flopped almost over an eye while the other stuck straight up, matching her slender, upright whip of a tail that I saw all day around the place, at times seeming to march around on its own as she explored the meadows, her nose to the ground.

The meadow grass was taller than she, so I'd trained her to run behind me in the track I'd made; that way, I pointed out to her, we did as little harm as possible to the flowers and grasses. We then went into the beech wood where slender columns of sunlight between the trees sparkled with golden dust and the birds were riotous with song far above us. She held back at the fence at the road, afraid we were going somewhere there'd be a car, but I coaxed her forward, inch by inch. She was terribly frightened, but even so she looked up at me with trust. She made me want to cry. Oh, how could people be looked up at like that by something small and harmless and ever choose to hurt it?

Min was full of excitement about her first ever poker game.

'So I turned over the card, Rosie,' as a long and rambling story finally ended, 'and you're not going to believe this, but it was the seven of spades! The others had to pay up there and then!'

'I was reading the other day,' I said, 'that it's hard for trees to put down roots as they grow older; that rooting is a juvenile trait. But you're doing great with the roots, aren't you? Admittedly, you're not a tree.'

'Why don't you go away on a holiday to somewhere nice,' she said, 'instead of making smart remarks? You're doing nothing.'

But I'd only been waiting to astound her. 'I can't go anywhere,' I said, 'I'm receiving four goats to mind on Friday.'

'You're *what?*' Min said incredulously.

'And a pig the vet wouldn't pass the last time. Underweight. A depressed pig. It's the charity Andy Sutton works for – they give Irish animals to families in the Third World who have nothing. It means the family can earn money and send their children to school. These ones are waiting to go.'

'Do they send them in twos?'

'The rabbits they do, but I won't be keeping rabbits – rabbits don't need a lairage. That's what your place is now: it's formally been turned into a lairage. Andy says Stoneytown is the ideal place. It's only seventy minutes from Rosslare Harbour and there's no other animals here that might contaminate them. And there's plenty of grass. Andy fixed it up.'

'Well I never! Andy, of all people! Will you be paid?'

'No, I won't be paid!' I said crossly. 'It's a charity, Min. But it's great. I like animals – I think the Creator had a wonderful time inventing them. If there is a Creator.'

'The Creator created people too, Rosie. You're not Saint Francis, you know. You don't have to spend your whole time with animals. And it's not safe out there, not for a woman your age.'

'That's the point!' I said triumphantly. 'That's why Andy did it! It got me hooked up, so it did – temporarily, but who cares? There's a cable now from the camp to the house and up the lane as far as the woods. There's three switches in the house. I'll have pumped water. I have a toaster.'

'God almighty!' she said, awestruck. 'A toaster in the old house! Where did you put it? There's nowhere to put it.'

'Where would you put it?' I asked, well aware that it wasn't long till she'd be back, criticising everything in sight. 'There's a shelf beside—'

'Where's Tessa these days?' she cut across me sharply.

'Tessa's in Dublin, doing her counselling. She's coming down soon.'

'And Andy?'

'Andy's out at the well this very minute, putting in the pump. But he's on his way to Dublin, too.'

Min is not the only person in our family who doesn't necessarily tell the other person what they want to know.

I wouldn't mind a poker game myself, I thought, after I rang off. It seemed to take a long time to make it home from the phone-box because I avoided the darkening woods by coming back the roundabout way, through the old camp and then up onto the ridge above the Milbay estuary. The dog was snuffling to and fro in its paradise of rabbit smells and I wasn't going to hurry her. Instead I threw my head back to follow the drama going on in the great arc of sky above us. The first stars were out, but small and determined clouds were moving into position as if they had been sent to extinguish them, and by the time I was at the bottom of the slope and going through the yard, they had done their work. Had taken for themselves the high empyrean and its ice-white light and sealed us below on earth under a ceiling of soft cloud, which rippled as a small breeze rose up, and a mild rain silently began to fall.

It was a good night in the house, though the dog was made uneasy by the electric light. I'd have to purchase lampshades.

'The ambiance has become quite urban, all of a sudden,' I remarked to her. 'And do you notice the new sounds? The kettle gathering steam? The click of that moth against the light bulb?'

I ate with an unfamiliar neatness, now that I could see what I was doing. And, last thing, boiled a kettle of water and brought the basin out in front of the range to wash myself.

But as I turned off all the switches and checked the dog's bowls, the pain I'd been trying to ignore broke through.

I went upstairs then and climbed heavily into bed and lay on my side with my fists over my face and tried, as hard as I had ever tried, to be accepting.

Was it never to be, then? Was it all over? Why was it all over for me? Why? How could it be that it was over, the sucking and whispering, the fleshy languor that slowly took on speed, the hungry mouth on skin, the bone of shoulders, hips, the dark body-shape rearing up above me, against the light? How could I bear it if it never happened again? And maybe it never would. There might be no one ever again. Maybe this was it. A glimpse. That sudden heat immediately stifled. Never again to splay on a crumpled sheet, unashamed, kissing in joy and gratitude.

Just because of age! I jumped from the bed and stuck my tear-stained face into the mirror and grabbed my hair and yanked it back from my forehead. There! There! Grey at the roots. Is it just because of that? Just because of that?

On Tuesday Andy brought the goats over. The first thing I thought about them was how if the wind shifted around to the west, their smell would hit the house and that would be the end of gracious living. They were the most ancient-looking living things I'd ever been anywhere near. I was amazed that beings so distant would do anything at all for humans. And yet they were got out of the truck and into the near field without a bother. Andy had been out there all day putting up a barbed wire fence, except for lunchtime when we ate our sandwiches with the door open to the calls of the wading birds whose feet left delicate hieroglyphics along the mudflats. Gulls floated into a wind just strong enough to hold them immobile against the blue sky. A few inches from the threshold, the delicate wagtails were bobbing away, and beyond them a pair of robins watched for crumbs with bright eyes. I pointed them out to Andy. Weren't the eyes just like Min's?

He told me that goats are the most welcome of all the animals No-Need sends out, because as well as being providers of milk and meat they clear scrub. I told him a little-known fact, that barbed wire was invented by a nun. He said the nun must have been trying to keep goats.

Then he went off and came back, this time with a large pig in a crate in the back of the truck. My first pig.

She wasn't even a big pig, but I immediately christened her Mother Ireland, though I knew no one around was likely to get the joke.

Andy told me to keep an eye on her, but she didn't seem in the least disturbed by arriving at her new home. Nevertheless, instead of doing any of the jobs I needed to do, I hung around the yard all afternoon, watching the dog quivering with intent as she crouched on the flagstones where a corner of the yard had been blocked off with planks to make a kind of sty for the pig. In the sty, Mother-I was lying on her side, snuffling peaceably. The wagtails, stiff and briskly nodding, like diplomats, busied themselves around her. At last the dog leapt onto the wall and, in a few quick steps, jumped down into the sty. I ran forward to separate the animals but to my astonishment found the dog spreading herself out along the dirty-pink flank of the pig, who gave a few surprised oinks, after which they both fell into sleep.

If only a man and a woman could lie down together as easily!

I was still a bit disturbed by the moment with Andy on the shore the previous week. As if there were something tragicomic about it – the sudden flash of animal truth, as immediately denied. What if it had been his penis that had been glimpsed, rather than my breasts? I'd definitely have remembered it. I'd automatically have 'placed' him as it were – I mean, I might've thought, Wow, that's small, or Wow, that's big, or Wow, that's crooked; I'd have thought *something*. And he must have done a similar compare and contrast on my breasts. And I couldn't say I minded. The truth was that walking along with the towel over the worst of my tummy, and the rest of me glistening with water, was probably as good as it was ever going to get. I mean, if I'd been dry, he might have seen the blackish pigment spots that were collecting between my breasts and on the skin below my neck. Not to mention a horrible little transparent tag of flesh, like something that'd grow on the roof of a cave, which had recently appeared on my neck itself.

It was having any reference at all to sexuality, in my relationship with Andy, that was upsetting me. It just wasn't right. I'd never thought about it before, but now that I did I had to recognise that in the unlikely event of being naked with Andy Sutton, I would have many problems with becoming excited. The first one might well be hot flushes. Not only were they bad enough in themselves, beginning with painful prickles in the soles of my feet and swelling upward to engulf the whole of me in a tsunami of sweaty heat, but I also needed to recover from them. For they also rolled through the inside of my head, leaving it, it seemed to me, a blank, yellow space. They took up *time*. I might be able, after a while and if he stroked me, to become warm and wet inside – the Creator had been quite good about that. Even hotel porn movies had their effect. But I would never be able to melt unless I knew I were melting him.

And how on earth could I take a melted Andy with the seriousness you need for lovemaking? I'd be embarrassed for him. I'd be put right off. I didn't like it when his face got sloppy after a few drinks, never mind anything more. And what if he started talking? Saying things that were supposed to be erotic and instructing me to do this and that to him? I'd die.

And yet... His hands on the water pump were so competent.

And where was I going to find any man to make love with if I didn't find one at home? How high could I set the bar? When I came back from Macerata after that last awful visit to Leo, I swore that I'd never again go with a man unless I was sure he wanted to be with me. But where was this entirely new, magically perfect lover supposed to come from? I was a woman of mature years, living in Dublin with her aunt. I couldn't realistically expect to set conditions for lovers.

18

The man in the Milbay hardware shop was trying to figure out how many yards of LED lighting I needed. Enough anyway to snake it out the window over the sink in Kilbride that was always open for Bell, and winding it through the last of the Petunias, stick it with duct tape on the wall of the yard to read WELCOME HOME MIN.

'I don't think I can oblige Her Majesty,' the man said – the two of us still fell around laughing at my Marie Antoinette joke. 'Your humble servant hasn't got anything that'd stretch that far.'

Just then the door crashed open and the same old man came in who'd told me about Stoneytown in the garda barracks months earlier.

'Bad cess to whatever bastard put in the sewer-pipe in this town,' he proclaimed. 'The whole fuckin' system is backed up again.'

'That would be a Bailey's job,' the hardware man said.

'Bailey's?' I said. 'Do you remember Bailey's? My grandmother, Mrs Barry, was the bookkeeper there for years.'

'Mrs Snooty Barry!' the old man said, just as the hardware man replied, 'Of course I remember Bailey's; sure Bailey's was going till the Sixties.'

The old man regarded me narrowly.

'Are you not the woman that was in the station there a while back?' he asked. 'The one who said the madman beyond in Stoneytown was your grandfather?'

'That's right!' I said, beaming at him.

'C'mere, Missus. How many grandparents are you looking for? Do you look for one in every place you go?'

'Now Paddy,' the hardware man cautioned.

'Mrs Barry's son was my father. He married my mother,' I said. 'After they met in Peamount. They both had TB, only no one knew she had it; she was just working there in the laundry.'

'Are you telling me,' the old man went on, amazed, 'that Mrs Barry's son married a girl from Stoneytown? Is that what you're trying to tell me?'

'They were Travelling people, really, the Stoneytown people,' the hardware man tried to intercede. 'Or so I always heard. And you never heard of them marrying away from their own.'

'Well, that beats all!' The old man was still astonished. 'I never heard the like. Mrs Barry, that looked down her nose at everyone that went into Bailey's! Mrs Barry had a son married a tinker!'

I consoled myself for my apparent déclassé status with a slice of apricot tart with cream in the Nook; then got online to Markey in the library computer room.

From: RosieB@eirtel.com
To: MarkC@rmbooks.com
Sent: 11.35 a.m.

'Thought' No. 9: Food
Everyone should eat food that's as clean and fresh as possible and not too much of it. That's true all through life.

But a meal itself offers the older person, who may have had to adapt to other people's tastes and timetables for many years, a new pleasure: the pleasure of eating alone. He or she can eat what they like, and above all, when they like: brie and grapes in the middle of the night, bacon and eggs at tea-time, a salad halfway through the morning.

But there's a Golden Rule:

Do Not Let Your Standards Fall.

Lay a proper table.

Have a starter or a dessert as well as your entrée – or two desserts and no entrée!

Have a glass of wine.

Eat when there's something you want to see on TV. Or save the day's newspaper to read with dinner.

Be conscious! Savour your freedom!

(150 words)

Then I googled the weather forecast, the one for fishermen, that I was sure the meteorologists tried harder with. That in turn made me wonder about the weather on the Saturday of my picnic, which I nervously wanted to be perfect in every way. But I went home and refused to let the nervousness grow.

I didn't hear a thing from Markey for several days. Finally, a message arrived:

From: MarkC@rmbooks.com
To: RosieB@eirtel.com
Sent: 3.44 p.m.

I'm sorry, Rosie, to have taken so long to respond to your 'Food' Thought. There was a small financial/professional crisis here last week after the tenants of the apartment above the bookshop disappeared, leaving a tap running in the bathroom, which led to a fall of wet plaster onto some fairly valuable books, etc, etc. I also took the grandkids to Disneyworld last weekend, and after promising them not to bring the laptop, I cheated of course and spent a lot of time in the hotel's Business Centre. You would have spent all the time there.

But Rosie, I have to tell you that you're back-sliding.

This eating alone stuff is completely alien to the average American. Solodining.com, for example, is one of many websites for singles which offer help with eating by yourself because they assume that if you're on your own you need help.

And did you know that something called the Virtual Family Dinner will be a reality in many kitchens in 3 to 5 years time? The technology is almost there. I saw this in the AARP journal for elderly people – how they've nearly perfected a system whereby a computer, once it sees Mom preparing to serve food, 'automatically looks up a directory of extended family members to find someone who might be available to chat, and then projects that person's life-size image onto the screen…'

The kind of thing you need to say is, 'Try This Stay-Young Food Plan!' What people want is not so much food as gourmet conversation pieces. A lot of our neighbours, for example, are into flaxseeds. No way are flaxseeds food. They wouldn't read either while they eat because (a) they don't much like reading and (b) they have to remember to chew each mouthful thirty times so as not to eat too much in order to (c) not have the rest of their lives ruined by growing F*T.

F*T is what matters. You cannot recommend dessert. I know people do eat dessert, but they wish they didn't.

From: RosieB@eirtel.com
To: MarkC@rmbooks.com
Sent: 4.05 p.m.

Do it yourself Smarty-Pants, if you're so smart. I don't care, we haven't even got a contract. I have a whole birthday party to prepare.

And I do not want to seem in any way to support the fat-fascists who police the American people.

So boo sucks to you.

Rosie

The summer was already on the turn when Min and I spoke the following Saturday, and I noted it was that bit darker by the time I got to the phone-box. I began by tactfully approaching the issue of social class, as touched on, to say the least, in the hardware shop. But she wasn't interested. She wanted to talk about her new friends. There was Luz, of course, and Bud next door who always gave Luz a lift when she had to go to the hospital about her breathing, and there was Helen and Lou, and Maya who was 'Hispanic' – a word I never thought to hear pass Min's lips – and Maya's 'partner' – another new word – Tuk, but Tuk's people were Inuits and he was away on his fishing boat most of the time, though when he was a boy he grew tomatoes, even though the weather was terrible where he came from. And there were her friends from the Catholic church, too, and those from the pub.

I found myself thinking, as Min talked on, about all the people all over the world I'd known and liked and loved. And who I didn't know any more, though I'd been the one who until the last drifting-apart had emailed and sent birthday cards. One night in a pub in Sydney, I'd finally registered how much you have to pay for not joining the majority. A couple who'd been my buddies when I taught there five years earlier had had a child since I last saw them, and now they'd gone home early – even though they had a babysitter, and even though I'd booked a special dinner to celebrate our seeing each other again.

If I'd put more care into thinking about them and their present life, I told myself, I'd have known a whole evening away from the child was too much to ask. But they hadn't stopped to imagine me, either. It hadn't occurred to them how there was nothing I could do, once they were gone, but sit on in the pub and mourn.

'But your American friends aren't real friends,' I interrupted Min, because I was envious, and because her newfound confidence suddenly seemed perilous. 'They won't be like Reeny. They haven't even got houses. They have lives of their own – you couldn't rely on them.'

'I know,' she said. 'Sure didn't you come home? Stands to reason you wouldn't have come home, had you somewhere you were enjoying yourself more.'

I stopped myself from whining: Are you not glad I came home? Are you not grateful? 'You're my aunt,' I said instead as lightly as I could manage. 'You're my only living relative. You're supposed to think well of me. It isn't because I'm not popular that I don't have all that many friends. Lots of people were very fond of me. There are people who are fond of me all over the world. I just never settled…'

'It's all to come for you, Rosaleen,' she said, speaking suddenly in that same voice of love and comfort I'd heard the night she cured my earache. 'Wait'll you're my age and you'll have your own gang, too. You're only a wee girl, still.'

And with that she switched back into the superior tone she always took with my current Robinson Crusoe existence.

'The well?' she cried. 'Give me a tap any day! But all the same, that's water like they don't make any more.

It's a holy well too, you know, I forget what saint. The old women thought – you know the way old women go on with their oul' nonsense, not that it was their fault, they'd never been anywhere – anyhow the old women thought the well water would stop a baby dying, but an awful lot of them did die.'

A car went past with its lights on, striking the trees that were so dark here, and writhing tonight in a cold wind.

'Do you think it's too windy for me to grow tomatoes?' I asked, to keep her on the line.

'How would I know?' she said. 'Don't ask me! I never had a tomato in my hand till I was fifteen. We had to eat seaweed, would you believe that? We worked worse than slaves. Have you ever picked seaweed in a broken pair of your father's boots, slipping and sliding, and tearing your hands and knees and ankles on the rocks in the rain? *Sleabhcan*, it was called. That was the harvest we got. Seaweed. I must tell Luz. Thank God I never thought of that for years. There's two things I learned about gathering *sleabhcan*: how to do it, and how to forget I ever did.'

She started to say goodbye. That she was going with Luz to a craft fair where everything was made out of wood.

'Either wood or whales,' she said importantly. 'Every single thing.'

'How do you mean, made out of whales?'

'I'm not sure which part of a whale,' she said, losing a bit of confidence.

'Well, I hope the whales don't smell,' I said. 'There's

the carcass of a badger just beside where I leave the car, in that bit of overgrown quarry just the other side of the hill from the house.'

'I know that cave,' Min said, 'that's where we used to leave our sacks. Every woman stuffed her own sack with hay or bits of heather to sit on while we were cracking the quarry stones.'

'That was a good idea...' I began.

'If you took another woman's sack, she'd go for you. There were terrible women there. I saw them rake each other's faces with their nails, or trip or push each other down onto the rocks and kick.'

'Oh!' I winced.

'Once in winter I saw some of them drench another woman's sack in a puddle so that it froze into ice overnight, and when she went to the quarry in the morning they beat her around the head with it till the blood ran down.'

'They loved a fight,' she said, as if it were a perfectly natural thing to say. 'Even if there was no trouble with the sacks, the women sometimes still fought like devils and the men would shout them on.'

'Oh, Min!' I breathed in dismay.

The dog was pressed against the side of the box, willing me to come out.

'Oh I know,' she said. 'They were bad oul' days sure enough. But if you're from a place ... if everyone knows your people. Like the women there, they were very rough women but they knew my mother and her mother. They had great memories too, most of them. They could tell you every word of a film even if they only saw it twice. We always sat on for to see the films twice. The man in the cinema was raging, but once when he got the guards, they said he couldn't throw us out. There was no law against staying there all day.'

She was still laughing reminiscently when she said goodnight.

'Come, Love!' I called to the dog. 'Please stay near me!'

We slipped through the fence and trotted through the woods as fast as we could.

Had my grandmother fought other women and stood there panting with her face covered in mud and splinters of ice and blood?

Had my mother?

The third and final Saturday I was jiggling with impatience, waiting for her call. It was a warm evening, with swallows darting and skidding across the road, but once again the childish pinks and blues of the late summer sky were succumbing to dark drifts of cloud. Why did the County Council put a phone-box in such a lonely place, tucked in here behind a half-moon of grass gone to seed, under a hawthorn hedge full of rustlings? I imagined the birds preparing to tuck their heads under their wings to sleep. And I was tired myself, having run the whole way – over the hill and along the track and across the meadow and through the beech woods – in sudden panic that Min might ring early.

The dog moved off to snap at the bees still working away in the weeds, while I propped the door of the box open and watched the bell – a round, metal bell, wired to the ceiling – which would vibrate for a split second before the ring began. *Ferruginous* was what Proust's translator called the sound of the bell that announced Swann's arrival. Could you use that word for any metal, I idly wondered, or would it have to be iron?

The bell moved and I grabbed the handset. 'Hello, Min? Min! I have something amazing to tell you about the Point!'

But first I made her wait: by telling her in laborious detail how I'd gone into the Spar supermarket in Milbay – which is where Bailey's used to be – and Nana Barry's flat had disappeared, too. And how when I was walking past the window of the ESB place on my way to the library, I'd stopped and made a hideous face, sticking out my tongue at the kettles, and lamps and fridges because no way had I forgotten the engineer who wouldn't give me electricity.

'Hope he saw me!' I told her.

'Is that what you have to tell me?'

'No. Wait. Remember I was telling you about reading about Stoneytown in the library? And finding out that the people who were moved into Milbay then gradually disappeared, and maybe some of them went to America because the fellow that crashed his plane was a Yank and he invited them?'

'Of course I remember! Is that what you're making a song and dance about telling me?

'*Wait*, will you?'

'According to my research, there was a photo in the *Milbay Herald*. However, the trouble was there hasn't been a *Milbay Herald* newspaper for donkey's years. Well,

I found the *Herald* archive! The woman on the library desk has got to know me, I've been hanging around the place so much that she let me go down to the basement to search for myself. And Min, there's a photo! I never thought I'd see a photo of Stoneytown! There's a fella with a crew-cut in a flying-suit, holding his helmet, with a big grin all over his face. And the background is very blurry, though there's loads of people there; but in front of him are children, hanging on to him, all around his legs. I can't make them out very well; they're just barefoot children with a blur for a face and black smudges for eyes, but you'd know which one was you!'

'Well!' Min said, sounding as if she were completely at a loss. 'Well! Oh my God! The airplane man!'

'And there's a caption underneath the photo in the actual newspaper. Are you listening?'

'Of course I'm listening!'

'*"Mr Charles 'Ginger' Novitzky of Duluth, USA,'* I began reading from my notebook, '*"was a welcome if unexpected guest in Milbay this week when his aeroplane on a training flight from Prestwick developed engine trouble and the intrepid airman was compelled to land his apparatus on grassland to the east of Trumbull's Woods, a manoeuvre which was watched with the utmost interest by a crowd assembled on Milbay Quay."* So, I've a request in to try to locate the original photo,' I ended proudly, 'so as to get a good copy.'

'Read that out to me again,' Min said after a pause. I think her voice was trembling, but you can't be sure at six thousand miles.

I read it again.

'That's right,' she said slowly. 'Ginger. That's right.

Your ma and me slept with our ma in the bed up in the loft, and the airman slept in the settle bed and our father slept in the chair. But they didn't sleep much – my father took out the poteen and I could hear them talking away. Talking about the war. Was your mother in the photo? Your mother thought he was like something out of the pictures—'

'I don't know, Min. You tell me when you come home. I don't know what she looked like.'

'Read it out to me again.'

I did.

And suddenly she told me the story she'd never told me.

'Your ma got America into her head and I think she got it from that fella. The way he came down out of the sky. She had to run anyway because she heard one of the women say the next year when our mother died that whoever got Noreen Barry would inherit a fine house, so she knew they'd soon begin to make a match for her. So she began to steal coins from the coats of the men who played cards in our father's house, one or two every time, and kept them in a cigarette box that had a picture of a river on the front. God love her, she thought she had enough to go to America the day she ran off. We were after seeing *Mister Deeds Goes to Town* and she was mad to go there herself. Anyway, I helped her. I brought her good skirt and her hat and a fresh cake of bread to the woods where she had a bag hidden in a hollow tree-trunk and she got the bus to Dublin, no bother. But I thought she was in America, those next years. I didn't know till my father told me to go up to

Dublin to mind her baby that she wasn't there. That she was never there.'

We were both silent. It was dark outside now and I wanted to cry.

After a while Min asked me how were the goats faring and how was the dog – but her heart wasn't in it. She said she'd talk to me same time next Saturday and I said there was no next Saturday – that next Saturday she'd be home because it'd be the day of the party. And then we said goodnight and goodbye and mind yourself and God bless, and that was that.

I walked back by the road and the track. Clouds thin as wood smoke drifted evasively past the moon and collected at the borders of the silent sky. I saw that the evening star had come out, a lone point of light at the edge of the vault. The same star that always seemed to me to be sending out a universal signal – Hello? Hello? Is there any other star out there to keep me company? Poor Keats. 'Bright star, would I were steadfast as thou art…' He bitterly regretted not having made love to his girl before he became ill. But you go on regretting, of course, even when you don't die young.

The dog brushed against my leg – as if something must have frightened her. If Leo had had so much as a dog, I suddenly thought. But Leo had nothing except the inside of his head, and nobody except his sons whom he hardly ever saw.

I tried to put humanity in perspective. Looked up earnestly to try to see things from the stars' point of view – to grasp my unimportance, Leo's unimportance, and everyone else's, compared to the cold, immense distances of space. But though I knew that the universe was indifferent to me, I could not make myself feel that indifference. I could not help but be warmed by the natural world, even if it was cold. I liked it that the dog asked for my protection. I liked the dark silhouette of the woods. I liked it that the shapes around me were familiar shapes. I took pleasure from the way the lines of white foam, where waves were rolling onto the shore, seemed purposeful simply because they were bright things moving with regularity in the dark.

And I couldn't believe that what I did or didn't do was of no consequence, even though I knew that the universe couldn't care less. What I did about Leo had to matter. It just couldn't be right to leave someone to rot away by himself on the Adriatic coast of Italy. People contact each other all the time. Soon enough it would be winter.

On Monday morning, Andy and the vet turned up to have a look at Mother Ireland.

'Not a thing wrong with her,' the vet said, when he was having a mug of tea. 'She's going to make a lot more people happy when she's dead than she ever did alive.'

'Ah no,' I said. 'She makes me happy. She makes the dog and the cat happy.'

He glanced at me, and I saw him take in a middle-aged woman with a month's grey roots, wearing canvas deck shoes worn through at the big toe, saying a sentimental thing. I saw him deciding not to bother to comment. Which made me appreciate Andy, who smiled at me and gently said, 'They all have to go before the winter, Rosie. Anything that isn't shipped out in the last load has to be slaughtered.'

'When's the last load?'

I'd thought maybe late October. Even early November. I knew Andy went to Africa with No-Need during the winter to teach people who received the live-stock how to manage it. I knew he and Pearl had their Christmas celebration, when he took her to dinner in the fanciest place in Dublin and they opened their presents, some weeks before real Christmas.

But I received a shock when he said, 'Round about the beginning of October. Maybe even sooner.'

I looked at him but he was looking away, out at the sea.

'Don't take her away till then!' I begged, though I knew the vet was standing there, contemptuous.

There was a pause, during which the vet closed up his little case with an aggressive snap.

'OK. No harm to leave her when she's doing so well,' Andy said. And then, as if to cover over his indulgence, he said, 'No-Need has been invited into Laos. A pair of rabbits can send a whole family of kids to school there. I have to have the shots next week.'

Laos.

'C'mon, Rose,' Andy broke the silence that had hung on after the vet bustled off. 'Follow me as far as Milbay and we'll have a cup of coffee in the Nook before I head off.'

I saw the dog's little forefeet disappear from the

crack in the door jamb as we got up to go, where she'd been anxiously watching for clues as to who was staying and who was not. She hated anyone to know she was watching and thought I couldn't see her, never grasped that a leg or a tail sufficed, even when I couldn't see her face.

'I wonder what will become of Min's place, all the same,' Andy said in the coffee bar. 'All the land around me at home in Carlow is going for housing, and why wouldn't Milbay be the same? But maybe she'll want to keep it when she sees it?'

'Min hates Stoneytown,' I said. 'She hates history, as a matter of fact. She doesn't think there should be a past. I bet she doesn't know that the States were once owned by England or anything else about them, and that suits her down to the ground. I just hope she'll settle down when she comes home after all her traipsing around. I hope she won't fall sick again.'

'How do you mean, sick?' he said.

'She wouldn't eat. She wouldn't get up.'

'Maybe she wasn't well...'

I looked at him until his eyes fell.

'Alright,' he said grudgingly. 'She was becoming too fond of a drink as well.'

'She wouldn't talk to me!' I cried.

Andy amazed me then by picking up my hand and holding the palm tenderly to his cheek for a second.

'Poor Rosie,' he murmured. 'Sure there was nothing wrong there that couldn't be got better. She's a great woman, Min is, and you're a great woman, and the best of nieces, only you worry too much. And pay attention to what I say for once in your life, because I know a lot about women.'

I watched him walk away, a thin, quick, ordinary man who fitted in exactly with the people coming and going in this little Irish town. A fundamentally mysterious man, though most times I could read him like a book. I knew, for example, that he'd arranged to have the vet there when he told me about Laos, so that whatever my reaction, I'd have to be restrained. I knew there was something more than that on his mind, too. He hadn't asked me to follow him all the way to Milbay to have a general chat. But whatever it was, he'd decided not to say it.

There he was, starting up the steps to the car park. Wearing exactly the same forgettable clothes as everyone else, and balding, like all the other nearly sixty-four-year-old men around. How come so many American men of the same age had full heads of hair? All those senators, with their lovely heads of white hair. It could hardly be the milk, could it?

On impulse, I went up to the library and stood close behind a girl browsing the *Friends* website, breathing heavily until she relinquished the computer, and I managed to make it print out a note I'd written to Leo. The woman behind the desk gave me a brown envelope and stamp and slipped the letter in with the library's urgent outgoing mail, while I dropped a euro into the collecting box on the counter. For the homeless. Which Leo, of course, was.

Milbay / Kilbride. Telephone 1-387-3896.

My dear Leo,

I sent you a message in June about the place I've been camping in this summer – the old house that my grand-father built on the tip of a peninsula on the south-east coast, where he used to be the overseer of a quarry. I've been happier there than I've ever been anywhere in my life (though, do you remember the little house in the sand dunes near Ostend? That was a happy place, too, wasn't it?). But the idyll is coming to an end. The place is the property of my aunt and she has no interest in it and above all she wants the money it will undoubtedly fetch.

However, to celebrate my aunt's return from the USA, and to express my gratitude for the wonderful summer I've had, and to gather my friends (and to mark a birthday, though it's not an important one), I'm going to give a little picnic lunch at the house on the 5th of September (death of Flaubert) – a Hibernian fête champêtre.

Is there any chance, Leo, that you'd be free and feel well enough to come over? There are direct Ancona–Dublin flights at this time of year and I've just looked them up and there's one with lots of seats on the 3rd. They're also ridiculously cheap, so I've paid for an Ancona–Dublin flight in your name (details attached). But THERE'S NO PROBLEM if you don't use it.

I know how little you go about these days, and I'm nervous at asking you even to consider the idea. But it would mean a lot to me to have you here. I misunderstood matters, the time we met in Macerata; I hadn't realised that the time has come for us to have a different kind of friendship from what we had before. But I do want a friendship, if you feel the same way. And I could put you up in Kilbride in my aunt's house – she's away till the day of the picnic.

If you come, bring your ombrello – piove sempre, *as you said the time you were in Dublin when we borrowed Tessa's house.*

Ring my Dublin number and I'll pick up the message from a coin phone here. (There is no phone service in Stoneytown.)

But very, very good wishes, whatever you decide.
Rosie

19

First thing on Tuesday morning, I rang Tessa and humbly asked her to come down to help me with the party. She was Miss Efficient, after all. And there were a few matters on which I needed her advice. My bottom, for example, was beginning to stick out and I'd end up looking like the Venus of Willendorf if it didn't stop. Was there anything I could do about that? And what was the story with chocolate? I never bothered with chocolate all my life, but just two nights ago I'd actually walked all the way to the car in the dark to drive to the petrol station for chocolate. Still, if she as much as used the words 'overweight' or 'diet' I'd undoubtedly want to hit her.

She was just like herself. 'Sure I'll come down,' she said. 'Parties were never your strong point.'

'It has to be perfect, Tess,' I said. 'I want it to be like the end of *The Marriage of Figaro*. And I want Min to be so charmed and impressed by Stoneytown that she won't sell it.'

'Who's coming, to begin with?'

'Well, Leo might be.'

'That's all we need for a great time! Doctor Death himself.'

322

I controlled myself with a deep breath. 'And I want something pleasant and good to happen where our poor ancestors had to live such awful lives. I want the place to be a different place from when Min was young – even from when the dog was young, because the dog is probably a descendant of a quarry dog and even...'

'Have you a fridge down there, more to the point?' she interrupted.

'And even leaving the quarry workers out of it, I want the theme of my celebration to be the same as Mozart's comedies.'

She tried to let that pass, but curiosity got the better of her. 'Oh, yes?' she said vaguely.

'Forgiveness,' I explained.

So, three days before the picnic, as I came out to the yard to give Mother Ireland some dandelion greens, I heard a yell from above and there she was, making her way down the ridge in her pointy-toed, high-heeled boots, carrying enough bags and boxes to open a store.

'Andy gave me directions and a key to the gate,' she beamed at me. 'Wow!'

It was like the Mediterranean that day, and she must have thought as much, looking around at the sunlit yard, at the little leaves, like twists of green crêpe paper, on the gnarled old apple trees, and the blue of the sea on the horizon.

'It beats Corsica hollow,' she said, 'that's for sure. And the whole place is great for a party. But what has you inviting Leo? I mean, won't Andy be here? He's always here when I'm looking for him.'

'He is not. But even if he were, what of it?'

I love how open her face is. Chagrin and amusement were vying with each other across it now, and it was like seeing the two states in their purest form.

'I want to know how you put up with it,' she said, 'if he's courting you.'

I must have gaped at her.

'I want to know how you cope with the boredom, Rosie,' she continued on, going a bit red, but determined. 'I'm not a bookworm like you, but even then he doesn't know what I'm talking about. He's never read a book, as far as I can see, except about being your own vet. He's never heard of Mitterrand or Lou Reed or Solzhenitsyn – well that's not fair, Solzhenitsyn, OK – but he's never heard of Andy Warhol or James Connolly or Seamus Heaney or Billy Joel. He doesn't like the telly. He says he's always in Africa or has jobs to do around the house or the farm so he hasn't the time to spare, and so only reads a paper on a Sunday. But that leaves us nothing to talk about. Like, I'd love to go to Tuscany and I'd love to go with a man, but when I said it to Andy he replied, "Where's this now Tuscany is?"'

She was spluttering now with several kinds of tension.

'Andy was the only prospect I've got, and I'm very fond of him and always have been, and we get on great about everything except talking. But now he's hanging around you, and I just can't believe it. You! I mean, I bore you, and I'm not that bad. But Andy wouldn't even know. I mean, you've had more men than I've had hot breakfasts. You've been around—'

'Hang on!' I cried. 'It's ten in the morning, so we can't start drinking, but let's have a pot of strong tea. We have to calm down.'

So we made tea and brought it back out, and opened the petits fours that were supposed to be for the party. Bell crept out of whatever cranny she'd been hiding in and sipped from a saucer of milk.

'Why would you like to go with a man?' I asked Tessa.

'Go where?'

'You just said. Tuscany, for example.'

'Oh,' she said, slowing down and looking up at me uncertainly. 'You know. The usual. After a good lunch, and all that.' Then she said hurriedly, to cover up, 'And the way people look at you if you're with another woman. Two oul' biddies is what they think.'

'But would Andy want to – I mean, lunch or no lunch…'

'I thought you'd know that,' she said. I looked at her suspiciously but she wasn't sneering.

'I've never as much as exchanged a peck on the cheek with your cousin,' I said loftily, leaving out the kiss I'd given him at my makeshift table over getting the electricity.

'Yes,' she said, fixing me with her honest eyes. 'But what do you think?'

She was my loyal friend, so I didn't bother making the return of 'what did I think about what?'

'I think he's wonderfully tender for a man; you've only to see him with a cat or a dog. But I don't know whether tenderness is what you want.'

'Is it what you want?'

'What I want ?' I looked around and took a big gulp of tea. Then drawing breath, I said, 'What I want is a lover who is a good man, a man who cares about me, who likes me and enjoys me and who likes Min and you and Peg and dogs and cats and who loves Ireland. And I want him to be a bit remote as well and very, very good at managing life and fundamentally detached so that I never think I own him, and absorbed in whatever it is he does, but open to new experience and such a good fit with my way of looking at things that we talk till we fall asleep and wake up laughing and kissing. More than kissing.'

'Do you by any chance want him to be good-looking as well?' Tessa asked after a pause.

'Yes!' I shouted. 'And to be vigorously but sensitively heterosexual, and to have had no woman before me, including no mother now I come to think of it, and of course no children.'

'Money?' she said.

'I'm not that bothered about money,' I said.

'That's OK then,' she said. 'You shouldn't have any trouble finding someone.'

We laughed so hard then we nearly rolled about on the flagstones, and Bell took off again, disgusted.

We made a great team, cleaning the house. The best tip, of course, for when things are bad was: 'Give Something a Thorough Clean'. I left Tessa to work by herself while I found the pink notebook and wrote that down. In fact, I was so turned on by the instantaneous psychological effect that housework has that I packed all the cleaning stuff into a box to do a spring clean in Kilbride when I went up to Dublin next day.

We went to bed early, and the dog snuffled down ecstatically between our backs and Bell spread out on the pillow beside me and stuck her tail practically up my nose. We'd exhausted ourselves cleaning every inch of the house and yard, and Tess had barely said goodnight before she was asleep. I said a '*My soul doth magnify the Lord*' to thank Whoever or Whatever there might be for the great good fortune of sleeping beside a friend and dear animals to the sound of the slow sea. Many, many times in my life I wouldn't have believed that I would ever be so lucky.

But one thing kept pulling me back into wakefulness.

Cleaning out all the apertures of the iron range had set us to talking about the housework the women of earlier generations had done, which led in turn to talking about Andy's devotion to his mother. But then Tessa had happened to remark – and I was struck, because she usually refused to admit that any action could bear any analysis – that all the same, he never let his mother speak.

'She does all her talking when he's not there. You watch her, Rosie, next time you're with the two of them. You know she's very emotional and she exaggerates a bit and nobody minds because she's such a decent old soul? But he minds, and he has her scared to open her mouth whenever he's there.'

'How do you mean, scared? He's the softest man I ever knew.'

'He is with us. But with her he just grunts when she

asks him something, and he doesn't answer her if she tells him anything about what she's feeling or asks him anything about what he's feeling. The most he does is grunt. So then she gets the message and shuts up, or she lets him talk about what mileage the car should be doing, or what the weather'll be like tomorrow.'

'But he wouldn't be like that with a wife, would he?' I asked. I'd had bosses all over the world who wouldn't allow women to use their own language and undermined their confidence by taking away their fluency and making them speak like men. 'Not if she was someone with a life of her own.'

'It depends, doesn't it?' Tess said. 'Wouldn't it depend on whether he thought he owned the wife? It could bring a person down, that,' she ended, thoughtfully.

'Yeah,' I said. 'It could make a person more lonely than just their lover not knowing who Salman Rushdie is.'

'Who's Salman Rushdie?' she said.

And we went back to laughing.

The following morning we went for a swim, Tessa in a proper suit, me in panties and a T-shirt. After, we boiled a couple of eggs in the electric kettle for breakfast. Then we finishing planning the menu for Saturday, which would include Tessa's salmon mousse, and a big bowl of summer pudding.

'Raspberries for sauce,' I said to her. 'Remind me. Frozen will do fine. And cream. Sunday'll be time enough to start thinning down.'

Then we left food and water for the dog and after

putting Bell in her travelling basket we tripped over the ridge.

'All we need is dirndl skirts and we could be the Von Trapp girls,' I remarked, to which Tessa pointed out that the hills were, in fact, alive with the sound of music, the morning so still that we could hear a Beatles song playing somewhere across in Milbay. '*I wanna hold your hand …*'

'Still powerful, isn't it?' I said to her, but she wasn't listening.

'I don't know what you see in him,' she said, and I knew who she was thinking about. 'But then no one ever knows what anyone sees in anyone.'

'I know what they see in George Clooney,' I said.

'Fair point,' Tess said.

I watched Leo walk slowly into the Arrivals hall in a beautiful linen suit that instantly marked him out as not Irish. It made my heart tighten with pity, that a man so recently commanding could have so quickly become so frail. And he was only five years older than me! He carried nothing but an overnight bag and a briefcase, but still he seemed weighed down, and I squeezed under the barrier to run forward to help him. He held me away from him for a moment to scan me. Then he bent and said quietly, 'I am so pleased, always, to see your bright face.'

I could not return the compliment, but I leaned up on tiptoe and rested my lips against his. His appeal had never had anything to do with vitality – though maybe it was because he was so inexpressive on every other level that he had managed to pursue a silent, erotic life with such amazing focus and intensity. But I'd always thought him beautiful in an old-fashioned way; I'd always thought he had the same kind of distinguished style as Ingrid Bergman's husband in *Casablanca*, a thing I never said to him, first of all because it was perfectly possible that he'd never seen the movie, and second because we never did say anything personal to each other. We were as polite as colleagues, as if what we revealed of ourselves in bed rendered any other kind of statement redundant.

But the bed years were over. And up close I saw again what I'd seen in Macerata: that though his skin was tanned and his fine hair impeccably groomed, and he smiled and murmured as he always did, the half-moons under his eyes were even more puffy and blue-tinged. He was not a well man.

'I'm so glad you came!' I said, as I led him out, and I couldn't have meant the words more.

On several languid evenings in Stoneytown, I'd gone back over rooms I'd lived in, and people I'd known and lovers I'd trembled at, who were now gone out of my life as completely as if they'd sunk beneath the waves with Atlantis. That there was a great chance now this would not happen to Leo and me felt like a precious thing, even with the passion drained from our relationship. I had a chance, now, to make something out of what had always before come to nothing.

'How many years since I was here?' he said, lifting his head and smiling at the boisterous Irish wind and the sky full of scurrying clouds. 'One of my very favourite small capitals, in spite of the idiosyncrasies of your brass players…'

A reference, that, to the time three years before, when Tessa lent us the house that had been empty since her parents' deaths, and we went to the only concert in the city that weekend – a performance of Beethoven's Ninth – where the horn player hadn't so much played his solo as wrestled it to the ground and kicked it around. Leo had been fascinated that such a thing could happen. But then, Leo was so orderly that he had an exaggerated regard for its lack.

'Are you hungry?' I asked, as I tucked him into my car and stowed his bag. 'We could go north, to Skerries – there's a simple little place on the harbour where they cook fish straight off the fishing boats.'

'Maybe not drive so much?' he said.

'You're tired, my dear,' I said. 'I can hear it. But it's dinner time and I came straight from the country and there's no food in the Kilbride house. Hey, there's a converted schoolhouse place not more than ten minutes from here where they really know how to cook. Will we try that?'

But when we were queuing to enter the car park at the brightly lit Old Schoolhouse Restaurant he touched my hand and said, 'Maybe not, Rosie. I had something to eat in Zurich. Maybe we'll just have a little picnic, no?'

'Tell you what,' I said. 'We'll call in to the Sorrento on the way home and order fish and chips. How about that? You go in and order them because fresh chips take ten minutes, and I'll put the car away and join you.'

By the time I'd parked the car and dropped his bag into the kitchen and put a match to the fire and walked up to the chipper, he was leaning on the counter, deep in conversation with Enzo. Now I came to think of it, Enzo was a kind of Swiss Italian, from somewhere near Lugano. They each had a glass of Enzo's dreadful red wine in their hands and were gravely discussing its properties, while Enzo's young wife, who in her day had inspired such reckless devotion in Mr Colfer, served the usual crowd of teenagers.

Doctors, they were onto now. Enzo's back. Enzo's back and the pain in it. Enzo's back and the ointment he got his wife to rub into it every night.

'*Food,*' I whispered to Leo. 'I'm starving!'

Enzo heard, and began wrapping two big smoked cods in batter and shovelling chips into bags.

There were *arrivedercis* all around. Leo was to call up any time to try the white. Mrs Enzo was glowering terribly, but the men, shaking hands in farewell, hadn't even noticed.

I liked walking down the street with him, arm in arm, except when one of us burrowed into the bag for another chip. He was as hungry as I was, I noticed. The busy place seemed delightfully peopled after Stoneytown, and every other window we passed revealed what was going on in the front room like one dramatic tableau after another. Various neighbours greeted me and nodded at Leo. Mrs Beckett, who must have been at the vodka, called from her doorstep, 'Who's the fella, Rosie? Is that his pyjamas he's wearing?' But she didn't have her teeth in, so Leo wouldn't have understood her. The lights were on in Reeny's, but I knew she was in Spain, which was just as well or I'd have had her commentary to deal with, too.

'Nice people,' Leo said approvingly. 'And Ireland – I had forgotten. It is so far north that the light is quite different. So odd that there is light in the sky so very late.'

He loved Min's house. I put the fish and chips out on plates and got salt and vinegar and as we ate he looked around at everything, murmuring 'Perfect, perfect', whether the scarlet Busy Lizzie in its china pot, the little blue armchair, the rag hearthrug, the tin dresser, the yellow curtains. But I saw him return to look unsmilingly several times at the stairs, rising steeply beside the fireplace.

In a moment of inspiration I ran in next door to fetch Monty, and together he and I brought my brand-new bed down the stairs, putting it under the back window where there'd be lots of air, if Leo wanted air.

'And just hold on...' I ran upstairs and came back with the fabulous sheets I'd bought in Manhattan after encountering the bed linen in the Harmony Suites. 'There!' I said. 'And look—' I opened the back door onto a sky of rich mottled turquoise, deepening to navy blue. 'There's a toilet here that we put back in for my dad a year or two after the modernising Council took it out. Isn't that handy? What's more, it is not raining. *Non piove sempre.*'

Bell crept in from the yard past my legs.

'Puss, puss,' Leo said politely.

She looked from him to me, from me back to him, then stalked back out. I slammed the door after her so, to let her know she wasn't welcome anyway if she couldn't be pleasant to a guest.

Leo washed the plates and even made instant coffee

– though he practically held his nose, drinking it – after which I brought him down hangers for his suit and his spare trousers. These he hung off the hook behind the door. He then put on his pyjamas and brushed his teeth at the sink, which he then cleaned scrupulously before getting into bed. I read the paper in front of the fire. We were as cosy as an old married couple.

I was standing up to go to bed myself when I remembered something that had been nagging at the back of my mind.

'Leo,' I said, 'did you pay for the fish and chips? Because I didn't.'

So long a silence followed that I turned to look at him. He was sitting up in bed, propped on every pillow I could find, his sombre eyes fixed on me.

'What's wrong?' I said.

He didn't seem able to speak, so I sat on the chair beside the bed and took his hands.

'What's wrong?'

'I have no money, Rosie,' he said.

'You have no money?' I repeated stupidly. My classy man! Three boys at Downside! An adviser to the EU Council of Ministers on cultural matters! 'You don't have the price of *a fish supper*?'

'No. Nothing. If you had not pre-paid my ticket…'

'Oh, no!' I cried out in pain – not about the money, but that I had believed he'd come for my sake.

'*No*, Rosie!' he said, having intuited my dismay. 'I would have had to borrow the money, but I would have come for your birthday in any case, my dear girl! You can't imagine what it meant to me to receive your letter.'

334

Then, visibly mustering all his energy, he whispered, 'I could not bring a suitcase. There was a problem with the lady of the house where I had a room. All I could take was what might fit in my bag, only my notes and the typescript and some CDs because the signora would have seen. Perhaps she will keep my clothes for me, but I think not, as she was very angry. Also, I do not at present know how I would find the money to pay her.'

'But, Leo…'

A horrible thought had come into my head. All the meals and rooms! All the Martinis and cappuccinos! Oh God, the phone bill at the *pensione* that Christmas in Ancona – I had meant to pay him back but I never did.

'How long has it been like this? Since when have you had … this problem?'

'It was not so bad at first,' he began. Then he must have again read my face. 'Don't, Rosa,' he whispered. 'I chose not to explain to you. It was my choice.'

'Is that why you wouldn't go into the Old School-house? But what will become of you?' I said, and held his hands to my lips.

'My wife is a very good mother,' he said, 'and I think maybe she will soon see that she should talk to the father of her children, and when we talk we will arrange something. My wife has always been wealthy, but there are many valuable things in the house in Lucerne that came from my family, which I am entitled to sell. But I have to wait until she speaks. As a husband, I am entirely at fault.'

'But you're not well!'

'I am tired. That's all.'

'Well, stay here! Look how comfortable you are now!

Min, my aunt – remember? – will be back tomorrow and when I explain that you need a rest she'll be the soul of hospitality. And meanwhile…' I rummaged in my bag for my wallet. 'Meanwhile, Leo, here are all the euros I have and I'll take out more tomorrow— '

His eyes were closing. Last thing he mumbled was something about Mozart's father, laughing as he went off into sleep, and thinking, I decided, about the music Leopold wrote for the horn, and what the horn player we'd heard massacring the solo in Beethoven's Ninth would do to it.

From: MarkC@rmbooks.com
To: RosieB@eirtel.com
Sent: 10.04 p.m.

Chico called a few days ago. I think he's having cold feet. He said Celtic moment still out, World moment by now also out, Latin American moment in.

I said we'd have the whole 10 x 150 words to him within the very near future. He said the words didn't matter; what matters is a synopsis he can give to the sales people. They don't read anything else.

Any chance you could send one?

From: RosieB@eirtel.com
To: MarkC@rmbooks.com
Sent: 10.54 p.m.

Ten Thoughts for the Middle of the Journey explores, in an intimate, reader-friendly format, that passage in life's journey when the questions of youth are no longer relevant, and the answers of age are still in the future.

You have reached the rich, fertile plateau of the middle years.

Now Is YOUR Time!

Do you want to use it to advance in wisdom and joy? Then let these deceptively simple 'Thoughts' be your companions.

Read! Reflect! Rejoice!

From: MarkC@rmbooks.com
To: RosieB@eirtel.com
Sent: 11.04 p.m.

You are a genius. I've sent that on to Chico.
Confidently awaiting fame and fortune.
Markey

20

The next morning, Friday, I made mugs of tea for us and sat beside Leo's bed while he drank his, and Bell glared at us from across the room. He kissed my hand when I brought some toast.

Not a bad way to start the eve of your birthday celebration, I thought. I mean, this is a world expert on Brahms we have here. None of your Six-Pack Joes. 'Gosh,' I said. 'Thank you. Now, how are you today? Would you be able to go up to the shop for me?'

I taught him the words 'batch loaf', and shortly after he set off for the Xpress Stores. He took so long that I was showered and dressed by the time he came back, his eyes sparkling, and commenting happily on how it was like going to fill your pitcher at the well in some oasis, there were so many people standing around talking. How everyone had been very welcoming, asking him where he was staying and how was I, and how was Min doing in America?

Uhuh, I thought. There goes the last of my reputation.

While he was washing the dishes I went onto my laptop and sat back to receive more praise from Markey.

And there it was, sent just after I had turned off my laptop last night.

From: MarkC@rmbooks.com
To: RosieB@eirtel.com
Sent: 11.30 p.m.
URGENT!!!

Rosie, ol' pal, make sure you're sitting down.

I sent Chico the email with your brilliant synopsis and got an out-of-office reply that didn't mention when he'd be coming back.

So I called Louis himself.

He said, 'Chico is no longer with the Louisbooks family.' He said it in a tone of voice so formidable that I saw at once why he's a multimillionaire and I'm not. Anyway – Chico's gone.

I took a deep breath and said that was a pity, that you'd done a fantastic job of putting together some thoughts that explore in an intimate reader-friendly format that passage in life's journey when the questions of youth are no longer relevant, and the answers of age are still in the future.

He said that was certainly a fine achievement and he congratulates you on it. He said his people tell him there's some overcrowding in the inspirational books sector. The smart focus is on collectibles.

Tea-towels, for instance, he said. The gift shops are crying out for cherishable tea-towels. Would we have a tea-towel idea we'd like to pitch?

I said I'd get back to him. Have a nice day, Louis, I said.

I was aware that it was only three o'clock in the morning in Seattle, but I could not contain myself.

'Markey!' I shouted into the phone, so loudly that Bell cleared the window from the armchair without touching the sill. 'Markey, how could they do this to us! Capitalist pigs, that's what they are! We should have had a lawyer.'

'Rosie!' He was nearly as loud and couldn't have been asleep.

'What?'

'Calm down!'

'How can I? When the biggest…'

'Rosie, that can wait. Now. Are you calm? You are? Well, there's a little bit of a development about Min. Nothing at all to worry about and I was going to leave it till morning to tell you, but now that you're here – the cops in Portland found my card beside the bed in Min's trailer and they called me about an hour ago, and I was of course able to assure them that I know the lady all my life, how she's a respectable senior citizen, etc. etc…'

'What were *cops* doing in *Min*'s trailer?'

'Apparently they'd paid a visit – not a raid, more a kind of pastoral visit – to the trailer park because according to the cops it's a bit of a 24/7 drinking den and there'd been a few small disturbances there. Apparently there are a few party-hearty Inuit there and some Mexicans and Guatemalans who've also been around the block, though the average age of the party-goers is well over seventy. But it seemingly wasn't about charging anyone with anything. Rather the Health and Safety Bureau had asked the cops to go in because the old folk were taking no notice of fire warnings and things like that. But when the sweep got as far as Min's trailer, they found it empty. There's no reason for that, is there? She's on a perfectly good tourist visa, isn't she? But anyway there was no sign of her or Luz. No passport or clothing, and her money – the cops checked, and she'd just been paid a month's wages by the Galway Bay Saloon and bid them goodbye.'

'Oh don't worry, Markey!' I laughed with relief. 'I know where she is. She's on her way home! She's coming to my birthday picnic tomorrow. I'm only praying the food won't go off, the weather is so gorgeous. But about that rat Chico and his—'

'Rosie Barry! We can talk about that tomorrow. My partner, who is unfortunate enough to sleep on the phone side of the bed and who has never met a single Barry, has been woken twice so far tonight on Barry business—'

'Oh, I'm sorry, Markey! Sleep well! Call me when you can, OK?'

I tried to explain to Leo: old friend Markey, Celtic wisdom selling point, promise of deckle-edged inspirational booklet for stacking beside cash-registers for impulse buyers – are you following me, Leo? He wasn't following me. So I sent him back up to the Xpress for the materials for a spaghetti carbonara for our lunch, though he could not hope to find words, he said when he came back, to express adequately his contempt for the little packet of grated cheese known in Kilbride as 'Parmesan'. To say nothing of the curious texture of Irish pasta. Then Bell, in spite of everything, could not control her greed at the smell of bacon frying, and came skidding back through the window. Which reminded me that Monty might like to come and eat with us, so I went and knocked on his door, and talked him into coming over to have some spaghetti, knowing if I'd just called over the back wall he'd have been too shy.

All his life Monty had glanced at himself anywhere there was the possibility of a reflection, and I watched with fondness now as he stood anxiously in front of his hallway mirror, which showed the athletic body that once looked great in jeans had become a pouter chest cinched low at the waist. And thinning hair which he quickly flicked with the comb he always kept in his back pocket.

'How's your ma?' I asked. For it was Reeny who had kept him going, even though Peg was his girl.

'My ma has a Spanish fella,' he said plaintively.

I managed to say 'Is that so?' instead of 'I know, and I think that's terrific and the least she deserves, and here's hoping he's halfway decent and speaks English, but even if he isn't and doesn't that's still good news – for you're forty-something years old and it's time you two let each other go.'

I remember thinking once, as I walked back to my seat in a plane full of businessmen waiting for the dinner service, some of them with napkins tucked under their chins, that it was like walking down a kinder-garten between rows of innocently expectant babies. Monty was like that. I always saw in him the plump little boy who had stolidly watched television in our house while his abandoned mother cried her heart out in his. You can see the child in men much more easily than in women.

'How was the bed?' he said heartily to Leo who looked quite startled by the bonhomie.

'Perfect!' Leo returned, making, with his thumb and forefinger, a little gesture to denote perfection that would have attracted considerable derision from the guys who propped up the bar in the Kilbride Inn. 'Such comfort! And the quiet, marvellous!'

'Is it noisy, then, where you come from?' Monty said, making a great conversational effort.

Leo said, 'Of late years I have been living in Italian towns and it has never been quiet for a single moment. But I hope to return to my family home in Switzerland…'

'Switzerland!' Monty said enthusiastically. 'I was over there not long ago for the Open! I never saw a course the like of it!'

'Did you play?' Leo enquired, and I thought at first he was thinking about a musical instrument. But it turned out that his son, the fifteen-year-old, the one he trusted to bring his wife around in some way, was Captain of Golf at his English public school.

Which it turned out was enough for Leo to be taken under Monty's wing as a sporting confrère. Before I knew what was happening, he'd gone back next door to fetch his clubs, and coats for the two of them, so that he might take Leo out to Portmarnock to show him a typical Irish links course.

'It's ideal for a chap that's feeling a bit under the weather,' Monty assured me. 'He needn't set a foot outside the golf cart, just breathe in the sea air while I get in a practice round.'

I looked helplessly at Leo, shrouded in a purple, polyester anorak, emblazoned 'TEAM', whose sleeves came down as far as his fingertips.

'Rosie,' he reassured me, 'this is a very good thing to do because when next I meet my boy I will have many things to talk about to him.'

'But you'll be away for hours!' I wailed. 'And I have so much to do in Stoneytown!'

'Well, you go on down there,' Monty said, 'instead of putting pressure on us. I'll look after Leo and introduce him to a few of the lads and feed him – they do a great steak in Portmarnock. Have a few pints. Early bed. Then he can come down to the picnic with me tomorrow.'

'But what about Peg?'

'Peg's going down with Tess.'

'*Mais ça va très bien,* Rosie!' Leo said. 'I will be absolutely content with those arrangements.'

Monty smiled proudly as if he personally were responsible for Leo speaking French.

I ran after them, out to where Leo was slowly climbing into Monty's car.

'Are you OK for money?' I whispered urgently. 'You have to stand your round—'

'*Qu'est-ce que c'est?*'

'Monty! Explain to our *ami* here about the Irish round system, will you? And look after him. And—'

'See you tomorrow!'

'See you tomorrow!'

I spent the afternoon cleaning Min's house and hosing down the yard and leaving the fire laid with a box of matches beside it, walking happily in and out of the buttery shapes the sun made on the floor. What's more, the Schubert song came on the radio that I thought of as my private signature tune because I played it every time I decided it was time to move on from wherever I was. I sat in the doorway and listened, enchanted as ever. It was the last song Schubert ever wrote, and I knew it well because I had it on tape in the days when people played tapes. 'The Shepherd and the Rock' it's called. For some reason the shepherd part is always sung by a soprano, who tells the world that with deep grief she is consumed, her joy is at an end, and all hope on earth is lost.

'I am so lonely here,' she mourns, and the clarinet mourns with her.

And then – I sprang over to the radio and turned up the volume – in a dizzy, charming and completely unmotivated reversal, that every time I heard it made me smile helplessly, 'Spring is coming,' she suddenly bursts out. 'Spring, my joy! Now I will make ready to go journeying.'

I used to play it to start me off on my own journeying.

And I stood up in Min's backyard there and then and made a vow. All that was over. A decision had taken up solid residence in me when I wasn't even thinking about it. I'd go journeying still, but I'd go to come back to a home.

The thing that made me walk away from Hugh

Boody, the thing that left me with friends everywhere and nowhere, the thing for which I had willingly paid in loneliness, was the freedom to pursue the wonderful. I followed it around the globe. It was the Iguacu Falls and Cologne cathedral and the coral underworld of the Great Barrier Reef and every place I hadn't yet been. It was the possibility of suddenly becoming a writer of wise mini-essays that strangers would pay me a huge sum for and even greater strangers would read and ponder.

But now I was just as excited by the ordinary. I'd loved, for example, putting out my breakfast things in Stoneytown the night before, just a mug and a plate and a knife and a spoon, but placing them beside the kettle, ready, was a great pleasure to me. I loved bringing in laundry from the line and dressing the bed with it, the sheets carrying a subtle layer of chill from the breezes that had dried them. I loved last thing at night checking the bolts of the barn and sheds, with the dog, then putting the bar across the inside of the back door. The dog would show off by scampering ahead to the next thing in the sequence. I loved it that we did the same thing every night, and so, I knew, did she.

And so I'd tell the others when they toasted me at the picnic: I'm not back, I'd say, the way you've often seen me. I'm home. If I go away again, it will be no more than an excursion.

Right! Get a move on! Yes, I'd been to the super-market, yes I'd packed the plates and glasses, yes I'd trapped Bell who was sulking in her basket on the passenger seat, and yes, I'd draped my white shift that I bought in Mykonos over the back seat, that I estimated would last five minutes in Stoneytown before something happened to it. Leo's second pair of linen trousers hung on the back of the door, long and thin like Leo. Wasn't infatuation the nearest thing to sunny weather? Wiping out everything else when it's there, and completely gone when it's not?

The phone rang.

'Oh Min! Oh, that's just *great*. You caught me just as I was going out the door! I was a bit worried because Markey told me this morning that the cops in Portland had been on to him – they found his card in your trailer. And I was also afraid that you'd be a bit surprised to find a strange man in your house when you got here. But do you remember that I had a friend – a man – who phoned me from time to time, and who you always said sounded as if he was reading the news? Well?'

'The cops rang *Markey*? What in the name of God had them doing that? Sure what has Markey to do with anything?'

'Well, what have the cops to do with anything! I mean, why didn't you tell someone you were leaving the trailer place? Why didn't you let me know—'

'C'mere, Rosie!' She cut across me briskly. 'You never exactly killed yourself letting *me* know when you were moving from one place to another.'

'But I was never involved with the police—'

'Neither was I! That's why I got out of there! I didn't want to go down to any police station to take a talking-to from men young enough to be my grandsons. And Luz minds her own business. Luz doesn't want anything whatsoever to do with any cop. What had we done?

Nothing! Plus the rent was paid up and I had my wages in my pocket, so we moved on. Why not, may I be so bold as to ask?'

'But why were the cops involved at all?'

'Because this country is crazy! All the rich people are thin with their nerves in bits and afraid of their shadows, while all the poor people are fat and everyone tries to stop them enjoying themselves. Did you know that if you buy a bottle of vodka here – which is for nothing, I can tell you, compared to those crooks in the Kilbride off-licence – you have to keep it in a paper bag? And you can't open it in a car? In a car! We were doing no harm to anyone and the next thing the people that own the trailer park landed on Tuk and Maya with a list of bad things we're supposed to have done the length of your arm. I'm disgusted with America, so I am. The people here are nice, but the laws are disgusting.'

'Well, you're on your way home. It doesn't matter now,' I said. I couldn't keep rebuking her. Anyway, I had so many things lined up to show her and so much to ask her that it just wouldn't do to be fighting with her. And Leo was living in her kitchen.

'Where are you, anyway?' I asked, because it suddenly occurred to me that she mightn't yet have reached New York.

'I'm in Duluth,' she said.

'What? *Where?*'

Then suddenly I remembered. The airman. The airman who ditched his plane. He was from Duluth. 'But…'

'The voice on the card I'm phoning on is after saying

that there's only fifty cents left, and Rosie, I don't know what's the score about making it to New York to catch the Dublin plane.'

Her voice sounded as nervous as it ever got.

'We have a room in a place for kind of respectable homeless people – transients is the name for us – and we have our own bathroom and all, you should see the tiles, they're better than the ones Reeny brought back from Spain. But it took us a good while to find it, and I have to find out where the radio station is, and Luz and me were having a drink across the road where the man asked did either of us want a shift in the kitchen tonight, and I said I would because Luz still isn't—'

'But it's my birthday tomorrow,' I began – before I felt my blood run cold. 'And your visa! Your visa, Min! Doesn't your visa run out the day after tomorrow? That's why you have to come home now! You *have* to. You have to leave the States before midnight tomorrow. Isn't Duluth near Canada? Go to Canada! Ring Markey and ask him what to do, go on – Markey'll help – Min, go *Business Class* if you have to.' I was shouting while she was shouting back. 'Ring me tomorrow, Min,' I cried, 'if you don't make it as far as Stoneytown.'

'I'll ring you tomorrow, Rosie,' she cried back, 'at the phone-box, when it's 9 o' clock where you are. I'll find out when that is where I am. I have the number written on my specs case.'

'Ring Markey! Mark Cuffe, Seattle.'

'I know,' she said. 'I will if I have to.'

Then she – who had never been a predictable woman – said the single most surprising thing she had ever uttered to me.

'I thought maybe Daddy might have come here,' she said. 'The airman invited everyone.'

'But your daddy would be over a hundred years old!'

'I don't care,' she said. 'I was going to ask on the radio. Someone might remember him.'

21

It was a Saturday morning for many a heartfelt '*My soul doth magnify the Lord*'. Since when was I as lucky as this?

I was seated out on the bench above the shore, in a sweater over my linen shift from Mykonos, reading a few pages of Proust, when a shout sounded from the ridge above. A postman! The dog couldn't believe her luck and raced up the slope to crouch at his feet.

'Do you think the weather'll hold up?' I called to him.

'Not a doubt of it! Here, overnight delivery. Sign here,' he said once I reached him. 'That's the low pressure over Biscay, that is,' he gestured at the sky. 'That'll be here for weeks.'

A small, thick envelope. Who'd thought of me?

'Ah, just today will do me,' I said, as the postman gave the dog an amiable pat and departed. 'Nice to see the old house back on the round,' he called back over his shoulder.

The stamps were American and the return address was Seattle; the gift was a mock-up of a little book, a deckle-edged birthday card with the words of my nine

'Thoughts' on tiny pages. How had Markey timed it to arrive on my birthday? Such confidence in the postal system! Easy to see he hadn't spent his adult life in Ireland.

The little thing looked sweet, unfinished as it was. Well, even if this was all I got out of my big idea it was something.

The dog had barely recovered from the postman when there came the sound of another car. What is more, she took to Leo from the moment she saw him walk slowly down the cart track, Monty hovering protectively behind him. It must be his sandals, I remarked, because Leo wasn't a person to ingratiate himself with a dog and he did little more than nod at her in return for her enthusiasm. Lovely Italian sandals with covered toes they were, and Leo said grandly that he'd send a pair first thing, after Monty had praised them, just write down the size and the colour. He mightn't have any money, but he hadn't an impoverished person's mindset either. He was very taken too by Mother Ireland and addressed some compliments to her in Italian, at which she started oinking wildly at the attention, prompting the dog to climb up on the wall of the sty to monitor that. But then she tore herself away from the pigsty to investigate the noise of yet another car, and crouched, alert and immobile, as Andy appeared, carrying a cake-box by a string between his teeth and a bottle of champagne in each hand. She headed up the slope, followed by Bell, who loved Andy. Then there were more car sounds, and in a couple of minutes Tessa and Peg appeared on the horizon.

The dog began running around in circles. You could see her thinking, this situation requires *maximum* battle-readiness. But Bell lost heart and leapt up onto the roof ridge and huddled there as if she had no intention of ever coming down.

The place looked like heaven in the sunshine as I showed everyone around. They exclaimed at everything. The perfect little stage-set home I'd set up within the shell of the house, and its wondrous distinction – electricity. The dishes sparkling in the wavering light reflected from the sea. The scrubbed steps up to the half-loft with its candles in glass shades beside the bed. My neat Elsan toilet in the whitewashed stone shed and the cerise geraniums in old iron pots that flanked its wooden door. The barn, where the dog's basket lay on the stone floor, protected by bales of straw from the breeze off the sea. The thick, mossy walls of the orchard and the aged apple trees, their tops sheared perfectly flat by the wind, their leaves still the colour of green candy. The slate path I'd made down to the shore with its edging of white pebbles. The trestle table Andy had put together in the yard at the back of the house, away from the sea, where everything basked in the absence of wind. The bench I'd dragged there, and the homemade wooden chairs I'd found in the other ruined houses, padded with old blankets.

The dog finally settled down, hostess-like, to preside at the picnic, surveying us from the grass of the slope with her tail curled around her in parenthesis, her eyes shining with interest.

Monty had brilliantly brought a bucket full of ice, into which we'd put the wine and champagne while we were having our tour. He looked very well today, I thought, as he loosened the corks – as if a bit of a tan, light clothes and his feet in deck shoes made him feel better about himself. And he was wreathed in shy smiles, too, now that Leo and he had formed a mutual admiration society, based, as far as I could see, on mutual incomprehension.

Screeek – Popp!!

'That's what men are for!' I said. 'Opening champagne bottles! Opening zips. Opening…'

'It's an awful pity Min isn't here,' Peg said. 'Why did she never tell us she grew up in a beauty spot?'

'But she might be here,' I said. 'It's early yet. And even if she doesn't make it further than Dublin, she's going to ring me tonight at nine.'

Peg didn't usually drink, but today she was knocking it back, as if she had something on her mind. She wasn't known for a great interest in animals, either, but here she was becoming extremely emotional about the little black dog. She called her down from her grassy post on the slope to grasp her head and point out to us the way her eyelashes curved upwards like a movie star's. The dog looked up at her adoringly. But when there was a delay because Tessa's *tarte flambée* wasn't crisping in the oven, and Tessa wouldn't let us start with anything else, the dog went off with Monty and Andy, Monty, needless to say, needing to check out Stoneytown's potential as a pitch-and-putt course.

Leo then exchanged his beautiful white shirt for one

of my T-shirts and went into the kitchen to fix a salad, while the three of us women laid the table.

As soon as Leo was out of earshot, Peg started telling Tessa and me about her father's latest escapades. How he'd taken his trousers down in front of the bus queue and the bus conductor had radioed for the gardaí. And how he'd gone into the Londis supermarket and taken a packet of chocolate biscuits off the shelf and stood there and eaten the whole lot.

We were laughing heartily before I noticed that Peg was white with tension. 'The day-care centre doesn't want him back,' she said, beginning to sob. 'What am I going to do?'

I gave her a hug, then, hoping to give her a chance to pull herself together, I asked Tessa, 'And yourself? How is your significant older person?'

'Auntie Pearl's fine,' she said. 'Just don't mention Laos to her; she's making a novena it won't happen. But don't say that to Andy because she doesn't want him to know she's broken-hearted. There's two of them in it, when it comes to pretending everything's hunky-dory.'

By now Peg was pouring herself another glass of wine.

'She was supposed to be going on the Diocesan Pilgrimage to Fatima again,' Tessa went on, 'but she couldn't because she's doing the flowers for a neighbour's daughter's wedding. Twenty thousand euro the idiotic bride is spending on one lousy wedding.'

, 'What was the Third Secret of Fatima?' Peg said woozily. 'There's one for you now!'

'That there's no God,' Tessa said. 'They opened the

envelope and inside was a piece of paper that just said *Ha ha ha!*

'That's not it,' I said. 'It came true when what's-his-name the Bulgarian fellow tried to kill the Pope. The secret was that someone would try to kill the Pope.'

'Was it?' Peg said, open-mouthed. 'Did it specify a Bulgarian?' Though she had a hard time saying 'specify'.

'I thought he was Turkish,' Tessa said.

'I wish the chaps would come back, and we could eat,' I said. 'You're becoming a bit tousled, did you know?'

'Doesn't matter,' Peg said. 'The hell with them.'

'Who lived here?' Tessa said. 'That's what I don't understand. I mean, why is this house here? When there's no road.'

'I did a lot of research in the library in Milbay while waiting for the teenagers to tire of trying to access porn on the computers,' I said, 'and apparently the terraced row of houses was built for farm workers sometime in the early nineteenth century, after which they abandoned the place and nothing happened here except smuggling. The First World War then stopped the smuggling, and then my grandfather and the other people came here, sometime in the 1920s. They came from west Waterford, and the older people were Irish-speaking. But they weren't craftsmen. They were more, apparently, like Travellers, like maybe one extended family or small tribe within the Travellers, and they were only here because there were houses they could winter in. And it seems they worked the quarries because they were too cut off out here to go around mending things, the way Travelling men used to do, or peddling little bits of this and that like the women. But the more I tried to find out, the more I realised that I'm not properly educated about Ireland, if you know what I mean.'

'No, I don't know what you mean,' Peg cut across me, quite aggressively. 'All that sounded like education.'

'What's up with you, Peg?' I asked, taken aback. We often fought but I seldom saw her this angry.

'I know what you mean,' Tessa said to me. 'You don't have the right qualifications. I'm thinking of getting a qualification in business administration, myself. There's no money in counselling, and that's what women need, money.'

'That's not what I meant,' I began.

'Or a man with money,' Peg said.

'No!—' Tess was beginning.

'C'mere, Rosie,' Peg cut across her – 'what happened to the book you were going to write? *Laugh Your Way to the Grave in Ten Easy Stages?*'

'Oh, why'd you have to remind me?' I said. 'It didn't work out. The Americans who were supposed to do it – one disappeared and the other doesn't want it. He wants a tea-towel instead.'

'I have a great tea-towel I got in Canada,' Peg said. 'You know your man, maybe he's a Bulgarian too, his name is Khalil – Khalil something begins with a G. They're really deep sayings, I keep it with the good silver, I'd never just dry something with it.'

'I have "If",' Tessa said. 'Y'know? "If you can keep your head when all around you…" It's pinned to the wall. And I have one with a recipe for Irish soda bread that I got in Texas. And I have "Go placidly amid the noise and haste".'

'I'm going to buy that one!' Peg cried. 'I saw it in my sister-in-law's! *Desider*-something it's called. It's a great one too.'

'*Desiderata*,' Tessa said.

'Hey, where's the Frenchman gone, Rosie?' Peg was tiring of tea-towels. 'Yours is a real gentleman, at least. But is he growing the salad or what?'

'He's not a—'

'I never saw a man so improved,' Tessa announced. 'He used to look down his nose at everyone, but now he has the manners along with the looks of Hugh Boody. Do you remember Hugh Boody? There was a gentleman! There was a man in a million! And not a word, not one word, Rosie Barry, did I receive from you of sympathy when my Hugh died. Peg came to the funeral, didn't you, Peg? Though God knows it was the least you could do. But you, Rosie... I'm not blaming you about the funeral because you were in Australia. But when you came home, when you came home and I – *I*, not you – brought up the subject, not a word, not a single word...'

'I didn't know what to say—'

'Ah for Crissake, Tess,' Peg interrupted, 'that was umpteen years ago! What's so special about being dead? Sure we'll all be dead any minute now!' She stood up in a dazed kind of way. 'C'mon and we'll go for a little siesta! Just ten minutes? Then we can have our dinner, and if the lads aren't back, that's their lookout.'

'OK,' Tessa said. 'Good idea.' And the two of them went in, giggling their way up the ladder to the loft.

Then Leo ventured back out of the scullery.

'They talk a lot, your friends,' he said. 'Irish people talk a lot.'

We sat there like Darby and Joan in the warm back yard, our faces lifted to the sun, as he informed me that my transistor radio was not what is meant in general by an 'apparatus for the reproduction of sound', and that the noise that emanated from it 'had nothing to do with music'.

'It's a miracle I like classical music at all, Mister,' I replied. 'Take a look around you. This here is where my people are from, this is where my mother and Min were reared. Here, Stoneytown. Not downtown Milan. Note the absence of symphony orchestras.'

It was all so peaceful that I didn't even rebuke the dog who, having returned from its walk, was standing on a chair, one paw delicately extended to the table, calmly serving herself some Brie. Instead I poured myself half a glass of wine. No, a quarter. There was a lot of the day still to go. *Tips for the Bad Times, Or How to Survive Life*: Do not hit the bottle at your own parties.

Leo had taken out the beautiful notebook he used when he was listening to music. I saw on several pages the quick drawings he'd made: the front of the house from the shore; the kitchen-room with its range; the back of the house, with the yards and the sheds around it; and the gable end that was nearly hidden by the high wall of the orchard.

'I'd do very little with this house,' he said confidently. 'It is quite perfect of its kind. But look, Rosa,' he made a quick mark on the steep roof above the front door.

'Here, since these roof flags must be re-laid anyway, I'd take the opportunity to recess a deep balcony, almost invisible frontally, but angled to share the light, brought through a back wall of glass to the bedroom.'

'But Leo…'

'And here…' He turned to the sketch of the blank gable wall. 'I think you might make another entrance here, away from the prevailing wind. You could move the animal shelters to here, too, and the pig houses could be dispersed among new apple trees. I'm afraid the existing trees are too old to save.'

'Leo, I don't own the house! And Min wants to sell it. So stop!'

'Oh, I'm sorry, my dear,' he said. 'I had forgotten about ownership. It is simply that the refurbishment of this house presents a challenge one can't resist contemplating.'

'I'm very glad you came to Ireland, Leo,' I said warmly. 'Have I made that clear? And some day…'

'But Rosa,' he cut across me, 'did you not say yesterday that some Americans who must be insane were giving you money? Why not buy the house with that? Those are unexpected funds, are they not?'

I must have given him a fright when I jumped to my feet, knocking over the old chair and shouting at the top of my voice, 'Monty! Andy! Where are you? One of you. Come! Quick! Quick!'

And when Monty appeared at the top of the hill I didn't even pause to explain what I was doing.

'Monty, have you got a few euro coins? Give me a ride to the phone-box on the main road, will you?'

At the phone-box I did the deed while Monty turned the car.

Only I rang Markey's office, because if I woke him up at home yet again, he'd bite the nose off me.

'Darling Markey, this is a message to you as my agent, a business message, urgent, urgent! Will you respond to Louis and ask him how much he'd pay for the text of a tea-towel? I hadn't realised that they can be really meaningful to people. It's not such a crazy idea to write one. If he comes up with any kind of sum, I could offer it to Min as a deposit on the old house and then pay her the rest as I go along from whatever salary I receive in my next job. Could you talk to Louis today? Because Min is on her way back, and it would be wonderful to sort this out on my birthday! Not that it's not wonderful anyway – our little book is lovely and receiving it was the best present ever, even if there are only Nine Thoughts and even if Louis doesn't want it. You made my day and it's a lovely day! I leave it to you, Markey...'

The phone went dead. Euros all gone.

Well, the important things had been said.

'Hi! Where are the girls?'

Andy waved happily up at Monty and me from where he was sitting at the table with the dog at his heels. He seemed to be pointedly ignoring Leo, but it turned out Leo had nodded off behind his sunglasses, his long fingers neatly folded in his lap. A man of his elegance, having to sneak out past his landlady and leave his clothes behind! To be unwell and tired, and have to do that!

'He's exhausted, the poor fella,' Andy said.

Tessa burst through the back door. 'This tart is as ready as it's ever going to be, as the actress said to the bishop,' she carolled. 'Fetch the plates, somebody!'

Leo woke up and took some mousse and salad and asparagus. But when he started to doze off again, I said, 'Did you ever hear of the Mad Hatter's Tea Party? Remember the dormouse? The dormouse was always asleep and finally the others put him into the teapot. If you don't watch out, I'll put you into the teapot.'

'Leave me be,' he said peaceably. 'I do not know what anyone is talking about and I cannot shout like your friends. And I am very willing to go into the teapot. I did not know how I would possibly tell anyone about my financial situation, but now that I have told you I am a happy man.'

He pulled his panama hat over his face then, while I folded an extra blanket between his back and the chair, and off he went for another sleep.

Meanwhile everyone else got even louder.

'You know, it will actually break my heart to lose old Min', I heard myself say, while slicing a pear.

'But you're not losing her, she's only—'

'I am losing her. She'll be different when she comes back from her adventure.'

'But you're fifty-six years old, for crying out loud!'

'It doesn't make any difference how old you are. The woman who runs the Sunshine Home was telling me that they all cry for their mammies. The older they are, the more they cry for them.'

'What do they want?' Peg said, beginning to laugh. 'If my mother was alive, she'd ask my da if it would be OK with him if she answered me. What about you?' she turned to Monty. 'Do you still need your mammy too?'

We could all hear the unmistakeable sneer in her voice.

'My mother was going to bring me back some cork tree saplings from Fatima,' Andy quickly said. 'But she didn't go in the end. Cork trees are very interesting.' The conversational gambit had been aimed at no one in particular and no one responded either, but I smiled my thanks at him for trying to cover up the tension. 'I'll be calling for my mother,' he continued, his face as red from a couple of glasses of wine as I'd ever seen it. 'I was round with her this morning – that old Renault of hers is acting up and she had flowers to deliver.'

'I warned her myself about the Renault,' Monty began.

'And I had a cup of tea with her after, and there was a bit of a shake in her hand – you know, like elderly people get? I got a right shock when I saw that. She's in great form but she's over eighty years old. I was wondering whether I should bring her out to Laos with me. She says she doesn't want to go, but what do you think? Would she be better off there than here?'

No one ventured an opinion.

He finished off, helpless but proud. 'She's everything to me,' he said. 'Like they say, a man's best friend is his mother.'

'Poor Pearl!' I muttered to Tessa. 'Mothers whose sons love them that much might as well be in jail.'

But Tessa was suddenly bleak. 'I wouldn't mind being her,' she muttered back.

The plan had been to have a second dessert of bananas fried on the stove with brown sugar and cream and rum, but there weren't nearly enough bananas because, it emerged, Peg had given a handful to Mother Ireland for a treat. But Peg said she'd make up for it later with a surprise. So we had a bowl of cornflakes each to keep us going and to sober up. And then we went for a small stroll, at Leo's pace.

There was an outpouring of oinks from Mother Ireland when we passed the sty, no doubt an appeal for more bananas. 'A cadenza,' I said to Leo, which made him laugh. It was wonderful to hear, as he'd never laughed, and barely smiled, that last time in Macerata.

The goats were in the first field, including three kids, pure white, with mad, golden eyes. All of sudden my spirits dipped and a chill passed through my heart. From the first time I saw them the gorgeous kids had reminded me of the children I'd never had. And every time I saw one I had to fight the desire to hold it across my belly and feel its living body pulse against my flesh.

Nobody knows what I'm feeling, I thought, as I stood at the fence with the others and waited for the ache to pass. Which means I don't know what they're feeling. Which then makes it all the more precious that we go to trouble to be together.

The first breeze of the coming evening lifted Peg's fine blonde hair.

'Leo is tired,' she said. 'Let's go back. My surprise is I brought frankfurters and rolls, if anyone's interested.

And mustard. The nice runny sort.'

'That's my girl!' Monty said, earning him a look of such despair from Peg that I wished I hadn't seen it.

'You can see the moon even though it's full daylight,' Tess said. 'Why's that? I should have gone to college.'

'I could murder a hot dog,' Andy said – at which the dog looked up at us enquiringly, as if she'd heard her name.

I took Peg's hand then and ran down the track with her as if we were girls, though I couldn't help but notice how awkwardly we ran.

'Are you OK?' I asked.

'He's been going with someone else,' she whispered urgently. 'She thinks he's God almighty and that's what he wants. She's twenty-eight...'

As I held her head for a quick kiss I could feel the sweat in her hair.

Leo had fallen back, walking so slowly, so I waited for him at the house.

'Would you like to go back to Kilbride with Monty?' I asked him quietly. 'It's only 5 o'clock and you've had enough, I think. Would you be all right in the house on your own? You could go up to Enzo for your supper.'

'But of course I'll be alright,' he said. 'I am so content in that house.'

'The key's in the door,' I said. 'You know – you put your hand in for the string. But knock first because Min might be there. If she is, tell her I'll be up at the phone-box tonight at 9 o'clock sharp to hear her news. And I'll see you in Dublin in the morning, Leo, and we'll have a lovely breakfast.'

After we came across the yard to the open back door, I went slowly around collecting glasses and plates, savouring the evening, before I stood at the gable end for a moment to look at the tide coming in. I liked the way the scallop of foam at the water's edge spilled first forward and then, languidly, spread sideways. I then joined the others where they'd built up a flaring fire in the range, and ate a frankfurter that Peg fished from the pot of boiling water, with the breeze sifting through the open front and back doors, from the sea to the hill behind, as if we were in a temple.

'Min never saw this room again after she was fifteen,' I said. 'She came here once with my father on his motorbike, but they couldn't get into the house. They had to sleep in the barn.'

'There'd be mice in a barn!' Peg shuddered. 'My God! There's probably mice here, who could've jumped on me when I was having that nap! I think you're crazy to sleep here, Rosie.'

'No mice, I think. I hope.'

'I don't think Rosie is crazy at all,' Tessa said loyally. 'It's so peaceful here.'

Monty was singing to himself:
You-ou-ou may say I'm a dreamer,
But I'm not the only one…'

Last thing, I took Leo aside and carefully explained to him how to coax the TV remote control into receiving *France-Inter*, and where to find the dark chocolate I'd hidden from myself in the *Collected Shakespeare*. And that

I'd bring fresh bread when I came in the morning.

Then the dog and I – and Bell, tripping along twenty paces to the rear as if pretending she, too, were a dog – escorted the others up to the ridge on their way to the cars. The place had never looked more beautiful. Behind us, the whole horizon was filled with shimmering sea, and underneath our voices, as we talked and laughed, was the sound of shingle being combed by waves, dragged slowly upward, then, in varied exhalations, as slowly released.

'It's a peninsula, this…' I began.

'I know it is,' Monty said happily. 'I was just saying that to Leo, here. And that's what makes all the difference, with the road going past. Forget your pitch-and-putt, there could be one of Ireland's finest links on this very spot.'

'I heard Min using the word "island" just recently, when she told me about my mother running away. She said my mother got out of the island when she was fifteen. And when I looked it up, she was right. The name of all this sticking-out bit of land in Irish is *Oilean Aoife* – Eva's Island. But according to the dictionary, '*oilean*' can mean either island or isolated place.'

'That's right,' Monty said. 'Castleisland in Kerry isn't anywhere near the sea.'

'Jesus, Monty, you're full of information today,' Peg said.

'Eva's Island is a great name for a course,' Monty said.

'Does *everything* have to be about golf?' Peg all but screamed.

We all fell silent then, as the slap and fizzle of water against rock rose from the shore. Ethereal wood pigeons, white and grey like the air, wafted towards the woods.

'Your mother got away,' Monty said thoughtfully, 'but then nothing happened.'

'It depends on what you mean by "nothing",' I said, as I ran ahead the last few feet to the top of the ridge and turned and threw my arms wide like a conquering hero, and did a little soft-shoe shuffle, laughing down at them.

'Am I nothing?' I cried.

To which they all shouted, 'No!'

The breeze was blowing the hair on all five heads in the same direction – so that you'd think, to look at them, that they belonged together: that they were all in the same little gang. But I knew how many hesitations and questions there were between them – and between me and them. And it made me like them all the more: that I knew how every one of them found it hard to get life right, and still they were willing to make a celebration, still they were generous. Three men, two of them balding. Two women past childbearing age. And myself, well past it. Yet I was moved by our middle-aged selves much more than if we had been young. It seemed a wonderful thing that we had come out of our separate lives and gathered on the top of a ridge for no reason but that we were friends.

And of course I snivelled happily when they sang 'Happy Birthday To Rosie'.

Back at the house I tidied up and made myself a stiff tea, then started out early for the phone-box so as to be there at 9 o'clock.

Already a dramatically crimson sunset suffused the west. Great plumes of purple and gold cloud spread along the horizon even as, out to sea to the east, the sky had resigned itself to an even grey. The breeze had dropped with twilight, and I'd never before known the sea to be so still. It lay like a silkscreen in greys and silvers and blacks: single clouds overhead doubled by their shining reflections, the rocks along the edge of the shore replicated in the water like two sides of a paper cut-out, the broken pier standing black above its double, and, across the mouth of the river, the distant bulk of Milbay shimmering slightly below its immobile self. Even the wading birds at the edge of the shingle, who never stopped chattering, had fallen silent.

A band was playing, far away. There must be a wedding in the hotel up the estuary.

I walked up the cart track, with the dog half-invisible in the dusk a liquid presence around my feet. Yet when a homing wood pigeon flew low over my head, she leapt up and gave a menacing growl.

You are protecting me, my little dear, I told her silently, and I want you to know I know it.

But she didn't stay for my pat on her silky crown. She melted into the coming night.

Ahead of me in the dark of the woods, something white seemed to be moving. Was it a head of pale hair, the head turned sideways? Or was it a face? It seemed to be moving deeper into the dark trees. But no! It was coming down the track. It was coming towards the house!

My heart soared! My ears sang! I began to stumble forward. Yes! She'd pulled it off! She must have got a taxi to the station and caught the train straight to Milbay…

A goat it was. Restless and greyish-white as it moved across the dark grass. I could hear its low bleating now.

I watched as fleet of foot it ghosted down the track, but once it saw me it jumped onto the bank of the meadow, and disappeared among the shadows there.

I waited in the grass of the lay-by for the last time. It would be a solemn moment when I picked up the handset. Surely Min and I had been changed by our phone-calls? And this old box was more than it seemed: you went into it as your ordinary self but came out better able to understand the other person. I would not reproach her today for all the worry she'd caused me by coming home via Duluth. I wouldn't say how it hurt me that she'd missed my birthday. I could be generous…

But when she said 'Hello' in exactly the same voice as usual – not a hint of apology – I couldn't restrain myself.

'Where are you?' I barked. 'Where? Are you at home? If you're there, that man with the foreign accent is my friend Leo who I used to go and see and—'

'What in the name of God is that fellow doing at home?'

'So you're not there?'

There was a silence.

'You're not at home?'

When she still didn't say anything, I actually felt my

belly tighten and a wave of nausea rise from it.

Then, 'Ah, Rose…' That was all she said. But in such a caressing voice.

It was left to me to say it so: 'You're still in America?'

'I am.'

'But you have time! It's only the afternoon there. You can make it out before the visa expires. You can go anywhere.'

'Rosaleen, I know that. I understand the whole thing. But I can't go home yet.'

'If you don't come home you'll be breaking the law,' I said urgently. 'You'll land in awful trouble. And if they throw you out, you'll never be able to enter the States again. You'll never see Luz or Carmen or Maya or Tuk or any of them, ever again. It's different since 9/11 – they don't care what your excuse is, you can't re-enter if you don't stick to the dates they write down. You'll be on an American government list. The immigration people won't care that you're old – they're always arresting old people for being terrorists because old people pay for their tickets with cash…'

'I know all about that,' she said. 'That's what's wrong with Luz, she came in from Mexico years and years ago and she can't go out again because then she couldn't return. She's stuck here. But that's the whole reason why I can't take off and leave her. She went into hospital here last night, and we had to pay, and she's not a bit well and nearly all our money is gone. Even buying this phone card I wouldn't have done, only it's your birthday. I have to stay in America and take a job. You know she smokes in bed? That was the whole cause.'

She told me the story then.

They had used the Catholic network again in Duluth. Had asked the manageress of a motel where they could find a nice priest, and he'd found them a studio with kitchen facilities, in a city hostel for transients. They'd had a great time yesterday watching television in the day room and playing cards. Min's intention was to go on local radio to find people from Stoneytown. Everyone thought that was a great idea because everyone else there would like to find their people too. She then did a kitchen-assistant shift in the bar across the road where she worked until they stopped serving food at 11 p.m. and she got twenty dollars into her hand.

She heard there'd been a complaint about a smell of smoke when she got back to the hostel, but each apartment had a heavy fire door and no light had gone on in the alarm system in the manager's office.

But Min couldn't open the door to their room.

And when the manager opened it with the master key, the place was thick with black smoke, and Luz lay up against the door, unconscious.

The fire brigade came and the medic with the team rang the Emergency Room to prepare, and Min heard him say that Luz's vital signs were OK but she had superficial burns along one arm.

'And Rosie, I brought her here. Duluth was all my idea. And it was a terrible experience for her. Because do you know what else he said?' Her voice was breaking into sobs. 'I heard him telling the Emergency Room to check her badly bruised hands, as all her nails were broken and there were scratch marks on the door.'

372

22

I tried Markey at once, but there was no reply either at his house or his work so I could only leave messages. Then I ran back through the woods, stumbling and cursing, to throw a few things into a bag and close up the house. I begged the dog to come with me. Tears were rolling down my face as I told her I needed her. But she would not – she could not – climb into the car. I drove to Dublin then, listening intently to a programme about frogs and refusing to think about anything else, so that I was more composed by the time I got to Kilbride.

It wasn't Luz who was the cause of the waterfall – barely dammed – of tears, though I could hardly bear to think about that poor woman's fear and panic. It was, simply, that whatever might happen in the long run about an appeal to the Immigration Service, Min wasn't coming home today.

From: MarkC@rmbooks.com
To: RosieB@eirtel.com
Sent: 4:30 a.m.
Subject: THERE'S NO NEED TO WORRY.

I'm on my way. Billy has medical qualifications and he's coming with me to take care of Luz.

If she's well enough, we'll put the pair of them in the apartment over Rare Medical Books. Otherwise they can come home with us.

Don't thank me! I mean that. Your aunt was very good to my ma. I am glad to repay.

Best love,

Markey

I stayed beside the phone for two-and-a-half days while the scare and its fallout were looked after. I tried not to think about my own situation, because when I did, I was gripped with fear that I'd been away so long the dog would have surely taken off.

I explained that finally to Leo, and went back to Stoneytown. With my heart beating so hard I was nearly sick, I parked the car in the cleft of the small quarry and dragged myself up and over the ridge. Eyes cast down, I got as far as the gate to the yard before I dared look up. And there she was, looking back at me. Waiting at the back door. We were as shy as new lovers.

After I fed her, I walked the headland with her, watching – like someone condemned to hang might watch a calendar – how autumn invades the summer. There were still skeins of dog roses in the hedges along the cart track, but the once-green blackberries were turning scarlet on their way to turning black. Vivid spikes of montbretia delineated every hedge and wall, and the foliage on the verges tangled and flopped of its own overweight, but trapped fallen leaves now tinged with brown the scrub of bushes and saplings along the edge of the woods.

I tried to see my ageing body as a thing that might unite me with the natural world. To see my own autumn as a time of rich colour, together with the leaves of gold and scarlet that littered the ragged meadow. Wasn't there some harvest for me, too, somewhere? – like the No-Need goats who pushed their heads through the fence along the cart track to gorge on blackberries and rosehips. What was the point of mourning for those states I could never have again: youth, passion, un-critical enthusiasm, buoyant hope? Couldn't I accept that some partial measure of these was worth having, even if I couldn't have their entirety? Couldn't I imagine a state of well-being that didn't require them?

From: MarkC@rmbooks.com
To: RosieB@eirtel.com
Sent: 3.15 p.m.

What's going on? I got some guy when I called this morning who said you'd gone back to Stoneytown. Who was this fellow? I heard Ireland had immigrants now, but I didn't know they spoke textbook English with cultured European accents.

Anyway, Rose, your prayers paid off. Billy says the old ladies will be fine in the apartment downtown while he monitors Luz's chest problem; he's having lab tests done, and X-rays. She's unable to smoke at present, as well as not wanting to, having received the fright of her life. Though if she does start again, we'll have to find them somewhere else to live, for obvious reasons – the books have had enough.

They've both taken quite a knock I think. Billy says Luz's healing will take a while – maybe months. But we're fine with that. Min meantime is very quiet though physically she's fine. I haven't got on to Louis about the tea-towel thing yet, because we've been so busy. When I do, you and I will talk again about making an offer to Min. But Billy says not to do anything for a good while, as it's really important to keep things quiet.

I stayed on in the old house. There came one beautiful last day of summer at the end of September, when I again walked the length of the ridge with the dog. At the end, directly across from Milbay, the springy turf gave way to a deep gouge in the hill, its wide, leafy chasm the haunt of big, white butterflies, like handkerchiefs languidly waving. The rock across from where I crouched was streaked with guano, where a pair of peregrine falcons whose harsh, other-worldly cries I often listened out for had built their lair. Far below, seven or eight cars were parked on the floor of the quarry, across which one little group, a mother, three children and a small dog, were slowly making their way. Little realising that they were being watched by me, and perhaps by the falcons too, floating immensely high above where they could see everything, town and river and sea, meadow and fields, and even down between the grasses of the meadow, its tiny shrews and moles.

Next day the temperature dropped and there were

no more butterflies. I went into Milbay and bought two men's sweaters, then rang Leo to instruct him to turn on the central heating in Kilbride and not to be afraid to keep it on; if I found him there without it on, I'd evict him.

But of course, he'd been comfortably warm until fairly recently. And he'd never worried about heating bills. He thought I was being very strange.

From: MarkC@rmbooks.com
To: RosieB@eirtel.com
Sent: 4.00 p.m.

Call me, will you Rosie? Leo – we've got to talking now, and after I told him I grew up in the back lane, he told me he walks that way on his way to train the ladies' choir! – anyhow, he says he's heard from you so I know you're OK, but it would be reassuring to hear your voice.

I have to say, things are working out well so far. I don't know what Min might be saying to you on the phone, but we're delighted with our lady guests. Luz is still very weak, but she gets up most afternoons for a few hours and cooks the most delicious Mexican food. Every few days we eat with them, and then have to take a cab home because the ladies really love their tequila and wine. Most nights we end up singing – Billy downloads songs from the Internet on his laptop with which to impress the three of us.

Min is supposed to do the housework but she says she's finished with housework – what she likes is business. Scholarly book-buyers from all over are asking me now who is that Irish lady who's minding the store; that she sure is one of a kind. And she's changing my life, I can tell you. She writes everything down, and in a ten-minute call every morning we set things up for the day. I can leave everything except the actual book-buying and price negotiating with her.

I told her this morning that she's the best argument I've come across for the existence of a caring deity, and she was chuckling all day.

One afternoon there was fresh graffiti on the door of the middle house of the ruined terrace. I knew that soon someone who had already found out that you can reach Milbay Point from inland would also discover that you can climb from where the track ends halfway along the edge of the big meadow, and along the ridge down to the house below. Or that you can come out of the woods and continue down the cart track beside the fields, and so come to my yard. Some day soon someone might brave the 'Keep Out' signs and come the extra mile around the back of the deserted village and eventually stand on the ridge and wave down to me.

I hoped that whoever came would be mothers with children, not boys with beer cans.

From: MarkC@rmbooks.com
To: RosieB@eirtel.com
Sent: 6.35 p.m.

Louis called me this morning! It was with reference to a letter from Delia Bacon to Emerson about your man Melville, but I turned the conversation (urbanely, I felt) to tea-towels.

'What did you and your writer have in mind?' he said.

I said we'd be in touch with a very brief proposal; that we'd expect a contract before we went further; that this is a highly competitive environment and that good tea-towel texts are vulnerable to piracy.

Whaddaya think of that!

Signed, your agent,

Speechless in Seattle

I called Markey to congratulate him on his quick thinking, and we fell around laughing for the first time in ages.

Beep beep beep.

The last of my euros went in.

'You know,' I said, 'life must make people very unsure. It seems all you need to do, to turn a commonplace observation into valued guidance, is sound as if you're absolutely certain. Lay down the law. But how can anyone be certain about anything? Of all the things I recommended in the 'Thoughts', the only ones I'm sure about are that it's important to enjoy your food and OK to love a dog.'

'And that everyone needs friends,' Markey said.

'Oh, yes,' I said. 'That, too.'

'*Old* friends,' he said.

'You just want to hitch your wagon to my star,' I said, and he was starting to laugh again, six thousand miles away, when the line went dead.

Next day I responded indirectly to Louis.

From: RosieB@eirtel.com
To: MarkC@rmbooks.com
Sent:11.45 a.m.
Private and Confidential

Dear Mr Cuffe,
I have tested the following in the field and am delighted to say it has been found both 'witty' and 'wise'. I would be open to production offers depending on (a) the level of quality envisaged for the product – I am not interested in anything less than excellence; (b) the marketing plan and budget; and (c) the size and prestige of the stores to be supplied. Please emphasise to your principal that copyright protection applies.
  Yours truly,
  Rosaleen Barry

Attachment # 1: The Wise Woman's Tips for the Bad Times

  1. Count your blessings.
  2. Fix your hair.
  3. Tidy your purse (or car, or truck).
  4. Establish as best you can your exact financial position, even if it is dire.
  5. Do a good deed for someone else.
  6. Smile at everyone you meet – they won't know you don't mean it.
  7. Don't be aggrieved because life is unjust. That's just how it is.

8. Do not listen to romantic arias/ hit the bottle/ call your ex or risk anything else emotionally disturbing.
9. If emotionally disturbed, do not sit down. Keep moving.
10. Find a baby. Ask permission. Make the baby laugh.

From: MarkC@rmbooks.com
To: RosieB@eirtel.com
CC: LouisAusten@Louisbooks&Collectibles.com
Sent: 2.36 p.m.

Dear Ms Barry,
My principal wants to know how many more of these you could supply. He has in mind a three-towel deal.

From: RosieB@eirtel.com
To: MarkC@rmbooks.com
Sent: 2.53 p.m.

Tell him YES for God's sake, Markey! Fast! Tell him there'd be no problem with future texts. Don't I happen to have Ten Thoughts for the Middle of the Journey to hand? They could readily be adapted to Five Thoughts for Two Different Parts of the Journey, i.e. the beginning or the end – or no journey at all, if the journey moment has passed! Whatever Louis wants!!

But don't forget what Yeats said when they phoned to tell him he'd won the Nobel Prize for Literature…

From: MarkC@rmbooks.com
To: RosieB@eirtel.com
Sent: 2.58 p.m.

OK, OK, what did he say?

From: RosieB@eirtel.com
To: MarkC@rmbooks.com
Sent: 3.03 p.m.

'How much? How much?'

From: MarkC@rmbooks.com
To: RosieB@eirtel.com
Sent: 3.35 p.m.
ARE YOU SITTING DOWN?

$10,000 each for three. Outright, flat-fee, no royalties.

$30,000 dollars = €22,000 @ current exchange rates.

Take off my agent's fee and you have €20,000 to play with.

How do ya like them eggrolls!

From: RosieB@eirtel.com
To: MarkC@rmbooks.com
Sent: 3.55 p.m.

He sure must want that letter to Emerson!

No, seriously – that's just great. WOWEE!

I drove all the way to Dublin to ring Min because this was no conversation to have with the phone beeping for euros every few minutes.

'Well!' I said, bursting with excitement. 'What do you think?'

'Oh, you heard the news did you?' she said. 'What do *you* think?'

'I think it's marvellous. I was—'

'Marvellous for some people,' she said threateningly. 'Not all that marvellous for others.'

'Are you talking about me?' I asked. 'Because if so you've got the wrong end of the stick. I'm—'

'No I don't mean you! Though you'll have to give a helping hand.'

Next thing Peg's name had got into the conversation, which remained hopelessly confused until I finally established that Min was talking about Monty, who had apparently named the day for marrying his secret girl-friend, a single mother aged twenty-eight with a little boy.

This was such an interesting bit of Kilbride news from abroad, followed by her amazement that Markey's Billy hadn't been a woman's name, that I had to work to catch Min's attention for the offer of €20,000 as a down payment on the Stoneytown house.

'We could ask an estate agent to value it,' I said, when she didn't answer at once. 'Though how anyone's going to value a worthless house on a priceless site, I don't know.'

But this Min was a different woman from the Min prior to the fire in Duluth. She'd only paused because she was so delighted. Absolutely and totally delighted to sell the whole thing for €20,000. In fact, she offered 10 per cent off for good measure.

'And good luck to you with the oul' kip! You could have it for nothing, only Luz and myself might buy a little place. She could buy a place back home near her daughter for what you're giving me. But I don't want to go to Mexico till I figure out how to get back here. I'm working in the vintage medical book business, you know, and I'm doing great.'

'But Min, what about Dublin! What about Kilbride! You can't just start a business life, never mind a Mexican life, at the age of seventy next month.'

'Why not?' Min said. 'Look at Monty. He's starting off where that bastard of a father of his left him, isn't he? That little boy is nearly the same age as Monty was when his own father walked out. Well, why can't I start off from where I was when I left my father? I was supposed to go to America. And I would have gone if you hadn't come into the world.'

'Oh I'm sorry, Min.'

'*Don't* be sorry. Not one thing about my life would I change, Rosie. Not even the hardship. I tell you with my hand on my heart. Not one thing, Rosie.'

Part Five

Winter

❧

23

All was well. Everyone was well. You'd think I'd have been happy. But instead, a darkness far worse than any I'd ever known came over me, as the autumn turned colder and colder.

I didn't care about anything. I didn't want to be bothered about anything. I slept long into the morning. During the day, I'd walk with the dog along the shore to see what the equinoctial gales had washed up, but even when there was something pretty or useful, I left it lying there. There was a dolphin, too, decomposing in the inlet where it had been trapped above the high-tide mark. It smelled bad, but I went past it every day anyway, because that was my route. Sometimes I met people. They'd begun to come over from Milbay in boats to take away stone and roof-flags and iron latches and cut-stone lintels and anything else that could be carried from the houses at Stoneytown. Even a couple of the ranges went – I knew that because entire front walls were being demolished now.

I think I looked normal enough when I came upon scavengers. I smiled and nodded, anyway, and went past with the dog. There was nothing to stop them doing what they were doing and it was legal enough; apparently the County Council was going to make a seaside park from the main road out to the Point, so Stoneytown could be said to already belong to the people.

As long as they didn't come near me, that's all I cared about. As long as no one climbed over the collapsed houses on the shore or walked all the way around the back and came near me. I couldn't be blamed for what I might do or say if they came anywhere near my place. And no one did come before the bad weather began, after which I welcomed every day of wind and rain. The worse the weather, the better chance I had of going from morning to night without even having to say 'hello'.

Winter closes in very harshly on that eastern coast. A crew of men, who were demolishing the buildings and taking up the old runway of the Air Corps camp, knew I was in the house and waved to me when I drove in and out to Milbay. I had the company of the noise of their machines during the day. The dog would come back from visiting them, smelling of the ham from their sandwiches. But it got dark around four o'clock in the afternoon as November began, and after they went home the wind seemed to rise along the hostile shore.

The Creator put curlews on earth to show human beings what desolation sounds like, I thought.

'It doesn't matter,' I said, when Andy came down to the house to announce that he and his mother Pearl would be going to Laos. 'I don't know what matters at the moment, except that you've brought the cold in.'

Indeed the influx of freezing air when I'd opened

the door was almost enough to make me resent his visit. See what he'd done? He'd helped my adversary! The range hardly seemed to radiate any heat into the air at all. I'd fill the grate with coal and wood and what warmth there had been would vanish before they began to burn. I'd scurry upstairs to the bed, which Andy had helped me shift across the loft to where the stovepipe came up through the floor. I'd burrow in under the duvet, and the dog would take up her post beside me, and sit there, her noble little head alert and watchful, while I listened to the rain speckling the roof, or the wind whining around the house and slapping the waves against the rocks. I'd warm up soon enough. But once I was warm, I'd remember that I was more lonely than I ever thought a person as restless as I could be. And I'd wonder: what happened to the me who had packed her own bag and got the taxi to whatever airport by herself? I used to know to rise early in the summer, and to make a fire and open a bottle of wine on rainy nights, or to read Henry James when I had to wait outside the offices of people who gave out work permits, and people who should allow me a tax rebate, and people whose stamp on a paper had let me enter or leave this place or that. I once knew how to slip out of bedrooms at dawn, closing the door noiselessly behind me. I could walk for a long time along the edge of highways and never look up when cars slowed down. I used to know how to manage by myself.

I called my state 'loneliness', but it was more like sorrow. I'd stare into the dark trying to think about the future, but the past would seep in and suffuse the future with regret. Why had Sister Cecilia died before I ever got around to thanking her for all that she had given me? I'd remember things like that, like when I was sick and she came to the house to teach me my words for *The Mikado*, and how she sat beside the bed and held my hand in both of hers and, for a minute, stroked my hair. And Lalla. How long is that – to say to yourself, 'This is the end' – if you jump from a high balcony onto rocks below? And my Dad. I'd recall his face, the last summer we were in The Hut, when I'd been up to the Harbour Nook to fetch three iced cupcakes for our tea, and I was coming out from under the viaduct where the railway crossed the road. He was there watching for me, sitting on a bollard because he was already too tired to stand for long. And his face as he looked at me, before he could compose it, was desolate.

Don't let Min die! I'd say to the dark. I can manage almost anything that's likely to happen, but Min must not die.

But Min is as happy and well as you've ever known her! So what's all this about dying?

She mourned my father a very long time. Even after the first few months – even a year, two, three years later – she might at any time stop whatever she was doing and sit down to gaze, dry-eyed, at the television, in-different to what it was showing. I was amazed at how quiet she was without him, she who had always been so brisk and unsentimental with him. I hadn't realised that her talkativeness needed his silences. That her energy was based on his weakness. That her certainties needed his doubts. I had thought of her and my Dad as separate beings, never realising that they were also each a half of a couple.

Maybe, I thought, though we are not a man and a woman, nor a parent and child, she and I, too, are a couple. And that's why I long to see her: her small hands on the handle of her shopping bag, her black eyes and her cloud of pale hair, the light, awkward, almost adolescent way she walks. She and I make up a whole. Or if not that, we're parts of the same whole.

She still rang the phone-box every Saturday, but at 4 o'clock my time, because of the early dark.

One time she told me about the party there'd been for Markey and Billy's twenty-fifth anniversary; only nobody had ever described Billy to me, so that I had no picture, however often he was mentioned, of the person Markey had been able to love.

'It was in a ballroom on an island so we all had to go on the ferry; you should have seen what the wind did to the ones who'd paid a fortune to have their hair done. A few of them had silver slides in their hair because that's the silver anniversary, you know, twenty-five, but a good few of them, the slides I mean, flew off into the sea. There was one lady fell down the stairs trying to keep in out of the wind, but lucky enough she was a doctor herself. But do you know what I did? Guess! I stuck silver crystals all over Luz's walker! That super-glue's great stuff. You'd think it was covered in diamonds. You could see it in the dark. She did great on the walker. We might go down to near Mexico for Christmas, now she's mobile.'

I was so taken aback that I said nothing, but Min

didn't notice, and sailed on. What could I have said, anyway? That I'd been more or less relying on visiting her at Christmas so as to help me out of this slump? That I already had a printout of flights to Seattle from the library computer, and was only waiting to discuss them with her?

She'd surely remark how there were tens of Christmases when I didn't come home to Dublin, nor even thought of asking whether that suited her or not, nor enquired what was she doing herself? Wasn't it not so long ago that I'd gone to meet Leo in the dreary little *pensione* near the docks in Ancona where we didn't manage to make love, and I had run out of things to read after twenty-four hours, and couldn't find anything in English anywhere except a Reader's Digest Condensed Book about a baseball player who'd survived a heart attack?

I'd relied on her, but still I'd made every decision without reference to her.

And it came to me as an insight: who was she being now, but me? Where had she learnt to do what she was doing now, but from me? It was as if we had been sisters, only I had gone out into the world first, and when she was finally ready, she'd followed. Which possibly meant that I was with her still, seeing as I was her presiding example.

And I missed her so much that I found that almost a consoling thought.

Could there be something physically wrong with my heart? Could a person have cancer of the heart? Why not? I jammed my fists into my chest to try to divert the ache. How can emotions, things you can't see or touch or even name, have so physical a presence? And what was wrong, anyway? Nothing was wrong. Min never missed a call. Leo was still in Kilbride and seemed to be very well. The last time I'd rung Tessa, she told me Andy and Pearl were almost ready to leave for the Far East, though neither of them was saying anything about what they really thought about that, and she hadn't seen Peg for a while because old Mr Colfer wasn't well, even by his standards. And that she herself was never better.

'And how are you, Chicken?' she asked.

'I'm doing fine,' I said.

I didn't say, I'm afraid of something bad happening. I'm afraid someone will die. If I wake with my hip hurting, I immediately think it's a symptom of leukaemia, or if I pee more than usual I think, well that's it now, I'm diabetic.

I tried to fight back with my old self. I'd tell myself jokes. Snail comes into a bar, and barman throws him out. Two weeks later snail comes back in and shouts, 'What did you do that for?' Man walks into a bar with a slab of asphalt under his arm. 'A beer for me, please,' he says, 'and give me one for the road.' Or I recited all the poems I'd learnt by heart, of which there were many, ever since I'd impressed Markey by learning 'Portrait of a Lady' and 'Marina' in the first week of our T.S. Eliot phase.

But I was more and more enfeebled by the cold grey days of rain and the nights full of the muted noises of nature gone wild in the darkness, humanity forgotten. I couldn't escape the cold for long. I had to brave it to go down and stoke the fire. I had to bring in fuel. I had light and tap water, but I couldn't run a heater, or even an electric blanket, off the minimal power supply I had, and, of course, nothing like a hot plate, so I was still cooking on the camping gas or on the top of the range. I'd fry an egg to put between slices of bread because that was the quickest hot meal I knew. I'd hurry with the dog out the back door where she and I would be as quick as we could about our business, but the cold would strip away the warmth I'd built up under my pants and tights, and when she ran back to me, shivering, I'd be shivering too, trying to pull my layers of clothes up with stiff fingers.

Back up in the loft, I could feel the cold still rising from the dog's coat. I thought very often about the men, women and children who had worked the quarries in this season. Of my poor mother! Who didn't even have electric light, and I'd start crying again. The dog must have thought I was a being with a bucket of water behind her eyes.

Finally I tried to lift myself out of the Slough of Despond.

I got the vet to come to the house and after I tricked the dog into letting him catch her, he sedated her. I brought her up to Kilbride then and tried to help her to come to terms with living there.

I was so intent on her that I hardly noticed Leo, except to register that the house looked very nice but in some way different, and that the phone was always ringing for him, and that he had a lump of real Parmesan the size of a brick for grating onto the pasta that his friend Enzo had brought him back from Italy.

But at the end of four days even Leo, who practised detachment from all creatures great and small, was utterly distraught. And I never, ever, wanted to see again an animal as unhappy as that little dog was in the city. She dragged herself on her belly across the yard to the wall of the shed and would not move from there to eat or even poop. And she jumped with fear, even on the fourth night, at a car-door slamming or anything with an engine going past on the other side of the wall. And Bell was afraid of her too, though they'd co-existed in Stoneytown without a problem.

I got her sedated again, and bitterly angry at myself for putting her through such an ordeal, went back to Stoneytown where for a few days I hardly let her out of my sight.

But we could not go on like this forever. I called the vet again, to bring the dog to the Bide-a-Wee Kennels in Milbay, where within an hour she jumped a wall that the woman there told me no dog had jumped in twenty years, not even one of the big dogs. It took half-a-day for me and the woman to find my little companion, shuddering, underneath a hedge.

The woman said she was not suited to kennel life. She said it might be a case of having to have her put down.

Not long after hearing those words, and not thinking straight due to sleeping tablets and anxiety, I suddenly thought there might be someone who'd look after her down in the docks area of Milbay, where The Hut used to be. Someone there who might say, 'Oh, leave her here and she'll be fine, this is a happy and safe place!' So I drove straight there from Stoneytown in thick, grey rain. The watchman let me in to the wharf, and I drove along narrow lanes between house-high stacks of shipping containers to where The Hut used to stand. There was no grass left. There was no shore, just a concrete embankment where the shore had been. There was no one at all around except the watchman, and he was young and didn't care whether I lived or died, much less the dog.

So she and I went back out to the Point and resumed our life there. The weather remained cold, but it now turned still and bright. On some days, it was even warmer outside the house than in, so I'd swathe myself in sweaters and scarves, and putting two pairs of socks on under my boots, sit and read on the bench outside the front door in the afternoons. It was like going to Las Vegas out there, after the bed in the loft. Often the band was playing in the hotel up the river; it seemed that the dancing at winter weddings started around three. I loved the kind of music they played: 'The Tennessee Waltz' and 'The Rose of San Antone' or '24 Hours from Tulsa'. Oh, America in songs! Such a great and vast place for heartbreak!

I could listen, and at the same time read my Proust and laugh and cry with the people of the book as if I were one of them – as if, were I to walk into one of their soirées, the narrator would remember who I was. I read with perfect credulity: appalled, for example, on behalf of the narrator when he discovers that Albertine, according to Andrée, had had 'furious desires' for women, even though it was my third time to reach that point in the plot and I wasn't shocked by lesbianism in the first place.

Perhaps what really disturbs me, I thought, is the whole idea of finding out something astonishing about a person after they are dead. And yet, that even a translucent life will turn out to contain a secret seemed, now that I knew something about the world, only natural.

But just as the weddings across the estuary were coming into their swing, I would hurry inside. Before that moment when the sun sank below the horizon and life went out of the scene like a revelation of bleakness – I was better off without revelations of that kind.

When the weather turned wintry and I was still down there at the Point, Tessa drove down to see me. I'd happened to mention I'd be in Milbay that Wednesday, and so she waited in the Harbour Nook till she saw me walk past. Still, I didn't give in to the *fait accompli*. I had coffee with her but I asked her not to come out to the house. I said that if she was my friend she was to listen to me; to hear that I didn't want to be with anyone; that I didn't want to talk or smile. That I couldn't. And she was not to use her better vitality to overrule me. She was to trust me and leave me alone.

'But if you're sick…'

'I'm not sick,' I said, and I heard an echo of Sister Cecilia's voice telling me that Min was not sick, that time she came to the house to talk to her after my Dad and

I became frightened by her fantasy of leaving us to become an opera singer.

And now, as then, Sister Cecilia helped me. Because I went on thinking about that time, trying to learn from it. Did I know what it was I was now missing, the way Min's unconscious had known for her? I remembered seeing a news item around that time, about Maria Callas walking out of a performance in Rome, and reading it out to Min because we both loved her on the radio. I said that no one ever wrote anything about Callas except bad things, but what about all the languages she knew and her understanding of music and drama? So Min knew too that there was hard work in the world that, unlike her own, underpinned something beautiful and emotionally persuasive. A great singer who contributed to the glory in the world.

If there was one thing Min had never known, and never would, it was glory.

'I'm not in despair,' I said to Tessa as I walked her to her car. 'I just have to stay till I know what it is I'm missing ...'

She gave me an exasperated look.

'You're going to be the worst counsellor in the world,' I said. 'Do you know that?'

'Probably,' she gloomily replied.

But she was being near-incredibly sensitive, given a track record that had seen Peg and me repeatedly calling her Pol Pot. She went on faithfully sending emails, which I read whenever I got to the library. And in which she talked about things I could manage, like that she'd had her Prada shoes heeled and now she could hardly walk in them, so maybe they were meant for people so rich they never got anything mended. Or that Leo was the hit of the century in Kilbride and that since he began training the ladies' choir there were women always knocking on the door with little gifts, like a fresh-baked cake of bread or a few last flowers from the garden or CDs or books. Reeny told her. Reeny was watching it all.

'The one thing Reeny wants to know,' she wrote, 'is why Leo is still wearing his linen suits? Does he not get cold, or has he skin like leather?'

I emailed back, adding not to expect a reply except once in a while: 'There's never any news here'. But that wasn't true. I had my own news: whether, for example, the range had behaved well that day or chosen to smoke. Or whether, when the dog had gone off to visit the men working on the camp demolition, I had decided to go up to bed and climb out again when I heard her scratch at the door, or to wait downstairs instead.

Look what I possess, I said to myself. I have a very good friend in Tessa, and I have other friends. I have my beloved dog. I have enough money to last till I find a job, and when I find a job I'll have this house to spend my earnings on. I'm very well apart from pains in my hands. Leo is faring better – every time we speak his voice is stronger, warmer. Min is having the time of her life. What more can a person ask?

But oh! my whole self seemed to cry out, they can ask for more than that! They can ask to be great. To be good. To do good. To be desired. They can ask for the void inside to be filled. They can ask that their mother come back, their father come back, their aunt – that someone love them and know them and care for them and help them on the last part of the journey…

Then the way Markey would laugh gently at me came back to me, and I calmed down.

'What's this?' he'd asked when I once said mournfully that I wasn't yet ready to go gentle into that good night.

'For Pete's sake, Rosie!!' he'd yelled down the phone. 'You're a relatively young person in the best of health. You're not going anywhere. Gimme a break!'

24

The fact is, there was never a tide in the sea that didn't turn. And inside me too, a change began. A few things happened to make me feel that I wasn't heading towards an endlessly receding horizon any more. I was making for shore instead.

One day there came a whistle from the ridge, and there, again, was the postman.

'There's mail for you, Missus,' he shouted down.

The dog was thrilled to have a visitor and scurried around him as I ran up the slope without stopping for breath.

'Nice day now,' he said, and I said, 'Better than yesterday, anyway', so pleased to exchange a proper greeting.

The mail was a card from the dentist and a letter from the Electricity Supply Board, saying that my supply would be cut off at the end of the month, as it was a special connection for the conduct of a lairage that could not be used for anything else. I walked to the phone-box through the winter woods to inform Andy. In drifts and corners and under bushes where the light didn't reach, fallen beech leaves lay still frozen from the night's frost: assemblages of beautifully precise shapes, all ochre with crisp white edges.

What would I do? Could I advertise for a home for the dog, and leave her? Was there any way I could go back to work and still have her?

Andy came down the next day.

'I had to see you anyway,' he said. 'To say goodbye. And to bring you a few things Pearl thought might be tasty, if you're not eating...' he pulled up short.

'It doesn't matter,' I said to him. 'I eat plenty.'

He went on then about me quitting there and going back to Min's house to let Leo feed me up with pasta. But I told him what was true, that the thought of going anywhere was still impossible.

'Well,' he said, 'eat anyway. We shouldn't stop eating today because we're afraid of what we'll be doing to-morrow.'

'Well, we *should*,' I said.

'Should what? Stop eating?'

'We should be afraid,' I cried.

'Rosie,' he said, 'don't stay here. Have the place done up if you love it that much. But leave, Rosie. Now. There's builders that could start this side of Christmas because there isn't much outside work in it. Give it up, Rosie. Let it go.'

'I want to stay here,' I said stubbornly.

'Is it because Leo is on Kilbride? Because if it is...'

'No! Oh no, Andy, not at all! That's one of the good things, Leo's being there. It's good for Leo and it's good for me and it's good for Bell and it's good for the house. I just want to stay here till I think of something else to do.'

And I eventually persuaded him to go in to Milbay to see the electricity people and to try to order Proust's *Jean Santeuil* on an inter-library loan, in case I got to the end of *Remembrance* and had nothing more to read.

Everything was bathed in the low sunlight of a still, cold afternoon, when I opened the door to him again and he tottered in, a sack of coal between his arms and a box of groceries balanced on top.

'Put the kettle on,' he panted. 'Library half-day. Fella from the ESB on his way – he's coming out to have a look around as a favour. I told him I couldn't make you shift out of here and you couldn't stay on without power, so he said he might be able to swing a temporary social-welfare thing.'

I expected him to bustle around as usual, but he was aware, I think, that we had only a few more minutes alone. So he put the box down and stood there, looking at me. I almost asked him not to speak, so tense was his face with effort.

'I know you think I shouldn't be taking Pearl so far away,' he began.

'That's what a few people think, probably,' I murmured.

'I don't mind the others,' he said, his face perfectly candid. 'But you...'

Knock! Knock!

The fine-looking man from the ESB filled the door, smiling in a big sheepskin coat: the same brown-eyed engineer with the carefully combed hair who'd turned me down in the spring.

'My God!' he said. 'The best view in Ireland you've got here!'

I hadn't washed my face since yesterday and my hair for I didn't know how long.

'Look!' he cried. 'There!'

Something moved on the rocky shore below. Ah, seals – three seals on the black rocks beside the stream from the hillside that ran out under the wall and down through shingle to the water. They'd come out to bask even in so weak a sun, a large one, a medium-sized one, and a baby seal on its own flat rock. As it calmly turned its white face from father to mother, and mother to father, I was momentarily pierced by a vision of family, where a little one is perfectly protected by larger ones.

The dog was quivering with anxiety on the threshold, watching the seals with maximum suspicion, but unwilling to leave her humans unguarded.

'Seals are good luck,' Andy said. 'Aidan, isn't it?'

'Indeed and they are. Aidan, that's right. Pleased to meet you,' he turned and shook my hand amiably. 'Though we met before, didn't we? Aren't you the quarryman's granddaughter? I think I remember you coming in to the office about this place, but that was before the cable got put in for the animals. Now! Who's going to give me the guided tour?'

The two of them went out then to look at the pump – the man, Aidan, tut-tutting at something: 'That'll freeze,' he was saying to Andy – as I stood for a moment at the door. A last reflection of light was coming from below the horizon, but the rocks where the seals had been had become a shadowy mass. I closed the door, shivering, and went to put on the kettle.

The dog padded happily behind the two of them as they examined every switch and socket, inside and out, from the loft to the barn, and marking the dust on the floor in front of the range with a mass of paw marks and footsteps.

Aidan only took off his coat when he sat down to the table-made-out-of-a-door for his tea. I had fruitcake to offer, too, from Pearl's care-package.

The body is everything, I thought again, looking at them. The way each man moved and talked and looked at me so differently, because they were each so differently made and felt so differently about themselves. And how Andy with all his delicacies and kindnesses had faded away as Aidan's presence filled the room.

'I was saying to Andy here,' he said 'that there's something we could do for you. Anyway, it's either that or throw you in jail for pretending you're a goat that didn't take the boat at Rosslare.'

'I'll go to jail happily if I can bring the dog,' I said. 'Jails are warm.'

'The dog looks fitter than you do,' he offered.

'Who asked you your opinion?' I said.

He boomed with laughter at that.

He considers me so old that I can't possibly misinterpret him, I thought. And he's right, I don't. If I were still young enough for him to fancy me, the air in this room would be singing. But look how friendly things are between us, just because there's no chance of him wanting me. I never thought of that – how that's a good thing about growing older. The way women and men retrieve each other. And things go back to where they were before everyone went mad with suspicion at the age of thirteen or fourteen.

'Can you follow me back to town?' he said to Andy. 'You'll have to sign off on the change of use.'

'No problem,' Andy said, though he looked miserable.

'I'll be back in a minute,' Aidan said. 'I just have to fetch something from the van.'

Andy began folding his scarf carefully under his chin, adjusting it so that one part crossed the other part in perfect symmetry.

'I was just going to say to you...' as if struggling to force the words out. 'That I have to bring Pearl to Laos because she's old now, and I can't go anywhere without her. I couldn't take the job if I thought she was on her own, and might fall sick and be asking for me, and it's right out in the sticks, this place where I'm going, and I mightn't make it back in time. And I have to go. Anyone who knows what No-Need could do for the place – they'd have to go.'

'I understand,' I said. I nearly said 'I understand, Andy,' but the near-rhyme would have made me smile and he was too tense for that.

He looked straight at me for the only time in the conversation. 'Is it a country that you're interested in yourself?' he said. 'Laos? A big traveller like you?'

'I was thinking more of Myanmar,' I said. 'If that's the direction I head in whenever I get myself going.'

I said it matter-of-factly. I didn't presume to be gentle. Nor was it sufficiently clear whether there'd been an invitation or not.

Aidan came bustling in the front door.

Andy looked down and whispered, 'Tell Tess.'

Ah. So Tessa had said something to him.

'This here's an electric blanket,' Aidan said. 'Best on the market. They probably said you can't use one, but you can, you've a big safety margin there. In a few days I'll ask one of the lads to come out to have a better look around than I got.'

'Mister…' I began.

'That's a present, that is,' he said. 'Sure Milbay wouldn't be there at all if it wasn't for your granda's quarry.'

I wrapped my head in a scarf and walked with them to their cars.

Aidan leaned out of his window. 'We can look after you better now,' he said, 'that we know you're a person, not a lorry load of sick sheep!', before he moved off bumpily, delighted with his own wit.

Andy hugged me for a long minute, our cheeks warm where they touched, our breath visible in the dark air.

'I wish you so much luck and happiness, Andy, I can't tell you how much.' I meant it from the bottom of my heart. 'And your wonderful mother, too. Come back safely.'

He didn't say a word – because he couldn't, I think. Then he too drove off.

I climbed back over the ridge into a new world.

The sea was flooded now with pale light from a moon that hung huge and low above the horizon. The roofs below me – the house, the barn, the sheds –

shone in its light. Music came across the silvery water. Was that the hotel band? Was it a dance night? No, someone was playing an old recording of – oh! – one of Min's big songs from the Saturday nights in Granny Barry's parlour. I used to mouth what I could manage of the fabulous words when I was nine or ten years old:

'When they begin the beguine
It brings back a night of tropical splendour...'

The dog and I stayed at the front door for a minute, looking out across the shore, where flashes of white marked the seagulls moving noiselessly in and out of the darkness.

'So don't let them begin the beguine.
Let the love that was once a fire remain an ember.
Let it sleep like the dead desire I only remember...'

I couldn't help it: my heart turned over with pain. I missed Min. I missed my Dad. I missed those nights when the two women sang at the table and the swallows swooped across the evening sky beyond the open windows behind their heads. I missed the past. I missed my childhood. I missed my youth. I missed a companion. I ached with missing. And the gold of the lights of the town began to smear and dazzle as if rain had come out of nowhere.

But it wasn't long until – after some thought which I recognised had the virtue of not being about myself – I invited Tessa to brunch.

'Brunch?' she said. 'In Château Misery? I could bring croissants, I suppose, but do you even have coffee down there?'

'Coffee wouldn't taste right, made on a range,' I said. 'And tea doesn't go with croissants. Would scrambled egg and crispy bacon not be good enough for you?'

'Too many calories,' she said. 'My whole day would be wrecked.'

'I could make potato cakes.'

'Oh well, that's different. Potato cakes are worth it.'

'But you bring fruit, Tess. Cities are the only place you can find fruit any more, and I have such a craving for it.'

She came on a day of high, bracing wind, running down the cart track from her little car like an athlete, and sweeping me into a hug that twirled us back into the house.

'Don't ever do this to us again!' she said, half-laughing, half-serious. 'Disappearing. Heading off by yourself...'

'I'm on my way back,' I said.

And it was so. Not because there'd been a single big turning-point. Instead, small things, gathered together, seemed to have been stepping-stones out of the darkness. The gift of the electric blanket from someone I'd once been angry with. The offer from Andy that maybe was an offer and maybe was not. The brunch, and everything to do with it: suggesting it, shopping for it, cooking it, and then laying the table, sweeping the room, arranging branches of red-berried rowan in a jug, and building up the fire in the range as a setting for it.

I was opening the bags we'd brought in from Tessa's car.

'This is the first food I've looked forward to for I

don't know how long,' I said. 'I was afraid that I'd never care again. But in the last few days I've been imagining melons.'

'In that first bag there,' Tess pointed, 'honeydew and galia. And apricots from Syria and strawberries from Zimbabwe and Cox's Pippins from New Zealand.'

'I grated Irish raw potato into Irish mashed potato to mix with flour from Ireland for the potato cakes, which will be swimming in low-fat butter so we can use twice what we'd use if it wasn't low-fat.'

'Would you mind telling me how you got so thin, if—'

'The picnic was the last time I was hungry, I think. I know I've lost weight – my jeans are loose on me – but I tell you something, Tess, and I bet you've never heard a woman say this before: I'm not glad. I'd be willing to put every pound back on again, and more, if it meant I'd be greedy again the way I used to be. Because I got a glimpse in the last couple of months of what it's like to lose your interest in living and I didn't like it. It must be a particular danger of middle age – that when you fall out of the world where you were fancied by people and fancied them, you become in-different to a whole range of other things. You have to work at keeping your links to sensuality and—'

'Rosie Barry!' Tess interrupted, disgustedly. 'Is there anything on earth that doesn't remind you of sex!'

'Oh don't be such a *peasant*, Tess. Sensuality isn't sex. It's feeling. It's relishing certain sensations enough to seek them out.'

'And you derive that from *potato cakes*?'

'Cheap sarcasm will get you nowhere,' I said loftily. 'And it must be a great bond between a couple, greed must,' I continued. 'Couples where both people are greedy have meals to plan and restaurants to talk about. I mean, some couples have nothing at all to talk about.'

'I don't know about that,' she said. 'Peg and Monty both loved their food, but that hasn't stopped him running off with a young one who looks as if she never had a square meal in her life.'

'How is Peg?' I said.

'She's very bad,' Tessa said. 'If it isn't one of you, it's the other.'

I was watching her start her eggs, which I'd flavoured with sorrel and a tiny bit of wild thyme.

'These,' she said emphatically, 'are the best scrambled eggs I've ever eaten.'

'Like I said,' I repeated with heavy emphasis. 'Some couples have nothing to talk about except food.'

She looked up innocently. 'What's wrong with you?' she said. 'Why are you talking like that?'

'Andy was here the other day,' I said.

Her face flushed. 'Oh, so that's why you're talking about couples! I knew there was something between you and him.'

'There was not. I told you. Never. It's the very opposite.'

'What would be the very opposite?'

I reached across and took her hand and held it. 'He told me to tell you that he has to go to Laos because he's needed there, and he has to bring Pearl because he's afraid to leave her. That's all he said in words. But the way he said, "Tell Tess" – there was something about it. I can't exactly put my finger on it. He was trying to say something else. But you know Andy, he just can't get things out.'

'Like what things?' she said. By now a blush had spread to the whole of her face.

'I don't know,' I began.

I didn't want to tell an actual lie. Besides, if she and Andy did get together, they'd find out. But I was more than willing to be suggestive.

All my life I'd kept Hugh Boody's offer to make me his mistress hidden at the back of my memories. I knew that though I could say I wasn't guilty – that I hadn't done anything to invite it and that I'd rejected it – I was guilty. There was something about the person I was that had attracted him in the first place, and made him confident I wouldn't be outraged at the offer. Maybe, too, I should have told Tessa about it. I wasn't sure. But I felt that if I helped her now go after Andy, I might somehow make up for my private knowledge of Hugh.

Not for the first time, Tessa picked up, in a way, on what I was thinking.

'I've been fine up to now,' she said. 'I always thought Hugh Boody was enough for my lifetime, because we were so happy together. But now I'd give anything for someone to grow old with.'

'I know,' I said. 'Me too.'

I laid my head on the table and she took my hand and squeezed it and said, 'Ah, *don't*.'

We were silent, but the room was not. Outside, the wind was whipping the tide onshore, while the coal in the fire shifted and the dog, asleep on the floor in front of it, made a soft, regular, breathing noise.

'Which one's Laos?' she said.

'It's the one beside Vietnam and up a bit. Remember how Kissinger and Nixon and that shower of liars bombed it when they were desperate.'

'But I'm a trained counsellor,' she said. 'I'll be graduating next month.'

'People have problems in Laos too, I dare say. I mean, English-speaking Laotians probably have lots of problems.'

'But is going out there what Andy meant?' She was definitely having cold feet. 'What way did he say "Tell Tess"?'

'He just said it – strangely. He would have seemed normal to anyone else, but I knew it was strange.'

'What exactly do you mean, strange?'

'Just – strange.'

We looked at each other.

'Listen, Tess,' I said vigorously, 'usually when someone says "what have you to lose?" it turns out that you have lots to lose. But in this case, I really think you should go out, just for the experience. If it doesn't work out between you and him, what the hell? What have you lost? Just go and be your energetic, wonderful self and see what happens. Don't be trying to live up to love – do you love him blah blah; does he love you blah blah. Love is too hard.'

The blush was back again.

'Damn it all,' I said, 'you're his cousin and poor old Pearl is your aunt, and you have every right to turn up in the jungle to help her settle in, and what's more she'll probably fall to the ground and kiss your feet. And when you're there, you'll see can you make something happen. Wear your shorts. You look cute in shorts.'

'But what'll I say I'm doing? What explanation will I give?'

'Say you just happened to be passing and you thought you'd drop in,' I suggested, and we split our sides laughing.

25

'He's in heaven!' Peg cried down the phone, sounding so distraught that for a split second I thought she'd murdered unfaithful Monty. But the Orpheus who finally brought me up from the underworld of that house on the Point turned out to be Mr Colfer, of all people, the late Mr Colfer, that is.

One of the workmen from the airfield had called out to me from the ridge that I was to ring Peg Colfer: it didn't matter what time, day or night. And that her dad was 'in heaven' was how she'd announced his death to me when I did ring. She hadn't wanted to say 'dead'.

'He just said, "I don't feel so good." And when I looked again he was lying back so uncomfortably that I knew. I just knew, Rosie!' She burst into bitter tears.

I did my best to soothe her, and said that of course I'd be home in time for the Removal, and of course I'd be at the funeral the following morning. She sounded so distressed that I only wanted to be there for her, quite apart from the fact there'd be no forgiveness, ever, for anyone who missed either ceremony. At the same time I didn't feel ready. I was nervous about leaving the dog. I was nervous about everything.

I stopped in Milbay to have my grey coat pressed while I had an emergency wash and blow dry. My legs were shaky, but it gradually came back to me: how to buy a sheaf of flowers, how to buy a pair of gloves, how to agree that it wasn't a bad oul' day now, thank God. I put make-up on in the hairdresser's and ended up looking so bright and neat, along with having lost so much weight, that I couldn't resist sticking my head around the door of the ESB office and asking was Aidan in?

He wasn't.

On the way to Dublin, I gave myself a severe talking-to. Give up! I said to myself. Stop all that stuff! What did you want, anyway?

I wanted him to think I'm attractive!

Why? Why?

You know why!

The funeral was from the Gardiner Street church, and I was held up on my way there by the lights opposite the Gresham Hotel. I knew well which window it was of the room where I'd lost my virginity to Dan the American professor – I'd sought it out in the months afterwards, when I was still expecting a letter from him. I thought of him as 'The Professor', though he was a bit Beach-Boy-looking, with his blonde hair and tanned skin. Had he been older, he would have been nicer to me. He'd have written a few sentimental letters. Many a professor had. Still, given that losing your virginity must almost by definition be a shocking experience, I was lucky. Dan was nice enough, and he had been careful.

And the truth was that it had been only partly me, young Rosie Barry, having great trouble pulling her skin-tight jeans down over her hips, who lay there on the bed. For 'The Dead' was as real, at least to me, as reality, and therefore I was Gretta too, though instead of turning away, preoccupied, from Gabriel, I was kissing him all over the face.

I had defences when I was that age. Lalla and I had boasted often, for example, that we would never give our happiness over to a man, and I had believed that I never would. And though I haunted churches praying that Dan would write, I hadn't believed in a God who listened, not since my dad died in spite of all my implorings. I also didn't believe because Markey and Flaubert didn't. And though I wanted letters from Dan, I couldn't receive them at home without awful risk, and I also couldn't receive them at Boody's because the other girls would have seen the American stamps and given me a hard time. So I wasn't altogether devastated by his silence.

But I'd often wondered whether that hour with him had affected the whole of my life. Why, for example, had I not married when I was young, like most people? Might I have married if I'd been a virgin?

Oh, when, as Tessa says, will I get over sex? I couldn't wait for the lights to change so as to leave O'Connell Street. When? It was thirty-five years since I scurried to meet Dan along that pavement there, yet today exactly the same shallow-breathed excitement had gripped me again, walking from the hairdresser's to the ESB in the hope that Aidan the engineer would be there.

Tell my body to get over it! I snarled at myself. *It's not me, it's my body that won't. That can't.*

Maybe I would never be free until, like Mr Colfer – there in the coffin drawn up at the foot of the altar steps – my chrysalis of flesh fell away. I tried, as I always did and with as little success as usual, to imagine where the Mr Colferness of Mr Colfer was now, since it was patently not in his emptied body. After my dad died, I used to imagine him floating above me; high up, but not so high that we were not still in touch with each other. But what if the spirit went down? What if it burrowed into the earth because it could not bear being dis-incarnated? Or what if it stayed on the same level as the living, so that when we walk around we push through thick crowds of spirits? Might my mother be walking beside me and I not know it? And what of the elements of spirit that were personality, that equipped a person to live in a human body among people? Where did they go? Were they just waste? I had known Mr Colfer as long as I'd known anybody; indeed, the day I ignored Min, who was threatening not to allow me to go to school, and ran up to his shop and burst in and announced to him that I knew how to read, he kindly gave me an orange. Where was his uniqueness now? Was it just a flourish of creation, like the million different patterns on the wings of birds?

Peg was absolutely grief-stricken. Her sobs all through the prayers sounded so heartfelt that I began to cry, too, just from empathy, till Tessa gave me a disgusted look. At the end, as the priest came down to the coffin to sprinkle it with holy water, and swing the incense-boat around it, asking that perpetual light might shine upon their father, the sobs of his family became hysterical, and Peg, blinded with tears, had to be half-supported down the aisle by her brother who was back from Canada.

We huddled against the wall of the church behind Tessa's umbrella as we waited for the family to shake hands with sympathisers and drive away. Tessa had shrugged off her coat for a moment, to show me the impressive scab on her arm where she'd received her injections for Laos. But my mind, as I pointed out to her, was on higher things.

'Isn't it extraordinary,' I said, 'that we all treat this kind of thing as if it were ordinary? This is a public occasion, but look at how private a thing it shows a family is! We've no idea what the weights and measures within that family were; what made all his children love Mr Colfer so much. I mean, as far as most people are concerned, he bullied Peg's mother, and made a holy show of himself over Enzo's wife, and it took him ten minutes to sell a person a box of matches. Why did Peg devote herself so to looking after him? Now he's gone and she's too old for a baby. Unless she goes to Italy to what's-his-name the crazy gynaecologist. I mean, that's the simplest way to make sense of having been born. Have a child. Join the gang. Did you not notice, when they were going up for Communion, how the generations lined up, queuing up like divers to climb onto the board? These few years are the time of Mr Colfer or your parents. And after that generation jumps off into the afterlife, then it's Min's, and then it's you and me and Andy and our lot. The thing is, we have no children, Tessie, you and me, so unless we're geniuses, which we aren't, there's no real point to us. You move along, then you line up for death and dive off, having left children behind to grow up and grow old and come out onto the diving board themselves. If you don't have babies, you're not leaving anything behind. You're just a spare.'

'For Crissake,' Tessa groaned. 'The world is full of babies! If you want a baby, why don't you go off and help some baby that already exists? It'd make a change from the dog. Neither you nor me ever wanted a baby, as far as I know, because if we did, what was to stop us having one? And anyway, Rosie, what the hell do you want us to do about it at this stage? Spend the rest of our lives apologising?'

'Well,' I said stubbornly, 'I still think that's all humanity is: teams of people queuing up to jump off into death. So you have to distract yourself. If you can think of anything to distract yourself with, which at the moment I can't.'

'But maybe there's something on the other side?' Tessa said. 'And even if there isn't, even if this life is all there is, isn't that more of a reason, not less, for enjoying every minute of it?'

I took her literally, and so the two of us had a great day, before I finally got back to Min's house after about a million drinks with the entire population of Kilbride in the pub on the square near Glasnevin Cemetery.

Oh, the difference between coming into an empty house and a house that was alive!

Dazed as I was, I could see that Leo had made the place his own with great artistry. All Min's little ornaments had disappeared, and he'd brought the plain, black rug down from beside my Dad's bed, and done away with the rag rug. He'd also tied the yellow curtains back to no more than narrow stripes on either side of the windows, and pampered the Busy Lizzies which now glowed coral red between the yellow stripes. Everything was as linear and simple as it could be, except for the fire, which moved gloriously through all kinds of flaring and receding radiances. Some Swiss dish involving potatoes, cheese and ham scented the air. Bell – who, Leo said, slept at the foot of his bed but would otherwise have no dealings with him – twisted over on her back, asking for her tummy to be rubbed, and when I sat at the table, she leapt onto my lap.

Leo had been listening to a Schubert quartet when I fell in the door, red-faced and garrulous, and he went back to it now to quieten me down, while I ate the supper he had served me.

'Now listen to the cello line,' he instructed. Or, 'Here Rosie, this is where he recapitulates the opening phrase…'

'You're wonderful,' I said, and I meant it. 'What do I have to do to persuade you to move in for ever?'

He smiled at me, serene. 'I regret that I am not available, my dear. My good son, my Benjamin, has been pointing out my virtues to my wife, and she and I have just begun a discussion, comparatively amiable in tone, about the possibility of my renovating the stables at the house in Lucerne for my own use. I have been studying soundproofing in Kilbride Library.'

Well!

'I'm very pleased for you,' I said sincerely, 'though you could have easily opened the first boutique hotel in Kilbride and made a fortune.'

Upstairs I found the chilled mineral water he'd left beside Min's bed where I was sleeping, and a bunch of freesia that, tiny as it was, lightly perfumed the air, and I saw that he'd even ironed the sheets.

Well! He and his wife were sensible people, making the best of the time they had. Everyone should be so sensible. And have so much money, of course.

I was longing to go to sleep but I couldn't resist going online now that there weren't any hyped-up adolescents queuing behind me for the computer. Anyway, I was missing my conversations with the friend of my youth.

From: RosieB@eirtel.com
To: MarkC@rmbooks.com
Sent: 11.05 p.m.

How are you, dear Markey, and how is all your Noah's Ark? I've just been at Mr Colfer's Removal and the wake afterwards, and I have had rather a lot to drink. But Leo and I have not been idle. We searched Min's kitchen and turned up a towel with a 300-word 'Irish Mother's Prayer' on it; another with a map of Paul Revere's Ride; another with an account of the Boston Tea Party and a recipe for Boston Baked Beans; and a fourth with the complete rules of the Texas Hold 'Em poker game. Min also has oven gloves with a chunk of Beatrix Potter on the backs. Needless to say, I'd never noticed all this reading-matter before.

Leo then made some sensationally strong coffee which has given me lift-off. So, herewith, seven miniaturised 'Thoughts'. They're for the Middle of the Journey but, oddly enough, they're not melancholy. Whatever has come over me? I have no trouble finding these positive things to say. In fact, I stand by them.

In the Middle of the Journey:

1. The dizzy highs and awful lows stop taking up all your energy. You discover what an empowering place a plateau is.
2. You face both ways, now. You can reach back to vigour, and forward to wisdom.
3. You're probably at the peak of your earning power and so the practical aspects of your life run smoothly. This itself is a new freedom.
4. You know what you want. You also know that just because you want it doesn't necessarily mean you should go for it.
5. You have the perspective of experience now, which can show you meaning and beauty where you never perceived it before.
6. The you that was acted upon is in the past. Now, you act.

7. Unnecessary struggles fall away. The fight against yourself is over. At last, you and yourself can be friends.

Bye now. Must go to bed, to rest in peace, like Mr Colfer.

26

I'd have stayed on in Kilbride for the comfort of
it, only I was anxious to return to the Point. I
knew the dog would be waiting. I could see her
in my mind's eye, crouched in expectation once she
heard the car, her head cocked anxiously until she
identified the person who arrived over the ridge. But
first I had to wait till the buffet meal in the inn that
followed the funeral was over, and everyone had
hugged Peg, and I could arrange to see her on her own.
I hadn't been able to communicate with her so far,
except to squeeze her hand and pick some bits of lint
off her black coat.

'Come out to the new house,' she said. 'I've to go to
the graveyard with my brother to look at the flowers
but I'll tell him you're waiting for me – that way we
won't have time to be discussing the inheritance.'

The bungalow, given over by Monty to Peg, was newly
painted, but the ground around it hadn't been
landscaped, and I had to pick my way through part of
a wild field to reach the porch. Peg, still in the black
dress that suited her blonde hair, led the way into the

conservatory, where a couple of armchairs from her father's house sat like doll's house pieces in the expanse of tile. I hugged her for a moment and she mumbled, 'It's just that I'll miss him so much.'

But she was all cried out, she said; she wanted a break, and she poured us each a tumbler full of champagne. 'I can't get drunk because there's a family dinner tonight where I'll need my wits about me, but champagne doesn't really make you drunk.'

'I'll remember to tell that to the guards if I get pulled over,' I said, and we clicked our glasses in a toast to her father in heaven and to us on earth, that we'd all have Happy Days.

'Gosh, Peg,' I said. 'God forgive me for saying it but bereavement becomes you – you look absolutely, fabulously well. And black is your colour—'

'I know,' she said smugly. 'Twenty pounds down. The secret is suffering.'

'Even the dark shadows under the eyes, they're so chic with fair skin! Your furniture, on the other hand…'

'Yeah,' she said. 'It looks really terrible. But I took it so the others wouldn't, once I knew that my da hadn't said anything about it in the will. The others are receiving more than they deserve, anyway – you know he left the house to us all? I have a leather suite on order. Monty always said we'd have leather because we might have pets.'

'Did you speak to him at the funeral?'

'I certainly did,' she said. 'I said "Hello, Darling", and winked when he skulked past with the child bride.'

'We seem to be coping with things in opposite ways,

you and me,' I said mildly. 'I'm stuck for something to do to cheer myself up, whereas you – well, all I can say is the worm sure has turned! You've come out with all guns blazing, if worms can carry guns.'

'I'm changing,' she said. 'I wasn't satisfied with the way things were, like you said I was the night we all went to *Babe*. I thought I was, but I wasn't. I'm glad now that Monty the Rat took off. Like father, like bloody son. The only difference between you and me now is that you're ahead of me in life. I'm learning to drive, whereas you can drive already. And you know how to dress whereas I'm only starting. I want to know where you got those sheer black tights; don't think I didn't notice. And I'm going to sign up for bridge as soon as they have a new class, but you're doing bridge already, or you're supposed to be. I'm even thinking of buying a dog.'

'Peg!' I shouted, and I hauled her up and danced her around in a big sloppy embrace before dumping her back into her chair again. 'Peg! Look no further for a dog! You can have a loan of mine! You can practise having a dog on my dog, and if you're very good you can even have a small share in her! You can mind her till the spring comes, till the house in Stoneytown has floors and ceilings and I can go journeying back there!'

'The little black dog?' she said. 'Hey! That's not a bad idea. Not bad at all. Remember the way she loved me the minute she met me? But I never heard her name. What's her name?'

'Her name is a secret,' I said. 'But she doesn't need a name, same as she doesn't need a soul. She already is purely and simply herself.'

'I'll call her "Herself" then,' Peg said. 'Tell Herself she's going to have a great life here. She's going to have what Monty would have had, the rotten creep: a personal, private handmaiden.'

'Just keep her away from twenty-eight-year-olds,' I said.

It was the momentum of banter that led me into saying what I shouldn't have. Peg's face winced in pain, and she had to pause before she could smile up at me. I smiled back, but our wryness was just a pose. What was funny about the twenty-year advantage Monty's new woman had? Nothing. It was an advantage, pure and simple. All nature was on its side. The older woman might have her heart broken, but there was nothing she could do to weaken its power.

'It's hard, you know, Peg,' I said to her at the car. 'That's all there is to say. Being a woman who's growing older on her own – there's no way around how hard it is. I'm sure it's hard for a man, too, but it's a different hard.'

'*You* manage,' she said, 'and you're six years older than me. Nobody's sorry for you.'

'I'm sorry for me,' I said seriously. 'I don't know how I've ended up with nobody, but I know I'd love somebody. I'd love to be the first person in the world some other person thinks of. I'd love to have someone to tell everything to. I'd love to go asleep and wake up beside someone…'

'It has to be the right someone,' Peg said.

'That's what you think when you're young,' I said. 'But I don't know. I'm not so sure. I'm starting to look for another job, and this time I'm going to hold out for

428

something useful. I was thinking of teaching English in Myanmar for six months for a start. Could you manage Herself for six months? You know Myanamar – that used to be Burma? It's a military dictatorship. It must be a help to the resistance to have some English. But I can't help thinking that if only I had someone, I wouldn't need to put all that effort into living my life. I could just look after him, not always be making my plans and doing everything by myself. I've had enough of myself.'

'I still think it has to be the right one,' Peg said stubbornly.

'Makes no difference anyway,' I said. 'Even if anybody would be better than nobody, I haven't got an anybody.'

'Rosie Barry!' Peg wailed. 'You came out here to console me, so how come you end up crying and I end up having to look after you?'

'It's because you're an angel,' I said, kissing her goodbye. 'How did I guess that you're an angel? It's because you're a blonde! Did you ever see a brunette angel?'

From that point on, I was ready to resume a normal life. On a brilliantly blue day, with an offshore wind that whipped the foam from the waves back into the sea, I went to consult my emails for a final time at the Milbay Library. Inside, handfuls of dazzling diamonds rattled every so often against the little windowpanes, as another sunlit shower shuttled over. Nature herself was being exuberant today, and I too felt well and reckless.

From: RosieB@eirtel.com
To: MarkC@rmbooks.com
Sent: 10.05 a.m.

I was seated here the other day, Markey, idly reading the obituaries at the back of the newspaper, when I noticed how they often say that the deceased person had been the 'best friend' of the bereaved.

And I thought, self-pityingly, how no one will ever claim that for me, that I was their best friend...

But then I thought — what would it be like to be your own best friend, yourself?

I thought about my friends and what I feel about them. I want to support them. I never want to hurt them. If there is something about them I think would be better changed, I approach them with affection and care — at least I hope I do. But basically I'm fond of them as they are, and if they want to stay the way they are, that's fine with me...

And then I suddenly saw that I've never been as kind as that to myself. Instead I've always ordered myself to change, instructed myself to improve. I've never approached myself with love. And, Markey, it was as if at last I understood. Loving yourself is not selfish indulgence. Love can open you up. Love can soften you, so that you can escape the old moulds. Love is a delicate, nurturing attentiveness. And when you direct that attentiveness at yourself, the frail shoots of a new you can slowly gather strength.

So I'm leaving Stoneytown with that insight tucked under my sweater.

I wanted to tell you, dear Markey.

Best love,
Rosie

From: MarkC@rmbooks.com
To: RosieB@eirtel.com
Sent: 10.12 a.m.
Subject: THANKS

Thank you, dear ol' pal, for being so open. It helps me to get something off my chest.

Rosie, I had to learn to not be harsh, when I came to the States. Harsh truth doesn't energise here; it hurts and bewilders people. You and I come from the slash-and-burn Kilbride school of human relations, but people here don't.

This brings me to my sincere regret about the way I left Ireland. Do you remember, when we were at the South Bull Wall? I saw that afternoon how hurt you were that I hadn't told you I was preparing to leave. That night on the boat to Holyhead I made a vow not to hurt anyone that way again; in fact for years I consciously tried to carefully share with other people, because of what I did to you.

So here is one of your middle-aged miracles: that I have this opportunity to tell you that I'm still sorry for what I did.

Why not come to Seattle and I'll show you around? Min is a great woman, but she is not you.

Best love,
Markey

I gave the dog a Valium because I was fed up paying for the vet to come out, and when she fell asleep I pulled her on the cart to the car and laid her on the duvet on the back seat with boxes of household stuff wedged all around. With any luck I'd reach Peg's before she woke up.

Leo was going back to Switzerland tomorrow, though he said he'd be visiting Dublin often. As a going-away present he'd done plans with detailed drawings for the house on the Point, in fine ink on sheets of handmade paper, which were lovely things in themselves. I went around the house, now completely empty for the builders, with his sketches in my hand. If my money stretched to it, The Barry House, as he called it, was going to have a glass wall on the yard side, a deep balcony faced in stone under the roof on the sea side, oak wainscoting throughout, plus under-floor heating from a geothermal installation deep in the first field, and an extra metre of old stone on the surrounding walls. Leo had even drawn the stones of the walls, along with copious notes. What the man didn't know about the effect of under-floor heating on limestone tiles, or how to double-glaze original windows, or how to clean out and restock an old apple orchard while constructing a comfortable house among the trees for at least one pig, wasn't worth knowing.

I'd tacked cardboard over the part of the old plaster on which some forebear had once kept a desperate calendar. That wouldn't be touched. And I'd written on the wall beneath the marks, with a thin sable brush dipped in Indian ink:

These marks found by
Rosaleen Barry
on re-opening her grandmother's house
Spring, 2003.

Leo had also done a special drawing for the builders of how that portion of old plaster should be protected behind a shallow perspex box, then covered over with new plaster when the spaces between the roof beams were re-done. Let someone else find it some day.

Hurrying then, I packed the car with the last bits and pieces. Toaster. Despised transistor radio. Humane mouse-frightening apparatus and Pepcid AC. Plastic shoes for wearing when examining rock pools. Rubber boots. Car mats. I'd burnt anything I didn't want to bring into whatever came next. I'd even burnt the cutting of Hugh Boody's obituary. If I was ever run over by a bus, Tessa might discover I carried it, and wondering about it could damage her life.

Then I went back up and stood on the ridge where everything was soaring with vitality – my hair, my scarf, the chilly wind, the scudding blue sky.

And I said a prayer of thanks there for the place, the house, the people, the animals, the birds, the fish. I said thank you to my grandfather and my mother and father and my aunt Min. I said thank you to Andy and to Aidan the ESB man and to Tessa and Peg. I said thank you to Markey and Billy and Luz. And I repeated the thanks every so often, as I drove to Dublin.

Though I could hear the mocking laughter still.

I'd been an unafraid child when I started at infant

school, sweeping room-shapes in the pine-needles and dirt of the schoolyard with branches laboriously twisted from the straggly evergreen trees. I'd shoo the other girls out of my imaginary parlour with a sudden flash of temper or, just as capriciously, like the most gracious hostess, invite them in to visit. For a while the other girls followed me, and we'd all be making house-shapes in the dirt. But a time came when they'd turned away in unison from my games – like grown women turning away, with commonsense shrugs, from a person too eccentric to be taken seriously.

Those mocking voices had their influence still. I had known it would strike them as affected, to be offering such ecstatic thanks left, right and centre.

But the hell with them.

'*My soul doth magnify the Lord…*'

I changed over to conventional thanks, however, when I saw the trouble Peg had gone to for the dog. She'd installed a big cage so that she might feel secure, and filled it with toys and a plush bed. And over the mesh door a plaque read HERSELF. But even better was when Peg, without fussing, opened the conservatory door and let the unimpressed dog out to begin her exploration of her New World. We stood there in our coats, like proud mothers outside a school playground, and watched. The little dog was a bit groggy at first and mooched around near us, looking up at me, then at Peg, then at her surroundings. But soon the straight black tail was all we could see above the grass, until the whole of her reappeared in the distance, sniffing and turning and scooting into the hedge, disappearing for a while, then running back to check that we were there, before taking off again.

'I thought you said she was afraid of noise?' Peg said, as another plane, wheels down, underbelly gleaming silver, screamed over us on its approach to Dublin airport.

The dog was happily digging a hole.

'Wow, Peg! Guess what? I never thought of it, but she comes from an Air Corps camp! That must be the one noise she doesn't mind.'

It's a sign, I thought. A sign I've done the right thing.

Leo's wife had sent him a ticket. Air France, Business Class. Just about the most expensive ticket there is. Reeny told me that when I met her going in her door as I was going in mine. 'He's not there,' she said. 'He's up in the Sorrento saying goodbye to Enzo. Everyone knows he's going and there's weeping and wailing among the fans. I'm one of them myself because he's gorgeous and a gentleman, only he played awful oul' music all the time. Anyhow, I have a fella in Spain, thank God, so I can keep a grip. But the poor oul' bats from the choir, they never knew anything like him. The way they go on about him you'd think he was a mixture of Padre Pio and what's-his-name in *South Pacific*, you know, the good-looking foreign one with the white hair. Half of them used to knock on the door with presents for him, and the other half used to leave theirs on the window sill. I saw a seagull today trying to tear open something wrapped in tinfoil there, so I dropped it up to Mrs Beckett's window sill. Let them figure that one out!' she said with a raucous laugh.

I went up to the chip shop to tell Leo I was home. There he was, leaning on the counter, where he bought me a choc ice while he and Enzo finished a conversation about a tisane for Leo's *mal di gola* and what best to do about Enzo's stiffness in the *dossa*. Then Enzo brought out from the kitchen a jar of the truly terrible wine his grandfather made in the hills above Bellinzona, and insisted Leo take it with his best wishes.

He kept on murmuring about his *mal* this and *mal* that as we walked down the street, but he was keeping very well, as far as I could see, nothing like the derelict he'd been in Macerata. And happier, even, than he'd ever been when we were having our affair, which was something I'd have to think about someday when I was thinking about what part sex had played in my life. But I didn't want to think about that yet.

Maybe his calm came from age; and maybe I'd be like that too, when the years and a bit of bad health slowed me down. Maybe I'd be content with days like his, which, it seemed, consisted of his thinking about his health, thinking about the essay he was writing on Schumann, thinking about buildings and remodelling them, and thinking about his family, especially his youngest boy. Though he'd also trained the ladies' choir twice a week and had given a couple of illustrated talks on musical topics in Kilbride Library, to overflow audiences, and he'd taught several children the first steps on the tin whistle. And he'd also taken several of his ladies to various concerts.

'How is the beautiful Peg?' he asked when I told him

about my day. I said she seemed a bit better, and how the dog was going to have a wonderful time.

Peg was one of his ladies. He'd taken her to a concert in the National Concert Hall, where she told me the manager there was all over him, and how the conductor had even turned around and waved to him when he was leaving the stage.

He must have invited Peg for her gift of looking up from under her lowered eyelashes like the late Princess Di, because music was wasted on her. I asked her what they'd heard and she said the one that goes louder. Which some people might have had trouble identifying as Ravel's *Bolero*.

But that last night I was the lady in possession, and very content to be so, with the raw dark outside and the warm kitchen illuminated by the scarlet Busy Lizzies.

And Leo who expertly revived the fire and poured some of the *vino di casa* into his decanter.

'We shall listen to some music,' he said contentedly.

'Rosa?' he murmured, a couple of hours later.

After washing up our pasta plates, he'd gone outside, then brushed Enzo's wine off his teeth in the scullery and discreetly undressed. And now he was standing in the middle of the room smiling at me. Wearing his pyjamas with the thick, satin piping, which were once a really splendid affair, but threadbare now from washing.

'*Rosa mia*?' He stood there in the kitchen with the dresser behind him, the cat sitting on the end of his neat bed, and the bedside lamp, that had a fly caught in its shade for years, casting a yellow light on the pillow.

Human beings are marvellous at believing in themselves.

'Are you serious?' I said. He wasn't one bit embarrassed, which took a lot of the embarrassment out of it for me, but I could feel myself blushing all the same. We were different people from the people we'd been. This me was shy all over again.

'But...' I said.

'It would be such a nice *arrivederci*,' he said softly.

It would have been ridiculous to say no.

But I wasn't committed when I began: I lay on the outside of the blankets with my funeral clothes on. But I did, somehow, eventually, arrive between the sheets. Nude. I'd always envied couples who'd been together a long time for exactly the way this was – cosy and commonsensical. I put an arm here, you put a leg there, you do that for a while, I do this for a while. God knows Leo and I were as good at the technicalities as anyone, though he took things very slowly, and there was a lot of resting on our sides. And when it came time to move things on, it was me who did the heavy lifting. But he had an absolutely unshakeable confidence in himself, despite his energy being low.

We were close. We kissed each other lightly most of the way through, to say thank you. And in the end, nature took over and we stopped being so nice and we did conjure up a thin, perfect sweetness that was like the voices of the sopranos of long ago.

The whole thing didn't even disturb Bell, seated watching the fire.

But afterwards, after Leo fell immediately asleep, I

had to deal with the turbulence that swept through me.

I didn't switch on a light, but I raked the fire, and put on a bit more coal, and sat over it in my sweater and panties with the cat on my lap.

I had to say to my heart: stop hurting, stop stinging, calm yourself, there is nothing to be done about your restlessness and regret. I knew that making love is good for a person, and I knew I should be grateful because a lot of single people my age (and for all I knew married people) didn't get a chance to do it half often enough. And I was grateful. But Time had been in the bed with us, my tummy resting on Leo's sharp hip, his arm across me as thin as a bone. And Time's hard lesson about how little other people can do for a person's aching heart was being repeated to me now. I couldn't say to Leo: mourn with me that lovers grow older. I couldn't say: being so close to you makes me desperately lonely for someone I could be even closer to.

A person has to grow up instead and not hurt other people.

It was my problem. I alone carried the memory of what had once been, of how much glory there was in the world as I imagined it when I was young, when it seemed to me that I entered through passion into a huge realm, when it seemed that sometimes I broke away from earth into the universe and shimmered with being. When I never questioned what I was. When I believed in everything.

Oh, give it back to me! I begged the silent, shadowy room. Oh, give it back! Give me my life to live again with what I know now! Give me back a beginning!

The phone beside me gave its initial half-ring and I picked it up before it could wake Leo.

'Yes?' I whispered.

'What's wrong with you, Rosie?' Min said vigorously. 'Cat stolen your tongue?'

At which Bell jumped off my lap, as if recognising the voice of her real mistress.

Min was dying for a gossip. She said nobody had told her anything. She wanted to know (a) who was at the funeral, and (b) what size was it, and (c) what about Peg – how was she getting along?

'Everyone' was the answer to (a), and 'very big' was the answer to (b).

And yes, public opinion in Kilbride had been horrified when it turned out that Mr Colfer left the house to all three children, and Peg's brother and sister had it up for sale before their father was even buried, with an auctioneer's sign actually on it when the funeral cortège passed.

'No!' Min breathed.

'But Peg didn't take it lying down. She took every stick of furniture out of the old house so the brother and sister had nowhere to sit. She's out in the new house now and she has my dog out there. She'd already got a solicitor and threatened to sue Monty for damages for ruining her life, though she settled for him making the builders finish the bungalow behind the airport in double time, which he's made over to her. Her thinking of taking an action against Monty for not marrying her didn't seem very women's lib to me, but she told Tessa that nothing is too low for her to stoop to when it comes to that man. Like, you're not going to believe this, but she found out the new wife's address and wrote her to say watch out: that Monty has a flatulence problem.'

'He has a what?' Min said.

Now I was in trouble. I couldn't use the word 'fart' with Min.

'You know,' I said. 'When you eat beans or something like that and noises come out.'

Silence.

'Noises come out of your body,' I said desperately. 'You know.'

'*Peg* did that?' Min said, disbelievingly. 'But Peg's a real lady!'

'Not now she isn't. When Monty told her back in September they were finished, she put a wasp in a matchbox and posted it to him, only it flew out and stung Reeny. Reeny told me that at the funeral. Peg'd put a little bit of tuna in the box for it to eat.'

Min sighed wistfully. 'There's always great news from home,' she said.

'Well, what about you?' I asked.

'That Markey is crazy!' she began happily. 'The feet are falling off me. Did you know that when the middle of Seattle kept flooding, they just built a different middle on top and left all of the old one there underneath? They didn't bother to knock it down! It's still there, all the little streets and the stores – that's *shops* – and the streetlights and all! Can you believe that? He took me to see it today. I couldn't believe my eyes! Can you imagine, Rosie, if there were two Kilbrides, one on top of the other! But it was a terrible long walk all the same.'

'That's Markey all right,' I said. 'I must have walked a few hundred miles behind that fella.'

'He has brains to burn,' she said. 'It was like listening to the television. It must have been from his father he got them because his mother was no great shakes in the brains department, though she was a very nice lady. Billy is the same as Markey, only Billy is quiet, but he has Luz on the mend. She's not the better of the fire yet, between you and me, but please God it won't be long. I made her a solemn promise that as soon as she's up to it we're going down to the border to have a look at Mexico. Do you want to come, Rosie? They don't really have Christmas in America because they're Protestants, but they're all Catholics in Mexico, even the Indians. Luz explained it all to me. We could have a great Christmas. And you could help us. Her or me can't go over into Mexico but you could – you could help take her grandchildren back to the place where Luz once saw them. There's a big pipe underneath the desert in that place, wherever it is, and her daughter sent the children down the pipe to come across – she tied red ribbons around their necks so Luz would know who they were. They just came to the end of the pipe, which comes out underneath a cliff, and they waved up at her and then they went back. If the children came across again, we could throw their Christmas presents down to them.'

'Well, Min!' I said. 'It looks as if you're having great adventures!' I could think of nothing else to say. I was stunned at her inviting me to join them.

'I am,' she said proudly. 'I used to not want any

adventures because look what happened to my sister – your ma. She went off to have an adventure – you should have seen the smile on her face when she waved to me from the bus – and the next thing we hear the priest comes to say she's looking for her letters of freedom to be married in Dublin. "Don't give them to her," my father said. "She should come home here and marry one of the lads." "I have to give them to her," the priest said. "She's old enough. And she's in the family way." And the next thing, I saw the priest coming up from the pier through the snow, and this time she was dead.'

'That had nothing to do with adventures,' I said. 'That was because men ruled the world, that's why. Every big bully like your father thought they could just push girls and women around…'

'He was not a big bully!' she said. 'He was a good man. Look how long he waited for me. And you!'

'How do you mean, waited? Where?'

'You saw it in the letter from the government about the house,' she said. 'It was in the dates there. It's there in black and white. He was there in the house and he wouldn't give it up till near the end of 1948. Well, you were born in September 1947. He was waiting. He told me to bring you back. He made me swear I'd bring you back.'

'And why didn't you?'

She didn't say anything.

'Why didn't you?'

I waited, and the silence got longer and longer.

So then I knew.

But though words formed on my lips, I didn't say anything more.

Some day I would. Some day I'd ask her about the time she and my father came down to the house on the Point on his motorbike and they'd slept in the barn. 'How did you keep warm?' I'd ask her.

There was a pause. She must have known that I'd heard what she didn't say. But the only remark I made when we were saying goodbye, about the past that was suddenly so different, was: 'I could have grown up in Stoneytown!'

'Sure what's wrong with you?' she said. 'You're grand the way you are.'

I fished my bra and my black skirt out of Leo's bed as carefully as I could, but he woke for a moment and smiled at me.

'Thank you,' he said, turning over. But then he mumbled: 'Did you say, Rosie darling, that Flaubert died on your birthday? Flaubert did not die in September.'

'Thank *you*,' I whispered back. 'That's OK about Flaubert. Go to sleep.'

'All the same,' he said, closing his eyes, 'we did very well for people our age.'

'Well, we did,' I said, kissing his cheek nearest to me. 'But no matter how much we talk it up, no one ever says that middle age is wasted on the middle-aged.'

I went upstairs and in a few minutes I was in Min's cool bed. I turned off the light, and with a beautifully precise jump, Bell landed at my feet, settling beneath them like one of the little dogs that prop up the feet of medieval knights on tombstones.

I lay there, fully awake, thinking about the day just passed and what I had learned from it. The music of 'Lady in Red' crept in again from next door, though turned down very low, and I envisioned Reeny dancing with herself, up and down the kitchen, eyes half-closed, her wine glass elegantly balanced in her outstretched hand.

How was it that I had never said to myself, 'Min loves my dad'? How come I just accepted that the two of them were as they were? Was it because I was only on the verge of puberty myself, when my dad died, that I hadn't become alert to all that there might be between a loving man who knew he had not long to live and the young woman who shared everything with him?

Why had I never noticed anything?

Or had I noticed?

And the dry, slight tension around my own eyes as I looked into the dark reminded me of something.

In The Hut, some nights, there'd be speckles of rain on the hard tin roof. Other nights soundless misty rain would surprise me when I woke up and went out to pee, hopping down off the railway sleeper that was the front step, knowing exactly where there was a patch of grass thick enough to stand on in bare feet. It was never completely dark, even when cloud covered the moon. The streetlights of Milbay stretching down the quay dimly illuminated the white strip of crunchy sand below the outcrop of turf where I squatted.

Some of that same light came in through the little window and helped me find my tiptoeing way back past the mattress in the front room where my dad slept, and through the partition to the bed I shared with Min. And once or twice I saw, as I passed my father's pillow, that his eyes were wide open in the dark. And when I was climbing into bed, that Min's eyes were wide open, too.

I thought nothing of it, then.

But on this night my heart swelled for those two people. I didn't know why they could not, or would not, move towards each other, and I didn't know what they knew about each other either. But I knew they lay awake in the dark, eight feet from each other. Able to hear each other breathing.

I turned on my side and closed my eyes.

They had stayed where they were. They did not leave me, when I was a little girl, for each other. They stayed, one on each side of me, sturdy pillars, between whom I was safe.

That's the thing to remember, I thought, as the first swirls of sleep rose into my head. 'Thought' No. 10 should have been about love. Love is at the centre. Remember that, now that you yourself have to start again. Remember the way they loved each other and the way they loved you, and think how many different kinds of love there are. You can't have back what you had before – nothing of before is going to come back and be the same again. But it's not just moths and snowflakes and waves and stars that are different from each other, no matter how many of them there are. Loving, and being loved, comes in infinite shapes and patterns. Who knows what it will look like next time? Remember that.